Praise for Dale Brown

By Dale Brown

DALE BROWN

PRICE OF DUTY

A NOVEL

WM

WILLIAM MORROW
An Imprint of HarperCollins*Publishers*

PRICE OF DUTY. Copyright © 2017 by Creative Arts and Sciences LLC. All rights reserved. Printed in the United States of America. No part of this book may be used or reproduced in any manner whatsoever without written permission except in the case of brief quotations embodied in critical articles and reviews. For information, address HarperCollins Publishers, 195 Broadway, New York, NY 10007.

First William Morrow premium printing: November 2017
First William Morrow hardcover printing: May 2017

Print Edition ISBN: 978-0-06-244200-0
Digital Edition ISBN: 978-0-06-244198-0

Cover design by Richard L. Aquan
Cover photographs: © Yevgen Timashov/OffSet/Shutterstock (Red Square); © Michael Warwick/Shutterstock (flag); © Shutterstock (computer code)

William Morrow and HarperCollins are registered trademarks of HarperCollins Publishers in the United States of America and other countries.

17 18 19 20 21   QGM   10 9 8 7 6 5 4 3 2 1

Price of Duty is dedicated to the people who are truly on the edge, both geographically and emotionally: the citizens of the former Soviet Baltic and Eastern European states that are on Russia's western periphery. They are no strangers to being under the control of the resurgent and aggressive Russian bear, and they naturally seek help from the West to avoid being swallowed up once again. But if the West is unable, indecisive, or simply refuses to help, they have little choice but to band together and fight until help comes.

This story is also dedicated to those who fight on the world's newest, most vital, and least understood battlefield: the world of computers and networks. It will take a new generation of cyber warriors to fight on this battlefield, and we as a nation need to do much more to prepare our young people to fight and win in cyberspace.

ACKNOWLEDGMENTS

Thank you to Patrick Larkin for all his hard work.

CAST OF CHARACTERS

AMERICANS

STACY ANNE BARBEAU, president of the United States of America

EDWARD RAUCH, president's national security adviser

KAREN GRAYSON, secretary of state

LUKE COHEN, White House chief of staff

JAMES BUCHANAN NASH, CIA director

SCOTT FIRESTONE, admiral, U.S. Navy, chairman of the Joint Chiefs of Staff

RAYMOND SATTLER, special agent, Federal Bureau of Investigation

KRISTIN VOORHEES, intelligence analyst, National Geospatial Intelligence Agency

IRON WOLF SQUADRON AND SCION

KEVIN MARTINDALE, president of Scion, former president of the United States of America

BRAD MCLANAHAN, Cybernetic Infantry Device (CID) pilot and XCV-62 Ranger pilot, Iron Wolf Squadron

PATRICK MCLANAHAN, Cybernetic Infantry Device (CID) pilot, Iron Wolf Squadron ground operations unit, former lieutenant general, U.S. Air Force (ret.)

WAYNE "WHACK" MACOMBER, commander, Iron Wolf Squadron CID operations, former major, U.S. Air Force Special Operations Command (ret.)

IAN SCHOFIELD, commander, Iron Wolf deep-penetration unit, former captain in Canada's Special Operations Regiment

SAMANTHA KERR, operative, Scion Intelligence

MARCUS CARTWRIGHT, operative, Scion Intelligence

DAVID JONES, operative, Scion Intelligence

ANDREW DAVIS, Iron Wolf deep-penetration unit, former sergeant, U.S. Army Special Forces

MIKE KNAPP, Iron Wolf deep-penetration unit, former sergeant, U.S. Army Special Forces

CHRIS WALKER, Iron Wolf deep-penetration unit, former sergeant, U.S. Army Special Forces

SKY MASTERS AEROSPACE, INC.

HUNTER "BOOMER" NOBLE, Ph.D., chief of aerospace engineering, Sky Masters Aerospace Inc.

CHARLIE TURLOCK, Cybernetic Infantry Device (CID) specialist, former captain, U.S. Army National Guard

JASON RICHTER, colonel, U.S. Army (ret.), Ph.D., chief executive officer

TOM ROGERS, remote piloting specialist

RUSSIANS

GENNADIY ANATOLIYVICH GRYZLOV, president of the Russian Federation

SERGEI TARZAROV, president's chief of staff

GREGOR SOKOLOV, minister of defense

VIKTOR KAZYANOV, minister of state security

DARIA TITENEVA, foreign minister

IVAN ULANOV, president's private secretary

COLONEL GENERAL VALENTIN MAKSIMOV, commander of the Aerospace Defense Forces

IGOR TRUZNYEV, former president of the Russian Federation and former head for the Federal Security Service (FSB), currently chief of Zatmeniye ("Eclipse") Consulting Group, a private espionage firm

MAJOR GENERAL ARKADY KOSHKIN, chief of FSB's Q Directorate

COLONEL VLADIMIR BALAKIN, chief of security for Perun's Aerie cyberwar complex

MAJOR LEONID USENKO, Special Surveillance Unit, Main Intelligence Directorate (GRU)

CAPTAIN KONSTANTIN RUSANOV, GRU Special Surveillance Unit

CAPTAIN ARTEM MIKHEYEV, GRU special technical officer

COLONEL YEVGENY PERMINOV, GRU liaison officer

AHMAD USMAEV, warlord, Chechen Republic

MAJOR PAVEL BEREZIN, detachment commander, Vympel ("Pennant") Spetsnaz unit

CAPTAIN ANDREI CHIRKASH, detachment second in command, Vympel Spetsnaz unit

TIMUR SAITIEV, Chechen fighter

YURI AKULOV, former FSB officer, currently an operative for Zatmeniye Consulting Group

IVAN BUDANOV, senior nuclear supervisor, Atomflot

DR. NIKOLAI OBOLENSKY, software lab directory, Nizhny Novgorod Research Institute of Radio Engineering (NNIIRT)

MAJOR GENERAL VIKTOR POLICHEV, Aerospace Defense Forces, senior military aide to Colonel General Maksimov

TARAS IVCHENKO, former FSB officer, currently an operative for Zatmeniye Consulting Group

MAJOR GENERAL KIRILL GLAZKOV, commander of the FSB's V Directorate

LIEUTENANT MIKHAIL KURITSYN, Vympel Spetsnaz unit

MAJOR ALEXEI RYKOV, Su-27 fighter pilot

SERGEANT IVAN ANANKO, Vympel Spetsnaz unit

SERGEANT DMITRY SAVICHEV, Vympel Spetsnaz unit

LEONID PEROV, former FSB officer, bodyguard for Igor Truznyev

CAPTAIN FYODOR GOLOVKIN, commander, Kipiyevo radar outpost

COLONEL RUSLAN BARYSHEV, Su-50 fighter pilot

CAPTAIN OLEG IMREKOV, Su-50 fighter pilot

MAJOR GENERAL ANATOLIY KAVERIN, commander, 2nd Aerospace Defense Brigade

POLES

PIOTR WILK, president of Poland; former general in the Polish Air Force and commander of the 1st Air Defense Wing

KLAUDIA RYBAK, prime minister

JANUSZ GIEREK, minister of national defense and deputy prime minister

MAJOR NADIA ROZEK, military aide to President Piotr Wilk, attached to Iron Wolf Squadron as copilot and systems operator for XCV-62 Ranger

MAJOR GENERAL MILOSZ DOMANSKI, Polish Land Forces

COLONEL PAWEŁ KASPEREK, F-16 fighter pilot and commander of the Polish Air Force's 3rd Tactical Squadron

MAJOR DARIUSZ STEPNIAK, head of presidential security detail, Bureau of Government Protection (BOR)

JAROSŁAW ROGOSKI, senior vice president, PKO Bank Polski

MARTA STACHOWSKA, chief technology officer, PKO Bank Polski

CAPTAIN TOMASZ JAGIELSKI, F-16 fighter pilot, 3rd Tactical Squadron

GENERAL INSPECTOR MAREK BRZEZIŃSKI, commander, Polish National Police Force

MAJOR GENERAL CZESŁAW MADEJSKI, deputy commander, Alliance of Free Nations (AFN) Northern Air Operations Center

CAPTAIN JERZY KONARSKI, Northern Air Operations Center

MARIUSZ BRODSKI, senior investigator for PKBWL, Poland's aircraft accident investigative agency

KAROL SIKORA, sergeant, Polish Special Forces, attached to Iron Wolf Squadron deep-penetration unit

ROMANIANS

ALEXE DUMITRU, president of Romania

MARKU PROCA, control room supervisor,
Cernavodă Nuclear Power Station,
Unit Two

NICOLAE DIACONU, senior plant operator,
Cernavodă Unit Two

ION MORAR, senior plant operator, Cernavodă
Unit Two

VASILE ENESCU, emergency coordinator,
Cernavodă Unit Two

BALTIC STATES

SERGEANT EDVARDAS NOREIKA, State Border
Guard of Lithuania

COLONEL REINIS ZARINŠ, Latvian Air Force
intelligence officer attached to AFN's
Northern Air Operations Center

SVEN KALDA, prime minister of Estonia

LIEUTENANT COLONEL INAR TAMM, Estonian
Air Force

KALMAR AIRLINES

KAARLE MARKKULA, captain, Flight 851

TUOMAS SAARELA, first officer, Flight 851

PRICE
OF
DUTY

PROLOGUE

PERUN'S AERIE CYBERWAR COMPLEX, IN THE URAL MOUNTAINS, EAST OF PECHORA, RUSSIA
Late summer 2018

Wrapped in stillness and silence for over three hundred million years, the mountain's vast inner recesses now echoed with the measured clatter of boots and echoing voices. Construction units, laboring around the clock for months in brutal conditions, had carved out an intricate network of tunnels and connected chambers—piercing layers of solid rock already ancient when dinosaurs roamed the earth.

Surrounded by heavily armed bodyguards, Gennadiy Gryzlov strode briskly along a brightly lit passage, heading deeper into the warren called Perun's Aerie by its makers. He found the word choice entirely apt. Perun was the old Slavic god of war, fire, and mountains, famed for hurling lightning from clouds like those that so often shrouded the jagged, icy peak soaring two thousand meters above their heads.

Sentries in thick overcoats and fur hats snapped to attention as Gryzlov passed, presenting arms with a flourish and the click of highly polished boots. With thinly veiled amusement, the forty-two-year-old president of the Russian Federation glanced at the shorter man stolidly keeping pace with him. "Colonel Balakin's soldiers appear disciplined and alert, Koshkin. I trust you can say the same about your Q Directorate people?"

Major General Arkady Koshkin nodded. "Yes, Mr. President, I can," he said confidently. His mouth twisted in a slight smile. "While I admit that the dress and mannerisms of my *komp'yutershchiks*, my tech geeks, are sometimes a bit eccentric, their expertise and ingenuity are remarkable. The weapons they are forging for us prove this beyond question."

Like most senior officers in Russia's Federal Security Service (the FSB), Koshkin wore civilian clothing rather than a service uniform. Eyes bright with intelligence and ambition gleamed behind thick spectacles. Long ago, he had concluded that cyberwarfare—the use of computer technology as a means to attack and disrupt the vital infrastructure of an enemy power—was the next true revolution in military affairs. Facing skepticism and hostility from slower-witted and more conventionally minded superiors, he had worked for years to win converts among the ranks of his nation's rising political leaders.

Now those tireless efforts were coming to fruition. He had been given command of a new and highly secret unit within the FSB. Organized at Gryzlov's personal orders, Q Directorate was responsible for all covert cyberwar action conducted beyond Russia's borders.

They came to an intersection and turned right, ending up at a solid steel door. Koshkin pressed his palm against a biometric panel. The door swung open, revealing an enormous room crowded with racks of computers and other electronic equipment.

Flat-panel displays dominated the chamber's walls. Power conduits and fiber-optic cables snaked their way toward a large bare patch in the middle of the tiled floor.

Gryzlov swung around, taking it all in. He nodded toward the open space. "That's where your supercomputer will go?"

"Yes, Mr. President," Koshkin said. "It's a new T-Platforms machine, faster and more powerful than any of their previous designs. The unit will be installed, tested, and fully operational in a matter of weeks."

"Very good," Gryzlov said. "What about the rest of your infrastructure?"

"Mostly complete," Koshkin assured him. He took out a tablet computer and tapped its small screen. One of the large wall displays flickered to life, showing a detailed, three-dimensional schematic of the Perun's Aerie complex. A chamber deep in the heart of the facility glowed green. "All internal and external power needs are met by a compact 171-megawatt KLT-40M naval nuclear reactor. As a result, this complex is, effectively, entirely off the grid, connected to the outside world only by deeply buried and highly secure communications links."

The Russian president nodded. He moved closer to the display, studying it intently. "And your primary defenses?"

"Virtually impregnable," Koshkin replied. He tapped his tablet again, bringing up a new map, this one depicting the narrow valleys and steep slopes surrounding Perun's Aerie. "An interlocking web of sensors—IR-capable cameras, radars, motion detectors, and the like—ensures that no enemy can approach undetected, either by air or on the ground." More areas glowed red on the big display. "Behind the sensor network, Colonel Balakin's engineers have sown dense, carefully camouflaged, minefields. These barriers will channel any attackers into kill zones covered by antitank, machine-gun, and mortar fire from concealed bunkers."

"And if the enemy attacks from the air?" Gryzlov asked with deceptive mildness. Before taking over his family's highly profitable oil, gas, and petrochemical companies and then going into politics, he had been a serving officer in Russia's air force. And he knew from bitter personal experience the kind of horrific damage precision-guided bombs and missiles could inflict.

"Our close-in air defenses include hidden SAM and antiaircraft batteries in pop-up emplacements sited high on the mountain above us," Koshkin replied. "In addition, Colonel General Maksimov has obeyed your orders to station interceptors at

Syktyvkar, including his first operational Su-50 stealth fighters. We have a direct secure link to those air units, and fighter jets can be overhead in twenty minutes."

Gryzlov stepped back from the display. He clapped the shorter man on the shoulder. "*Otlichnaya rabota!* Excellent work!"

"Thank you, Mr. President," Koshkin said, striving to conceal his sense of relief. In public appearances, Russia's youthful, good-looking leader radiated charm, confidence, and calm. Those closest to him knew the fierce temper and manic, often uncontrolled, rage that lurked behind the façade. Failing Gennadiy Gryzlov always carried a high and painful price.

"And the other defensive measures I ordered?" Gryzlov asked. "Are they operational yet?" Koshkin hesitated, and Gryzlov's eyes narrowed in suspicion—he did not like having to draw out bad news from his subordinates. "Well?" the taller man demanded.

"Colonel Balakin informs me that work on them is running somewhat behind schedule," Koshkin admitted. "But since the need for such backup defenses seemed so remote, neither of us felt it was wise to divert the necessary manpower and resources just now."

Gryzlov's mouth tightened, and his gaze turned cold. "That was a decision well above your pay grade, General." He watched the FSB officer's round face turn pale and then went on. "Whether or not you believe my orders are *wise* is irrelevant. Understand?"

Koshkin nodded.

"Then you will obey me," Gryzlov snapped. "I want those troops and weapons and explosives in place as soon as possible. No more delays! No more bitching and whining about money and resources. You and Balakin are soldiers in the service of Mother Russia, not pissant junior accountants! Is that clear?"

"Yes, sir."

"Good." The Russian president's angry expression softened slightly. "So far, you have done reasonably well, Arkady. Don't screw up at the end, eh?" His smile grew warmer and more genuine. "After all, you want the chance to test these shiny new cyberweapons of yours, yes?"

Koshkin snapped to attention. "Yes, Mr. President."

"Then keep me informed of your progress," Gryzlov said. "And tell Colonel Balakin to pull his thumb out of his ass and obey my orders . . . *all* of my orders."

ABOARD THE PRESIDENTIAL SUKHOI SUPERJET 100, OVER RUSSIA
A short time later

Powered by two massive turbofan jet engines, the sleek, modern passenger airliner climbed smoothly through clear blue skies over northern Russia—bound westward toward Moscow at just under five hundred knots. While most Superjet 100s carried around a hundred passengers, this one was different. The plane had been purchased as a transport aircraft for Russia's leader, so its main cabin was almost empty, occupied only by a few luxurious leather chairs reserved for VIPs, a couple of rows of business-class-style seats for the president's military and civilian aides and bodyguards, and a well-stocked bar and galley.

Gennadiy Gryzlov swiveled his seat to face Sergei Tarzarov, his chief of staff. "So, what did you think of Koshkin's new Q Directorate playground?"

Tarzarov, a thin, plain-looking man, was cautious. "The facility is impressive enough," he allowed. His mouth turned down. "As it should be at the cost of several hundred billion rubles."

Gryzlov grinned to himself. Tarzarov was renowned for his shrewdness and cunning. For decades, the ruthless old man had survived and prospered as the ultimate Kremlin insider—as the man who made and unmade heads of state, cabinet ministers, generals, and intelligence chiefs. One by one, his rivals vanished. If they were lucky, they were merely driven into political oblivion. Those who were not so fortunate, or who were perhaps more dangerous, ended their days in a gulag or an unmarked grave.

But for all his cleverness, Tarzarov was a dinosaur. Like so many steeped in the old ways, he measured a state's power chiefly by its military strength—by the numbers of bombers, tanks, artillery pieces, and nuclear-tipped missiles it could field. He was blind to the overwhelming strategic advantages waiting for those who first mastered the new digital battlefield.

"You believe we are wasting Russia's resources?" Gryzlov pressed.

"I do not doubt that Koshkin's promised new weapons will be useful in their own limited way and at the right time," Tarzarov said slowly. He shrugged. "But I am not sure we need them now, Gennadiy. And at such expense. Our position in the world is strong and it grows stronger with every passing day."

"Oh?" Gryzlov raised an eyebrow. His voice grew cooler, laced with biting sarcasm. "Have you forgotten how the Poles and their high-tech American mercenaries handed us our asses last year?"

"There were certain tactical setbacks," the older man admitted. "But we achieved a strategic victory. We now hold all of eastern Ukraine, and the NATO alliance lies in ruins."

"Save the bullshit for the gullible masses," Gryzlov retorted, his patience fraying. "McLanahan and his Iron Wolf Squadron bombers and fighting machines kicked the snot out of two of our tank armies, destroyed dozens of our most advanced combat aircraft, and then wiped out the best part of a tactical missile brigade."

"But now Patrick McLanahan is dead," Tarzarov reminded him quietly. "Shot down by one of his own countrymen—as you demanded. And this act of cowardice by the American president, Barbeau, has spelled the effective end of NATO. No one trusts the Americans anymore."

"McLanahan may be nothing more than burned ashes scattered across Poland," Gryzlov growled. "But his Iron Wolf mercenaries and their Polish paymasters are still very much alive. And their continued existence threatens our power in Europe and around the world. You've seen the intelligence reports. Poland's so-called Alliance of Free Nations is fast becoming a rallying point for all those who should fear and obey us."

Tarzarov fell silent. Much as he hated to admit the younger man's point, he could not deny that the Poles with their freelance American military and technical experts remained a thorn in Moscow's side. Despite a yearlong campaign of black propaganda, secret bribes, and thinly disguised saber rattling, Russia had failed to win back the allegiance of any of the former Soviet puppet states in Eastern and central Europe. The members of Warsaw's new defense pact were showing far more resilience and cohesion than he had expected.

Gryzlov read his thoughts. He nodded. "Now you see it, Sergei. Too often we have seen victories snatched away by weapons and technology beyond our capabilities. That must stop. It is high time we made our enemies dance to a tune of our choosing, not theirs."

Reluctantly, Tarzarov nodded. "Perhaps you are right, Gennadiy." He sighed. "But I fear the consequences if word of your plan leaks out. The damage to our international position could be severe."

"True enough," Gryzlov agreed, with a quick, predatory grin. "But one must be willing to take risks in any high-stakes game. Empires are not won by fearful men."

He glanced away, staring out across the vast and empty sky. "Still, I agree that secrecy is vital. For now, at least." He turned back to Tarzarov. "Tell me, Sergei. Can the FSB successfully conceal the existence of Perun's Aerie from foreign spies?"

The older man frowned. "Koshkin's security and his *maskirovka*, his deception plans, are good. Very good. But good enough to hide so large a facility from the West?" He shrugged his narrow shoulders. "*Babushka gadala da nadvoye skazala*, '*to li dozhdik, to li sneg.*' My grandmother told fortunes and said, 'It will either rain or snow.'"

It was an old Russian proverb meaning basically, "Who can say? Maybe yes and maybe no."

"Then let us hope it will snow," Gryzlov said enigmatically.

With that, Russia's president fell silent, staring out across the heavens as the Superjet 100 sped west.

CHAPTER 1

**NEAR SILIȘTEA GUMEȘTI,
SOUTHERN ROMANIA**
Late fall 2018

Clouds covered the night sky, obscuring the stars and the new moon's pale sliver. Deep in a patch of woodland east of an old Romanian military airfield, a twelve-foot-tall, humanlike machine stalked through the darkness—moving with catlike grace and quiet despite its size. Suddenly it stopped, crouching low beneath the spreading branches of a massive oak tree.

The machine's six-sided head swiveled from side to side atop its broad shoulders, carefully probing the surrounding forest. At rest, it faded from view, becoming almost invisible both to the naked eye and to thermal imagers.

Inside the cockpit of the Cybernetic Infantry Device—a human-piloted combat robot—Brad McLanahan opened a secure channel. "Wolf One to Wolf Two. I'm in position and standing by."

"Two copies," a cheerful female voice replied. "I'm roughly three hundred meters to your right. So what is your evaluation of the tactical situation, young Jedi?"

Brad grinned. Five years ago, Charlie Turlock had taught him how to pilot these incredible fighting machines. Gutsy and combat-experienced, the former U.S. Amy National Guard captain and current Sky Masters CID specialist was still a teacher and robotics enthusiast at heart. She loved everything about the combat robots she had helped design, build, and steadily improve. That was why she was here now, serving as a covert adviser to the Iron Wolf and other Scion forces helping Poland and its allies.

It was easy to understand Charlie's enthusiasm, he thought. Every time he strapped himself into a CID, he experienced a sudden rush of power, perception, and sheer freaking speed so unbelievably intense that it was almost sexual.

And why not? he thought. Covered in highly resistant composite armor, the robot's micro-hydraulically-powered exoskeleton was stronger, quicker, and more agile than any ten men put together. Feedback from a special haptic interface translated its pilot's gestures into exoskeleton motion, enabling the machine to move with un-canny nimbleness and precision. Sensors of all kinds, coupled with a highly advanced computer interface, gave a CID's pilot astonishing situational awareness and the ability to aim and fire a remarkable array of weapons with speed and pinpoint accuracy. In basic terms, a single Cybernetic Infantry Device was more mobile, carried heavier firepower, and possessed significantly greater recon capability than an entire conventionally equipped infantry platoon.

Focus, Brad told himself sternly. Piloting one of these babies made it way too easy to get caught up in the thrill ride, losing track of the mission at hand. He concentrated more fully, allowing his CID's neural interface to show him the composite imagery crafted from its wide range of passive sensors. Several slowly pulsing yellow dots blinked into existence on his display.

"I count at least ten fighting positions occupied by enemy infantry deployed across our line of approach, about two hundred meters out," he told Charlie. "They're dug in really well, completely covered by antithermal IR camouflage suits or netting. But I'm getting multiple heartbeats through my audio pickups and seeing several thermal traces of respiratory CO_2." He smiled. "I could light 'em up with my radar to see what kind of heavy weapons they're manning, but that would probably give us away."

"Indeed it would, Wolf One," Charlie replied. Her tone was amused. "But I suggest you refine your scans a bit. I think you're seeing the worm, not the hook."

Slightly nettled, Brad did as she suggested, mentally commanding the CID's systems to tighten up its sensor readings, briefly concentrating on one sector. His image of the larger environment grew slightly fuzzier as the computer honed its focus. More data flowed through his conscious mind at the speed of thought.

"*Skurwysyn*. Son of a bitch," he muttered in Polish, seeing what she was getting at. After living for more than a year in Poland, he was commenting and even beginning to think in Polish. Those heartbeats he was picking up were way too regular, as were the CO_2 traces. "They're decoys."

"Yep," Charlie agreed. "Probably some kind of dummies wired up to simulate human cardiac and respiratory systems." Now she sounded admiring, but just the tiniest bit smug at the same time. "Our friends out there are getting clever. Just not quite clever enough to beat the software and hardware tweaks my guys and I built into that Mod IV CID you're riding."

"It is a sweet machine," Brad agreed absently, widening his sensor fields again. If the enemy had its decoys positioned out front, then logically its real strike force should be stationed on a flank, ready to hammer anyone pouncing on the bait.

"Gotcha," he murmured. Several of the huge oak trees off to his left were very subtly *wrong*, just slightly too symmetrical to be natural. They were hollowed-out fakes large enough to conceal a heavy-machine-gun nest or an antitank missile team, he realized. Seen by a human eye, that camouflage was near perfect, but not when pitted against a CID battle computer with its lightning-fast ability to discern and analyze patterns. There were also several patches of ground near the trees that didn't quite match the predicted natural rise and fall of the landscape. Those were probably foxholes covered with camouflage cloth, he decided.

Quickly, Brad highlighted the enemy positions he'd detected and sent the imagery to Charlie's CID. Their computer systems simultaneously compressed and encrypted signals before transmitting them in short, millisecond-long bursts. Together, this combination of compression, frequency hopping, and encryption allowed CIDs operating together to communicate freely, without the risk of enemy interception.

"Wolf Two copies," she replied. "What's your plan, Wolf One? Flank the flankers? If you go about half a klick due west, you could—"

"Negative," he said, edging backward, moving unhurriedly enough to stay hidden from view. Like the Mod III before it, his CID's armored "skin" carried an overlay of hundreds of small, hexagonal thermal adaptive tiles. Made of a special material, these tiles could change temperature with amazing rapidity. Using data collected by its sensors, the CID's computers adjusted the temperature of each tile to mimic its surroundings— displaying the heat signatures of trees, bushes, buildings, and even other vehicles. When moving slowly or at rest, the robot was practically impossible to detect using infrared or other thermal imagers. At high speeds, the camouflage system broke down as the CID moved through too many different heat textures too quickly and drained its power supplies.

"C'mon, Brad," Charlie said persuasively. "Between the thermal system and the new chameleon camouflage plates we've added, you can sneak right in on top of those guys and shoot the crap out of them. It'll be a great test of the system. All you've got to do is take it nice and easy. No fuss. No muss. No burned-out batteries. Right?"

She was right about that, Brad knew. This new CID also wore thousands of paper-thin electrochromatic plates layered over its thermal adaptive tiles. Derived from a highly advanced technology the Poles were experimenting with for a main battle tank they were designing, they represented the most significant upgrade Charlie and her Sky Masters team had crafted onto the new Mod IV CID. Put simply, they gave the robot a chameleon-like ability to blend with its environment. Its onboard computers continuously monitored the terrain through which it moved, using tiny voltage changes to alter the mix of colors displayed by each electrochromatic plate.

But there was another way to deal with this planned ambush, one that might be a heck of a lot more fun. So he kept retreating, moving back about five hundred meters in silence, blending with the shadows. At last, satisfied with his position, he slid a 25mm autocannon out of one of his weapons packs and checked the ammunition load. "Okay, Wolf One is weapons live," he radioed Charlie. "Stand by."

"What the heck are you playing at, Brad?" she said, exasperated. "You can't lay down effective fire from your current position—not unless you're planning to waste enough ammo to chop down half this forest first!"

"You know what your trouble is, Charlie?" Brad asked.

She sighed. "I'm afraid to ask. But go ahead. Tell me."

"Despite all those years you spent under my dad's command, you still think like a ground pounder," he said. "But I'm a McLanahan to the bone, so I know you should fight using all three dimensions whenever you can."

"Oh no," Brad heard Charlie groan.

"Oh yeah!" he said, grinning like a madman. Then he took a deep breath, getting set and making sure those hidden enemy fighting positions were locking in tight on his battle computer. Three. Two. One. *Now!* Autocannon at the ready, he sprinted forward—accelerating with every stride, racing through the woods at ever-increasing speed. Shattered branches, leaves, and clumps of torn brush whirled away in his wake.

Guided by his commands, his CID's computer threw a series of markers across his display, continuously adjusting them as his speed picked up. Two hundred meters. One hundred and fifty meters. Seventy-five. Ten. The last marker flashed green.

And Brad jumped, bounding high into the air at nearly seventy miles an hour. The huge fighting machine came crashing down through the trees, hit the ground still running, and leaped again.

This time Brad landed right in the middle of the enemy position. He dug in his heels, braking to a stop in a huge cloud of dirt and dust, and then spun rapidly through a complete circle—firing precisely aimed bursts into every foxhole and hollowed-out tree concealing hostile troops and weapons. Flashes lit the woods in all directions, strobing eerily in the darkness.

At last, his autocannon whirred and fell silent. *Blank ammunition expended*, the CID's battle computer reported.

Still smiling, Brad opened a channel, careful to set his electronically synthesized voice to normal human volume. "So, what about it, Captain Schofield? Have you and your merry gang of backwoods bandits had enough for tonight? Or shall we make it the best two out of three?"

Cautiously, a soldier, clad from head to foot in a leaf-and-branch-studded sniper's ghillie suit, stood up in one of the foxholes. Before joining the Iron Wolf Squadron to fight the Russians last year, Ian Schofield had been an officer in Canada's Special Operations Regiment. Now his own teeth flashed white in a rueful, answering grin. "I think you've made your point, Brad. As has Ms. Turlock." He shook his head in wonder. "That new Mod IV CID of yours is a damned good piece of gear. I'm just glad my lads and I won't be the ones facing it in real action."

MAIN CONTROL ROOM, UNIT TWO, CERNAVODĂ NUCLEAR POWER STATION, ROMANIA

That same time

Surrounded by several other large, industrial-looking buildings, two domed concrete cylinders rose above a countryside otherwise dotted with fields, orchards, and a few small villages and mid-size towns. Sited on a canal that fed into the Danube River, the Cernavodă Nuclear Station's twin seven-hundred-megawatt heavy-water reactors supplied 20 percent of Romania's electricity.

First ordered during the Ceaușescu regime, Unit Two only came on line eighteen years after the brutal communist dictator's overthrow and execution. Three more planned reactors had been mothballed at the earliest stages of construction.

Like all Canadian CANDU-6 designs, both operational Cernavodă reactors relied heavily on automated computer control systems, first to maintain safe and efficient power production and then to shut the reactors down in an emergency. The plant's operators stressed the advantages these advanced digital systems offered over the less sophisticated, manpower-intensive control measures used in competing reactor designs. From a purely technical standpoint, their claims had merit. Increased automation meant fewer human-induced errors, lower costs, and safer day-to-day operation.

Unfortunately, those same computer systems also created a path—a hidden breach in all the defenses and barriers intended to protect Unit Two from accident or attack. A breach that ran straight into the reactor's hellishly radioactive, high-pressure, high-temperature core.

In a peaceful world, this overlooked vulnerability would never have mattered.

But the world was not at peace.

Control room supervisor Marku Proca yawned

once and then again. "*Isus*. Jesus," he muttered, fighting down a third jaw-cracking yawn. He blinked rapidly, distractedly running a hand through his thick mane of white hair. Night shifts were always a bitch.

One of the two younger men stationed in the control room glanced away from the computer displays on the operator's desk. "Want another coffee, boss?"

Wryly, Proca shook his head. "No thanks. My kidneys are already floating." He nodded toward the displays. "So? Any problems?"

The third man, a senior plant operator named Nicolae Diaconu, shrugged. "No. As usual, everything's nominal." He pulled a safety logbook closer and jotted down a few notes, checking the time as he signed it with a flourish. "There, you see! Twenty-two thirty hours and all's well."

At that moment, unnoticed by Proca or his two subordinates, preset logic bombs detonated inside the computers tasked with monitoring Unit Two's independent automated emergency shutdown systems. Malicious code covertly embedded in their operating software suddenly went live, surreptitiously taking control while leaving routine operations seemingly undisturbed. Within milliseconds, the hijacked computers began sending precisely tailored viruses through fiber-optic links connecting them to other machines.

Down and down the linked hierarchy of computers these pieces of malware rippled— methodically seizing every system in their path as they moved closer to their primary targets. There, at the very heart of each of Cernovadǎ's two emergency shutdown mechanisms, lay three very small, very simple digital machines.

These "trip" computers had one function: they constantly cycled through data sent from sensors embedded in the reactor core, coolant systems, and the containment building. When any two out of three of these tiny computers sensed temperatures or pressures or other anomalies beyond parameters set in their simple programming, they were expected to "trip" the reactor—safely shutting it down in seconds.

But now viruses latched on to their very basic code and went to work, swiftly cutting away those parts of each program that "read" incoming sensor data. Stitched in their place were endlessly repeating loops of false data—all showing a range of perfectly safe temperatures, pressures, coolant flow levels, and neutron power.

In a matter of seconds, both of the elaborate automated systems designed to shut down Cernavodǎ's Unit Two were out of action, securely cocooned in an illusory digital world where nothing would ever go wrong.

Now a small subroutine in the rogue program controlling one of the commandeered computers activated.

Beep. Beep. Beep.

Nicolae Diaconu closed the logbook he'd just finished signing and glanced at his display. "I've got a minor flag from one of the test and display computers," he told Proca. "Says it's getting

an error reading from a neutron flux detector in
Zone 11."

"Just one?" Proca asked. There were nearly two
hundred separate vanadium and platinum-clad
flux sensors set throughout the reactor core.

Diaconu took a closer look. "Only one detector," he confirmed. "NFS-11A."

Proca shrugged. "Follow normal procedure.
Have the DCC test the same sensor. Let's see if
we've got a genuine equipment failure or just a
programming glitch."

"Already on it," Diaconu said, keying in a command to the plant's main "X" Digital Control
Computer.

Neither man ever realized that this routine
request for a diagnostic check on sensor NFS-
11A was the detonation trigger for yet another
logic bomb, this one buried deep inside the control computer's core operating software. Line
after line of malicious code spooled through the
computer, rapidly taking command over specific
programs used to manage the reactor and its associated systems. Another virus flashed through
a link into the identical "Y" DCC running in
standby mode, turning it into a slave clone of the
hijacked master computer.

In a perfectly timed, sequenced, and calibrated
digital assault taking less than thirty seconds
from start to finish, Unit Two's human operators
lost control over their seven-hundred-megawatt
heavy-water nuclear power reactor—and all without the slightest warning.

CERNAVODĂ UNIT TWO REACTOR CONTAINER BUILDING
That same time

Now fully in command, the sabotage programs running in the reactor's digital control system kicked into high gear. Over the course of the next few minutes, dozens of valves and actuators opened and closed in a carefully orchestrated sequence. Thousands of gallons of deuterium-laced "heavy" water and ordinary light water used to cool and control the reactor drained away. Steel-encased cadmium rods used to adjust the fission reaction slid out of the core and locked.

More valves opened. Pressurized helium gas reserves set aside to force emergency supplies of cooling water and gadolinium nitrate—a chemical that could poison and stop the fission reaction—into the core in a crisis vented uselessly into the cold night air outside the containment building.

As its control mechanisms were ruthlessly and systematically stripped away, power levels inside the reactor started spiking. Temperatures inside thousands of uranium fuel bundles rose fast, heating the heavy water still surrounding them to the boiling point. This, in turn, caused the fission reaction to climb even faster.

As minutes ticked by without human intervention or even awareness, temperatures and pressures inside Cernavodă Unit Two's core climbed dangerously. Fuel bundles melted, sagging closer and closer together. Hydrogen gas began boiling off the super-heated zirconium alloy cladding around each bundle.

Through all of this, the computer-driven displays inside the control room showed no signs of trouble. Separate analog-driven contact alarms should have gone off as the reactor went haywire, lighting up in a dazzling cascade across control panels. Instead, these backup alerts fell prey to yet another weakness in Cernavodă's automated systems.

Concerned that human operators could be overwhelmed by the hundreds of alarms that might be triggered in any real crisis, the plant's designers had installed alarm prioritization software. In an emergency, this program deliberately suppressed all minor alarms. In theory, this allowed control room operators to focus on the most serious threats they faced. What its creators failed to anticipate was the unauthorized insertion of a single line of malicious code, one that automatically defined *all* alarms as minor.

And so Cernavodă Unit Two's highly trained and dedicated control room personnel were left essentially blind, deaf, and dumb—with no way of knowing that their reactor was racing out of control, accelerating toward a catastrophic meltdown.

MAIN CONTROL ROOM
A short time later

Marku Proca checked his watch and sighed. Half an hour left until he could reasonably take another coffee break. He stretched back in his chair, concentrating on keeping his eyes open. Sure, Diaconu and Ion Morar, the other operator, were both capable guys, but it wouldn't do them any good to see him slacking off on shift.

His direct line to the turbine room buzzed.

"Proca here," he said.

"What the hell's going on down there, Marku?" a voice demanded, barely audible over the earsplitting whine of huge machinery spooling down. "We're not getting near enough steam. Every goddamned turbine I've got is shutting down!"

Proca sat up straighter, suddenly wide-awake. "What?"

"We're going dark, Marku! Your fucking reactor must be off-line. So why don't I see any trip alarms?"

Proca stared at the displays showing Unit Two's status. Everything on his board showed the reactor operating well within normal parameters. Nothing *was* wrong. Nothing *could* be wrong. In its essentials, nuclear power generation was a simple process. A fission reaction produced heat. Water circulating through the core to cool and control the reaction turned into steam. And that steam drove turbines, producing electricity.

He started to sweat. If one or more of Unit Two's steam generators had blown out, that was bad. Very bad. But the only other possible explanation was even worse. What if they were facing a massive rupture in the reactor's cooling system? A major loss-of-coolant accident, or LOCA, was the primary nightmare for any nuclear plant.

"Marku?"

"We're checking," Proca snapped, dropping the phone. He spun toward Diaconu. "There must be something wrong with the primary DCC. Switch control to the 'Y' computer. Now!" The younger man immediately obeyed.

His action set off two more pieces of malware buried in their computer system.

Immediately an alarm shrieked, accompanied by a flashing red icon on Diaconu's display. "I've got a major fire warning in the secondary control area!" he yelled. "The SCA's automated sprinklers are activating!"

"Oh, shit," Proca said. Unit Two's secondary control area was designed to maintain safe operation of the plant if an accident wrecked the main control room or otherwise rendered it uninhabitable. But now, triggered by the false fire alarm, torrents of high-pressure water sluiced across the SCA's computers, equipment panels, and other electronics—setting off a destructive chain of short circuits and overloads.

Bad as that was, the complicated sequence of valve openings and closures set in motion by the second piece of malicious code was far more deadly.

In seconds, the superheated steam still boiling away from the reactor found itself funneled into just one section of pipe—a section that ran right over the main control room. Under computer control, another valve at the far end spun shut. As more and more steam forced its way into the bottlenecked pipe, its internal pressure climbed higher and higher. Forced far beyond its structural limits, the steam pipe suddenly ballooned, cracked, and then blew apart.

Jagged steel splinters sleeted outward from the burst pipe—shredding everything and everyone in their path. Marku Proca had just time enough to see Diaconu and Morar hurled aside in a spray of blood and bone. And then he broiled to death a fraction of a second later when the temperature hit more than six hundred degrees Fahrenheit.

Safe in a shielded area behind the wrecked control room, Unit Two's hijacked computers continued executing their carefully laid-out sabotage programs.

CHAPTER 2

**THE SCRAPHEAP, FORMERLY SILIŞTEA
GUMEŞTI MILITARY AIRFIELD, ROMANIA**
A short time later

The Iron Wolf Squadron CID piloted by Brad
McLanahan strode into a huge darkened
hangar. Behind him, two big doors rolled shut and
overhead lights snapped back on, revealing ultramodern aircraft of various makes parked across a
vast concrete expanse.

The locals believed the old Romanian air base's
absentee foreigner owners were content to let it
rot. That was exactly what Scion, the private military corporation run by former U.S. president
Kevin Martindale, wanted them to believe. The
Scion and Iron Wolf personnel stationed here
called it the Scrapheap—reflecting its decaying,
disused external appearance. But behind the peeling paint, rust, and piled-up rubbish was a fully
equipped operating base jam-packed with sophis-

ticated aircraft, drones, combat vehicles, weapons, communications gear, and sensors.

Near the far wall, a second CID already stood motionless. Still wiry and lithe in her midthirties, Charlie Turlock, dwarfed by the twelve-foot-tall machine, had her strawberry-blond head inside an open panel on one of its spindly-looking legs. Two harassed-looking technicians stood next to her.

Brad moved up beside them and ordered the robot to crouch down. With the main hatch clear, he climbed out and dropped lightly to the concrete floor.

"I don't care what you've been told before," he heard Charlie tell the techs. "But in my book there is no excuse for sending one of these machines out into the field with systems operating below spec. And right now this leg's main hydraulic assembly is pegging out at ninety-four percent of its rated efficiency. That is *not* acceptable."

"Ms. Turlock," one of the techs said stiffly. "With all due respect, Major Macomber says—"

Scowling, Charlie whipped her head out of the open panel and turned on the tech. "Do *I* look *anything* like Whack Macomber to you?"

"Nope," Brad said, coming up beside her with a quick grin. "He's at least twice as big and four times as ugly."

Charlie laughed. "Flattery won't get you anywhere, McLanahan." Her eyes gleamed with amusement. "Besides, I hear you already have a serious flame back in Warsaw. Which would explain those Polish phrases I hear you trying to rattle off so nonchalantly all the time."

Brad nodded, feeling his face turn just the slightest bit red.

He and Major Nadia Rozek had been thrown together last year, when the newly formed Iron Wolf Squadron helped fight off a determined Russian attack on Poland. Since then, he'd realized that the beautiful young Polish Special Forces officer was a force of nature—tough-minded, fearless, and intensely passionate. Her current duties as a military aide to Poland's president, Piotr Wilk, tied her to the capital more than she would like, especially when Brad's own assignments took him farther afield. But whenever they could, they spent every waking and sleeping moment in each other's company. And a relationship he'd first imagined was just a whirlwind "girl in every foreign port" kind of fling now showed every sign of turning into something a heck of a lot more serious.

Still smiling, Charlie took his arm. "C'mon, Brad, you can buy me a glass of wine at the canteen and then keep me company while I write up my report on tonight's exercise." She waggled a stern finger at him. "A report that will include a full and honest evaluation of that crazy-assed stunt you pulled off."

"Yes, ma'am," Brad agreed, relieved that she was letting him off the hook.

She glanced back over her shoulder at the two technicians. "And in the meantime, you guys are going to bring that unit up to one hundred percent status ASAP—even if you have to pull the whole leg assembly and replace every power coupling and fluid line. Got it?" Glum-faced, they nodded.

Once they were out of earshot, Brad asked, "Kinda hard-assed, weren't you?"

"Yep." Charlie nodded. "But that's one of the reasons I'm out here in the Romanian boonies instead of kicking back in my nice cushy Sky Masters lab." She shook her head. "Look, Wayne Macomber's a rocking, socking soldier and a damned fine tactician, but you and I both know he doesn't much like CIDs. He'll fight in them when he has to, but basically they give him the creeps."

That was true, Brad knew. He'd often heard the big, powerfully built Iron Wolf ground forces commander bitching about feeling like a slave to the "damned unholy gadget" whenever he piloted a CID. "So?"

"So he's got kind of a blind spot when it comes to their proper care and feeding," Charlie said quietly. "The Russians may still be licking their wounds from last year, but they'll be back—and probably sooner rather than later. And when they come, you're going to need every CID and other piece of high-tech military hardware you can scrounge as a force multiplier. So you're gonna want everything in tip-top fighting condition, not sidelined for repairs because someone figured 'good enough' would cut it. That's why your dad wants me to tighten things up on the maintenance side."

Surprised, Brad looked at her.

She shrugged her shoulders. "Yeah, I know the general's still alive and kicking." She snorted. "I always knew Patrick McLanahan was a steely-eyed hard-ass. I just never figured that he'd find a way to make that literally true." She shook her head in wonder. "Three years riding a robot full-time. Man, I wouldn't have bet that was possible. Or sane."

Brad nodded slowly. Very few people knew that his father, critically wounded during an unauthorized mission against the People's Republic of China years ago, had actually survived. Fewer still knew that only a CID's life-support systems kept him alive. Piloting one of the huge machines sustained his crippled body, but it could not heal him. Patrick McLanahan was trapped, forced to interact with the world entirely through the CID's sensor arrays and computers.

Brad sighed, fighting down the painful blend of regret and relief and anger that hit home whenever he thought much about his father. It was always hard seeing the bold and daring man who'd raised him pushed off into the shadows—robbed of all normal human contact in an eerie world of binary 1's and 0's. But now it felt even worse.

During Russia's recent attack against Poland, Patrick McLanahan had revealed himself to Gennadiy Gryzlov and to Stacy Anne Barbeau, the new American president. Both were horrified to learn that the man they considered an enemy and a threat to world order was still alive. But neither political leader had known his true condition.

Both Gryzlov and Barbeau were sure he was dead for real this time—shot down by American F-35 fighters along with the rest of the Iron Wolf bomber force flying back from an all-or-nothing strike against a Russian ballistic-missile force set to blast Poland off the map. That callous act of treachery had been the price demanded by Gryzlov for agreeing not to drag the United States into a war Stacy Anne Barbeau feared. It was a price she had been gullible enough and cowardly enough to pay, even at the cost of shattering the NATO alliance.

"Sorry, Brad," he heard Charlie say softly. "I know it sucks." She rested her hand lightly on his arm.

He forced himself to smile and squared his shoulders. "Now about that drink you wanted—"

"Captain McLanahan!" he heard someone call out.

He looked around, seeing a Scion staffer hurrying down the hall toward them.

"Yes?"

"You're needed in the communications center, sir," the man said tersely. "There's a secure call for you from Mr. Martindale. He's got President Wilk on the same line. Priority Alpha One. All Scion and Iron Wolf stations are going on full alert."

Brad felt cold. Short of a surprise air or missile attack on Warsaw or some other allied population center, he couldn't imagine much else that would trigger that kind of move.

"I'll tag along, if you don't mind," Charlie said. Her mouth twisted in a sly grin. "You know I always hate to miss a party."

ABOARD AN XV-40 SPARROWHAWK TILT-ROTOR, OVER ROMANIA
A short time later

"*Tak, panie prezydencie.* Yes, Mr. President," Brad McLanahan said, speaking loud enough into the mic to be heard over the pounding roar of the Sparrowhawk's huge propellers. "I'll do my best."

"Very good, Captain," Piotr Wilk said gravely. "You should know that this appeal for our help comes from the very highest levels of the Romanian government. President Dumitru himself assures me they have no other hope of averting disaster. Unless someone can get inside Cernavodă and manually activate whatever shutdown and emergency cooling systems survive, his experts believe the reactor containment building will rupture—"

"Spewing radiation across Romania and a hell of a lot of central Europe," Brad said impatiently. "With respect, sir, the situation's pretty clear."

"All normal and fucked up, yes?"

"As per usual," Brad agreed. The Polish president's grasp of American military slang kept growing by leaps and bounds.

The Sparrowhawk banked sharply, slowing fast as its propellers swiveled upward, turning into rotors. Through the cockpit windows, he caught a glimpse of what appeared to be a large industrial complex, eerily bathed in spotlights. Flashing blue and red lights showed a sea of emergency vehicles—fire trucks, ambulances, and police cars—surrounding the power plant.

"We're at the reactor site," he reported. "I've got to go, Mr. President. It's time to suit up."

"Understood," Wilk replied. "Good luck." He paused, and then said carefully, "There is one more person here who wishes to speak to you. She is . . . most insistent."

Brad swallowed hard. "Hi, Nadia," he said, trying to sound casual.

"You will be careful," Nadia Rozek said crisply.

"You realize that I'm planning on walking into a nuclear reactor that might already be melting down, right?" Brad asked.

"Yes," she said huskily. "That is *why* you will be *very* careful, Brad McLanahan."

"I'll try," he promised.

"*Kocham cię.* I love you," Nadia murmured. "So I will be extremely angry if you get yourself killed unnecessarily. Understand?"

"Yes, ma'am," Brad said quickly, feeling a lump in his own throat.

The Sparrowhawk touched down in the middle of a hurriedly cleared field. Groups of nuclear plant technicians, policemen, and soldiers waited nervously at the edge of the landing zone, their faces lowered against the sudden rotor-blown hail of dust and dead grass.

Charlie Turlock tapped him on the shoulder. "Time's up, smooth talker," she said, with a grin. "But remind me later to give you some pro tips on soulful romantic chitchat."

"If there *is* a later," Brad said, unstrapping from his seat and moving back into the troop compartment, where the support crew was already prepping his CID.

"Well, yeah, there is that," Charlie agreed. "But have a little faith, okay? That machine can take one heck of a lot of heat and radiation and keep on ticking just fine. Trust me."

Brad nodded, knowing she was right. Five years before, Charlie herself had piloted a CID into a burning federal building gutted by a terrorist's "dirty" bomb packed with iridium-192. Sighing, he climbed through the CID's main hatch and squirmed into position in the cockpit, waiting patiently while the robot's computers synched with his central nervous system.

The hatch sealed.

"Wolf One is up," he said as status reports, data, and images gleaned by the CID's sensors began pouring into his consciousness. His audio pickups immediately tamped down the otherwise overwhelming sounds of barely contained chaos—blaring klaxons, sirens, and frantic radio calls from emergency crews trying to cope with a disaster far beyond their training or ability to control.

"Shutting down thermal adaptive and chameleon camouflage systems," he radioed. There was no point in wasting the limited power stored in his lithium-ion batteries and hydrogen fuel cells. He couldn't expect to hide from impersonal forces of nature like radiation, heat, and pressure.

"Copy that, One," he heard Charlie say. Wearing a headset, she stood at the edge of the Sparrowhawk's lowered ramp, ready to guide him out of the aircraft. "Right, big guy, let's go greet the puny earthlings. But now that you're fully visible, try not to scare the shit out of too many of the locals, okay? We're going to need all the help and technical advice we can get."

CHAPTER 3

EQUIPMENT AIR LOCK, CERNAVODĂ UNIT TWO REACTOR CONTAINMENT BUILDING
A short time later

Cautiously, Brad McLanahan moved into the huge air lock. Ordinarily used to transfer new fuel bundles and other heavy equipment into the containment building, it was just big enough for his CID to stand upright. His radiation and temperature sensors ticked up slightly, but not beyond the expected range. He relaxed a little. The inner containment seals were still holding. For now, anyway.

Behind him, a massive steel door swung slowly shut. It locked into place with a rhythmic, repeated series of solid-sounding *CA-CA-CA-CLANK*s.

"The outer door is sealed, Wolf One," a tense voice confirmed through his headphones. Scarcely two hours ago, Vasile Enescu had been at home, comfortably asleep in his own bed. Now, as the senior surviving emergency coordinator, the middle-aged Romanian nuclear engineer found himself neck-deep in a catastrophe no one had ever imagined possible. There were no drills, no intensely rehearsed response plans to fall back on.

The rapid-fire briefing Enescu gave Brad before he entered the air lock quickly made it clear that the Romanians knew next to nothing about conditions inside the containment building or the reactor itself. Without functioning control rooms and computers, they were entirely dependent on readings from a handful of external gauges—readings that seemed to show the unthinkable, a complete failure of both automated shutdown systems *and* all of the emergency cooling systems.

"I'm ready to open the inner door," Brad said. "Stand by."

He moved closer to a keypad set next to the door. Carefully, using his CID's powerful, articulated metal fingers, he punched in the security code uploaded into his computer—along with all of the nuclear plant's schematics and operating manuals.

The pad display flashed red: *Acces Interzis*. Access Denied.

"Swell," Brad muttered. He tapped the keys again, double-checking the code.

Again, *Acces Interzis* blinked back at him.

"Either the door motors are on the fritz, or the lock mechanisms are disabled," he reported. "I'm resetting for manual operation."

Guided by the CID's computer, Brad yanked open a wall-mounted panel and quickly pulled several circuit breakers. The security keypad went dark. He moved back to the inner door, gripped the handwheel set in the middle, and spun it counterclockwise.

Slowly, the thick steel door swung away, opening into the containment building.

A blast of hot air roared into the air lock. A graphic flashed across Brad's display, showing the temperature spiking from a comparatively cool twenty-four degrees centigrade to nearly sixty degrees—140 on the Fahrenheit scale—by the time the door was fully open. At the same time, atmospheric pressure climbed to around 125 kilopascals, a little over 1.2 times the normal air pressure at sea level.

Brad winced. Given the situation, those readings weren't totally unexpected, but they were still a bad sign. Containment buildings were usually kept at slightly negative pressure, a feature meant to keep stray contaminated particles inside in case of any small leak.

He peered into the interior. It was pitch-black. All of the normal and emergency lights seemed to be dead. His computer compensated instantly, piercing the darkness with its blend of passive and active sensors. He shook his head in dismay, staring at a labyrinth of pipes, pumps, steam generator tanks, electrical conduits, cranes, and other equipment that filled the enormous building almost from floor to ceiling. Steel tracks used to guide new fuel assemblies to the reactor itself ran deeper into the maze.

Warning. Warning. Radiation count rising. Temperature rising. Atmospheric pressure rising. Estimated

time to catastrophic suit protection and systems failure:
Twenty minutes, the CID reported. A small timer
activated at the edge of Brad's vision, counting
down in jumps and skips as the computer continuously reevaluated its original estimate.

No time to waste, he told himself, feeling his
heart rate accelerate. His mouth felt dry. He
needed to get in, find out what was going on, fix
it if possible—and then get the hell out of this
deathtrap.

"Entering containment now," he reported.

"Understood, Wolf One," Enescu said. He
sounded even more worried now. Clearly, the
readings echoed from Brad's CID had him rattled
too. "Make for the vault. It is imperative that we
discover the reactor's current status."

"On my way," Brad replied. He swung down
off the tracks and moved deeper into the labyrinth, heading toward a colossal concrete block at
its heart. Twenty meters high and twenty meters
deep, this was the vault housing the fission reactor
itself. Green arrows lit up on his display, indicating the fastest route to his target, one of the end
shields. These steel shields, protruding out of the
vault, were the only parts of the reactor not solidly encased in concrete and carbon steel.

He ducked under a set of rails and carriages—
part of the machine used to insert fresh uranium
fuel bundles and remove spent ones—and came
face-to-face with a tall cylindrical shell. Behind
this shield lay the calandria, an enormous metal
drum containing the intricate assembly of pressure tubes, nozzles, compartments, and control

rods that made up the reactor core. Row after row of hundreds of capped metal lattice tubes projected horizontally through the end shield.

Whole sections of pipe fittings and tubes glowed with unearthly intensity. Rivulets of molten steel dripped slowly down the face of the shield, crackling and hissing in the darkness.

Warning. Warning. Rapid temperature increase. Pressure now 200 kPa. Radiation count climbing, his computer reported. The countdown clock blinked bright red and readjusted. *Fifteen minutes to protective shielding failure and lethal exposure.*

"You seeing what I'm seeing, Vasile?" Brad asked, staring up at the luridly glowing end shield.

"Affirmative," Enescu said, horrified. "*Lisus Hristos!* Jesus Christ! The damned thing really is melting down. We are losing whole fuel assemblies!"

"No kidding," Brad snapped. He swallowed hard, trying to stay calm. "So tell me what I need to do first."

"The secondary cooling system!" the other man said, after a moment's thought. "We need to buy time by dumping as much water as we can into the reactor as fast as possible."

"I thought all your pumps were off-line," Brad said, puzzled.

"They are," Enescu told him excitedly. "But there should still be a very large quantity of water left inside a big reserve storage tank at the very top of the containment building. Our high-pressure cooling system is disabled, but we can still use gravity to get water into the reactor!"

Brad's CID highlighted the water tank the other man was describing. "That's your dousing tank," he realized, studying the data flashed by his computer. "Isn't that supposed to tamp down some of the pressure buildup in here? Before the building blows apart under stress? I mean."

"Ordinarily, yes," the Romanian said, almost stumbling over words in his haste to explain. "But with the internal atmospheric pressures your machine is reporting, the dousing system should already be in action. So it must be off-line, too."

"Along with everything else in this joint," Brad growled.

"You *must* make cooling the reactor your top priority," Enescu said. "Unless you can do that, nothing else ultimately matters." Keys clicked as he typed furiously on his laptop. "I am transmitting a list of the valves you need to open, and those you need to shut off, *now*."

Green and red dots suddenly blossomed on Brad's display, each matching one of the valves on the list the Romanian had sent by data link directly to the CID's computer. They were numbered in order of priority—stepping down in a sequence from near the ceiling to a group of valves just above the top of the reactor vault.

"Wolf One copies," Brad said. He moved fast through the complicated jumble of pumps, generators, and other machinery, dodging and ducking to avoid smashing into pipes and conduits. He came out into a relatively open area near the edge of the huge reactor assembly and looked straight up. Reaching the catwalk leading to the first valves he needed to open meant climbing at least eleven flights of narrow, steep metal stairs.

Warning. Warning. Time to suit breach now ten minutes, thirty-five seconds.

"Screw taking the stairs," he muttered, shaking his head. Instead, he leaped straight up, grabbed a railing, started swinging back and forth, and then flung himself upward again—just as the railing crumpled and then tore away under the CID's weight. Up and up he went, twisting and curling from handhold to handhold as though the robot were a circus acrobat rather than a fighting machine.

One last jump took him onto the central catwalk. It shook, swaying under the sudden impact.

Brad bounded over to the first valve, spun it open, and turned away, ready to move on to the next one in the preplotted sequence.

WHIRR.

He whirled back and saw the valve closing again, driven by a power-operated actuator. Frowning, he cranked the valve open again and watched it closely a second time. "What the hell is this, Vasile?" Brad asked.

"That should not be possible," the Romanian said, stunned.

"Possible or not, it's damned well happening," Brad snapped. "What's the procedure here?"

Enescu hesitated, clearly thinking it through. "If you unscrew the access plate on the left side of the actuator motor, you should be able to uncouple the—"

Warning. Temperature now eighty-five degrees cen-

tigrade. Pressure at 225 kilopascals. Radiation rising. Hydraulic system function degrading, now at eighty percent. Sensor function partially impaired. Time to fatal suit breach now seven minutes, forty seconds.

"No way! I don't have time for anything complicated," Brad interrupted. He could actually feel the CID growing stiffer and less responsive to his commands. His visual displays flickered slightly, dimming just a bit as some of the robot's sensors failed.

Sweating inside the cockpit, he grabbed the actuator motor and ripped it off the valve. It sailed away into the darkness in a shower of sparks and torn metal.

"Or you could just do that," Enescu admitted.

Brad gritted his teeth and swung over the edge of the catwalk. In a blur of motion, he guided the CID downward through the tangle of piping and machinery, opening some valves and closing others. Crumpled actuators were hurled aside, clanging and clattering down to the floor far below.

He reached the last set of valves and cranked them full open. Pipes above him were humming, vibrating, as thousands of gallons of water poured along the path he'd opened into the reactor. He dropped the rest of the way, landing heavily on top of the vault.

WHUMMP. WHUMMP. WHUMMP. WHUMMP.

The massive vault shuddered beneath his feet. Four huge plumes of superheated steam erupted on all sides, hissing and boiling higher and higher. Immediately the CID showed external temperature, radiation, and pressure readings jumping dramatically.

Warning. Warning. Time to suit failure now five minutes, ten seconds. Brad swore under his breath.

"Those are pressure relief ducts," he heard Enescu babbling. "Temperatures inside the core must be so high that our cooling water is flashing into steam on contact. If the disks sealing those ducts had not ruptured, the calandria itself might have fractured!"

"*No, to pięknie,*" Brad snarled. "That's just swell." He sighed. "What's next? I'm running out of time real fast in here."

"You must manually release the SDS-1 rods," the Romanian said, referring to a group of thirty-two cadmium rods that should have plunged into the core the instant the reactor began running wild—shutting it down automatically. "With so many fuel bundles already damaged or destroyed, some of the rods may not be able to fully deploy. Even so, any rods that reach the core should greatly slow the fission reaction."

"Okay," Brad said. He scrambled toward a shallow rectangular gap on the top of the vault. That opened onto a concrete-stiffened steel box called the reactivity mechanism deck. Row after row of shutdown rod drives protruded above the deck.

He crouched down, ordering the CID's display to zoom in on those drive mechanisms.

"*Isus,*" Enescu said, seeing the images he sent. "The clutches between each motor and shaft have been de-energized, locking them in position. But this should only happen *after* a reactor trip, not before. This is—"

"Impossible," Brad finished for him grimly. "Yeah, I get it. Look, I'm starting to sense a really bad pattern here. How about you?"

"Yes," the other man said simply.

Suit failure in four minutes, the CID's computer reported calmly.

"Moving now!" Brad snapped. Hunched over, he scurried across the deck, systematically tearing away cables connecting the shutdown rods to their control units and motors. Freed from the locking mechanisms holding them in place, rod after spring-driven cadmium rod fell away— plunging deep into the steam-clouded jumble of twisted pressure tubes and molten uranium fuel slurry inside the reactor.

Radiation levels decreasing, the CID told him. *Containment building temperature and pressure still rising. Hydraulic system function down to sixty percent. Estimated time to catastrophic suit failure now less than two minutes.*

"I'm heading for the air lock," Brad radioed, moving carefully toward the edge of the vault. His eyes narrowed, looking for a clear path through the clouds of superheated steam still billowing off the reactor.

There.

He jumped down. And fell sprawling across the concrete floor when the CID's right leg refused to flex. "Shit!"

Partial hydraulic failure, the computer reported. *Emergency override inoperative*. Brad swore again, seeing whole sections of his system schematics wink yellow and then red. He forced the robot upright, hearing damaged servos and actuators whining shrilly in protest.

Dragging his CID's immobile right leg, he limped awkwardly toward the open air-lock door.

Warning. Warning. Chemical alert.

"You have *got* to be kidding me," Brad snarled at his computer. What now? He was right at the edge of the air lock, for Christ's sake! Exasperated, he swung around.

In his display, the clouds of steam venting off the reactor vault now glowed bright red. The CID's chemical sniffers were picking up a growing volume of flammable hydrogen gas mixed in with the water vapor, rising higher and higher toward the distant ceiling. His jaw tightened. Too much hydrogen accumulating up there could trigger an explosion powerful enough to blow the containment building apart.

"Tell me this isn't really a problem, Vasile," he said quietly.

"It is not a problem," Enescu said confidently. "We have a network of automated igniters spaced around the top of the containment area. They will burn off the hydrogen before it reaches a dangerous concentration."

Brad stared up through the maze of pipes and machinery. He shook his head in disgust. "Yeah, that would be great. Unfortunately, your fucking *automated* igniters aren't firing."

For a moment, there was stunned silence over the radio circuit. "*O Doamne!* Oh my God!"

Catastrophic suit failure in forty-five seconds.

Scowling, Brad took out his autocannon and loaded a single 25mm incendiary round. He backed up to the very edge of the open air lock. "Look," he told Enescu. "Right now I can probably set off the hydrogen pocket near the roof. But what I need to know and *fast* is if that's just going to blow the shit out of this whole place."

There was another long silence.

Twenty-five seconds. Twenty-four seconds. Twenty-three seconds.

"Our calculations show that any hydrogen flare or explosion now should inflict only minimal damage," Enescu said at last.

Seventeen seconds. Sixteen seconds.

"How sure of that are you?"

Fourteen seconds. Thirteen seconds.

"Only somewhat sure," the other man admitted.

Eleven seconds. Ten.

"Works for me," Brad said simply. He aimed upward, zeroing in on a bare patch of concrete on the containment roof. Then he squeezed the trigger. The autocannon bucked.

WHUUUMMMMP!

A bright orange flash overloaded his vision screens. They went black. In that same instant, a shock wave slammed into the CID. Servos howling, Brad stumbled backward into the air lock.

His displays flickered back online and he breathed out in relief. Both the roof and the intricate, interwoven assembly of pipes and machinery around the reactor appeared intact.

Seven seconds to suit failure. Six seconds.

Reacting fast, Brad dropped the autocannon, grabbed the heavy air-lock door, and hauled it shut. Then he frantically spun the handwheel clockwise. One after another, the door's locking mechanisms clicked into place—sealing out the lethal radiation and heat still emanating from the crippled reactor core.

Catastrophic suit failure averted, the robot's computer said coolly.

Wearily, Brad closed his eyes, ignoring the ever-lengthening recitation of the computer's list of damaged or destroyed components. Slowly and very deliberately, he slid down the side of the air lock. "Never again," he murmured. "I am never doing *anything* that crazy again."

"How much do you want to bet on that?" he heard Charlie Turlock say cheerfully over his headset. "Because you're a McLanahan, remember, and I've got my eye on a brand-new sports car that's *way* above my current pay grade."

OUTSIDE CERNAVODĂ NUCLEAR POWER STATION
That same time

Several hundred people milled around the edges of a kilometer-deep "emergency exclusion zone" hastily proclaimed around the damaged reactor. Policemen and some soldiers in riot gear were stationed to keep the onlookers—a mix of news crews and the morbidly curious—from getting any closer. Bright lights and logo-emblazoned vehicles marked the presence of television reporters jabbering away excitedly in half a dozen different languages, urgently relaying a mix of pure speculation, ill-informed guesswork, and wildly inaccurate information to audiences around the globe.

No one paid much attention to the small, three-man team working inside the back of a panel van parked near the outer fringes of the growing crowd. According to their licenses and ID cards, they were employees of EuroSlav News, a tiny, independent news agency whose business was selling content over the Internet and to small local papers across Eastern and central Europe. Behind the façade, however, EuroSlav News was a GRU front used both as a cover for intelligence gathering and as a means of disseminating covert pro-Russian propaganda to unsuspecting audiences.

One of the GRU agents, Captain Konstantin Rusanov, sat hunched over a bank of electronics equipment. Tasked with monitoring radio and computer signals from the plant, the short, dark-haired man was intensely focused. His mouth turned down suddenly as a new flood of signals reached his earphones and displays. He turned toward their team leader. "The Romanians and the Iron Wolf team have successfully prevented a containment breach," he said glumly, unable to hide his disappointment.

Major Leonid Usenko shrugged and stubbed out his cigarette in an overflowing ashtray. "That is unfortunate," he agreed. "But that reactor is still badly damaged, isn't it?"

Rusanov nodded. "Beyond repair, in all likelihood." He glanced at the third man, rail thin and balding, sitting next to him, busy watching over his own array of equipment. "Do you concur, Mikheyev?"

"I do," Captain Artem Mikheyev confirmed. He was a "special technical officer" assigned specifically for this mission. He smiled happily. "Best of all, the voice and video transmissions I've recorded should provide Moscow with much useful new data. Now that we've seen one in action, further technical analysis should teach us much about the strengths and weaknesses of these supposedly *invincible* Iron Wolf fighting machines."

CHAPTER 4

A few days later

Flanked by two AH-1Z Viper gunships, a Polish-made W-3 *Sokół* VIP helicopter came in low over the snow-dusted woods surrounding the base at Powidz. Rotors beating, it flared in for a landing right outside a large hangar. Even before its engines finished spooling down, the left-hand copilot's door slid back and Polish president Piotr Wilk dropped lightly onto the tarmac.

Moving fast, he crossed to the Iron Wolf hangar and headed straight for the conference room at its far end. Middling tall, trim, and not yet fifty, Wilk still carried himself like the veteran fighter pilot and charismatic air-force commander he had been before entering politics. There were many moments when he regretted leaving the military life he'd loved—of no longer being allowed to scramble into a MiG-29 Fulcrum or an F-16 Fighting Falcon and go head-to-head against his country's enemies. But those were also the moments when he reminded himself that true service to Poland and the cause of freedom required sacrifice.

In his case, that meant choosing the darker fields of statecraft, strategy, and diplomacy over the swift, exhilarating dance of air-to-air combat. And like so many Polish leaders before him, he faced the unenviable challenge of confronting Russia and its seemingly limitless imperial ambitions. Of defying an ancient enemy whose military and economic strength dwarfed that of his beleaguered nation.

But this time, Wilk reminded himself, Poland had allies. Not many, perhaps. Certainly not as the world conventionally reckoned numbers. But these were friends beyond price—friends who had already shown themselves willing to fight and die for a cause they considered just.

And these new allies had powers of their own, technologies, tactics, and weapons far beyond those used by other armed forces.

Kevin Martindale stepped forward, greeting him with a firm handshake. Once president of the United States, the gray-haired, gray-bearded American now ran Scion, a private military corporation. Last year, Scion's specialist commandos, pilots, and intelligence operatives served as the cadre for a new unit, the Iron Wolf Squadron. Using every advantage conferred by their high-tech aircraft, drones, and CID fighting machines,

the squadron had helped Poland's outmatched soldiers fight Russia to a draw—though only by the
narrowest of margins and at a high cost in dead
and wounded.

Wilk also knew that many of those who survived were paying yet another price for aiding
Poland. Caught backstabbing her own NATO ally
because she was afraid of the Russians, America's
president, Stacy Anne Barbeau, had retaliated by
seeking federal indictments against anyone who
worked for Scion or who had fought in the Iron
Wolf Squadron. She accused them of undermin-
ing U.S. national security interests and violating
laws that prohibited enlisting in a foreign army.
Legally, her claims were on shaky ground. In
practical terms, however, Martindale and many
of his fellow countrymen were effectively exiled
from their own native land.

He could only imagine the pain that must
bring.

"It's good to see you again, Piotr," Martindale
said quietly. "I wish it were in better circumstances."

Wilk nodded. "As do I."

With the NATO alliance fractured beyond
repair, thanks to Barbeau's malice and folly, he
and Martindale had been working for months to
build a coalition of the smaller countries from the
Baltic to the Black Sea. So far, their efforts had
met with more success than they had first dared
to hope.

Their new Alliance of Free Nations, the AFN,
now included Poland, all three of the small Baltic

states, Slovakia, Hungary, Romania, and even tiny Moldova. And the Czech Republic, though still formally outside the treaty, had expressed serious interest in joining its Eastern and central European neighbors. Even the Finns, although reluctant to openly risk angering the Russian bear prowling around their doorstep, were secretly willing to coordinate defense planning and other operations.

Backed by the hard-earned reputation of its Iron Wolf "auxiliaries," Poland was still the chief military power in this fledging defense pact. Nevertheless, the Scion weapons and advisers doled out to other frontline states had measurably improved their fighting forces. Compared to the Russians, the AFN nations were still horribly outgunned—in population, economic clout, raw troop strength, and access to high-tech military hardware. But now at least they had enough power and political coherence to deter anything but an all-out Russian offensive.

Or so Wilk and his fellow national leaders had hoped. "*Nie chwal przed zachodem,*" he muttered. "Don't praise the day until sunset."

Martindale grimaced. "Too true."

Over the older American's shoulder, Wilk saw a lean young woman in the dress uniform of a major in the Polish Special Forces coming in on the arm of a tall, broad-shouldered blond-haired man wearing the Iron Wolf Squadron's dark, rifle-green jacket. They looked intensely happy, though somewhat tired.

A fleeting smile crossed the Polish president's

face. "Major Rozek and Captain McLanahan!" he said, moving toward them. "I am very sorry I had to cut your leave short." His eyes twinkled. "But brief though it was, I hope you found your time together . . . restful?"

To his inner delight, both Nadia Rozek and Brad McLanahan actually blushed. After the brash young American nearly got himself killed at Cernavodă, Nadia had practically threatened mutiny unless Wilk allowed her to rush to his side. Supposedly, they'd gone skiing at one of the resorts in the High Tatras. Privately, he had his doubts they had ever made it farther than a hotel room bed, let alone strapped on any skis.

They saluted.

"Uh, yes, sir," Brad stammered out. "We had a great trip. It was . . . er . . . very relaxing."

Hiding a grin, Wilk returned their salutes. The younger McLanahan really was a terrible liar. Major Rozek was wiser. She said nothing, though a scarcely veiled warning in her blue-gray eyes suggested to Wilk that he might be skating on very thin ice, president of the Third Polish Republic or not.

He found Martindale at his elbow. "We're all here, Piotr," the other man said, guiding him toward a chair at a large oval table.

Wilk turned and saw that Wayne Macomber had come in behind him, accompanied by the huge Cybernetic Infantry Device piloted by Patrick McLanahan. Never one for formalities, Macomber sketched a salute and moved to his own chair. Without speaking, the robot simply stalked over to the other side of the room and silently swiveled to face the table.

That bothered him. The older McLanahan had withdrawn more and more from routine human contact over the last few months, seemingly content to communicate more by e-mail or text—and then only about questions of military strategy or weapons technology. He hoped that was simply an effect of the enormous pressure they were all under in trying to get the Alliance of Free Nations up and running before it was too late. If the other man's increasingly distant behavior was a symptom of something more serious—

With an effort, Wilk pushed his worries about Patrick McLanahan to the side. While the English poet John Donne had rightly proclaimed that no man was an island, the former U.S. Air Force general was still just one man among millions. And at this moment, they faced bigger and more immediate problems.

He nodded almost imperceptibly to Martindale, signaling him to begin.

"Before we move to a detailed discussion of the current crisis, I think it's best to lay out the bigger picture," the head of Scion said smoothly. "While President Barbeau remains unalterably opposed to our new alliance, there have been signs that other—"

"With all due respect, sir," Whack Macomber said, leaning forward with a shit-eating grin. "Maybe you should save the canned spiel for the politicians back in Warsaw and just tell us flat out how badly we're screwed."

Martindale closed his eyes in exasperation. "Are you *trying* to piss me off, Major?"

"Trying?" Macomber said innocently. "No, sir." He winked at Brad, who was clearly fighting a losing battle with a grin of his own. "I just thought we could save some time is all. Since we're all clearly doomed, that is."

Wilk couldn't help it. He laughed out loud. Even now, even after more than a year in their company, it still astonished him to realize how impudent some of these Americans could be in the face of power. It was both alarming and refreshing, the characteristic of a people who could just be foolish enough to tease God, but who might also be bold enough to kick the Devil in the balls.

"Fine," Martindale said wryly. "I'll be brief." He thought for a moment and then went on. "Okay, we all know that Stacy Anne Barbeau hates our guts."

"Especially yours," Macomber pointed out.

"Especially mine," Martindale agreed. "Even when I was president of the United States, we never saw eye to eye on the big national-security-policy debates. Or even on the little ones, for that matter. But right now she thinks I'm out here raising hell with the Russians for two reasons. First, so I can line my own pockets with profits from Scion military contracts. And second, to screw her politically by causing trouble overseas, when she wants to focus on her own domestic agenda."

"Which says much more about her own sordid inclinations than it does about you," Wilk said.

"Sure." Martindale shrugged. "But in this case, what matters are her actions, not her motivations."

He frowned. "Basically, as far as Barbeau is concerned, the Alliance of Free Nations is, and I quote, 'a reckless bunch of third-rate countries with delusions of grandeur.'"

"Remind me not to send flowers for her birthday this year," Wilk murmured dryly to Nadia Rozek.

"The good news is that Congress is still bucking her demands for broader economic and trade sanctions on the AFN and Poland," Martindale said. "A few congressmen think she was right to let NATO break up rather than get dragged into a war with Russia. Most believe that was an act of diplomatic cowardice and strategic idiocy. But *all* of them are furious that she crossed the line and actually helped the Russians against us at the end—especially without even consulting the congressional leadership."

"And the bad news?" Wilk prompted.

"She's tightening her executive orders to restrict trade with Poland and the other AFN countries. We'll challenge those in federal court, but it'll take months even to get a case heard . . . and presidents have a lot of wiggle room when it comes to restricting the sale of arms on national security grounds. For all practical purposes, it's now impossible for us to buy U.S.-manufactured military-grade equipment or technology, especially from Scion-affiliated companies like Sky Masters. At least directly and legally."

"What about indirectly?" Wilk asked.

"We have a few routes still open to us," Martindale said. "Some of the countries still in NATO aren't tagging along with Barbeau's trade restrictions. My sources in Paris, Rome, and London all tell me their arms industries will keep selling weapons and ammunition to the AFN—so long as our purchases are 'reasonably discreet.'"

"The Brits, French, and Italians make some decent gear," Macomber said. Then he shook his head. "But even their top-of-the-line equipment isn't up to par with what we were getting from Sky Masters. That ain't going to cut it."

Wilk knew the American Iron Wolf ground commander was right. Confronted by superior Russian numbers, Poland and its allies needed every technological edge they could muster if they were to survive another conflict.

Martindale nodded. "Indeed." He shot them a look. "On the other hand, we can use those friendly states as conduits to smuggle in material from Sky Masters and other suppliers in the States."

"At a higher price," Wilk said sourly. "Both in money and time."

"Necessity is a harsh and expensive mistress," Martindale agreed.

"Well, we shall do what we must," Wilk said. He shook his head. "My cabinet ministers and parliament will not be happy to see even more money funneled into defense at the expense of other priorities, but they know the stakes."

Brad sat forward. "What about the other allies? Can any of them chip in more money or credits?"

"I doubt it," Martindale said. "Hungary, the Baltics, and the rest are pretty strapped for cash. As it is, the rearmament programs they've agreed to at our urging are already straining their economies. If we're very lucky, they *may* be able to honor their existing commitments. Asking them to pony up more resources isn't in the cards."

"Unfortunately, I am afraid that we are already unlucky," Wilk said flatly. "I spoke to Romania's president Dumitru this morning. He informed me, with deep regret, that his country can no longer afford to meet even its current alliance defense obligations."

"Because of what happened at Cernavodă?" Brad asked, frowning.

Wilk nodded gloomily. "The Unit Two reactor there cannot be salvaged. It will take months of emergency cooling and containment before the Romanians can even begin to dismantle it—all at an enormous cost. Dumitru tells me the first estimates are in the billions of dollars." He spread his hands. "His government also feels compelled by pressure from its own people and from the rest of Europe to shut down the other Cernavodă reactor."

"How the hell are the Romanians going to replace twenty percent of their electrical generating capacity?" Macomber asked.

"They can't," Martindale cut in coolly. "Not on their own. They don't have enough spare oil- or coal-fired plants or hydroelectric dams to make up the loss. Which means the Romanian economy is going to take a huge hit—with factories shuttered due to loss of power, and rolling blackouts in the towns and cities."

"Just as we head into winter," Macomber growled. "That's not going to be fucking pretty."

"No, it will not," Wilk said quietly. "With the cold and darkness of winter looming, President Dumitru is gravely concerned that his government could be toppled by a wave of massive public unrest."

"With the Russians waiting hungrily in the wings," Brad said.

"True," Wilk said. "And naturally our *friends* in Moscow are doing their best to make things even more difficult for Dumitru. This morning they presented him with a virtual ultimatum. The Russians are threatening to cut off all natural-gas exports to Romania unless he accepts price increases far beyond Bucharest's ability to pay."

Martindale's expression darkened. "So there's the iron fist without the velvet glove," he said caustically. "I assume there's more."

Wilk nodded. "Dumitru was also handed a personal communication from Gennadiy Gryzlov promising to provide the energy supplies Romania needs, but only if he abandons the Alliance of Free Nations and signs a defense pact with Moscow."

"That's classic," a cold, electronically synthesized voice said.

Surprised by the sudden interjection, Wilk and the others swung toward the huge CID standing motionless by the far wall. "General?"

"Gryzlov never misses a chance to kick people when they're down," Patrick McLanahan continued. "That accident at Cernavodă was the perfect opening for him to make trouble. The Romanians can either kowtow to Moscow now, or do it later—

after a new pro-Russian government takes power. My bet is that Gryzlov is already in touch with leaders of the opposition parties in Bucharest."

Wilk nodded slowly. "A correct assessment, General." He shrugged. "Many of Dumitru's political opponents already favor the Russians, either out of conviction or sheer expedience."

"That son of a bitch in Moscow is pretty god-damned fast on his feet," Whack Macomber said. His gaze darkened. "Too fast, if you ask me. Which is why I've got a nagging itch that says the Russians engineered this whole thing."

"Your instincts are accurate, as usual, Major," Martindale said softly. "My Scion IT experts finished their preliminary analysis an hour ago. The computers at Cernavodă were hacked. That reactor was deliberately configured to melt down."

There was a moment of stunned silence.

"Which is why the plant's automated systems seemed to be fighting me every step of the way," Brad realized. "Like every time I turned a valve or tried to get through a door."

"Your report gave us the first clues," Martindale agreed. "Apparently, there were traces of malware in every significant operating system."

"But how?" Wilk asked. "Surely Cernavodă's designers were not foolish enough to connect their control computers to the Internet?"

"Not officially, no."

"Then—"

"Regrettably, there are many ways to infect a computer with malware, Mr. President," Nadia Rozek told him grimly. Wilk suddenly remem-

bered that her father was a software engineer who
specialized in Internet security.

"Major Rozek is quite right," Martindale said.
"Anyone with access to the plant's automated control systems could have implanted those sabotage
programs using something as simple as an easily
concealed USB flash drive or a microSD card
half the size of a thumbnail. Only the most sophisticated body scanners can detect them, and
Cernavodă did not have them."

"How many people had such access?" Wilk
wondered.

"Too many," Martindale said. "My guys think
that malware might have been put in place weeks
or even months ago. So the hackers could have
bribed a plant operator, either somebody still on
staff or planning to quit or even retire. Or maybe
they suborned someone else, someone who visited
Cernavodă in an official capacity. Like a contrac-
tor or an IAEA inspector, for example."

"Whoever did it is long gone," Patrick McLanahan said tonelessly. "Either conveniently dead . . .
or hidden away in Russia, far beyond our reach."

"Probably so," Martindale conceded. "I've ordered a Scion security team to work with the Romanian police to narrow down the list of possible
suspects. But it's not real likely that we'll ever get
our hands on whoever planted that malware."

Wilk scowled. "Then how do we prove the
Russians were responsible for this catastrophe?"

"We can't," Martindale said bluntly. "At least
not clearly enough to sway international opinion if it comes down to a United Nations piss-

ing match between us and Moscow." He shook his head in regret. "The code my experts have analyzed has similarities to malware they've seen before—to viruses created by a Russian hacker group called Advanced Persistent Threat 28, or ATP 28. But—"

"But these computer criminals often share their techniques and secrets with others around the world," Nadia Rozek said. "So such a similarity would not be sufficient evidence." Her eyes were ice-cold. "Not for President Barbeau and the other weaklings afraid to stand up to the Russians."

Martindale nodded. His own expression was equally bleak. He turned to the others. "Whether or not we can prove it is pretty much beside the point. What's more important is that this cyberwar attack on Cernavodă was perfectly planned and executed. And if Brad hadn't been close enough to intervene with a working CID, we'd be overwhelmed right now trying to deal with the physical and political fallout from a radioactive plume spreading across Europe on the wind. You can bet that millions of people would have been hightailing it away from Romania as refugees."

"The danger would not have justified so much panic," Nadia said stubbornly. "The accidents at Chernobyl and Fukushima showed that any significant damage would have been limited to those areas within thirty or forty kilometers of the plant."

"Maybe so," Martindale agreed. "But most folks aren't logical. Scientific studies don't carry much weight when they run up against generations of 'nuclear bogeyman' scare tactics." He shrugged. "As it is, we were fortunate Brad was in the right place at the right time."

"Sure," Macomber said. "Trouble is, now we're down one of the new CIDs we needed to bolster our forces. That robot is basically fried. Hell, just about every system is shot. To get the thing back up and running, we're practically going to have to rebuild every piece, from the actuators on up." He shot Brad a wry look. "No offense, kid, but you're hard as hell on expensive gear."

Brad did his best to look sorry. "Yeah, Whack, that *is* a bad habit. And it's one I'm trying real hard to break."

"No sweat, Brad," Macomber said more seriously. "Pain in the ass though you often are, I'm glad you came through in one piece. CIDs I can replace. Good pilots are a heck of a lot tougher to find."

Half listening to the two Iron Wolf officers banter, Wilk stared down at the table, gathering his thoughts. At last, he looked up at Martindale. "If we cannot prove that what happened at Cernavodă was a Russian attack, is there any point to announcing that the reactor was deliberately sabotaged?"

"Officially? Probably not, Piotr," the American said slowly. "That would only raise questions we can't answer right now." He allowed himself a quick, sly grin. "But we could leak the suggestion to some friendly journalists, off the record. God knows the broader public loves conspiracy theories. And even the hint that what happened was Moscow's fault might buy Dumitru and his government a little breathing room."

Wilk nodded. For months, Russian propaganda outlets—both official and unofficial—had been flooding the airwaves and the Internet with all kinds of wild stories about "warmongering Poland" and its "bloodthirsty, piratical mercenaries." Giving Gryzlov and his minions a taste of their own medicine couldn't hurt.

"But what if this was not just a single act of sabotage?" Nadia asked. Her mouth tightened into a thin line. "What if Cernavodă was merely the first salvo in a new Russian war against us? A war waged with computers rather than tanks and aircraft?"

"That, Major Rozek, is the billion-dollar question," Martindale said. He looked somberly around the table. "My guess is that we're not going to have to wait long to find out."

CHAPTER 5

THE WHITE HOUSE SITUATION ROOM, WASHINGTON, D.C.

The next day

Listening to Gennadiy Gryzlov preach at her over a secure video link with Moscow, U.S. president Stacy Anne Barbeau blessed the decades she had spent smiling winsomely at men she secretly despised. For years, she'd schemed, flirted, and backstabbed her way up through the ranks of American politics—serving in the U.S. Senate, as secretary of state, and now as president. Washington was littered with the still-breathing political corpses of rivals and former allies she'd first charmed, then outmaneuvered, and finally dumped by the wayside.

There was a time, she admitted to herself, when the younger Russian president's rugged good looks would have turned her on. But not anymore. Not since last year, when his threats and crazed nuclear saber rattling had pushed her into a corner, forcing her to choose between the safety and security of the United States and her personal pride.

She didn't regret seeing Poland and the other Eastern and central European countries drop out of NATO. In her view, letting them into the American-led alliance after the collapse of the Soviet Union in the first place had been a huge mistake—one that virtually guaranteed continued conflict with Russia and threatened U.S. interests without any concomitant gain. But the way NATO fractured had made her look bad, and it had hurt her politically here at home, where right-wing hawks were always circling . . . looking for any excuse to bash her as a weak-kneed woman.

Someday she would find a way to stick a shiv in Gennadiy Gryzlov, she thought silently. Someone so arrogant and self-assured was bound to give her an opening, sooner or later. For now, though, she concentrated on hiding her seething anger behind a diplomatic mask of polite attention.

"My government is grateful for your efforts to restore order in Europe, Madam President," the Russian said suavely. "And we share your view that this Alliance of Free Nations is a threat to the region's stability. After all, if it were not for pressure from the militaristic Poles and their black-market hired soldiers, the Baltic states, Romania, and the rest would gladly see reason."

Barbeau's eyes narrowed. "And just how do you define *reason*, Gennadiy?" she asked pointedly.

He smiled broadly. "I mean, of course, that

the nations of Eastern and central Europe could again assume their traditional role as neutral buffer states between the great powers—rather than serving the geopolitical ambitions of the Polish madman Piotr Wilk and your own former president, Kevin Martindale."

"Martindale's a criminal," Barbeau shot back, touched on a sore point. "His actions are in no way condoned by my government."

Gryzlov's own gaze hardened. "If I thought otherwise, Madam President, our conversation today would be proceeding along *very* different lines." He relaxed. "As it is, I am confident that our vital national interests coincide on this issue. Restoring the proper balance between NATO and Russia is the key to European peace and security. But this cannot be achieved unless we stop Poland's efforts to build a ramshackle empire. If not, we may find ourselves again dragged to the edge of an abyss because some petty Polish client state sees war as an alternative to domestic unrest or self-imposed catastrophe."

Barbeau regained her composure. She was not going to let this bastard rattle her again, she decided. Nor was she going to let him smooth-talk her into making any commitment she might regret later—like saying something Gryzlov could later claim gave him the green light for another military adventure against Warsaw.

"I agree that the instability of some of the countries in this new alliance worries me," she said carefully. "But I think you exaggerate the short-term risks."

"Do I?" Gryzlov replied, arching an eyebrow. "With the example of this terrible accident at the Cernavodă nuclear reactor before our very eyes?" He shook his head. "What more evidence do you need of the dangers posed by these backward countries?"

He raised his eyes as if to heaven. "If it were not for a miracle, your true allies in Western Europe— the Germans, the French, the Italians, and all the others—would even now be submerged by waves of refugees fleeing the radioactive contamination caused by Romania's criminal negligence."

Oh, good God, Barbeau thought disgustedly. How stupid did this clown think she was? "There are rumors that that reactor was sabotaged by Russia-based hackers," she said dryly.

"If so, the gang in Bucharest must be reading too many spy thrillers," Gryzlov said coolly. "Cernavodă's design and construction flaws and management failures are matters of record. Read the reports from the IAEA and other responsible organizations if you doubt me." He shrugged his shoulders. "Besides, blaming foreigners is always the first resort for any government eager to hide its own incompetence."

"Perhaps so," Barbeau retorted. "But blackmailing President Dumitru by threatening to cut off Russian natural-gas exports just adds fuel to that particular fire."

Gryzlov actually laughed. "What of it?" he asked. "Like any rational power, Russia will use whatever leverage it can to woo countries away from Poland's dangerous embrace."

He shrugged. "You should follow our example and further tighten your own restrictions on trade and commerce. Your Congress is too hesitant. Too weak-willed. You must show those now looking to Warsaw that the price of ignoring America is too high."

"What Congress will or won't do is an internal political matter," Barbeau snapped, stung by the Russian's barely concealed taunt. "It's certainly not any of your business."

"You have my apologies, Madam President," Gryzlov said, though without an ounce of genuine contrition in his voice. "You are correct. Your disagreements with Congress are not my concern." He smiled slyly. "But then neither should you criticize business decisions we make about our natural-gas exports to Romania. Gazprom is, after all, a wholly Russian-owned corporation."

For a moment, Stacy Anne Barbeau fought the temptation to unleash every expletive in her formidable arsenal. Slowly, with enormous difficulty, she regained control over her temper. Gryzlov had set a cheap rhetorical trap and she'd walked straight into it. That was bad enough. But arguing the point with him further would just put her in the position of someone wrestling with a pig: you both got dirty and only the pig enjoyed it.

She took a deep breath and forced herself to smile sweetly at the Russian. "I'll bear that in mind, Mr. President."

"Excellent!" Gryzlov said with a wide, false smile of his own. "In that case, I look forward to our next discussion. I am sure it will be . . . illuminating."

Once the connection to Moscow was broken, she sat glowering in silence for a few moments before spinning toward Luke Cohen, her White House chief of staff and longtime political adviser. The tall, rail-thin New Yorker had been hovering off-camera through the whole conference. "Well?"

"He's up to something," Cohen said flatly.

Barbeau snorted. "No kidding." She spun back to stare at the blank screen again. "And we'd damned well better find out what it is . . . before it bites us in the ass."

Frowning, she turned back to Cohen. "Pull together a special interagency group of economic, intelligence, and military analysts, including Cyber Command. Grab the best people you can find and get them focused on the situation in Eastern Europe. Tell them to flip over every goddamn rock from Moscow to Prague if they have to."

Cohen nodded. He hesitated. "Should I bring Nash in on this?"

"Christ, no!" Barbeau said. "With a lot of help from staff, that moron might be able to find Bucharest or Budapest on a map." She shook her head in disgust. "But I doubt if he'd know which was which."

It had taken her months, but she had finally been able to force out the last holdovers from the Phoenix administration—the chairman of the Joint Chiefs, Air Force General Spelling, and

CIA Director Thomas Torrey. Her replacement for Torrey, James Buchanan Nash, was an amiable nonentity, a former senator from Virginia. His onetime colleagues had confirmed him largely on the strength of his prior service in U.S. Navy intelligence. What most of them didn't know was that Nash had spent most of his short naval service on "detached duty" in Guam, supervising the base bowling alley because his superiors had seen that as the safest place to park a junior officer with solid political connections but severely limited competence.

Despite that, Barbeau had made him her CIA director because she'd wanted someone politically reliable heading the agency—someone malleable enough to do what he was told without protest. Jimmy Nash might be dull-witted, but he looked good on television and in front of congressional committees . . . as long as he had aides close by to feed him the answers to tough questions. Best of all, the new CIA director had never been part of that aging prick Martindale's faction or an admirer of the late, totally unlamented, and lunatic former Air Force Lieutenant General Patrick McLanahan.

"Okay, I'll keep Nash in the dark," Cohen agreed. "That won't be hard." He jotted down a few notes to himself on his ever-present tablet computer. "Anything else?"

Barbeau nodded. "Put the fear of God and the FBI into everyone in that working group. I don't want any leaks—not to the Hill, not to the press, and especially not to anyone connected with Sky

Masters or Scion. Whatever intelligence they dig up about Russian plans stays inside the White House. It doesn't go floating around. Got it?"

"I'll do my best," Cohen promised.

"You'll do more than that, Luke," Barbeau said sharply. "You either keep a lid on this or I'll find someone else who can. Is that clear?"

The New Yorker swallowed hard. "Yes, Madam President."

"That's just fine, Luke, honey," she said, relenting slightly. "And as soon as you've handled all of that, I want you on a flight to Moscow."

"Moscow?"

Barbeau nodded. "Get in touch with Gryzlov's people. Arrange a private one-on-one with that smooth-talking son of a bitch. Push him, Luke. See if you can get a read on what the hell he's planning."

THE KREMLIN, MOSCOW
A short time later

Major General Arkady Koshkin stood stiffly in President Gryzlov's outer office, trying very hard not to fidget. He was uneasily aware that the continued existence of both Q Directorate's cyberwar initiative and his own personal fate rested on the outcome of this hurriedly called meeting with Russia's mercurial leader. While the computer viruses his specialists had crafted had done enormous damage to Romania's Cernavodă nuclear plant, the results had fallen short of his more optimistic promises. He wished now that he had not so blithely assured Gryzlov that a total reactor meltdown and containment breach was inevitable and unstoppable.

A droplet of sweat rolled down his high forehead and dripped onto his spectacles. Nervously, he took them off, distractedly mopping at the thick lenses with his handkerchief.

The door to Gryzlov's inner office swung open, held by Ivan Ulanov, the president's private secretary. "You may go in, General," the younger man said. There were dark bags under his eyes. Russia's president kept late hours. "They are ready for you now."

Quickly stuffing the handkerchief back in the breast pocket of his suit, Koshkin hurried through the door. Ulanov closed it silently behind him.

Hands clasped behind his back, Gennadiy Gryzlov stood by the far windows, looking out across the darkened Kremlin. Minister of State Security Viktor Kazyanov sat bolt upright in one of the two chairs set squarely in front of the president's ultramodern desk.

Without looking around, Gryzlov said, "Sit down, Koshkin."

Sweating even more heavily now, the head of the FSB's Q Directorate did as he was ordered. Kazyanov didn't so much as nod in his direction.

Abruptly, Gryzlov swung round and sat down behind the desk. "I have been going over your report on the Cernavodă operation," he said, not bothering with any of the usual pleasantries.

Koshkin felt sick. "Mr. President, I—"

Gryzlov waved him into silence. "You and your people did well, Arkady," he continued.

Caught by surprise, Koshkin could only gabble, "But . . . the reactor . . . the containment building, I mean . . ." He forced himself to slow down. "I regret that our attack was not entirely successful."

"Calm yourself, Arkady," Gryzlov said patiently. "No weapon works perfectly the first time it is used." He shrugged. "And you certainly couldn't have anticipated that the Poles and their American mercenaries would react so quickly and so effectively to the reactor meltdown."

"No, sir."

"What matters is that we now know your new cyberweapons are as powerful as you promised," Gryzlov said. "Which is why we're going to use them on a much larger and grander scale."

"Mr. President?"

Gryzlov bared his teeth in a quick, wolfish grin. He tapped the slick surface of the computer built into his desk. The large LED display set into the same desk lit up, revealing the first page of a document marked *Top Secret* and headed *Operatsiya Mor*, Operation Plague. "Take a careful look, Koshkin. The time for tests and experimentation is over. Now is the time to put your prized theories into practice!"

Eyes widening, Koshkin leaned closer to the screen, rapidly skimming through the list of targets outlined in the detailed operational plan the president showed him, flipping through page after page with a flick of his finger across the display. He whistled softly in wonder.

"Well," Gryzlov demanded. "Can you execute this operation?"

Still astonished by the scope of his president's ambitions, Koshkin sat back in his chair, thinking fast. At last, he nodded cautiously. "We can, sir. Q Directorate has all of the essential cyberwarfare capabilities needed to strike these targets." He pursed his lips. "But hitting them with the necessary precision and speed will require some additional work to fully weaponize specific computer programs."

Gryzlov's expression soured.

"It's not a question of hardware," Koshkin hastily explained. "Between the new supercomputer at the Perun's Aerie complex and equipment at other sites, we have all the computing capacity needed."

"Go on," Gryzlov said, through gritted teeth.

"It's a matter of personnel, Mr. President," Koshkin said, sweating again. "To keep up with the proposed operational tempo after our first strikes go in, my directorate will need the services of additional special information troops. Coding is labor-intensive work and each attack demands malware individually tailored for the precise target."

"Very well," Gryzlov said curtly. "Present your requirements for more *komp'yutershchiks* to Tarzarov on your way out. He'll find the hackers you need."

"Sir."

"And inform me at once when you are ready to launch *Mor*'s first phase."

"Yes, Mr. President," Koshkin said, already moving toward the door.

"Oh, and Arkady?"

The head of Q Directorate looked back toward Gryzlov. "Mr. President?"

"Be quick about it," Gryzlov said. "Remember, no man is irreplaceable." His eyes conveyed all the warmth of the Siberian tundra in winter. "Do not learn that the hard way, eh?"

When the door closed behind Koshkin, Gryzlov turned his icy gaze on his minister of state security. "You were very quiet just now, Viktor."

Kazyanov actually squirmed nervously in his seat, an oddly unbecoming gesture in one so tall and powerfully built. "I did not wish to interrupt, Mr. President." He spread his hands in an embarrassed gesture. "This new cyberwar technology is not something I fully understand. At least not yet."

"Yes," Gryzlov said contemptuously. "That much is all too clear. Though perhaps I should expect more from you, since Koshkin is at least nominally one of *your* subordinates."

He watched the other man's face turn gray. Insulting poor, fearful Viktor Kazyanov really was about as dangerous as kicking a toothless puppy, Gryzlov decided. It might be enjoyable, but there really wasn't much sport in it.

"On the other hand," he said. "The reports

from your GRU unit outside Cernavodă were excellent." He shot the bewildered and frightened minister of state security a cynical smile. "It was fortunate that Usenko and his team were ready and waiting to catch a glimpse of one of these Iron Wolf machines in action, was it not?"

"You knew one of those combat robots would enter the damaged reactor building?" Kazyanov realized, unable to conceal his surprise.

Gryzlov shrugged. "Let us say that I thought it more likely than not."

"What game are you—" Kazyanov stopped himself in midsentence, obviously afraid that he was crossing onto dangerous ground.

Gryzlov let that slide. "But we still need more information about these Cybernetic Infantry Devices." The corners of his mouth turned down. "That bitch Barbeau, for all her high-minded prattle about international cooperation, still won't tell us all she knows about their design, their capabilities, and their weaknesses."

Kazyanov nodded. Every request they'd made to the Americans for more technical data on the CIDs had been shunted aside with a welter of unconvincing excuses, delays, and outright lies.

"So the answer is obvious," Gryzlov said. He tapped his desk. "We lure one of these machines out into the open again, this time for a closer look. Even at the cost of lives." Seeing the confusion on his spymaster's face, he sighed. "Think of chess, Viktor. This match is just beginning. And if we have to sacrifice a pawn or two to gain the advantage we seek, then so be it."

Baffled, Kazyanov decided to fall back on simple, unquestioning obedience. It was a habit that had served him well all his adult life. "What are your orders, Mr. President?" he asked.

And then, listening closely while Gryzlov outlined the gambit he had in mind, he began to understand. Outwardly simple in its details, the younger man's stratagem possessed a certain brutal elegance.

CHAPTER 6

OUTSIDE GROZNY, CHECHEN REPUBLIC, RUSSIAN FEDERATION
The next day

Ramshackle houses and huts dotted the steep, snow-covered hillsides above Ahmad Usmaev's walled compound. Rifle-armed guards, bulky in heavy sheepskin coats, patrolled the walls. Their breath steamed in the frigid air. Winter came early this high up in the Caucasus.

Inside the compound, Colonel Yevgeny Perminov held his arms out from his sides, hiding his disgust while one of the Chechen warlord's slovenly bodyguards frisked him for concealed weapons. Service in Russia's military intelligence arm, the GRU, often required dealing with unsavory characters. Seen in that light, the self-styled sheikh Ahmad Usmaev was not so different, although his coarseness, paranoia, and almost mindless brutality might be said to plumb new depths of depravity.

Usmaev was one of the cold-blooded killers Russia relied on to hold down its restive Chechen Republic. He and his kinsmen ruled over a large stretch of mountainous territory outside the capital city of Grozny. In return for generous subsidies from Moscow, Usmaev stayed loyal to President Khuchiev, another warlord put in power by Russia. In exchange, the Russians turned a blind eye to the methods he employed to terrorize the villages and towns in his grip—an orgy of murder, mutilation, rape, extortion, and hostage taking.

The bodyguard stepped back and nodded to Usmaev. "He is unarmed."

The warlord, a short, portly man wearing an intricately embroidered vest and a green velvet Muslim skullcap waddled forward to greet Perminov. "My friend, welcome again to my simple home! You honor me with your presence."

With an effort, the GRU colonel kept a straight face. Usmaev's "simple" home was a villa stuffed full of ornate, expensive furniture, priceless tapestries and carpets, and high-priced consumer electronics—all paid for by Moscow's largesse and the profits from his own reign of terror. He followed the Chechen into a palatial sitting area.

Usmaev plopped down on a plush, overstuffed couch and waved Perminov into a high-backed chair trimmed in gold leaf. Another of the warlord's guards deferentially returned the colonel's still-locked briefcase. It had been taken away from him at the gate and then run through an X-ray machine as a precaution against explosive devices or other hidden weapons.

After several minutes wasted enduring the customary round of utterly insincere compliments and platitudes, Perminov finally felt able to come to the point of his visit. "You have received my government's request, Sheikh?" he asked.

Sagely, Usmaev nodded. "I spoke to your superiors, yes."

"And you can provide the men we need? With the necessary weapons training?"

"As easily as I do this!" the warlord said, snapping his fingers. He lowered his voice. "Though I understand the risks involved are, shall we say, significant?"

Perminov nodded. "So I believe."

Usmaev smiled coldly. "I have a number of followers who are bored by the peace I have established here. They grow restless. And such restless men can cause a lot of trouble if they are not given the chance to act on a wider stage."

"That is true," Perminov agreed cautiously. "In this instance, the audience may prove unforgiving. Perhaps lethally so."

"That is in Allah's hands," Usmaev said with a shrug. His eyes glinted. "Who knows? Perhaps he will be merciful."

The colonel got the distinct impression the other man would be happier if the god he worshiped decided matters the other way. And perhaps that was just as well. "You understand that we are in some haste?" he asked. "I have an aircraft standing by to ferry your men to Moscow for further briefing."

"Of course," Usmaev said. He raised an eyebrow. "Assuming our other arrangements proceed smoothly, they can join you at the airport within the hour."

Perminov unlocked his briefcase and flipped it open so that the Chechen could see the contents. The case contained fifteen million rubles in cash, worth about two hundred thousand American dollars. "Please, Sheikh, accept this small token of our appreciation for your assistance in this matter," he said.

Usmaev's smile grew even wider. He nodded to one of his bodyguards, who stepped forward to take the briefcase from Perminov. "Your visits are always a joyous occasion, Colonel. I look forward to our next meeting."

"As do I," the GRU colonel said stoically. Much as he personally loathed Usmaev, there was no getting around the fact that the other man had one great virtue. Like many in this brutal, war-torn region, he would sell his own sister if the price were right. But unlike so many of his rivals, once bought, Ahmad Usmaev stayed bought.

And that, in the end, was what truly mattered to Perminov's masters in the Kremlin.

IZMAILOVSKY PARK, MOSCOW
That same time

Two men, both bundled up against the cold, strolled casually together along a winding, wooded trail. They were alone.

Izmailovsky Park, once the childhood home of the czar Peter the Great, was a favorite haunt of Muscovites in the summer and winter. During the summer, crowds sought its forest glades and ponds as a refuge from the city's heat and humidity. And in the snowy depths of winter, they poured in with their sleds, ice skates, and cross-country skis. But few people found the park's damp gravel paths and stands of barren, leafless trees very inviting on the dreary, gray days so common in the late fall.

All of which made it the ideal spot for a discreet rendezvous.

Igor Truznyev, former president of the Russian Federation, glanced down at his shorter, thinner companion. "You're sure you were not followed?"

The other man's world-weary brown eyes crinkled in wry amusement. "Should I ask the same question of you, Igor?" He nodded toward the desolate stretches of woodland lining both sides of the trail. "Shall we waste our time prowling about to see if anyone is lurking behind one of those birch trees? Or hiding beneath the fallen leaves?"

The taller man laughed softly. "A fair hit, Sergei." He shrugged his big shoulders. "I only worry that your protégé might find these occasional discussions behind his back somewhat disconcerting."

"Gennadiy may be more . . . confident . . . than you assume," Sergei Tarzarov, Gryzlov's chief of staff replied softly.

"He sees himself as invincible, you mean?"

Truznyev asked pointedly. "As so powerful now that he is immune to betrayal from his own closest subordinates and associates?"

"Perhaps," the older man said. "And why not?" He turned his gaze more directly on the former president. "Some of us know how narrowly we averted disaster in our war with Poland last year, but the masses do not. They idolize Gennadiy as the leader who retook eastern Ukraine for Mother Russia and humiliated NATO in the process."

For a split second, Truznyev saw red. What no one else knew, most especially not Gryzlov or Tarzarov, was that *he* had orchestrated that war with Poland—secretly funding a band of Ukrainian terrorists in the hope of luring his hated successor into a political and military quagmire. Then, or so he had fondly imagined, Russia's elites would see the terrible mistake they had made in backing a madman like Gryzlov. And once that sobering realization took root, they were bound to come, hats in hand, humbly begging him to reclaim their nation's highest office.

But his plan, brilliant though it was on paper, had backfired—foundering on human weaknesses he could never have anticipated. How could he have imagined any American president so cavalierly betraying a longtime NATO ally, let alone showing herself willing to buy Gryzlov's restraint by ordering the deaths of her own countrymen?

Grimly, Igor Truznyev fought to keep the cauldron of rage and shame boiling up inside from showing on his broad face. Why risk making Tarzarov suspicious now? If the veteran Kremlin insider saw the value of keeping in touch with those like Truznyev who were currently out of power, why rock the boat? Besides, these clandestine meetings gave him valuable insights into the otherwise secret deliberations of Gryzlov's government.

And if nothing else, Tarzarov's patronage over the past few months had lined his pockets quite nicely. In the years since he'd been forced out as Russia's leader, Truznyev had used his skills and his contacts to build a substantial business empire, including a highly competent private intelligence network. His plan there was twofold. Money was the mother's milk of political success, especially in post-Soviet Russia. But the dirty little secrets he and his personal agents uncovered were bound to be even more useful . . . when the day of reckoning with his political enemies came.

With that in mind, he changed the subject.

"I see from the news out of Romania that you've put my guys to work, Sergei." He winked. "I told you they were good. Maybe a bit unkempt and ill-disciplined, like so many young people these days, but still very effective, eh?"

"So it seems," the older man agreed tersely.

"But their parents and boyfriends and girlfriends keep asking me where on earth you've stashed them," Truznyev said, watching Gryzlov's chief of staff closely. "Naturally, I tell them I haven't the faintest idea."

A thin, utterly humorless smile flickered across Tarzarov's narrow, lined face. "I can only imagine how much pain it causes you to offer the unvarnished truth, Igor."

"Very funny," Truznyev said. He kept his eyes fixed on the other man. "Still, I hear rumors. Strange rumors. People talk of a mysterious 'treasure cave' being built out somewhere in the east."

"Do they?" Gryzlov's chief of staff said coolly. He shrugged. "*Slovo serebro. Molchaniye—zoloto.* Words are silver, silence is golden."

"That's easy enough for you to say," Truznyev noted acidly. "You don't have to deal with the constant whimpers and complaints. *'Please, sir, where is my boy Sasha? Where is my lover Ludmilla? Are they well? When will they e-mail me?'*" He scowled. "The litany never ends. And frankly, it's getting on my nerves."

Tarzarov looked back at him without any discernible emotion. "Then you tell them all they need to know."

"Which is?

"That their loved ones serve at the pleasure of the state, wherever the state requires," the old man said. "And that the sensitive nature of their current work demands total seclusion—for the time being."

"Yes, well, that won't exactly offer their families much comfort," Truznyev said.

"You surprise me, Igor," Tarzarov said. "I would not have thought you so sentimental."

"I'm not. I'm only tired of being kept in the dark."

"Oh?" The older man raised an eyebrow in disbelief. "You've been compensated for your assistance. In fact, richly compensated. True?"

"True," Truznyev agreed.

"Then be content with your pay, Igor," Tarzarov told him brutally. "And stop prying into state secrets that are no longer your concern."

For a moment, Truznyev stood rooted in place, transfixed by anger and shame. Once, with the mere wave of a hand, he could have exiled this dry stick of a man to Siberia or had someone put a bullet in the back of his skull. Slowly, he took another deep breath. *Patience*, he told himself. The time would come when such insults could be avenged.

He started walking again, keeping pace with Tarzarov along the winding path. With an effort, he kept his voice level. "I presume, then, that you have a specific reason for contacting me? Some further need for my services as a private citizen and businessman?"

The other man nodded. "I need more specialists."

Now, *that* was interesting, Truznyev thought. "How many exactly?"

"Perhaps thirty or forty more," Tarzarov replied. "Of the same type and with the same skills and abilities."

Truznyev whistled softly in surprise. "So many?" He shook his head doubtfully. "That's a tall order, Sergei. Gifted computer hackers are in high demand, especially in the private sector."

"The needs of various criminal enterprises do not concern me," the older man said flatly. "Tawdry schemes to steal credit-card numbers and drain bank accounts will have to wait."

Truznyev ignored the gibe. "So now that Gennadiy sees the damage a few lines of cunningly written code can do, he grows more ambitious, eh?"

"What the president intends is well beyond your need to know," Tarzarov reminded him. "The question is: Can you provide the people we require?"

"It will be difficult. And expensive," the former president warned.

"How surprising," Tarzarov said dryly.

Truznyev shrugged. "You can't expect iconoclasts like these *komp'yuternyye botanikov*, these computer nerds, no matter how patriotic, to flock to government service—especially now that the word's gotten around that you've put the first batch I found you in cold storage somewhere."

"And how do you suggest we overcome this . . . reluctance?"

"With money, of course," Truznyev said. "You'll have to up the signing bonuses you offer substantially."

"Which will increase your own referral fees," Tarzarov said tartly.

The former president shot him a vengeful smile. "Of course." He eyed the older man narrowly. "You may also find it necessary to reimburse certain . . . businessmen . . . at least those who rely on these experts in certain extremely profitable sidelines."

Tarzarov frowned. "You seriously expect us to pay off the *Mafiya*?"

"Why not?" Truznyev said bluntly. "It's been done before. And many times." He smiled again at Gryzlov's chief of staff. "As you know yourself, Sergei."

The older man frowned.

"Look, the math is simple," Truznyev pointed out. "You can pay off the crime bosses to keep them happy. Or you can waste even more time and money on futile police raids. Because we both know the police will never find anyone the *Mafiya* decides to keep for itself."

The older man sighed in exasperation. "Exactly how much is this all going to cost, Igor?"

"Well, that's an interesting question," Truznyev said carefully. "For a start, you'll have to at least double the signing bonus you offer each hacker. Figuring a minimum of thirty people, that'll mean—"

Deeply immersed in their discussion, he and Tarzarov moved farther along the walking trail, haggling over the price Russia's government would pay for its new "special information troops." What neither of the two men noticed was the very small, brown, birdlike shape silently swirling through in the sky above them. It was a palm-size glider, an ultralight spy drone equipped only with a sensitive microphone and a few cell-phone components serving as a communications relay.

OVER MOSCOW
That same time

Roughly one mile away, a Bell 407GXP light helicopter orbited slowly over the city at an altitude of one thousand feet. Private flights were ordinarily restricted to routes along the Moscow River, but this helicopter belonged to Tekhwerk, GmbH—a jointly owned German and Russian import-export company specializing in industrial and light-manufacturing equipment. Since the corporation helped the Kremlin obtain otherwise difficult-to-replicate Western high-technology machinery at reasonable prices, Russia's law enforcement and regulatory agencies often turned a blind eye to its activities.

The larger of the two men in the Bell helicopter's luxuriously appointed passenger cabin spoke to the pilot over the intercom. "How much longer can you give us here, Max?"

"About twenty more minutes, Herr Wernicke. I told Moscow Control that you wanted to check out some possible new factory sites from the air."

The big, beefy man who called himself Klaus Wernicke nodded appreciatively. "Good work. Keep us posted."

"Will do."

Wernicke looked across the cabin at his companion. "Everything okay on your end, Davey?"

"We've still got a good, solid signal from the Wren," confirmed David Jones, a much smaller and younger man than his superior. He wore earphones and clutched a small handheld controller. "With the thermals I'm picking up, I should be able to keep her aloft for another five or six minutes."

The big man nodded. The tiny Wren glider they were monitoring was the significantly more advanced version of a miniaturized reconnaissance drone originally developed by the U.S. Naval Research Laboratory. Called the Cicada, the Wren's predecessor was designed for deployment in mass swarms. Sown from manned aircraft or even larger drones, Cicadas were tasked with gathering intelligence on large-scale enemy troop movements using a variety of lightweight, low-bandwidth sensors. In contrast, this Wren had a much narrower and far more focused mission. It was tasked with keeping tabs on just one man, Igor Truznyev.

Although the Russians didn't realize it, Tekhwerk was ultimately owned, through an intricate web of holding companies, by Kevin Martindale and Scion. Profits from its legitimate operations were used to fund covert action and intelligence gathering inside Russia itself. And the need for frequent travel between Tekhwerk's dual headquarters in Moscow and Berlin and its other far-flung divisions provided invaluable cover for Scion agents masquerading as corporate executives and employees of the company.

Scion field operatives like Marcus Cartwright, for example.

Calling himself Klaus Wernicke, Cartwright had been running a surveillance operation against Truznyev for months—ever since Scion had captured and interrogated one of the agents the former Russian president used to foment last year's brushfire war with Poland. Made aware that Truznyev, a ruthless, wildly ambitious, and dangerous man, was still very much a player on the world scene, Martindale had ordered a close watch kept on him.

Unfortunately, it was a mission that had proved much easier to set in motion than to accomplish.

Before he became Russia's president, Truznyev had spent years in charge of the Federal Security Service, the FSB, one of the successor agencies to the USSR's feared KGB. When he'd been ousted from the Kremlin, many of the spy service's veterans had joined him in private life, going to work for the consulting group he'd founded. As a result, his personal security and countersurveillance people were top-notch, generously paid, and well equipped. All of which meant that employing the usual methods—tailing Truznyev through the Moscow streets or bugging his offices or hacking into his computers—would only have tipped him off.

So far Cartwright and his Scion team had only been able to track their target's major movements at a distance, without gaining any significant intelligence on his operations or current plans. For all the time, money, and effort they'd expended, their investigation hadn't picked up much more about Truznyev than could have been gleaned from reading the gossip pages of any Moscow tabloid or trade journal.

It had been enormously frustrating.

Until today.

Today, Truznyev had left his personal security detail behind and ventured out alone. He'd never done that before, not even when he paid visits to his various mistresses. Cartwright had immediately seen this as a sign that something big was in the wind. And free to act at last, his surveillance team had pounced, warily tailing the Russian right up to the edge of Izmailovsky Park.

But that was as far as they dared go. Inside the park's deserted confines, anyone who stayed close enough to tag Truznyev and his contact, let alone listen in on them, might as well paint *shpion*, spy, across his forehead.

That was when the Wren drone they'd launched from this helicopter had proved its worth. Floating down silently on the wind, circling slowly as it rode thermals rising from the ground, the bird-size glider had been able to intercept most of the conversation between Truznyev and his contact.

Best of all, the Russians would never know they'd been bugged.

Before the Wren ran out of altitude and airspeed, a twitch of its flight controls could send the little drone gliding away across the woods. Eventually, it would skitter down through the trees and crash-land somewhere in among piles of dead leaves. And even if someone else stumbled across it before one of Cartwright's people got there, the palm-size drone would appear to be nothing more than some child's cheap toy.

"Truznyev and this other fellow are saying their not-so-fond farewells now," David Jones announced, still monitoring the signals coming through his headset. He glanced across at Cartwright with bright eyes. "I don't know who he is yet, but I can tell you one thing for sure, he's a big enough fish to put the fear of God himself into our friend Igor. At least for a bit."

Cartwright bared his teeth in a hunter's triumphant grin. *Smile, Comrade Truznyev,* he thought coldly. *You're on candid microphone.*

CHAPTER 7

**KONOTOP AIRFIELD,
RUSSIAN-OCCUPIED UKRAINE**
The next day

The four-engine Russian turboprop touched down hard on Konotop's landing strip amid greasy puffs of black smoke from its landing gear. The aircraft rolled down the long concrete runway, decelerating fast as its pilot applied reverse thrust and braked. Similar to the American C-130, the An-12 was still the aging workhorse for Russia's tactical air-transport command.

Propellers spinning slowly, the aircraft taxied off the runway and over to a brand-new hangar erected after last year's surprise Polish attack had wrecked the base. It slowed to a stop and the rear clamshell door whined open.

Prodded out by a squad of armed Russian soldiers, several men emerged and gathered silently on the tarmac, blinking in the bright sunlight. Most were very young, though one gray-bearded fellow looked to be in his midforties. All of them still wore the sheepskin coats and high boots common in the Caucasus Mountains.

Spetsnaz Major Pavel Berezin strolled out from the hangar and stood with his hands on his hips for a moment, looking them over. His eyes narrowed in disgust. He turned toward his second in command, Captain Andrei Chirkash. "Well? What do you think?"

Chirkash shrugged. "They'll do."

"You think so?" Berezin asked skeptically.

"Any man can stop a bullet," Chirkash pointed out.

The major laughed. "That is so, Andrei." He shook his head. "All right, then, let's get these bandits and sheepherders sorted out and on their way. The sooner they're off my hands, the better I'll feel."

Chirkash sketched a salute and moved off to shoo the Chechens into the hangar.

Once the bearded men were inside, the guards marched them over to long, folding tables piled high with weapons, ammunition, explosive vests, other equipment, and clean, Western-style cold-weather clothing.

Berezin stepped forward. "Listen up! You were briefed on your assignment in Moscow last night. But here's where it gets real." He eyed the assembled Chechens. "Which of you is in charge?"

The oldest man stepped forward with a proud glint in his pale blue eyes. "I, Timur Saitiev, command this force."

Berezin nodded. "Very well, Saitiev. Get your

men changed and distribute those weapons and gear as you see fit." He checked his watch. "Your truck will be here at any moment."

"Yes, Major," the gray-bearded Chechen said.

"One more thing," Berezin told him. "Be sure to leave your personal effects here. Wallets. ID cards. Cell phones. Prayer beads. The lot." He smiled pleasantly, lying through his teeth. "We'll keep them safe for your return."

Stoically, Saitiev shrugged. "As you wish."

The Spetsnaz major had a sudden uncomfortable feeling the Chechen could read his mind and didn't give a damn. Then again, why should he? If Saitiev and his followers were already willing to strap on suicide vests to avoid capture, they must have few illusions about the mission they were being asked to undertake.

He turned away, hiding a grimace. Aspiring martyrs always gave him the creeps. Killing for a cause was one thing. That was man's work. But seeking out death deliberately? Berezin shook his head in disbelief. That was sheer madness.

IRON WOLF SQUADRON COMPOUND, POWIDZ, POLAND
Two days later

"Odarennyye komp'yuternyye khakery pol'zuyutsa sprosom," a deep, resonant masculine voice said.

"Gifted computer hackers are in high demand," a higher-voiced translator repeated, in English.

In silence, Brad McLanahan, his father, and the rest of the Iron Wolf command team listened carefully to the remainder of the recorded conversation sent by emergency courier from Moscow. Major Nadia Rozek, serving as President Wilk's personal representative, sat next to Brad. He found himself aware of her every movement, her every gesture, no matter how slight or fleeting. It was both exhilarating and completely disconcerting. Never before had he felt so completely connected to another person.

Nadia's mouth tightened as the digital recording came to an end. She turned to Kevin Martindale. "This second man? The one speaking to Truznyev? Do you know who he is?"

"My people couldn't get close enough to take a picture of him," the head of Scion said slowly. "But from the context and from Truznyev's general demeanor, we're pretty sure it was Sergei Tarzarov, Gryzlov's right-hand man."

"Well, it's nice to know that we're not totally paranoid," Whack Macomber muttered.

Martindale glanced at him. "Major?"

"The Russians really *are* trying to kill us," Macomber explained.

"Thank you for that incredibly deep strategic insight," Martindale said wryly. He looked around the table at the others. "I admit nothing we heard was especially earthshaking or surprising, but at least this offers us a glimpse of what's going on. And perhaps just as importantly, a sense of just *who* is making it happen."

That was true, Brad thought. Still, something

else in what was said had caught his attention. "This so-called treasure cave or whatever . . . the place Truznyev seems to think is the center for Gryzlov's cyberwar program?" he asked. "Do we have any leads on what he's talking about or where it could be?"

"None," Martindale admitted. He shook his head gloomily. "Since this hit my desk last night, I've had Scion analysts digging around in every Kremlin database we can access." The corners of his mouth turned down slightly. "Which isn't nearly as many as I would like. The Russians have markedly tightened their computer security protocols over the past twelve months."

"Yeah, and now we know why," Brad said. He frowned. Learning that the bad guys weren't complete idiots wasn't especially surprising, but it still sucked.

Martindale nodded. "Indeed." His fingers drummed softly on the tabletop. "Still, we've picked up a few pieces of the puzzle. Just not enough to paint any kind of accurate or even coherent picture."

"Pieces like what, exactly?" Macomber asked.

"Orders to various military engineering battalions, putting them on standby for what are labeled 'strenuous construction projects of the highest priority,'" the other man answered. "Along with similar orders to railroad construction units . . . and requisitions for huge amounts of reinforced concrete and other building materials."

"And where was all that stuff supposed to go?"

Martindale grimaced. "We don't know." He

looked frustrated. "Every message we've found so far ends with the same instruction: 'Additional directives will be transmitted *solely* in writing or by word of mouth from the senior command authority. No further records connected to this assignment will be maintained electronically. Violation of this order in the slightest degree will be punishable by death.'"

"Gryzlov knew we'd come poking around," Brad said grimly.

"So it seems," Martindale agreed. He shook his head. "In a contest like this, familiarity doesn't necessarily breed contempt. Instead, as you learn more about how your opponent thinks, you develop the ability to anticipate some of his moves. We've used that against Gryzlov in the past. Unluckily, though, it appears the learning curve works in both directions."

"This is not a *game*," a cold electronic voice said abruptly. "This is a war. A real war. And it is high time we started fighting in earnest, not just pussy-footing around."

Startled, Brad and the others turned toward the huge machine positioned at the far end of the table.

"Excuse me, General," Martindale said carefully. "I'm not quite sure I follow you. What, exactly, are you proposing that we do?"

"Kill Igor Truznyev," Patrick McLanahan said bluntly. "We should have done it sooner. He got a lot of good people killed last year for his own petty political ends. And right now he's funneling computer hackers to Gryzlov to organize more cyberwar attacks against us. We should wipe him off the map. Now. Before it's too late."

Martindale's face was impassive. Then, slowly, he shook his head. "I strongly disagree, General McLanahan," he said quietly. "On tactical, strategic, and political grounds."

"How so?"

"Tactically, it would be extremely difficult to eliminate Truznyev. Strategically, our surveillance operation against him is just now beginning to yield actionable intelligence," Martindale explained. He leaned forward in his chair, tapping the table with one forefinger for emphasis. "And politically, the assassination of a former Russian president by Scion, Iron Wolf, or Polish forces would be an unmitigated disaster. It would hand Gennadiy Gryzlov and Stacy Anne Barbeau precisely the evidence they need to smear us as warmongering lunatics."

"He's right, General," Whack Macomber said somberly. "Could we get some guys into Moscow to drop Truznyev? Sure. But making that kind of hit would be messy as hell. And the odds of getting our people out safely afterward?" He shrugged his broad shoulders. "As close to none as makes no damned difference."

"I concur," Nadia said firmly. She looked squarely at the CID. "I have studied the intelligence on this man with great care. Except in rare and completely unpredictable circumstances, like this clandestine meeting with Sergei Tarzarov, he surrounds himself with armed bodyguards, most of them FSB or Spetsnaz veterans. When he travels, he uses a wide variety of alternate routes, often employing decoy vehicles. To have any hope of success, an assassination attempt would require a sizable team equipped with heavy weapons. And any force large enough to complete the mission could never infiltrate undetected or escape successfully after the deed was done."

"Then I will kill him myself," the CID said tonelessly. "No weapon that Truznyev's goons carry can stop me."

Whoa there, big guy, Brad thought. What the hell had gotten into his father? "Dad, with all due respect, that's nuts," he said stubbornly. "Even if we could somehow slip a CID into Moscow on the sly, nailing Truznyev with one would be the same thing as taking out a full-page ad in the *New York Times* telling the whole world that we did it."

"Who cares?" his father said flatly, still not bothering to use the voice synthesizer program that most closely matched his natural human tones. "It's time to stop tap-dancing around Gennadiy Gryzlov and his thugs. Waiting like penned sheep while he makes his next move is an act of criminal stupidity."

Abruptly, the CID containing Patrick McLanahan swung into motion, prowling around the conference table. Around and around, the huge fighting machine stalked, the very image of armored, eerily quiet lethality.

"Killing Truznyev, right under his nose, practically within spitting distance of the Kremlin, will send Gryzlov the only kind of message he understands," the machine said forcefully.

"But, Dad, I—" Brad began, trying hard to think of some argument, *any* argument, that could break through whatever strange and murderous impulse held his father in an icy, implacable grip. He saw the anxious look in Nadia's eyes and knew the same fears were mirrored in his own gaze.

Martindale held up a hand to stop him.

"Well, your suggestion is certainly worth considering more carefully, General," the gray-haired head of Scion said hesitantly. "I suggest you work up a detailed plan for the operation. Once that's done, we can bring President Wilk into the discussion and—"

Sirens went off suddenly outside the hangar, rising and falling in unearthly, earsplitting wails.

For a split second, Brad sat frozen, taken completely by surprise. Time itself seemed to slow down, with separate milliseconds ticking by one after the other. Whose bright idea was it to schedule a defense exercise now, smack-dab in the middle of a crucial strategy conference?

Then a loudspeaker blared, *"Incoming! Incoming! Take cover!"*

WHAAMM!

An explosion somewhere outside rocked the hangar, rattling light fixtures and knocking over water glasses on the table. Dust hung in the air, eddying oddly as concussion from the blast rippled through the room.

Oh, shit, Brad realized. This was no drill.

His father's CID blurred into high speed, smashing right through the conference room's locked exit. Shattered pieces of door went flying.

Reacting almost as fast, Martindale dove under the table for cover.

Brad, Macomber, and Nadia kicked away their chairs and ran for the opening. Nadia already had her pistol, a 9mm Walther P99, out and ready. They darted through the hangar and out onto the airfield.

WHAAMM! WHAAMM! WHAAMM!

They hit the dirt as another wave of huge explosions slammed down across the base—blowing craters in the runway in blinding orange bursts. Debris fountained high into the air. Plumes of oily black smoke from burning buildings and wrecked vehicles curled across the Iron Wolf base.

"Goddamn it," Whack snarled, scrambling back to his feet. "We're being mortared! Some bastard out there has us zeroed in."

OUTSIDE THE IRON WOLF COMPOUND
That same time

Patrick McLanahan sprinted southeast through the woods beyond the base. Coldly furious, he tore through obstacles in his path instead of detouring around them, leaving a trail of jagged pieces of perimeter fence and toppled, splintered trees.

L-band radar countermortar scan complete. Firing battery located, his computer reported. Imagery flashed into his consciousness. The CID's sensors had traced the mortar rounds hammering the Iron Wolf compound back to their origin point—a large clearing near a farm road about three kilometers outside the airfield perimeter.

Warning. Adrenaline and noradrenaline levels spiking. Acetylcholine levels dangerously low. Serotonin falling. Immediate biochemical and neurotransmitter rebalance required. Initiating emergency medical protocols now.

With a low growl, Patrick overrode the CID's health-monitoring systems, shutting down its unwanted attempts to tamper with his brain and body chemistry. Increasingly, there were moments when stray elements in the machine's programming unnecessarily interfered with his fighting efficiency. Like now.

It was insane. Why should he slow his reaction time in combat? Unlike ordinary humans, he knew how to surf the rolling wave of his fury, using the emotion as a means of speeding up reflexes that were already lightning fast. It was another way to gain an edge over those too weak-willed and weak-minded to push these incredible war machines to their design limits.

Glowing trails slashed across on his vision display, highlighting new mortar rounds headed for the Iron Wolf base. For a split second, Patrick was tempted to drop into air-defense mode. His autocannon could sweep those rounds out of the sky before they did more damage.

Screw that, he thought savagely. Defense was a sucker's game. When someone hit you, you killed them. It was that simple. And that effective.

Brighter patches of sunlight shone at the edge

of his vision. He was closing fast on the enemy firing position.

Red lines suddenly zigzagged across the display. His sensors had spotted lengths of carefully camouflaged trip wire laced between trees along the edge of the woods. And each trip wire was tied into a powerful demolition charge.

That was clever, he decided. Those booby traps could have inflicted serious casualties on any conventional reaction force. His mouth twisted into a cruel smile. It was just too damned bad for the enemy that they were up against a killing machine, not a platoon of vulnerable human infantry.

Still sprinting at top speed, Patrick leaped high, clearing the tangle of trip wires in one long bound. He thudded down heavily in a field beyond the tree line.

Five hundred meters downrange, he spotted several men wearing civilian clothing gathered around a large tube with a baseplate and bipod assembly. *Weapon identified*, the CID's computer announced, transferring the data through his neural links faster than conscious thought.

He scowled. That was a Polish-made 98mm heavy mortar. Probably one of a pair that had gone missing last year, sold on the black market by a crooked Polish supply sergeant. *Nice*, he thought coldly. Nothing said the universe really was *not* a warm and cuddly place quite like getting the crap blown out of you with a weapon made by your own allies.

Crack!

A .50-caliber round slammed into the CID's

torso at 860 meters per second. Its enormous impact knocked him backward a step and shattered several of the robot's camouflage tiles. The bullet itself tumbled away, deflected by his composite armor. His jaw tightened. Damn it, that was enough.

It was time to do some killing, Patrick thought wrathfully.

A targeting cursor appeared on his display, highlighting a spot deep in a clump of trees off to the flank of the enemy mortar crew. *Two-man sniper team. Range five hundred and twenty meters*, the computer warned.

Reacting instantly, Patrick unlimbered his 25mm autocannon. He charged straight ahead, swiveling to fire on the move. A quick burst ripped the sniper and his spotter to pieces.

One of the bearded men serving the mortar looked up and saw him coming. His eyes widened in dismay. Yelling a warning, he fumbled for the assault rifle slung across his back. His startled comrades did the same, scrabbling frantically for the small arms they'd laid aside while feeding HE rounds into the mortar tube.

They were too late.

Patrick tore into them like a tiger pouncing on a flock of panicked goats. In a blur of purposeful, brutal motion, his robotic hands smashed skulls, shattered rib cages, and ripped screaming men limb from limb. Blood and broken bits of bone sprayed across the clearing and spattered across his armor.

At the end, one man tried to run.

"Not so fast," Patrick said coolly. He caught the fleeing man in a remorseless, implacable grip and casually spun him around. "You win the toss. You get to live."

His gray-bearded prisoner stared up at him in terror. "*'Adhhab 'iilaa aljahim, shaytan!* Go to hell, demon!" One hand scrabbled for a pull-cord detonator dangling from his coat pocket.

"You first," Patrick retorted. Without hesitating, he hurled the other man high into the air and crouched down, covering the sensor arrays on the CID's six-sided head with his arms.

WHUUMP.

The suicide vest exploded.

As the pall of smoke and grisly debris drifted away downwind, Patrick stood back up. A few more camouflage plates had taken a beating from the shrapnel packed into the vest, but his CID was otherwise virtually unscathed.

From start to finish, less than three minutes had passed from the moment the first mortar round hit the air base.

GRU SURVEILLANCE UNIT
That same time

Inside a nondescript panel van parked along a dirt road several kilometers away, three men sat transfixed with horror, watching the gruesome images streaming in from long-range video cameras they'd sited to cover the Chechen attack.

"*Presvataya Bogoroditsa*. Holy Mother of God," Captain Artem Mikheyev said shakily. "Unbelievable."

"Those poor fucking sods never had a chance," Usenko agreed. The major shook his head in dismay. "Not against that creature. Not against so much speed, firepower, and armor."

Konstantin Rusanov swallowed hard. "That machine's sensors must be incredible," he said. "Did you see how easily it avoided the trip wires the Chechens set? My God, the robot spotted them as easily as if they'd been wrapped in neon-red tape!"

Usenko pulled his gaze away from the monitors. "Pack your gear," he ordered. "The sooner we're well away from this place, the safer I will feel."

"Yes, sir," both of his subordinates said in unison.

"I hope our masters in Moscow find the information gained from this massacre of use," the major said sourly. He grimaced. "God knows I have no love for mindless brutes like those Chechen thugs, but even they deserved a better end."

CHAPTER 8

Powerful floodlights run off portable generators turned night into day for the teams of Polish military police investigators still combing the clearing. They were looking for clues that would help identify those involved in the mortar attack. Numbered yellow markers scattered across the field tagged pieces of evidence left in situ. More floodlights glowed in the distance, showing where another team was hard at work inside a large semitrailer truck they'd found abandoned along a nearby farm road.

Brad McLanahan stood in the darkness just outside the lit area, watching the investigators do their work. He avoided looking too closely at the row of black plastic body bags lined up for transport to the nearest morgue. He'd seen the battered and broken remains of the men his father had killed before they'd been discreetly tagged, photographed, and bundled away. He'd also seen the dried bloodstains spattered across the CID's torso and limbs.

Despite his warm uniform jacket, he shivered.

Nadia Rozek took his arm in hers. She nestled her head gently against his shoulder. Brad sighed. Her touch helped ease a little of the tension and fear he felt building up inside.

Martindale and Macomber finished talking to the grim-faced Polish officer heading up the investigation and came over.

"Captain Sojka says his best guess is that these men were from Chechnya or somewhere else in the Caucasus," Martindale told them. "Probably Islamist radicals. Apparently, they were all wired with explosive vests, but only one had time to set his off."

"Islamic radicals?" Nadia said. Her eyes flashed angrily. "Perhaps so. But I am sure they were doing Moscow's bidding this time, not that of Allah. The Russians have often used some of the Chechen factions for their dirty work."

"That seems probable," Martindale agreed. His face was troubled. "But I am still somewhat surprised that Gryzlov would authorize direct action against us like this."

Macomber snorted. "Why?"

"After their success in wrecking that Romanian reactor, I would have expected the next Russian move to be something subtler and more potent." Martindale shook his head. "A short mortar barrage on one Iron Wolf base? What could Gryzlov really hope to achieve with this kind of pinprick attack?"

"Yeah, well, I've got three dead troopers and a bunch more wounded who might see things a little differently," Macomber muttered.

Brad nodded. "Whack's right, sir. Short or not, that attack still did a heck of a lot of damage."

One of the mortar rounds had exploded right in the middle of a joint Polish–Iron Wolf recon team heading out on an exercise. Other hits had destroyed several aircraft on the flight line. Between President Barbeau's moves to restrict arms sales to Poland and the difficulty involved in evading her sanctions, finding replacements for those men and machines would be costly and time-consuming.

"Gryzlov is the kind of thug who never saw a weapon he wouldn't use," Macomber went on. "Sure, he may be planning to launch more of that cyberwar shit, but that's not going to stop him from hitting us anywhere and in any way he can." He frowned. "Plus, we made it fricking easy for him. Once the bad guys 'made' Powidz as our base last year, we should have upped stakes and deployed somewhere else."

That was true, Brad realized. They'd gotten lazy, too attached to the facilities and central strategic position the Polish air base offered. By continuing to operate out of a fixed and identified location, they'd made it possible for the Russians to plan and execute this terrorist strike.

"I take your point, Major," Martindale said

quietly. "Perhaps you'd better start scouting out a new base for the squadron."

"It's not going to be easy to find something now," Macomber warned. "Gryzlov's already got his reconnaissance satellites making routine passes over every military facility in the AFN."

Nadia spoke up. "I suspect the Russians also have eyes on us here." She shrugged. "Our Military Counterintelligence Service does superb work, but it is a difficult task to root out any deep-cover agents."

"What about shifting all of our operations to the Scrapheap?" Martindale suggested. "We're still flying under the radar there, aren't we?"

"Maybe," Brad said skeptically. "But I wouldn't count on it. Besides, while Siliştea Gumeşti's a good spot for ferrying in new aircraft and equipment and doing some training, it's badly sited for anything else."

The others nodded. Any units stationed in southern Romania would be too far away to effectively help defend Warsaw or the Baltic states—the most likely targets for any conventional Russian air or ground assault.

"Maybe we could find something closer to the border," Martindale said. He pursed his lips. "There are a number of decommissioned Polish military airfields out there. If we ran the same kind of cover op we used at the Scrapheap, we might be able to—"

"Excuse me," Brad said, interrupting. He took a deep breath. Putting off what he had to say wasn't going to make it any more palatable. "But

I'm afraid we may have another problem, a bigger and more immediate problem."

They all turned toward him, looking puzzled.

"My dad," he said. Swallowing hard, he waved a hand at the row of body bags. "He could have captured some of those guys. Or at least tried to."

"Those men were wired with explosives," Martindale said sharply. "They were ready and willing to kill themselves to avoid being taken prisoner."

Brad shook his head. "No dice, sir. You can't detonate a suicide vest if you're unconscious." He looked hard at Macomber. "Hell, all it takes is one powered-up tap from a CID's finger to drop someone. My dad knows that. *You* know that."

The other man nodded slowly and turned to Martindale. "The kid's right."

"Exactly," Brad said. "But instead he just waded into those guys and butchered them in the blink of an eye." He sighed. "Plus, you all saw him at the conference before they hit us. He was already keyed up beyond reason and primed to kill."

Slowly, reluctantly, Nadia and the others nodded.

"So let me get this straight," Macomber demanded. "You think the general is on the edge of going batshit kill crazy in that metal suit?"

"Yes, I am," Brad said quietly. "You know what piloting a CID in combat is like, right? About getting that weird surge of power and speed and awareness? The sudden feeling that you can do *anything* . . . and that nothing on earth can stop you?"

"Yeah," Macomber said. "But those are sensations you can learn to control. You just have to stay focused."

"For an hour, sure. Even for a day, maybe," Brad said. "But my dad has been stuck inside one of those machines for three full years now. Twenty-four hours a day. Seven days a week. He doesn't sleep. He's never off-line. Who knows what that's doing to him?" He swung toward Martindale. "Do you?"

The head of Scion shook his head. "No, I don't," he admitted carefully. "Your father's experience is . . . well, *unprecedented* is really too weak a word. But it's the only one that fits." He cleared his throat. "In the circumstances, I agree that your fears may be valid. The general has seemed somewhat distant over the past few months."

"And today?" Brad challenged. "What happened here wasn't exactly *distant*, was it?"

"No," Martindale said somberly, gazing at the row of body bags. "Far from it."

"But if this is so, what can we do?" Nadia asked. She tightened her grip on Brad's arm. "Outside a CID, General McLanahan will die. But the threat of a man possessed of such power and then driven mad by isolation . . . well, that is truly terrifying."

Now it was Martindale's turn to sigh. "That is very true, Major Rozek." He stood silently for a few moments, clearly weighing his options. Then he looked up at the others. "I need to make a trip to Nevada soon, for a couple of reasons—this new situation with our friend being one of them. Since I'm currently on Homeland Security's Most

Wanted and Least Liked list, arranging that will take a bit of doing."

He turned his gaze on Brad and Nadia. "But once I've got everything set, you two will be coming with me."

"Us?" Brad asked, confused. "Why?"

"Among other things, you are a pilot, aren't you, Captain McLanahan?" Martindale asked bluntly.

"Sure."

"Then let's just say that you're due for some flight time in a new aircraft," the head of Scion said coolly and cryptically. "As is Major Rozek."

NEAR THE PERUN'S AERIE CYBERWAR COMPLEX, DEEP IN THE URAL MOUNTAINS, RUSSIA
The next day

Even though he had watched the footage all the way through several times before, President Gennadiy Gryzlov still found the images of the Iron Wolf combat robot in action deeply disturbing. So much power, he thought darkly. But even with the knowledge that this power was in the hands of his enemies, the sight of such grace blended with such incredible ferocity was also strangely exhilarating.

When the video flickered to its gruesome end, he turned to Colonel Vladimir Balakin. The trim, dapper chief of security for Q Directorate's secret complex sat silent for a long while, plainly unable to hide his consternation.

"Well?" Gryzlov demanded at last. "Now that you've seen this imagery and read the general staff's analysis of these machines and their capabilities, what do you think?"

Pulling his wits together, Balakin replied slowly. "That . . . device . . . it is beyond anything I imagined possible." He looked sick. "I would estimate that it represents military technology of perhaps an order of magnitude beyond ours."

"So the generals tell me," Gryzlov said coolly. "Which is why you must be ready, Colonel."

Balakin visibly paled. "You anticipate an attack by machines like that? Here?"

"Anticipate? No, Colonel," Gryzlov said, shrugging. "Nevertheless I think it would be wise to be prepared for any eventuality."

"But our cover measures . . . the *maskirova* we've used to conceal even the basic fact of this complex's existence, let alone its location . . ." Balakin stammered.

"Yes, with luck, the Poles and their American mercenaries will never learn about Perun's Aerie," Gryzlov agreed patiently. "But I would encourage you not to trust solely to luck." His mouth tightened. "These mountains are littered with the bones of those foolish enough to believe fortune would smile on them forever. Do I make myself clear?"

Balakin licked lips that were suddenly as dry as dust. "Yes, Mr. President. You are perfectly clear."

"As for these Iron Wolf high-tech marvels," Gryzlov said soothingly. "Remember that the old ways have power of their own. So look to your defenses—*all* of your defenses."

The secure phone on Balakin's desk buzzed sharply. Hurriedly, the colonel grabbed it. "Yes?"

He listened for a moment and then handed it to Gryzlov. "It's Major General Koshkin, Mr. President."

"What is it, Arkady?" Gryzlov snapped.

"The first sets of our cyberweapons have been securely delivered and are in place," the head of Q Directorate reported.

"And?"

"There are no signs that any have been detected," Koshkin said. "*Operatsiya Mor* is ready to launch, on your order."

"Very good," Gryzlov said, relaxing. "You have again done well, Arkady." He checked his watch. "You will have my signed authorization to proceed as soon as I return to Moscow."

He handed the phone back to Colonel Balakin and sat back, happily imagining the unholy chaos his orders would soon create.

NIZHNY NOVGOROD, RUSSIA
That same time

Nizhny Novgorod, the fifth largest city in Russia, sprawled along the western bank of the Volga River about four hundred kilometers east of

Moscow. Founded in the Middle Ages, it served as a strategic border fortress against the Tatars of Kazan—successors to the Mongols of Ghengis Khan. Over the centuries, it grew into the trade capital of czarist Russia.

Renamed Gorky by Stalin to honor the author Maxim Gorky, the city took on a new role, as a center for Soviet military research and production. Foreigners were banned for security reasons. As a "closed city," it remained largely off-limits to non-Soviets until the communist regime collapsed.

Open again to international trade and commerce, Nizhny Novgorod was still home to some of Russia's largest and most important scientific and military research labs and factories. Chief among them was the Nizhny Novgorod Research Institute of Radio Engineering (NNIIRT). Operating out of a collection of unremarkable brownish-gray concrete buildings, this firm, part of the huge GKSB Almaz-Antey defense conglomerate, was responsible for the design and manufacture of highly advanced radar systems—including the target acquisition radars and software used by Russia's S-300 and S-400 surface-to-air missile units.

Not far from the institute, a pale blue UAZ delivery van sat parked along a quiet, tree-lined side street. Its driver, a morose-looking middle-aged man with a drooping mustache, sat placidly behind the wheel. From time to time, he took a drag on his cigarette while idly flipping through the pages of a local tabloid. Sandwich wrappers and a thermos on the seat beside him suggested that he was on a meal break.

The cargo space behind him appeared packed from floor to ceiling with shipping crates, boxes, and other packages. Those appearances were deceiving. All of the jumbled boxes and crates hid the entrance to a small concealed compartment.

Inside this tiny space, two people sat hunched over an array of computers and other electronic gear. Small fans hummed quietly, providing ventilation and cooling. Crumpled disposable coffee cups filled a wastebasket to the brim.

At last, one of them, a bleary-eyed young man, took his hands off a computer keyboard. He turned to his companion, a good-looking redhead, and shrugged his narrow shoulders apologetically. "Sorry, Sam. But it's no go."

Samantha Kerr frowned. "You're sure?"

He nodded. "Oh yeah. I can get into the business side of NNIIRT's computer systems without any problem, but the firewall for the software lab is just too darned good. I could probably break through by brute force hacking . . . but doing that would leave traces their IT guys would zero in on in a heartbeat." He spread his hands. "And I assume that would be bad?"

"Incredibly bad," she agreed wryly. "As in career-ending, up-against-the-wall 'you're going to be shot, treacherous *Amerikanskaya* Scion spies' bad."

"Yeah, so I'd kind of like to avoid the whole getting-executed-for-espionage thing," the younger man said. "It would upset my mom and dad and look bad on my résumé."

"Can the Russians pick up what you've done so far?" she asked.

"No way," he replied. "It's like I tried to pick the lock on that lab firewall, but only using nanoscale tools. Sure I left some traces, like scratches on a physical lock, but they're so small you'd have to know exactly where to look to spot them. A routine security scan won't pick anything up."

"Good," she said, leaning forward to peer over his shoulder. "So we'll do this another way."

"Meaning?"

"If we can't hack into the software lab from the outside, then we'll have to come in at the other end." She narrowed her eyes in thought. "You said you can hack into the institute's business systems, right?"

He nodded.

"So you can get inside their conference-scheduling software?"

"No problem," the younger man said. "What do you want to look at?"

"Every meeting set over the next week or two."

"I'm on it." His fingers flew over the keyboard. Dates and times and names scrolled rapidly across the computer's large LED display.

"There!" she said, pointing to a conference scheduled a few days out. "That's the one."

The younger man raised an eyebrow. "You're kidding me?" He looked closer. "'Systems Demonstration for FAVORITE/TRIUMF Target Acquisition and Identification Software Upgrade 19.17c'? Really?"

She grinned. "Sounds fascinating, doesn't it?"

Her grin widened as she took in his mystified look. "Check out the official guest list."

His eyes widened as he scanned through the list. "Whoa! Lots and lots of heavy hitters there. Geez, including some of the top brass for Russia's aerospace forces."

"Exactly," Samantha Kerr said with satisfaction. "So now I need you to add just one more name to that list." She opened a drawer and took out a set of identity cards, rapidly flipping through them until she found what she wanted. She handed it to him. "This one."

CHAPTER 9

NEAR THE CITY CENTER, WARSAW, POLAND
The next day

Warsaw's rush-hour commute was in full swing, with cars, buses, and trams choking the major streets. Sidewalks teemed with people streaming to work in office buildings, corporate headquarters, banks, and other businesses. Though temperatures hovered just above freezing, several days of intermittent rain had at last given way to a bright, sunny morning.

Strolling arm in arm, Brad McLanahan and Nadia Rozek joined the hurrying crowds, moving just fast enough to avoid being jostled. They were out of uniform, dressed in civilian clothing—warm winter coats, sweaters, and jeans. Martindale's message summoning them from Powidz the night before had stressed that they should be ready to travel "inconspicuously" and at short notice.

This morning, faced with an overseas trip of

indeterminate length, Nadia had decided to clear away some of the chores that had been piling up in her absence. Her service as one of President Wilk's military aides and as his personal go-between with the Iron Wolf Squadron left almost no time for everyday routines like paying bills, laundry, and shopping.

Brad's smartphone buzzed. He took it out and looked at the text message displayed on its screen: *Helo@Belweder. 1030. Flt out MinMaz 1100. No bags. M.*

"Ah, hell," he muttered, quickly entering an acknowledgment.

"Martindale?" Nadia asked quietly.

He nodded. "We've got a chopper flight out from the Belweder Palace in ninety minutes." The palace was the site of Piotr Wilk's working office. Given the Polish president's preference for fast travel, helicopter landings and takeoffs from its forecourt were fairly routine—not something that should draw a lot of attention.

"A helicopter flight to where?" Nadia asked.

"The air base at Minsk Mazowiecki, where we catch a plane to . . . well, who knows? But our final destination should be Battle Mountain in Nevada," Brad told her. He grinned uncertainly. "That's my old hometown, you know."

"So there go most of my errands," Nadia said, frowning in mild irritation. "Straight into the dumpster."

"I'm afraid so," Brad said. He showed her the text. "But, hey, at least we don't have to waste time packing. No luggage allowed, see?"

Nadia raised an eyebrow. "I'm being asked to fly to a foreign country without fresh clothes or even toiletries, and *this* is supposed to console me?" Her eyes flashed. "You have much to learn about women, Brad McLanahan!"

He winced. "Oh yeah . . . I guess that's true."

Laughing, she took pity on him. "Never mind. I am glad to be your instructor." She checked her watch. "If we hurry, perhaps I can unscramble the mess my bank has made of my direct deposits. There's an ATM just off Aleje Jerozomliskie."

Brad nodded. Jerusalem Avenue was one of the main east-west streets in Warsaw and they'd have to cross it on their way to the palace anyway. He shoved the smartphone back into his coat pocket and contritely offered her his arm again. "I'm entirely at your service, Major Rozek."

"Apology accepted, Captain McLanahan," she said with a warm smile.

Nadia's good humor lasted up to the moment they dashed between a stream of slow-moving yellow-and-red buses and saw the line of five people already waiting to use the automated teller machine. She slowed up. "*No, to pięknie.* Just great," she murmured. "If this day gets any worse, I may have to kill Martindale myself. Just to even the score."

Brad decided the better part of valor was keeping his mouth shut.

The elderly man at the front of the line shuffled forward, fumbling in his pocket for a wallet. Peering through thick reading glasses, he fumbled out his bank card and then gingerly inserted it into the ATM, almost as though he expected the machine to bite off his fingers. With that much accomplished, he slowly and with painstaking care punched in his four-digit PIN.

Impatiently tapping her foot at the back of the line, Nadia briefly closed her eyes in exasperation. *"Boże, daj mi cierpliwość."* She sighed. "God give me patience."

But before the old man could even select an option from the ATM's menu, brightly colored zlotys, Polish bank notes, started popping out of its cash dispenser. They dropped out in ones and twos at first, and then faster and faster, and in larger denominations.

For a moment, he stared in disbelief. "What the devil? What is this?" Then, frantically, he started grabbing at the bills as they emerged. "This machine has gone mad! It's throwing away my money! All of my money!"

More zlotys spewed out. Caught up in the brisk cold breeze, bank notes whirled away down the sidewalk. At first, only a few startled passersby snatched at them. Then as the haywire ATM kept disgorging cash, others joined in, scooping up bills as they slid along the paving and snagging them out of the air. More and more people turned to watch in astonishment.

"Is this some kind of crazy promotional stunt?" someone asked.

"Who gives a shit?" A younger man with a shaved head and multiple piercings laughed, holding up a fistful of zlotys. "It's real cash, see!"

Red-faced and shaking with rage, the old man

tried to tear the notes out of his hand. "That's mine," he yelled. "Give it back, you thieving skin-head!"

"Fuck off, Grandpa," the younger man said coldly, holding the zlotys high out of his reach with one hand and roughly shoving him away with the other. "I don't see your name anywhere on these bills."

"But they're coming from my account," the old man shrieked.

"Then go complain to your goddamned Jew bank." The skinhead laughed again. "Those Żyd moneylenders are your real problem, not me."

Several others in the gathering crowd nodded, though most looked disgusted.

That's enough, Brad thought grimly. He stepped forward. "I suggest you give this man his money back," he said, in halting Polish.

The skinhead laughed contemptuously. "Or what, dickhead?"

"Or I'll have to kick your ass," Brad said softly.

"Screw you, foreigner," the other man retorted. He tugged a switchblade out of his pocket and flicked it open. The long, thin blade glinted in the sun. "Maybe I should carve you up a little, to teach you some manners, eh?"

The crowd went very quiet.

Okay, Brad thought, *this just got real*. He rolled his shoulders and neck unobtrusively, loosening up. When the guy made his move, he'd have to slide to the right fast, deflect the knife with a rising left-hand block, and then . . .

"Please move aside, Brad," he heard Nadia say

calmly. He glanced backward, not wanting to take his eyes off the skinhead, now fearful about the sudden distraction . . . but moments later he obeyed. Nadia had drawn her concealed 9mm Walther P99 pistol. Smiling coldly, she stepped gracefully into a two-handed shooter's stance—aiming right at the skinhead's center of mass. "Drop the knife, *dupek*."

The other man's eyes widened in fear. His gaze flicked nervously from side to side, looking for support that wasn't there. He licked his lips. "Jesus, lady. Are you totally fucking nuts?"

"*One,*" Nadia said. "*Two—*"

One of the skinhead's friends grabbed his arm. "For Christ's sake, Jerzy. Let it go. Dump the knife!" He waved his cell phone. "I just heard from Eryk. Every damned ATM in the city is going nuts. Zlotys are flying everywhere, man. It's like manna from heaven. So who needs this shit?"

Blank-faced now, the other man let the switchblade fall out of his hand and slowly backed away. The crowd parted to let him through.

Satisfied, Nadia holstered her pistol, then knelt quickly, and scooped the knife off the sidewalk. She glanced at Brad. "Do you think that other little piece of scum was telling the truth? About all the ATMs running amok?"

Police sirens were wailing now, rising and falling in what seemed like all directions throughout Warsaw's city center. "Yeah," he said slowly. "I think he might have been."

She looked worried. "If so, that would be bad. Very bad."

Brad's smartphone buzzed again. He checked the text and looked up. "Yes, it sure would. And you're not the only one who's worried. Our flight time just got bumped up. Apparently, all hell is breaking loose, and Martindale and the president want us back at the palace right away."

PKO BANK POLSKI, PUŁAWSKA FINANCIAL CENTER, WARSAW
A short time later

Jarosław Rogoski stared at the computer screen with unconcealed bewilderment. In thirty-two years of service with the bank, including five as the senior vice president for retail banking, he had never encountered anything like this. Right now the monitor was displaying the details of just one of the millions of individual accounts owned by the bank's customers. But what it showed was, well, impossible.

Net Account Balance: 10,521.25 zł

The display flickered briefly.

Net Account Balance: 1,320,499.11 zł

Again, the monitor refreshed.

Net Account Balance: -10.05 zł

He looked up at the bank's chief technology officer, Marta Stachowska. "Something like this craziness is happening to every account?"

She nodded grimly. "Every single one that we've pulled up so far." She bit her lip. "The numbers jump wildly every second and, as far as we can tell, with total randomness. No matter what we try, we can't seem to freeze any of them."

"Oh my God," Rogoski muttered. He tapped the screen. "Is this problem connected to what's going on with our ATMs?"

"Probably." Stachowska looked sick. "I think all of our computer systems have been hacked, Jarosław." She lowered her voice. "Our phone and computer help lines are jammed with customers who want to know why their checking and savings and investment and retirement account balances are going nuts. People are starting to panic."

Rogoski felt the blood drain from his face.

Every banking executive dreaded the possibility of a panic-driven run on his or her institution as more and more customers pulled their money out in a frenzy. To help avert that, it was standard finance-industry practice to maintain cash reserves large enough to deal with any sudden rush of withdrawals. But now, with every automated record-keeping system in chaos, how could the bank let anyone withdraw anything from any account?

Suddenly another horrifying possibility occurred to him. "Christ, what about all the credit cards we've issued? Are those records affected too?"

Stachowska pulled up another screen and scanned the rapidly changing numbers. "Yes, they are," she admitted in a low, quivering voice.

Rogoski swallowed hard. "Which means that everyone who tries to use one of our cards—"

"Is being automatically declined," she confirmed somberly. "At the moment, every line of business we have—from individual banking and home mortgages to investment banking and commercial lending—is effectively dead."

He sat down hard, burying his head in his hands. "My God," he muttered. "We're ruined."

"If it's any consolation," Marta Stachowska said quietly, "it's not just us."

"What?"

"If what the news reports we're hearing are accurate, every financial institution in Poland has been hacked," she told him bluntly. "What's happening here in Warsaw is going on across the whole country."

OVER WARSAW
A short time later

In a whirlwind of rotor-blown dried leaves, the *Sokół* helicopter lifted off the forecourt. Narrowly clearing the trees and wrought-iron fence separating the Belweder Palace from the city, it began circling, steadily gaining altitude.

Brad McLanahan peered down at the Polish capital's mosaic of elegant classical architecture and gleaming, modern skyscrapers, of broad, tree-lined avenues and narrow alleys. From what he could see, traffic was at a total standstill. Crowds of people were pouring out into the streets, converging in agitated masses on a number of different buildings scattered throughout Warsaw's center. Flashing blue and red lights marked dozens of police cars trying to force their way along jammed thoroughfares.

"Those mobs are gathering outside every branch of every bank and financial institution," Martindale said grimly over the intercom.

Brad looked across the passenger cabin. The other man had his own face pressed to the nearest window. "Sir?"

"The banks have closed up tight," Martindale told him. "What choice do they have? With what appears to be some really nasty malware running wild through all of their computers, they can't make any transactions."

"Which means our whole economy is going to be grinding to a halt," Nadia realized.

"That's about the size of it," Martindale said gloomily. "Without operating banks, who can conduct business? Sure, there may be a few mom-and-pop stores that still deal mostly in cash, but everyone else relies on electronic transfers. It doesn't matter whether you're a worker bee using an ATM card or a credit card or a big corporation relying on a line of credit to fund some new enterprise." He frowned. "It's a damnably simple equation: without access to capital or credit, there's no real commerce. Not above a primitive, barter-style economy, anyway."

"So very soon no one will be able to buy food. Or pay for gasoline. Or anything else," Nadia said, looking deeply worried. "Not once they've used up any cash they have left in their wallets and purses."

Brad looked down at Warsaw's streets. The

crowds were growing fast. He could see thousands, maybe tens of thousands, of people, more streaming in from every direction. He glanced back at Martindale. "You think people down there are going to turn violent, don't you?"

"Yes, I do," the other man said flatly. "At least enough of them to make real trouble."

Thinking about the skinhead he'd confronted, Brad nodded. There were always fringe groups in any society, ready and eager to snatch any chance to raise hell. And as panic spread through Poland, with more and more of its citizens discovering they could no longer access their savings or use credit cards to buy necessities, it would take just a single small spark to set off an epidemic of looting, arson, and mayhem.

Something caught his eye just as their helicopter swung east, heading for Minsk Mazowiecki at 130 knots. White puffs suddenly blossomed in the air, right above a huge mass of people thronging a wide avenue lined by several major banks.

"The police are firing tear gas," Martindale said somberly. "It's begun."

OFFICE OF THE PRESIDENT, BELWEDER PALACE, WARSAW
Later that night

Polish president Piotr Wilk sat huddled with the two most important and influential members of his government—Prime Minister Klaudia Rybak and Janusz Gierek, his minister of defense. They were gathered around a conference table equipped with a computer and a flat-screen display.

Slightly muffled by distance and the stout walls of the palace, the constant wail of police, ambulance, and fire-engine sirens served as a backdrop to their tense discussion. Riot police were in action at multiple points across Warsaw, fending off the massive, panic-stricken crowds still trying to break into bank buildings. Other police units had their hands full cracking down on criminals who were setting fires and looting stores across the city.

Kevin Martindale looked out at them from the computer screen. His image was grainy. The American was flying west somewhere over the Atlantic Ocean aboard one of his private executive jets. Bouncing encrypted signals through multiple communications satellites made this secure two-way video link possible, though only by the narrowest of margins.

"I've spoken to the heads of every major bank personally," Klaudia Rybak said crisply. Before she became prime minister, her work as an economist had helped Poland transition from a failed Marxist state to a vibrant, increasingly prosperous nation. Most of the men and women who ran their nation's financial institutions were former colleagues or subordinates. "The situation is extremely grave. There is no doubt that all of their current account records are corrupted beyond any hope of salvage."

"Can they reboot their computer systems using stored backups?" Martindale asked.

The prime minister nodded. "They can. In fact, they must." Her expression was bleak. "But to do any good, each bank's IT specialists will have to systematically analyze each separate backup with enormous care. Only those made *before* these hackers inserted their malware will be safe to use."

"All of which means more delay before the wheels of commerce begin turning again," Wilk said sourly.

"Yes, Mr. President," she agreed. "But that is not all. Rebooting from earlier backups means that the digital records of millions and perhaps tens of millions of separate financial transactions will be effectively erased forever. Over time, paper receipts and records can be used to help fill in some of the resulting gaps, but not all." She sighed. "No matter how you look at it, the costs and economic disruption will be enormous."

"How much?" Wilk asked.

The prime minister shrugged. "It is impossible as yet to tell. But I suspect it will be somewhere on the order of eight to ten billion zlotys. And those figures may go much higher. The costs to our economy and people will certainly rise steeply for every day the banks remain closed."

Martindale whistled softly under his breath. Ten billion zlotys was close to three billion dollars at current exchange rates. It also represented close to 2 percent of Poland's annual gross domestic product. Taking that kind of financial hit once wouldn't tip the country's growing economy into a full-blown recession, but it was close. And it was all too likely that more hits were on the way.

"Can we prove the Russians did this?" Janusz Gierek asked. The white-haired defense minister's voice trembled with anger. "What is being done to track down those responsible?"

"Computer emergency response teams, CERTs, from our Internal Security Agency are examining copies of the corrupted software with all possible speed," Wilk told him. "And Mr. Martindale's experts from Scion are conducting their own independent analysis."

"To what result?" Gierek pressed.

"We have not yet uncovered any definitive evidence, Janusz," Wilk admitted reluctantly. "As was the case with the malware found inside the Cernavodă reactor, there are some elements in the code which suggest involvement by Russian hackers—but nothing more concrete."

"Who else besides the Russians would conduct an attack of such scope and severity?" Gierek snapped. "The Americans may have the ability to engage in cyberwarfare on this scale, but I do not believe that even their president, Barbeau, would act so malevolently."

"At least not without a little more provocation than we've given her," Martindale agreed wryly. "As a matter of purely personal revenge, Stacy Anne might be willing to see *my* corporate or personal accounts wiped out, but I doubt she'd risk the political and diplomatic fallout involved in taking out your whole banking system."

"If Moscow is responsible, then what is our response?" Prime Minister Rybak asked. "Can we take our case to the United Nations? Or press for compensation through the World Trade Organization?"

"I'm afraid going down either of those two roads right now would only play into Gryzlov's hands," Martindale said quietly.

Wilk nodded his understanding. They were faced with the same dilemma they'd confronted after the cyberwar attack in Romania. Without solid evidence directly tying Moscow to the malware-caused collapse of Poland's banking system, lashing out against Russia would only lend credence to claims that the Poles were paranoid.

Gryzlov could easily blame the catastrophe on criminals. For years now, gangs of hackers based in Romania and Russia and elsewhere had been stealing millions from banks and retailers and other corporations. Any claim that this most recent hacking incident was just more of the same would be readily accepted by those eager to stay out of any conflict between Moscow and Warsaw.

"If protesting to the international community would be a wasted effort, what exactly do you propose that we do?" the defense minister asked.

"I've ordered our computer response teams to help our banks and other businesses tighten their security," Wilk said, already knowing how inadequate his words sounded. "They will also apply special scrutiny to Internet portals and sites we suspect are vulnerable to Russian infiltration."

Gierek snorted. "Wasted time. And wasted effort. It's too late to lock the barn door now. The horse has already bolted."

Martindale looked apologetic. "Janusz is probably right, Piotr," he said. "If I were Gryzlov, I wouldn't have kicked this war off until I had more of my cyber bombs safely ticking away inside other targets."

"Then why not launch retaliatory cyberwar strikes of our own?" Klaudia Rybak asked. "Perhaps we could show Moscow this is a dangerous game by knocking out Russian government websites— or better yet, those important to industries and corporations controlled by President Gryzlov and the oligarchs who are his allies."

Piotr Wilk wished that he could do as she urged. Every bone in his body cried out for vengeance. His instincts as both a patriotic Pole and a former officer in its air force all told him that taking the fight to the enemy was the only way to win. Gallant defensive struggles waged against enormous odds might be the stuff of legends, but offensive action was the path to victory.

Sadly, in this case, wishes could not change realities.

Poland did not have either the resources or the time needed to develop the kinds of sophisticated cyberwar weapons Gennadiy Gryzlov was now using against her. And since the Russians had been systematically "hardening" their own computer networks against hacking, limited Polish cyberspace counterattacks were unlikely to penetrate their security. At best, any damage they could inflict would be minimal. At worst, a failed Polish cyberattack might leave traces that would allow Moscow to brand Poland as an aggressor state.

"Perhaps that is true," Gierek agreed after listening to his president's reasoning. He scowled. "We have spent the last year and billions of zlotys building up our conventional air and ground forces. Sadly, it now appears that we were only preparing to fight the last war instead of the one we now face, just like every other fool in history. We are no different from the French who wasted their resources on the Maginot Line or the Americans who thought they could refight World War Two in Vietnam."

The defense minister's bitter gaze turned toward Martindale. "But what of our allies in Scion? Are you equally unprepared?" His eyes narrowed. "Or do you have such weapons of your own you might share?"

"If we had cyberweapons that would help, I'd employ them in a heartbeat," the American assured them. He smiled ruefully. "Remember, we've tied our fortunes closely to yours. If Poland prospers, my people and I prosper. If you fall, we're going down with you."

"But your company's hacking operations are extraordinarily sophisticated," Gierek pointed out. "During our last conflict with Russia, my intelligence analysts were amazed by the information your 'tech wizards' pried out of the enemy's computer networks."

"True enough," Martindale said quietly. "But Scion's computer operations are primarily focused on intelligence gathering, not direct action on a strategic scale. Going off half-cocked now only risks exposing sources and methods my people need to penetrate the security screen Moscow has thrown around this covert war."

"Then why not modify this netrusion capability your Iron Wolf fighting machines and aircraft employ to blind enemy radars in combat?" the Polish defense minister asked stubbornly. "That is a form of weaponized computer hacking, is it not?"

"Because netrusion is a tactical option, Janusz, and a significantly limited option at that," Martindale replied. "Yes, we can hack into enemy radars—but only for a few minutes and only at relatively close range. That's a far cry from being able to pull off the same kinds of stunts Gryzlov and his guys are managing." His mouth turned down. "Look, I don't like this any better than the rest of you folks. But all I can suggest for now is that we'd all better buckle up. Because I'm damned sure this ride is going to get a lot bumpier real soon."

CHAPTER 10

ZATMENIYE ("ECLIPSE") CONSULTING GROUP, DOMINION TOWER, MOSCOW

That same time

Seven stories high, the all-white Dominion Tower was a remarkable piece of avant-garde architecture. Each floor was stacked above the others in an irregular, uneven pattern, creating a profusion of cantilevered balconies. At the building's heart, a series of interconnected staircases crisscrossed its soaring white-and-black atrium. Reviewers characterized the building's exterior as resembling something seen in a Jenga or Tetris game, while the interior reminded many of one of M. C. Escher's wilder drawings.

Igor Truznyev's Zatmeniye Consulting Group occupied the top two floors. While he found the Dominion Tower's name a hopeful omen for his future, the building's other tenants were its primary attraction. Even before it opened, Moscow's most successful information-technology start-up companies had rushed to lease office space in the new building.

Their presence served Truznyev's purposes in two ways.

First, the need to protect their precious intellectual property made these IT start-ups incredibly security-conscious. The physical and Internet safeguards they'd added to the complex dovetailed perfectly with Zatmeniye's armed guards, biometric locks, and the expensive, anti-eavesdropping film applied to all of its office windows.

Even better, their employees had served as an ideal pool of potential candidates when Sergei Tarzarov and his master, Gryzlov, had needed computer experts. Discreet poaching from the Dominion Tower's other tenants had helped Truznyev fill their quotas and line his own pockets with the fees Tarzarov paid him.

But now, watching the news reports from Poland, he was beginning to regret sending so many hackers into the service of his hated successor.

"Rioting continues virtually unabated in the heart of Warsaw, Łódź, Kraków, and other major Polish cities. While it is not yet known how many people have been killed or injured in the unrest, it is clear that Polish police have made thousands of arrests. In an effort to calm the situation, government officials have stressed that the banks will reopen as soon as possible, but they have so far proved unable to offer any firm schedule. Journalists gathered outside the official residence of President Wilk report that he is in urgent consultations with—"

"*Sukin syn!* Son of a bitch," Truznyev muttered, stabbing at his remote to mute the smooth, urbane tones of the BBC's late-hour newsreader.

Moodily, he leaned back in his leather office chair, watching images of angry mobs and looting flicker across the big-screen television mounted across one wall of his sleek, futuristic office. Much as he despised the Poles and their mercenary allies, nothing he saw made him happy.

He swore again, softer this time. It was bad enough that Gryzlov had succeeded in breaking the NATO alliance last year. That was a diplomatic and foreign-policy victory that had eluded generations of wiser and saner Russian leaders. But now it appeared that this cyberwar campaign of his might actually tear Poland apart and, at the same time, destroy the new Eastern European defense pact the Poles had forged. If so, the younger man would be more popular than ever—and virtually impossible for Truznyev to unseat, whether in an election or an inner-circle Kremlin coup.

That fact that Gryzlov was achieving these victories with the aid of computer specialists he himself had provided only rubbed salt in his wounds.

Truznyev shook his head, angry with himself. Helping Sergei Tarzarov find hackers had made sense, especially considering the sums the cynical old Kremlin insider had offered. But he had been foolish to do so without learning more about Gryzlov's plans.

Well, he thought bitterly, it was time he stopped acting out of ignorance. It was essential that he

uncover more details of Gennadiy Gryzlov's cyberwar operation, including the truth about this
purported "treasure cave." Otherwise, there was
no way he could accurately judge the younger
man's chances of pulling off yet another unexpected political triumph—let alone figure out some
way to discreetly sabotage the upstart president's
scheme.

He picked up his phone. "Vitaliy," he snapped
to his assistant. "I want Akulov and Ivchenko in
my office. Now!"

While waiting for his two most senior subordinates to arrive, Igor Truznyev contemplated
the orders he would give them. Yuri Akulov and
Taras Ivchenko were veteran intelligence officers.
In their youth, they had served with him in the old
KGB. When the Soviet Union collapsed, they'd
followed him into the FSB and later acted as his
eyes and ears inside the spy agency after he became
president. Faced with the choice of sucking up to
the new regime when Gryzlov took power, they'd
opted instead to stick with Truznyev.

He nodded to himself. Akulov and Ivchenko
were hard-nosed, competent, and thoroughly reliable. Each man still maintained a wide range of
personal contacts inside Russia's intelligence services and armed forces. Both also had extensive
experience in dealing with the criminal underground. Given enough time and money, he was
confident they could ferret out the information
he required. Equally important, he was sure they
could do so without tipping off Tarzarov or Gryz-

lov that he was poking his nose into their precious secrets.

"Let's just see what you're really up to, Gennadiy, you little prick," he muttered. "And then I will decide if it's worth the risk of throwing a little sand into your gears."

THE WHITE HOUSE, WASHINGTON, D.C.
The next morning

President Stacy Anne Barbeau looked across her Oval Office desk at Edward Rauch, her national security adviser. Her professional politician's smile stayed about as far south of her eyes as her deliberately thickened Louisiana accent was from the Mason-Dixon Line. "Just so we're clear, Ed, I don't want any bureaucratic bullshit. I want straight talk. If you don't know the answer to something I ask, you fess up like a man, you hear me?"

"Yes, Madam President," Rauch said quickly. With Luke Cohen on his way to Moscow, the slightly built, gray-haired man was in charge of the interagency working group tasked with analyzing the situation in Eastern and central Europe. From the deep dark bags under his eyes and the pallor of his skin, Barbeau judged he was taking his responsibilities seriously.

"Good," she said, allowing a little more warmth to creep into her expression. Rauch had spent most of his working life writing dry, academic papers on U.S. defense policy for different think tanks headquartered inside the Washington Beltway. Facing the real world, where there were no simple, black-and-white answers, must be a hell of a shock to his system.

"The usual Russian huffing and puffing aside, I assume we're pretty sure Moscow is behind this Polish banking meltdown?" she asked.

"We are," Rauch agreed. He shrugged his narrow shoulders. "Nothing else makes sense. Criminals with the skills to pull off a computer hack like this would have every incentive to be subtler. They could have gone in, cleaned out a bunch of high-value accounts, and then vamoosed, leaving no one the wiser."

Barbeau nodded grimly. Concluding that Gennadiy Gryzlov was screwing around with the Poles again wasn't much of a stretch. What mattered most to her was how much danger the Russian president's "virtual" aggression posed to the United States and its remaining interests in Europe.

Even with support from Martindale's Iron Wolf and Scion mercenaries, Poland and its allies were unlikely to win any open clash with Russia. But the Poles, in her experience, had never been an especially logical people. And real wars had a way of spreading uncontrollably. Seeing the Poles, Czechs, and others batted around by Moscow was one thing. Watching the violence spread to engulf long-standing American allies like the Germans was another.

She decided to cut straight to what worried her the most. "Are there any signs this digital war is going live?"

"No, Madam President," Rauch said decisively.

That was a surprise. Barbeau stared coldly at him. "I really hope you're not spitting in the wind here, Ed."

He shook his head. "Not in the least. So far, every piece of satellite imagery we've got and all of our NSA signals intercepts show *zero* unusual military activity on either side."

"None?"

"Not a peep, Madam President. All ground forces on both sides above the battalion level are still in garrison, without any sign they're moving to higher alert status."

Barbeau chewed on that for several seconds. "Okay, so if there aren't any tanks, infantry, or artillery on the move, what about Russia's fighters and bombers? Or the Poles? Gryzlov and Piotr Wilk are both so fricking air-minded that any clash between them is sure to start with bombing raids or fighter sweeps."

Again, Rauch shook his head. "Aside from routine air patrols, there's nothing going on that we can detect. Neither side appears to be preparing for serious combat."

Okay, that was weird, Barbeau thought. She didn't like it when foreign leaders started acting unpredictably. She would have bet money that Gryzlov's cyber attack was only the prelude to a conventional military offensive. And if not, she would have put just as much money down on the probability that Piotr Wilk would react violently to any Russian provocation.

Which left open one obvious and deeply disturbing possibility. If the Poles weren't willing to retaliate openly, they still had other options.

"So what's going on at Powidz?" she asked. Since learning last year that Kevin Martindale's Scion mercenaries, high-tech drones, aircraft, and combat robots were based there, the Polish Special Forces base had become a high-priority target for U.S. intelligence. Rauch hesitated. "Spit it out, Ed," Barbeau snapped. "I wasn't screwing around earlier, you hear? If you've got any indications that clown Martindale and his merry men are planning something, I need to know. And right now! Not later, when it's too late, and I've got Gennadiy Gryzlov screaming in my goddamned face."

"It's just that we're not sure how to interpret the data," Rauch told her warily. "Our satellites picked up signs of some kind of attack on Powidz a couple of days ago."

"*Before* this cyberwar hack against the Polish banking system?" He nodded. "Jesus Christ," Barbeau snarled. "And no one in your working group thought this was important enough to report to *me*?"

Her national security adviser winced. "Our best analysis was that this was only a pinprick raid, Madam President," Rauch said. "Based on the photos, it looks as though someone targeted

Powidz with a few heavy mortar rounds, but the damage inflicted appears to have been minor."

She gritted her teeth, fighting down an urge to savage the pallid little man. Firing him now would only draw press and congressional interest she didn't want or need. "Well, then, according to your best *analysis*, Dr. Rauch, who the hell fired those mortar rounds?"

"The NSA intercepted Polish military police transmissions indicating possible Chechen involvement," Rauch said cautiously.

Barbeau snorted. "For *Chechen*, read *Russian*," she said.

"In all probability," Rauch agreed.

"So let me get this straight," she said carefully. "First, the Russians plastered a really important Polish military base with mortar rounds and now they've hacked the shit out of the whole Polish banking system?" Rauch nodded. "And in response, the Poles are doing *nothing*?"

"Yes, Madam President. At least from what we can see."

Stacy Anne Barbeau blinked in disbelief. "Does any of this match up with your previous analysis of probable Polish reactions to renewed aggression by Russia?"

"No, ma'am. Not to the slightest degree," the national security adviser admitted.

"Should I be worried about that, Ed?" she asked carefully.

Rauch took a deep breath. "Oh, hell, yes, Madam President," he said. He grimaced. "Obviously, President Gryzlov has started a new war against the Poles and their allies, but all we're able to pick up so far are tiny flickers of flame and smoke here and there."

"Like a coal-seam fire," Barbeau realized. "The kind that can burn undetected underground for decades or even centuries."

He nodded. "Exactly. Right up to the moment it explodes onto the surface. Which is precisely what worries me about this situation." He looked back across the desk at her. "Either the Poles and their Iron Wolf auxiliaries are being uncharacteristically passive, or—"

"They're planning something big in retaliation," Barbeau finished for him. She shook her head in dismay. "Something really fucking big."

UNIFICATION HALL, COTROCENI PALACE, BUCHAREST, ROMANIA
That same time

In Foreign Minister Daria Titeneva's considered judgment, the setting for her private meeting with Romanian president Alexe Dumitru was impressive. A blend of ornate Venetian and French neoclassical architecture, the palace was a marvel of splendor and grace. While the nineteenth-century building had only narrowly survived the barbarism and architectural lunacy of the Ceaușescu regime, years of painstaking work had succeeded in restoring its glories, along with many of the artistic and historical treasures looted by the communists. Most of the palace was now a national museum, but one wing served as a residence for Romania's head of state.

Cotrocenti's Unification Hall, used for conferences with important foreign leaders and diplomats like her, was especially beautiful. White marble walls and columns bore intricate decorations in gold leaf, and a stained-glass ceiling showing scenes from Romania's history bathed the enormous room in natural light.

In stark contrast to the ornate backdrop, however, Russia's dark-haired chief diplomat found her host far less imposing.

Once tall and robust, Alexe Dumitru now seemed a pale and shrunken caricature of himself. The stresses and strains imposed by economic and political crisis were visibly aging him. Considered impartially, she supposed that was a shame. But it was largely Dumitru's own fault for deciding to turn his back on Romania's traditional ally, Russia, in favor of this half-baked coalition cobbled together by the Poles. Perhaps now he would see the error he had made and make amends to Moscow. And if not, Titeneva thought coldly, he would fall—bringing other, more sensible, men and women to power in Bucharest.

Donning a thin smile, she slid a thick document across the table toward the Romanian leader. "In light of recent events in Poland, I think you will find my government's most recent offer a very reasonable one, Mr. President."

Dumitru raised a skeptical eyebrow. "Oh?" He

glanced down at the front sheet of the proposed diplomatic agreement between the Russian Federation and Romania and then handed it off to one of his aides without reading further. Warily, he looked back at her. "Perhaps you would be kind enough to summarize what President Gryzlov now demands?"

"*Demands* is a harsh word," Titeneva said primly. She shrugged. "But I will not quibble over a mere matter of semantics." Still smiling politely, she leaned forward. "Stripped to its essentials, my government's revised proposal is very simple. We are still willing to supply your country with the natural gas it so desperately needs and to do so at a price your economy can afford—"

"If we break our agreement with the Alliance of Free Nations and instead sign a defensive pact with you," Dumitru said impatiently.

"Of course," Titeneva replied calmly. "Poland has made itself our enemy. Why should you tie your country's fate to that of Piotr Wilk's misguided regime? Will your people thank you for leading them down such a blind and dangerous path?"

"With respect, Madam Foreign Minister," the Romanian said stiffly. "Somehow I fail to see any difference between this 'new' proposal of yours and the ultimatum your master tossed at my feet eight days ago."

Titeneva shrugged again. "Why should there be any substantial change in our position? The relative balance of power between our two nations remains much the same, does it not? Without the energy supplies we alone can provide, Romania faces a bleak and unhappy winter. Warsaw cannot help you. We in Moscow can. Your choice should be an easy one."

Seeing Dumitru's face darken, she held up a hand. "But President Gryzlov is willing to make one additional concession, as a gesture of friendship."

"Which is?"

"The cataclysmic collapse of the Polish banking system should make clear the danger we all face from criminal computer hackers," Titeneva said, keeping any trace of emotion out of her voice. "Accordingly, the defense pact between our two countries would include a guarantee of aid from Russian cybersecurity specialists against this new terrorist and criminal threat."

Privately, she thought this move by Gennadiy Gryzlov, her occasional lover, was far more likely to anger the Romanian president than to woo him. Although she rarely sought out details of Moscow's illegal covert operations, only a fool could fail to draw the obvious conclusion. This was no different than having someone point a gun at your head and then offer to protect you. From himself. For a price.

But that was typical of Gryzlov, she decided. The Kremlin leader handled diplomacy the way he made love—brutally, without any attempt at subtlety or refinement. While she counted herself among those attracted by the younger man's displays of wild, almost unhinged passion, she strongly doubted many others on the world stage shared her attitude.

Somewhat to Titeneva's astonishment, Dumitru chose not to react with open fury to his Russian counterpart's newest bit of thinly disguised blackmail. She could see the anger in his eyes, but very little of it sounded in his voice. If anything, he seemed more tired and disgusted than outraged.

"Tell President Gryzlov I find his candor . . . *clarifying*," he said. "May I ask how long I am being given to consider your government's proposition?"

"This is *not* an ultimatum, Mr. President," Titeneva said, feigning surprise. "There is no artificial deadline."

"How reassuring," Dumitru said coldly.

She spread her hands. "Of course, it is also true that international events are moving with great speed. Proposed commitments of valuable resources that make sense on one day may seem unwise, or unnecessary, the next."

The Romanian met her gaze levelly. "Naturally."

Titeneva got to her feet. "I am expected to return to Moscow tonight." She stared across the table challengingly. "As a matter of common sense, I would advise you not to delay too long in deciding to accept our proposals." She smiled pleasantly, again assuming the role of an experienced diplomat rather than that of an extortionist's go-between. "I would be truly sorry if the relationship between our two great nations suffered because of any lingering ambiguity."

"You can safely assume that I completely understand President Gryzlov," Dumitru said bluntly. With equally contrived civility, he rose to escort her out of the palace. "You may assure him that I will consider his propositions with great care and in precisely the same spirit of friendship with which they were made."

So he will refuse us, Titeneva realized. Inwardly, she shrugged. So be it. For a moment, she was tempted to emulate Quintus Fabius, the Roman ambassador to Carthage who had openly offered its oligarchs the choice between war and peace. But why bother with such drama? she thought. All too soon, she was sure, Alexe Dumitru would have ample reason to regret his pigheadedness. Then again, so would the Pole Piotr Wilk and all the others across Eastern and central Europe who had joined him in defying Moscow.

CHAPTER 11

**HANGAR FIVE, MCLANAHAN INDUSTRIAL
AIRPORT, SKY MASTERS AEROSPACE, INC.,
BATTLE MOUNTAIN, NEVADA**
Several hours later

Hunter "Boomer" Noble swiped his key card
through the door lock, waited for it to *beep*
softly in approval, and stepped into the vast,
dimly lit hangar building. Waiting for his eyes
to adjust, he tugged off his gloves and unzipped
his jacket. It felt good to come inside out of the
icy, fifteen-knot breeze blowing across the long
airport runway. This late in the year, it got decid-
edly chilly out on the high desert of north-central
Nevada.

Gradually, his vision adapted, revealing more
than a dozen aircraft of varying sizes and shapes.
Hangar Five was used to store some of the many
experimental planes designed and built by Sky
Masters since it went into business. Most were the
brainchildren of Jonathan Masters, the company's

founder and chief scientist. His tragic death five years before at the hands of domestic terrorists had left a hole in Sky Masters' reputation for high-tech innovation and invention that Boomer and his boss, retired U.S. Army colonel Jason Richter, were trying hard to fill.

"But damn, boss, you left some mighty big shoes behind," Boomer murmured, staring along the rows of plastic-shrouded aircraft. Jon Masters had been brilliant, maddening, quirky, childish, and a hell of a lot of fun to work with. From day to day, you never knew if he was going to come into the lab brimming over with a new concept for a single-stage-to-orbit space plane or with the roughed-out specs for a radar system so sensitive it could pick up the flutter of a bat's wings at fifty nautical miles.

Jason Richter, Sky Masters' chief executive officer, was incredibly talented and quirky as hell in his own way, but he would never be another Jon Masters. You only ran across a guy like that once in a generation or two, and then only if you were very lucky.

He glanced down at his phone. Speaking of Richter, where the heck was he? According to the text he'd sent asking Boomer to meet him in Hangar Five, he should already be here.

Three figures stepped out of the shadows on his right and came toward him into the light. Two were men, the third a young woman. Jason Richter was not with them.

"It's nice to see you again, Dr. Noble," a smooth, assured voice said.

With a sense of almost resigned incredulity, Boomer recognized Kevin Martindale. Jesus, he thought bitterly. Wasn't there any level of security that could stop this guy? Or at least give some warning that he was on the way?

Martindale, a former president of the United States and current head of Scion, might still be one of Sky Masters' best customers—no matter how many wrathful executive orders Stacy Anne Barbeau signed—but the ease with which he popped in and out of even the company's most secure facilities was beginning to mightily piss Boomer off. He sighed. The ability to hack into the company's text-messaging system was just one more item on a lengthening list of spooky stunts the Scion chief seemed to delight in.

"My apologies for the small deception," Martindale said with a devilish twinkle. "But I thought making an appointment through regular channels might cause something of a stir in all the wrong places."

With an effort, Boomer controlled his annoyance. He was pretty sure the other man took perverse pleasure in startling the crap out of him, so maybe it was just best to let his irritation go. "Yeah, that's true enough, sir," he said with a dutiful smile. "I guess being on President Barbeau's 'Most Hated' list must cramp your normal travel schedule a little."

"It is occasionally inconvenient," Martindale agreed. "Still, my companions and I manage to make do."

Boomer's gaze moved past the gray-haired Scion

CEO to a much taller, broad-shouldered young man. His smile widened into a genuine grin. "Hey, Brad! Nice to see you again. You're looking pretty good for a stateless pirate or bloodthirsty mercenary or whatever nasty name the Russians are calling you these days."

Brad McLanahan smiled back, though Boomer thought the expression seemed a bit forced. No real surprise there, he decided. It must suck to find yourself effectively exiled from the United States, able to return only surreptitiously, sliding along in the slippery wake of someone like Martindale.

"It's a living, Boomer," Brad said quietly. "Besides, the Iron Wolf Squadron is a top-notch outfit—and Poland is a great country, one well worth fighting for."

That simple, heartfelt declaration earned Brad a dazzling smile from Martindale's other companion, a slender, dark-haired young woman.

Boomer's never-too-deeply-buried horndog instincts kicked into high gear. Now, *there* was one mighty fine-looking lady, he thought. He straightened up, squaring his own shoulders. "Why, hi there, ma'am," he drawled, sticking out a hand to shake hers. "The name's Hunter Noble, but you can call me 'Boomer.' I'm the chief cook and bottle washer around this joint, except when I'm flying one of our S-19 Midnight shuttles to space and back."

Brad rolled his eyes. "This is Major Nadia Rozek," he said. "She's in the Polish Special Forces, a military aide to President Wilk, and his personal liaison with the squadron." He leaned in close and dropped a very firm hand on Boomer's shoulder. "And *mine*," he said quietly.

The young woman laughed. Her bright blue-gray eyes sparkled with amusement. "Oh, I am quite sure that Dr. Noble will be a perfect gentleman whenever he is around me."

"Because if I'm not, Brad here will kick my sorry rocket-jock ass?" Boomer asked, smiling back.

With a predatory grin of her own, Nadia Rozek shook her head. "Oh no," she said sweetly in lightly accented English. "*I* will."

"Now that we've settled exactly who will kick whose ass, could we move on to slightly more serious matters?" Martindale said, mildly exasperated.

"Such as why you're poking your nose into this hangar full of old X-planes?" Boomer asked.

Martindale nodded. "On the nose, Dr. Noble." He turned and waved a hand toward the assembled aircraft. "We're here to check out one of Dr. Masters's orphans. One of his many advanced aviation projects that never found a loving home."

Orphans, huh? Boomer frowned slightly. That probably was the way most people would see the planes stored in this hangar.

Many of the aircraft, sensors, weapons, and other equipment invented by Jon Masters were in active service, either with the U.S. Armed Forces or with Scion and the Polish-allied Iron Wolf Squadron. But a lot of his designs had never made it into full production. They'd fallen victim to government and corporate budget cuts, to behind-the-scenes political maneuvering, or to cutthroat competition from the larger, more established U.S. defense contractors.

It was incredibly expensive to move any aircraft design off the drawing board and turn it into something you could actually fly. From a strictly corporate point of view, every dollar sunk into any canceled project was money down the drain. Which was why Helen Kaddiri, Jon Masters's ex-wife and the company's current president and chairman, often called Hangar Five "Never-Never Land" or "the Warehouse of Expensive Dreams."

Boomer's own view was very different. He saw the hangar as a place of as-yet-unrealized potential, as a well of innovation just waiting to be tapped. The experimental aircraft stored here incorporated revolutionary design concepts and technologies—concepts and technologies that could be applied to a wide range of new projects in the years ahead. Sure, maybe these particular prototypes and test planes hadn't found favor with the powers that were, but that didn't mean the resources expended on them had been wasted.

Which was probably why he suddenly wasn't thrilled at the prospect of seeing Martindale get his perfectly manicured hands on one of them. Scion's CEO had a purely utilitarian view of aircraft and weapons systems. They were just tools to be used, discarded, and even destroyed so long as he achieved his goals.

Boomer could sort of understand that attitude when it came to planes or weapons that were in production, finally rolling off the assembly lines after years of flight and systems testing. But every aircraft in this hangar was literally one of a kind. All the blueprints and design specs in the world could never come close to capturing the hard-earned knowledge each represented.

"Which particular X-plane are you interested in?" he asked reluctantly.

Martindale turned to Brad. "It's your show now, Captain," he said.

"Yes, sir!" Eagerly, the younger man moved deeper into the hangar. Boomer and the others tagged after him.

Brad stopped next to one of the plastic-covered shapes. "This baby," he said, pointing. "This is the one we want."

The aircraft he'd indicated was about the size of a Gulfstream 450 business jet, around the size needed to carry twelve to sixteen passengers or two-plus tons of cargo. But that was where its resemblance to any commercial design ended. It had a batwing configuration with four jet engines buried in the wing's upper surface.

Boomer's eyes narrowed in surprise.

Designated the XCV-62 Ranger, this was Jon Masters's design to meet a U.S. Air Force call for a stealthy, short takeoff and landing (STOL) tactical airlifter. While other companies like Northrup Grumman, Boeing, and Lockheed noodled around with scale-model prototypes to prove their concepts, Sky Masters had jumped straight to building a flyable test aircraft. But Masters's untimely death and later the Barbeau administration's vendetta against any company connected to Scion, Martindale, and Patrick McLanahan had strangled their bid in its cradle.

He looked back at Brad. "You have got to be kidding."

"Nope."

Boomer frowned. "Why not use the XV-40 Sparrowhawk we already sold you? That tilt-rotor's a sweet ride and it can land practically anywhere."

"Sure," Brad agreed. "But it doesn't have anywhere near the operational range we're likely to need." He went on, ticking off his reasons on his fingers. "Plus, it's not fast enough or maneuverable enough. And finally, with those big rotors spinning, her radar cross section is so high there's no way the Sparrowhawk can penetrate a high-threat air-defense environment undetected."

Still frowning, Boomer turned back to Martindale. "You guys still have at least one of the XC-57 Losers your guys flew in Iraq back in 2010, don't you? The Loser might have been designed as a bomber, but you know the mods I made turned it into one heck of an effective cargo airlifter or troop transport. Plus, one ugly mother or not, it's got all the range and airspeed you could possibly want."

"Unfortunately, the XC-57 is far too big for the mission we may have in mind. And it's certainly far too visible to enemy radars," Martindale said patiently. "Remember, Dr. Masters originally designed the Loser to fire hypersonic missiles well outside the range of any enemy air defenses. Stealth was the last thing on his mind."

Brad cut back in. "Look, Boomer, here's the deal: we're looking for an aircraft just large enough to carry a team deep into hostile territory and set down on a small, improvised runway. And we need to be able to do that, and get out again, without being detected." He patted the aircraft beside him. "The XCV-62 here fits the bill perfectly."

"If it's as capable as Dr. Masters claimed it would be, that is," Martindale added. He shrugged. "Of course, if that was all just marketing hype—"

"The Ranger is a damned fine flying machine," Boomer said firmly. He stared hard at the other man. "Though whether Brad's right about it being perfect for your needs depends pretty heavily on exactly what kind of cockeyed scheme you're planning now. Care to fill me in?"

Seeing the cool, impassive expression on Martindale's face, he sighed. "Never mind. Forget I asked. Most guys who say, 'If I tell you that, I'll have to kill you' are just bullshitting. But in your case, I figure you'd only be issuing a clear statement of intent."

Brad and Nadia both grinned at his quip. So did Martindale, though in his case Boomer was pretty sure it was more out of politeness and not genuine amusement. Like many powerful men, the former president rarely enjoyed being the target of someone else's wit.

"Anyway, this is all academic," Boomer went on. He shook his head. "There's no *way* Helen Kaddiri is going to let you fly that XCV-62 out of here. At least not at a price you can afford. Sky

Masters poured more than a hundred million dollars into the Ranger prototype. I don't care how much backing you've got from the Polish government, no one's going to approve paying that much for a single aircraft."

"Helen's a shrewd businesswoman," Martindale told him. "Shrewd enough to know the difference between a hundred million in sunk costs gathering dust in a hangar and thirty million dollars or so in cold, hard cash—or at least its digital equivalent."

Boomer stared at him. "She took thirty million? For the Ranger prototype? You're shitting me."

"Not in the least," Martindale assured him, smiling smugly. "Dr. Kaddiri has already verbally approved our acquisition. You can confirm that with her if you like." He smiled thinly. "But as a precaution, I would recommend finding somewhere safe from FBI, CIA, and NSA eavesdropping before you do."

"Yeah, well there's the biggest roadblock of all," Boomer pointed out. "Now that Barbeau's on the warpath against Scion, we've got the feds crawling over our facilities day and night—inventorying every piece of flyable hardware we own. With special attention being paid to advanced aircraft like the Ranger."

He turned toward Brad. "It already took a hell of a lot of finagling to smuggle out those last couple of CIDs your Iron Wolf guys needed, and those robots are small enough to conceal inside a shipping crate full of other crap."

"Your point being?" Martindale asked.

Boomer shrugged his shoulders. "That even if you're planning to strip the XCV-62 all the way down to its component parts, there's no way you'll get it out of Battle Mountain past the feds, let alone all the way to Poland."

"Sure there is," Brad said, with total confidence.

Boomer eyed him suspiciously. "How?"

"Nadia and I will fly it out."

Boomer felt his jaw drop open. Recovering fast, he shook his head. "Like hell you will."

"Why not?" Brad asked.

"For one thing, no matter how shit hot a pilot you are, you can't just hop into an airplane you've never flown before and handle it safely."

Brad shrugged his broad shoulders. "That's what full-motion computer simulators are for, Boomer. We can reconfigure one of the flight simulators in Hangar Two for the XCV-62 and squeeze in a few hours later tonight—when all the wannabe commercial-jet trainees are out in the bars or in bed."

Boomer nodded slowly. Much as he hated to admit it, that part of Brad's scheme made sense. Sky Masters owned some of the most advanced full-flight simulators in the world. And a sizable chunk of its revenues came from the fees its instructors and computer programs earned by teaching prospective pilots how to fly everything from two-seater turboprops to superadvanced fifth-generation fighter jets like the F-22 Raptor and the F-35 Lightning II. Plus, Brad had already proved himself a fast learner when it came to flying.

Then he shook his head decisively. "Even if you *can* figure out how to fly the beast in time, there's still no way you can pull this stunt off."

"I find your lack of faith disturbing," Brad said, deepening his voice.

"Very funny, Darth McLanahan," Boomer retorted. "Look, Brad . . . the Ranger is reasonably stealthy, okay? But against radar. It's not freaking invisible to the naked eye."

"So?" Brad asked innocently.

"So as soon as you taxi out onto the runway past those hangar doors, the friendly local FBI agents camped out on our doorstep are going to start screaming bloody murder. And once that happens, you are toast. Between the USAF Aggressor Squadron down at Nellis and the Navy Top Gun gang at Fallon, you'll have F-18s and F-16s coming down hard on your ass before you fly a hundred miles downrange."

"No, we won't," Brad said. He looked at Boomer with the faint hint of a barely suppressed grin. "Before Sky Masters built the Ranger, you put together a couple of full-scale design mock-ups, didn't you?"

"Yeah," Boomer said slowly, still not sure where this was heading. "That's standard aerospace-engineering practice. Mock-ups let us check things like aerodynamics and refine the human-factors stuff like figuring out the most efficient cockpit layouts."

"Do you still have them?"

"Well, sure. You know how Jon was. He never threw anything away if he could help it," Boomer said, shrugging. "So every piece of crap from the Ranger project is crated up in long-term storage somewhere at our facility here." His eyes narrowed. "Why?"

"Patience, Dr. Noble," Nadia interjected with a smile of her own. "All will be made clear soon enough."

Brad thanked her with a flick of his eyes and went on. "The XCV-62's engines are standard commercial types, right?"

Boomer nodded. "Yeah, they're off-the-shelf Rolls-Royce Tay 620-15 turbofans. You know the Sky Masters philosophy: never reinvent the wheel if you don't have to. Designing new engines for every airframe just adds cost, complexity, and delay."

"So if you had to, you could scrounge up some spares, right?" Brad asked.

"Sure. Why?"

Brad broke into an unrestrained, boyish grin. "You mean you haven't figured out my incredibly cool plan yet?"

Boomer winced. There was almost nothing he hated worse than being the last one to a party. He adopted an old man's quavering tone. "Show a little mercy to an aging wreck, okay? I'm hitting thirty-five later this year. I may still have the body of a Greek god, but my brain may be going soft."

At least that bit earned him a delighted laugh from Nadia. Even if she was obviously attached at the hip to one of his friends, it was nice to know she was paying attention.

"Fair enough, old man," Brad said, grinning

even wider. "See, here's how I see things playing out . . ."

While he listened to the younger man run through the details of his plan, Boomer found himself shaking his head in awestruck wonder.

When Brad finished, he whistled softly. "Man, up to now, I never figured I'd meet anyone more willing to push the envelope on seriously, bad-to-the-bone, balls-to-the-wall crazy than General Patrick McLanahan. I guess that means insanity really *is* genetic."

For just a split second, Brad's smile slipped.

Oops, Boomer thought. He'd hit some kind of nerve there. He wondered what it was.

"Does that mean you'll help us?" Brad asked quietly.

"Oh, hell, yeah," Boomer said, clapping Brad on the shoulder to try to get past the moment. "You can definitely count me in. Because, I mean, how could I possibly pass up the chance to wind up in federal prison on a count of grand theft of a top-secret stealth aircraft?"

CHAPTER 12

wo Polish F-16C Vipers slid through a clear night sky above the Polish capital. Since it was peacetime and they were operating in Warsaw's often crowded airspace, both fighters had their navigation lights on. Otherwise, their mottled light and dark gray camouflage would have rendered them almost invisible at anything more than a couple of hundred yards.

"Tiger flight, fly heading zero-nine-zero, climb and maintain five thousand meters," a calm voice said through Colonel Pawel Kasperek's headset. "Nearest civilian traffic is a LOT Polish Airlines 737-400 thirty-five kilometers away at your eleven o'clock and descending. No bogeys detected at this time."

Kasperek glanced back over his left shoulder through the F-16's clear canopy. There, well below his current altitude and far off in the distance, he could see the airliner's bright white anticollision strobes as it came in for a landing at Warsaw's Chopin International Airport. The regularly scheduled night flight from London Heathrow was arriving on schedule. He clicked his mike. "Acknowledged, Warsaw Operations Center, Tiger flight, heading zero-nine-zero degrees, climbing to five thousand."

Without prompting, Kasperek's wingman, Captain Tomasz Jagielski, piloting another Polish F-16, responded simply with "Two." Tomasz was a young but experienced F-16 pilot. Last year, before Poland's alliance with the United States collapsed, his skills and hard work were rewarded with a deployment to America's ultrarealistic war games known the world over as Red Flag. Red Flag was designed to give aircrew members their first ten combat missions, considered vital to survival in real combat, and Jagielski took full advantage of this rare opportunity, minimizing the partying and maximizing his studying, and won awards for his performance during the war games.

As a good wingman, Tomasz stayed off the radio unless prompted by his leader—he knew well the wingman's edict that he was expected to utter only three phrases without question: his place in the formation; the words "Lead, you're on fire;" or while in the bar: "Lead, I'll take the ugly one." But now Kasperek thought it was getting too quiet, so he clicked the mic button and spoke: "Doing okay, Tomasz?"

"Roger that, sir," Jagielski responded. Given his

cue to speak, he went on: "Too bad it looks like the Russians aren't going to come out to play tonight, though. I need another couple of kills to make ace."

Smiling under his oxygen mask, Kasperek tugged his stick gently left, pulling back a bit at the same time. His Viper rolled into a gentle turn and climbed at 340 knots. Young for his rank, the Polish Air Force commanding officer made sure he rotated through regular patrol missions with all of the pilots in his squadron. Seeing firsthand how each of them flew and reacted was crucial to his leadership style. If their current cold war with Russia turned hot again, he needed to know exactly what he could expect from the men and women under his command.

Jagielski, for example, was unfailingly aggressive. If you wanted someone ready and willing to tangle with an enemy fighter force, even badly outnumbered, he was your guy. By the same token, it was sometimes necessary to ride herd on him, as the Americans would say, in those situations where the slightest wrong move could accidentally set off a shooting war.

Polish F-16 and MiG-29 fighters patrolling along the border with Russia's Kaliningrad enclave often encountered Su-30s and Su-35s on the same kind of mission. Sometimes no more than a kilometer or two separated the rival forces. Flying in such close proximity to potential hostiles took nerves of steel. No matter how hard the Russians tried to provoke an incident—say by locking on their fire-control radars or maneuvering in a threatening manner—it was vital that Poland's pilots refuse to take the bait. President Wilk's orders were clear. If open hostilities began again, it was essential that Russia be seen as the aggressor.

Thankfully, tonight's mission should be far less nail-biting, the colonel thought. He and Jaglieski were slated for a routine patrol along their country's border with Belarus. For all practical purposes, the Belarussians were firmly under Moscow's thumb. Russian troops operated freely within the country's borders. So did FSB, SVR, and GRU spies. But last year's destructive Iron Wolf CID raids had shown the Russians the folly of stationing combat aircraft so close to the frontier. They seemed content to maintain a close watch over their own airspace and that of occupied eastern Ukraine.

Unfortunately, Kasperek thought coldly, it was equally evident that the Russians had found other ways to make his country suffer. He glanced aft again, seeing the lights of Warsaw spread out in a glowing arc along the black ribbon of the Vistula River. Fires still burned in a few places near the city's center, set by rioters in the aftermath of the bank system's collapse.

Resolutely, he turned away. He and his pilots could do nothing to stop the cyberwar attacks aimed at Poland. Their sacred duty was to keep watch over her skies, standing ready in case Moscow's conventional armed forces tried to take advantage of the political and economic chaos its computer hackers were creating.

Right now Pawel Kasperek and his wingman could see a huge expanse of their beloved country.

At 5,000 meters, their visual horizon extended out almost 250 kilometers. Besides Warsaw, patches of warm yellow light marking cities and towns like Lublin, Białystok, Łódź, and Częstochowa were plainly visible. Thinner strings of light traced out Poland's network of major highways and rail lines.

Abruptly, one of those bright blotches winked out, going black in an instant. Another followed seconds later. And then another.

"*Jezus Chrystus*, Tomasz," Kasperek said into his mike. "Do you see what I'm seeing?"

By now, a vast stretch of the countryside below them had plunged into sudden, near-absolute darkness.

"I do," Jaglieski radioed. His voice was tight. "The whole damned electrical grid may be going down."

NATIONAL POLICE HEADQUARTERS, PULWASKA STREET, WARSAW
That same time

Piotr Wilk was sure he had never seen the commander of Poland's national police force, General Inspector Marek Brzeziński, so weary. From the rumpled state of his blue-gray uniform and his disheveled white hair, it seemed likely that he'd been awake since the cyberwar attack on the banks occurred, or, at best, catnapping in his office.

Despite his obvious fatigue, however, there was no doubt that Brzeziński still had a firm grip on the situation. He turned to Wilk. "We are making progress in restoring order, Mr. President. Not as quickly as I would like, naturally. But progress, nonetheless."

He gestured toward one of the two large maps covering one wall of the emergency command center. It showed the city streets of Warsaw. Colored overlays were pinned across the map, each marking a different trouble spot. Black X's across many of them indicated places where police action already had quelled mobs or suppressed large-scale criminal activity like organized looting or arson. "Riot-control teams from the Preventative Police have now succeeded in regaining control over most areas of the capital. Hundreds of looters and hooligans are under arrest. Ongoing investigations by the Criminal Police should enable us to press charges against most of the worst offenders."

"Good work, Marek," Wilk said. He pointed to the other map, the one showing all of Poland. "And what about the rest of the country?"

"Even better," Brzeziński said. Unconsciously, he tugged at his loosely knotted tie, straightening it. "The disturbances in most other cities and towns were on a much smaller scale than those we saw here."

Wilk nodded his understanding. Warsaw lay at the center of much of Polish national life, of its economy, culture, and politics. Its growing wealth and prosperity drew many of the country's best and brightest. Unhappily, that same prosperity also attracted a number of troublemakers, an ugly mix of anti-Semitic skinheads and far-left anarchists, along with the more commonplace thieves, rapists, and murderers. When Poland's banks shut down and the streets filled with tens of thousands of fearful citizens, these thugs had seized the opportunity to run wild.

But now that the banks were beginning to reopen, however shakily and tentatively, the public unrest and panic should gradually subside. Without the cover provided by massive crowds of protestors, any skinheads, crooks, and anarchists still at large ought to hurriedly scuttle back to their squalid haunts.

Brzeziński agreed with his reasoning. "We hope to tamp down the last outbursts of violence and disorder by the morning, Mr. President," he said. "Or by noon at the—"

All the lights suddenly snapped off.

For a brief moment, Wilk sat frozen in his seat. Then he pulled out his smartphone and tapped its flashlight app, a move imitated by others in the command center. Startled faces appeared in the different beams, seeming strangely disembodied in the sudden darkness.

"I think your schedule may have to be revised, Marek," he said grimly. "Unless this is only a very local problem."

In less than a minute, emergency generators in the basement kicked in, restoring power to the headquarters building.

Wilk glanced down at his phone. Dozens of texts were already flooding in, from every ministry in his government. "Shit," he muttered. He turned toward the somber-faced man in charge of his security detail. "We're heading for the roof, Major," he said, rising to his feet.

Major Dariusz Stepniak frowned. "I think that would be most unwise, sir." He glanced up at the lights. "It's possible this power outage is intended to lure you out into the open. If so, there could be a sniper targeting the roof, hoping you'll make an appearance there. It would be safer to return to the Belweder Palace immediately."

With an effort, Wilk fought down the temptation to tell the other man he was being a paranoid idiot. Like all agents in Poland's BOR, the Bureau of Government Protection, its version of the U.S. Secret Service, paranoia was practically part of Stepniak's job description. It was his job to imagine the sniper on every rooftop, the pistol-wielding assassin in every crowd, the suicide bomber at every public gathering.

But that didn't mean it was necessary for Wilk to indulge every one of the major's fears.

He rose and jerked his head toward the door. "I'll just have to take that chance, Dariusz. If you're right and someone shoots me, you can tell me how fucking stupid I was. But in meantime, I need to see what the hell is going on outside for myself." He held up his smartphone, showing the sea of urgent messages, all highlighted in red, flicking onto its small screen. "Because whatever it is, I can assure you that it's really bad."

Minutes later, Wilk, Stepniak, Brzeziński, and a number of aides were on the roof of the five-story headquarters building, staring out across Warsaw's skyscraper-studded skyline. It was utterly dark, marked only by a few tiny points of light that showed other buildings with working emergency generators.

His phone buzzed sharply, signaling a Priority One call. "Wilk, here."

Prime Minister Klaudia Rybak was on the other end. Ordinarily perfectly cool and collected, she now sounded flustered and out of breath. "I've been in touch with the top people at Polski Siece Elektroenergetyczne," she said.

Wilk nodded to himself. PSE was the state-owned company in charge of Poland's national power grid. "And?"

"They say their voltage-control software is malfunctioning," the prime minister said quickly. "They don't yet know how or why, but their computer programs are apparently misallocating power—shunting power to portions of the grid that are already at maximum capacity and siphoning electricity away from areas that need it. Voltage surges all over the country are knocking out transmission lines and generators."

"How bad is it?"

She gulped. "Their best guess is that more than fifty percent of the country is already completely blacked out."

Wilk closed his eyes. He and the rest of his inner circle had all been on edge wondering where Russia's hackers would strike next. Well, now they knew. Not that it was any comfort, he thought bleakly.

"I'm afraid there's more, Piotr," she said.

"Yes?"

"Andrzej says he's getting frantic calls from his opposite numbers all across the Alliance."

Wilk felt himself tensing up. Andrzej Waniek was his foreign minister.

"They've been hit by the same kinds of transmission outages," she told him. "The Baltic states, Hungary, Romania, and the rest are all going dark."

IRON WOLF COMPOUND, POWIDZ, POLAND
A short time later

A slowly rising moon turned the woods around the Polish air base into a dreamlike world where pitch-black shadows mingled with splotches of pale gray light. Tree branches rustled, swayed by gusts of cold wind from the east.

Captain Ian Schofield, his senior NCO, Sergeant Andrew Davis, and Whack Macomber lay prone in a clump of brush growing over and around the charred trunk of a tree felled by lightning. They were on a shallow rise overlooking the perimeter fence. All three wore ghillie suits that included the most efficient antithermal linings available. While motionless, they were effectively undetectable by the human eye or most IR sensors. Despite that, none of them was under any illusion he could hide for long from the lithe gray-and-black shape prowling slowly along the fence several hundred meters away—not if it decided to come looking for them, anyway.

"Tell me again why we're out here, Major?" Schofield murmured into Macomber's ear. With luck, even the CID's razor-sharp audio pickups would have trouble picking out his whisper at this distance amid the noise of the wind whistling through the woods.

"We need you and your guys to keep an eye on CID One out there," Macomber said softly. "We're . . . well, let's say we're a little worried about the pilot."

"Worried as in you think maybe the guy's catching cold? Or worried as in he might go loco?" Davis growled.

Macomber shot him a sour grin. "The latter, Sergeant. As I suspect you'd already guessed."

"Maybe so," the noncom said with a glint in his eye. "But since you're asking us to keep tabs on a potentially homicidal maniac who just *happens* to be riding around in a practically invincible combat machine, I kinda figured it made sense to hear the bad news straight up. Without any of the usual HQ happy talk."

"Fair enough," Macomber agreed. He understood Davis. Like him, the sergeant was a seasoned veteran with multiple covert operations under his belt, first with the U.S. Special Forces and then with Scion and the Iron Wolf Squadron. And one of the first things anyone learned in Special Ops was to figure that whatever the rear-echelon guys told you was about 70 percent sugarcoating, 25 percent pure BS, and maybe, on a good day, about 5 percent fact.

Schofield frowned. "If this man could be a threat, why not simply wait until he climbs out of the CID and then send him in for a psych evaluation?"

"Because, in this particular case, that's not an acceptable option, Captain," Macomber said flatly, making it very clear to both men that he'd gone as far as he was going to go down that road. The fact that Patrick McLanahan was still alive, never mind that he could not survive for very long outside a CID, was a tightly held secret, even within Scion and Iron Wolf.

"Swell," Davis muttered. "Ain't nothing so joyful as being voluntold to babysit a killing machine."

This time it was Schofield who shot him a warning glance before turning back to Macomber. "Very well, Major," the Canadian said. "What are your orders if we do see this pilot going off the reservation? Do you want us to engage him?"

"Hell, no," Macomber answered. "I try not to send guys out on suicide missions." He shook his head. "No, if you spot trouble, you call it in to me or Charlie Turlock and then vamoose as fast as you can."

"And then what happens?" Davis wanted to know.

Macomber was silent for a moment. At last, he sighed. "Then Charlie and I gear up in other robots and do our best to put him down, without getting ourselves or anyone else killed."

* * *

When he'd crawled far enough back down the rise to be safely out of sight, Whack Macomber slowly climbed back to his feet. He winced as his knees popped. "Man, I may be getting too old for this snake-eating commando shit."

Charlie Turlock jumped up from the tree stump she'd been sitting on while waiting for him. She grinned. "Maybe so, Whack. That's why CIDs are so cool. You get a nice cushy ride and you let the robot do all the work."

"Yeah, they're just peachy-keen," he retorted. "Right up to that point where they drive you nuts." He jerked a thumb back over his shoulder. "Like the general, for example."

Charlie's mouth turned down. "We don't know that yet. Not for sure."

Macomber shrugged. "Maybe not. But it's for damned sure that he's getting awfully close to the line between sane and crazy—assuming, for argument's sake, that he's not already way, way over it." He looked closely at the slender woman. "You heard Piotr Wilk and most of the other AFN leaders have declared martial law, right?"

She nodded. The news coming down from on high wasn't good.

No one knew how long it would take the various national computer emergency response teams and Scion's technical specialists to flush the Russian viruses that were screwing up power transmission systems across most of Eastern and central Europe. That left Poland's president and his counterparts in an ever-worsening bind. The longer their people were left without electricity, the colder, hungrier, and more pissed off they were likely to get. In the circumstances, deploying military units to help maintain order and distribute emergency supplies was probably the least-bad option, but it certainly wasn't something anyone would celebrate.

"Well, our friend Patrick out there has been pinging Wilk, Martindale, and me every few minutes, telling us we should deploy the Iron Wolf CID force to stamp out any new riots," Macomber said grimly.

Charlie's eyes widened. "But that's—"

"Crazy, yeah," he finished for her. "See the problem?"

CHAPTER 13

THE KREMLIN, MOSCOW
That same time

Luke Cohen forced himself to look pleased when Gryzlov's long-suffering secretary ushered him into the Russian president's inner office. It took one hell of an effort. Serving as Stacy Anne Barbeau's White House chief of staff and longtime political confidant had put calluses on both his ego and his conscience, but dealing with this mercurial son of a bitch was even tougher.

First, Gryzlov had waited for days before replying to his repeated back-channel requests for a private meeting. Then, after Cohen flew all the way to Moscow, Russia's leader left him cooling his heels in the American embassy, pleading "the press of urgent state business." Now, more than a day later, he'd abruptly summoned the tall, skinny New Yorker to the Kremlin—ignoring the fact that it was already close to midnight.

Cohen decided he was getting really tired of dominance games.

Smiling broadly, Gryzlov crossed the room to greet him. "Mr. Cohen, as always, it is a great delight to see you." He shrugged apologetically. "I regret, of course, both the unavoidable delay and the late hour. But, sadly, my life is not my own."

Irked though he was, Cohen had to admire the other man's ability to lie his ass off without breaking a sweat. For a second, he was tempted to call Gryzlov out, just to see how the Russian would react. Instead, he settled for murmuring the usual diplomatic pleasantries while they shook hands.

Politely, the Russian president waved him into a chair and then sat down facing him.

"And now what can I do for you?" Gryzlov asked easily. He smiled. "Feel free to speak candidly. As you see, we are the only ones here. There are, as you would say, no inconvenient witnesses."

Cohen nodded, thinking fast. He'd met with Gryzlov last year, to covertly brief him on what turned out to be a disastrous attempt by U.S. Army Rangers to capture the Iron Wolf mercenaries fighting for Poland. At the time, the Russian had insisted on speaking his own language, relying on a Foreign Ministry official to translate for him. Cohen assumed that was because the Kremlin leader's English was rustier than his CIA bio claimed. Now it was clear Gryzlov had been playing some other game instead.

Maybe the Russian president had wanted a witness at last year's briefing as insurance against the

Americans getting cold feet and aborting their Ranger mission at the last minute. If so, the fact that he was willing to meet privately now could be a positive sign.

The theory was worth testing, anyway. Besides, the president had ordered him to press Gryzlov hard.

"President Barbeau is very concerned about the situation in Eastern and central Europe," Cohen said carefully.

"Yes, I know," Gryzlov agreed. "She told me so at great length during our last video conference." He shrugged. "Naturally, I share her worries. The political turmoil in this self-styled Alliance of Free Nations should trouble everyone who wishes to preserve peace and order in Europe."

Cohen hid a frown. If the Russian leader really wanted a frank exchange of views, what was up with all the phony-baloney platitudes? There was no way he could slink back to the White House and report he'd only heard the usual pile of diplomatic bull crap. Not if he wanted to keep his job. Not to mention his balls. Making allowances for her subordinates' failures was not one of Stacy Anne Barbeau's strongest suits.

He leaned forward. "Forgive me for speaking bluntly, Mr. President, but while that's a nice sentiment, it rings kind of hollow just now. Because you and I both know that Russian hackers are behind this wave of cyberwar attacks."

"Is this an official accusation by your government, Mr. Cohen?" Gryzlov asked. His expression was veiled.

Cohen shook his head. "No, sir. If it were, you'd be hearing it from President Barbeau herself." He looked the Russian leader squarely in the face. "But at this juncture, she would rather avoid unnecessarily increasing the tension between our two countries."

Gryzlov nodded in appreciation. "She is a sensible woman."

"Which isn't the same thing as someone who will turn a blind eye to what you're doing," Cohen said firmly. "You're playing a dangerous game, Mr. President. One that could easily spark a new war between Russia and Poland and its allies. Or create a terrible humanitarian crisis as governments and other civil institutions collapse across Eastern and central Europe."

The Russian reacted with an amused chuckle. "Your talent for melodrama is remarkable, Mr. Cohen." He shook his head. "As it happens, Russia is playing no such game."

"Our intelligence analysts say otherwise," Cohen shot back. "They say some of the malware used in these attacks bears clear signs of Russian origin. Apparently, the techniques the hackers use are like a set of digital fingerprints."

"Every country has its own criminals," Gryzlov said, with a shrug. "Mine, alas, is no exception." He smiled. "Perhaps your intelligence analysts should learn to discern between state action and criminal conduct."

"You can't seriously claim that a few crooks

with computers just took down most of the electrical grid in eight separate countries?" Cohen said in disbelief.

Gryzlov shrugged again. "How should I know what criminals are capable of?" He spread his hands. "Or it may be that this catastrophe is only evidence of criminal negligence by those in authority. Perhaps these power companies were skimping on necessary maintenance and now it has caught up with them. Widespread electrical outages are not uncommon, after all, even in more advanced nations."

Cohen snorted.

"You think that unlikely?" the Russian asked, raising an eyebrow. He looked speculative. "There is one other possibility, of course."

"Like what?" Cohen asked.

"That this power transmission crisis was deliberately orchestrated by Piotr Wilk and his puppets," Gryzlov said calmly.

For a moment, Cohen just stared at him, unable to believe he'd heard the other man correctly. "With respect, Mr. President," he said at last. "That is absolutely and totally crazy."

"Is it?" Gryzlov asked, with a cynical smile. "After all, these governments are under considerable pressure from their own people, who are unhappy at being dragooned into a war pact led by Wilk and his mercenaries. But now these blackouts have given the Poles and the others an excuse to declare martial law, have they not?"

He snapped his fingers. "So much for dissent or political protests now, eh? With the push of a few buttons and the stroke of a pen, these fascists have gained the ability to crush all opposition to their plans. In a day or so, the lights will come back on . . . but I strongly suspect you will see their soldiers and tanks still patrolling the streets."

Cohen didn't know whether to laugh or cry. The Russian leader was either off his rocker or, far more likely, just toying with him. Like most of those close to Stacy Anne Barbeau, he had no particular fondness for Piotr Wilk or Kevin Martindale, but he also knew they weren't idiots. Trying to pull off a Machiavellian maneuver like that was only a recipe for disaster, and both men were smart enough to know it.

For several more minutes, he sparred with Gryzlov, trying his level best to make the Russian leader understand the U.S. knew what he was doing and strongly disapproved. In the end, he came to the dispiriting realization that Gryzlov honestly didn't give a damn.

"Cheer up, Mr. Cohen," Gryzlov told him at last. "Nothing that happens in these tiny, troublemaking countries should have any lasting effect on the relationship between Russia and the United States. President Barbeau and I have worked hard to rebuild the ties of friendship and close cooperation damaged by past leaders." His eyes were cold. "Surely, neither of us would be foolish enough to jeopardize this progress. Not for the sake of a few minor countries so utterly inconsequential to your own great nation's genuine interests." There was a knock at the door. "Come!" Gryzlov snapped.

His private secretary came in, looking apologetic. "Mr. Cohen's embassy car is downstairs, Mr. President."

Gryzlov raised an eyebrow, obviously pretending to be surprised. "So soon?" He glanced at his watch. "Ah, I see. It's well past midnight. Where *does* the time go?"

The Russian president got to his feet, forcing Cohen to do the same. "While I regret that we were not able to come to a full meeting of minds tonight," he said, "I am certain that, eventually, you and President Barbeau will come to share my perspective on these regrettable, but relatively unimportant events."

He put his hand on the American's shoulder, gently but unmistakably guiding him toward the door. "Please, allow me to walk you to your car."

"That's quite all right," Cohen said tersely. Being given the bum's rush was bad enough. Seeing Gryzlov standing on the steps of the Kremlin's Senate Building waving a not-so-fond farewell as he drove off would only add insult to injury.

"Oh no," the Russian said, with a quick, slashing grin. "I insist. It will give me great pleasure."

It was an ambush.

Luke Cohen figured that out as soon as he and

Gryzlov walked outside into the frigid night air. Oh, his car from the American embassy was there all right. But it was surrounded by television news crews and other journalists. Bright klieg lights snapped on, spotlighting them. Cameras flashed in the darkness.

"Oh, shit," Cohen muttered.

"Courage, Mr. Cohen," Gryzlov said quietly, still wearing his practiced politician's smile. He gestured toward the crowd of waiting reporters. "It appears that someone leaked the news of our meeting to the press. I hope it was not one of your people. If it was one of mine, you may be sure he will get what he deserves." He shrugged. "In the meantime, we shall just have to make the best of it, true?" Helplessly, Cohen nodded. "Excellent," Gryzlov said. With the American still in tow, he stepped up to a bank of microphones.

"While I am surprised to see you all here tonight, perhaps it is for the best," the Russian leader began, favoring the assembled journalists with a dazzling smile. "First, let me say that the news of these terrible blackouts affecting our closest neighbors to the west is deeply unsettling. While Russia has justifiable grievances against a few political leaders in these countries, no civilized person can view the suffering of so many tens of millions of innocent people with anything but compassion."

He paused briefly for dramatic effect and then went on. "Accordingly, I wish to make it clear that Russia is ready to offer immediate economic aid and technical assistance to those in distress. For the time being, we are willing to set aside any disagreements we might have with their governments." Sighing, he shook his head. "At a time of such tragedy, petty political disputes must obviously give way to simple human decency."

Listening to Gryzlov's obviously prepared and practiced litany of falsehoods, Cohen tried desperately to keep the anger and humiliation he felt from showing on his face. Sure, this was a setup, but now that he was boxed in, all he could do was hope to get out without further compromising the United States.

"Is this offer of aid and assistance something you and Mr. Cohen discussed tonight?" one of the reporters asked.

Gryzlov glanced quickly at the American standing beside him and then turned back to the assembled press. "You must realize that I cannot answer such a question," he said with the hint of a smile. "Mr. Cohen is President Barbeau's White House chief of staff, and her personal representative to me in all matters concerning this sudden crisis. Our meeting this evening was entirely off-the-record. So it would be highly improper for me to reveal *any* of the substance of our private conversation. All I can tell you is that we had a very full and frank exchange of views on a number of issues."

"Including this sudden wave of cyberwar attacks on Poland and the other Eastern European countries?" a voice called out from the middle of the press gaggle. "The ones some say are the work of computer hackers paid by your government?"

Cohen recognized the skeptical face of Simon Turner, the BBC's longtime Moscow correspondent. He darted a glance at Gryzlov, half expecting to see the Russian leader irritated by this impudent, but extremely pertinent question.

Instead, Gryzlov laughed. He wagged a finger in mock reproof. "You have been visiting too many conspiracy-theory websites, Mr. Turner." He smiled broadly. "You should remember that Russia has long sought an international arms-control treaty to ban this form of warfare. My country's only interest in cyberweapons is purely defensive. Our energies and our resources are entirely devoted to safeguarding our computer networks against attack by others—not to inflicting harm on innocents."

The veteran BBC reporter wasn't quite ready to yield, however. "Those are fine sentiments, President Gryzlov, but they seem a bit out of touch with current events. A number of independent experts have verified that—"

"Anyone with access to a computer can write anything they wish," Gryzlov interrupted with a sly smile. He made a careful show of *not* looking in Cohen's direction before he continued. "But if it comes to making wild accusations, I should remind you that only one great power currently has a military unit specifically dedicated to creating such weapons. And the last time I looked, my government had no control over the Pentagon's Cyber Command."

Cohen felt his face flush angrily.

"Are you suggesting that the Americans are responsible for these attacks?" Turner asked incredulously.

"Not at all," Gryzlov said in mock surprise. "I merely point out the dangers of casting aspersions without facts."

With that, he turned away from the microphones and nodded to someone standing off in the shadows.

Cohen recognized Sergei Tarzarov, his Russian counterpart. Expressionlessly, the old man nodded back at Gryzlov, and then spoke a single word into his cell phone.

In moments, a small army of plainclothes Kremlin security officers poured out into the courtyard. Politely, but firmly, they shooed the TV crews and other reporters away.

When the journalists were all safely out of earshot, Gryzlov turned to Cohen. "I regret this awkward incident," he said perfunctorily, scarcely bothering to hide his amusement. "But I am afraid the impertinence and intrusiveness of the press is a cross that must be borne by all of us who live in truly free societies."

THE WHITE HOUSE, WASHINGTON, D.C.
A short time later

"That rat fucker!" President Stacy Anne Barbeau snarled, watching the footage from Gryzlov's "impromptu" press conference play across the big screen in the Situation Room.

When it finished, she spun around in her chair to glower down the length of the long table at her national security team. "Well, that tears it," she said bitterly. "Gennadiy Gryzlov may be a lying sack of shit, but he's also fricking clever. And right now he's running rings around us."

"How so, Madam President?" CIA director James Nash asked, plainly confused. "Nobody with any sense will buy the idea that *we're* behind the cyberwar attacks in Europe."

"Of course not!" Barbeau snapped. "But that's not the point, Jimmy." Nash looked hurt. She sighed, fighting for patience. After all, she was the one who'd opted for loyalty, not brains, in picking the former senator to head the CIA. It was hardly fair to expect brilliance from a man whose principal strengths were looking good on television and knowing how to read persuasively from a teleprompter.

"Look," she said, trying to speak calmly. "You're right that most European leaders will pin the blame on the Russians—right where it belongs. But this media ambush he just pulled on Luke still screws us over."

Barbeau saw Ed Rauch nodding slowly.

Good, she thought, *at least one of these clowns gets it*. But some of the others still looked unsure. "Follow the timing, people," she said flatly. "First, Poland's banking system gets trashed. Then hackers fry the electrical grid in most of Eastern

Europe. And now Gryzlov 'accidentally' reveals that we've been holding secret talks with the Kremlin the whole time. What do you suppose that will suggest to those with suspicious minds, like Piotr Wilk and his gang?"

"That we've either signed off on this Russian cyberwar campaign or, at the very least, that we're just standing on the sidelines, willing to let it happen," Rauch said.

"That's about the size of it," Barbeau agreed. "Which pretty much screws over any chance we could have used this crisis to strengthen our own position in Europe. Before Gryzlov's little press conference, we had a shot at peeling away some of the weaker members of the AFN by offering our help. Now we probably don't."

Secretary of State Karen Grayson frowned. "I guess I don't see the problem." She looked troubled. "I mean, I thought our policy was pretty much to hunker down here in the States while we rebuild the Air Force's bomber and fighter wings. You don't really want to expand NATO back into Eastern Europe again, do you?"

Barbeau stared coldly at the other woman until she wilted back into her chair.

Good God, she thought contemptuously, was her secretary of state really that naive? Couldn't she figure out the difference between a public-relations front and serious strategy?

"This isn't about expanding NATO, Karen," she said finally, regaining some control over her temper. "But there's a big difference be-

tween having the countries of Eastern and central Europe act as neutral buffer states that are
friendly to us . . . and watching the Russians frog-
march them back into submission to Moscow. I
may not want them tied to our apron strings, but
I'm sure as hell not happy at the prospect of seeing
Gryzlov calling all the shots in Poland, Hungary,
and the others the way the Soviets used to."

Rauch cleared his throat. "There might be a
way we could regain some influence in the region,
Madam President," he said tentatively. "And help
stave off this new Russian onslaught at the same
time."

"Which is?" Barbeau said sharply. From the
pained look on her national security adviser's face,
she was pretty sure he knew she wasn't going to
like his proposal.

"Given the changed strategic circumstances,
maybe we should ease off a bit on our arms restrictions," Rauch suggested. "I'm not saying we
should supply weapons to Poland and the other
countries ourselves. But if we looked the other
way while they bought combat systems and muni-
tions from Sky Masters and other companies . . ."
Seeing the expression on her face, he trailed off
uncertainly.

"Not a chance," she said. "The restrictions stay."
She shook her head. "I may be pissed off at Gryzlov's moves, but that doesn't mean I'm willing to
risk getting sucked into a war, of any kind, on the
side of the Poles and Martindale's paid killers."
Her mouth turned down in disgust. "Especially

since these so-called geniuses appear completely outmatched by Russia's cyberwar forces."

"Then what is our policy?" Rauch asked carefully.

"We look to our own defenses," Barbeau said. She frowned. "I hate playing a waiting game, but I don't see that we have much choice. Not after Gryzlov managed to poison the well so deftly just now."

She looked down the table at Admiral Scott Firestone, the new chairman of the Joint Chiefs. Unlike his predecessor, the short, stocky Navy man seemed content to leave high-level policy in the hands of his elected civilian masters. He rarely spoke up at these meetings unless asked a direct question. As a rule, she found that restful, though there were occasional moments when she wished the admiral would be a little more proactive.

"Pass the word to Cyber Command, Admiral," Barbeau said. "I want stepped-up efforts to harden our key computer systems. Now that we've seen what the Russians can do, let's not get caught with our pants down around our ankles. Is that clear?"

"Perfectly clear, Madam President," Firestone said.

"And tell your people to work even harder developing more of our own cyberweapons," she added coldly. "If that son of a bitch Gryzlov ever decides to sic his goddamned hackers on us, I want to be able to hit him back—and hit him so hard that he'll wet himself."

THE KREMLIN, MOSCOW
That same time

Sergei Tarzarov closed the door to Gryzlov's office behind him. His face was impassive.

The president looked up from his desk with a satisfied grin. "That went well, didn't it?"

"If you mean that you successfully humiliated Cohen, and through him, the American president, then yes, it 'went well,'" Tarzarov said. He frowned. "But I am not sure this was a sound political move, Gennadiy."

Gryzlov laughed. "You're such an old woman sometimes, Sergei." He leaned back in his big chair, folding his hands behind his head. "If Barbeau thought she could use our *Operatsiya Mor* to scare her former NATO allies back into Washington's arms, I've spiked her guns."

"And in the process, you may also have managed to persuade her that we are a dangerous enemy worth opposing," Tarzarov pointed out. "Rather than an equal with whom she can negotiate."

Gryzlov shrugged. "If so, who cares? Barbeau may be a foolish bitch, but the scales were bound to fall from her eyes sooner or later. Besides, what can she do?"

"The Americans have their own cyberweapons and computer specialists," Tarzarov said. "Is it not likely they will redouble their own cyberwar efforts, both to defend themselves and to act offensively against us?"

Again, Gryzlov laughed, but this time without

any real humor. "You still don't see what's going on, do you, Sergei?" His eyes were cold, full of calculated cruelty. "When I finish with the bastard Poles and their toadies, it will be Barbeau's turn to suffer. And when that day comes, she will learn that all the cyberweapons and computers in the world cannot save her."

CHAPTER 14

MCLANAHAN INDUSTRIAL AIRPORT, BATTLE MOUNTAIN, NEVADA
The next day

The evening sun sent long shadows slanting across McLanahan Airport's runway and hangars. It was setting fast, sinking toward the steep, rugged hills and peaks lining the horizon about thirteen miles beyond the Sky Masters field's fenced-in perimeter.

"Masters Three-Zero, McLanahan Tower," said the tower controller seated in front of six large high-definition monitors forming a panoramic video arc of the airfield. "Winds two-four-zero at twelve gusting to eighteen, runway two-five, cleared for takeoff."

"McLanahan Tower, Three-Zero cleared for take-off, runway two-five," replied the pilot.

"Masters Six-Two, taxi to and hold short of runway two-five via Alpha and Alpha One."

"Taxi to and hold short of two-five via Alpha and

Alpha One, Masters Six-Two," came the reply from
a second aircraft.

Hunter "Boomer" Noble stood in the center of
the airport operations room, behind the two controllers on duty. McLanahan Industrial Airport
did not have a control tower, but used a network
of remotely operated cameras and sensors to give
air-traffic controllers a precise and real-time view
of not just the airfield but all of the surrounding
Class-C airspace for thirty miles in all directions.
The controller did not use a normal radar display.
Instead, aircraft icons floated across the screens
along with their call signs, altitude, airspeed, and
route of flight. As the C-130 Hercules started its
takeoff roll, Boomer could see its route-of-flight
line extend off into the distance, first to the southwest and then to the south.

"Our friendly local G-man is on the way,
Boomer," the shift supervisor told him as he
clicked off from speaking with the facility's security watch commander.

Boomer nodded. He checked his watch. As
promised, FBI special agent Raymond Sattler was
right on time. It sure was nice to know that you
could count on *some* things in this crazy world, he
thought—especially from a government employee.

Ray Sattler and his team of dozens of agents
were ever-present fixtures at McLanahan Industrial Airport, Sky Masters Aerospace, and even
in the town of Battle Mountain. Plus, Sattler had
many more agents stationed at Sky Masters' facilities all over the country. When the Barbeau
administration tried to close down Sky Masters

because of its suspected support of Scion in Poland and Ukraine, Jason Richter and Helen Kaddiri hired the best law firms, lobbyists, and political operatives to challenge the government's sanctions. The government finally made a deal with Sky Masters: allow the Justice, Defense, State, Commerce, and Treasury Departments to closely monitor every aspect of Sky Masters Aerospace's operations, and the company could stay open. The government gave the job to the Federal Bureau of Investigation. And the FBI immediately sicced dozens of investigators, lawyers, and accountants onto the task of scouring every possible aspect of the company's operations. Sometimes it seemed like each and every Sky Masters office, hangar, workbench, and break room in dozens of locations had an FBI agent assigned to it 24/7. It was as if anytime an airplane, hangar door, or wrench belonging to Sky Masters moved, an FBI agent was there to monitor it.

The electronic lock on the door behind him clicked. Boomer glanced at the man behind a separate console. "Here we go, Ned," he said.

"Ready to rock-and-roll, boss," the operator responded. Boomer nodded. It was time to raise the curtain.

"Was that what you wanted me to see, Dr. Noble?" Sattler asked, nodding toward the monitor showing the big four-propeller cargo plane taxiing onto the runway. Sure, Sattler was a nice guy and very thorough, Boomer thought, but he was so damned *quiet* and too darned fast. Which made him scary as well. Boomer turned around.

Everything about the FBI agent, from his perfectly knotted red silk tie and dark blue suit coat to his neatly creased slacks and polished black wing tips, practically shouted "rising Bureau star slated for a headquarters job at the Hoover Building in D.C. any moment now."

"That old Four Fan Trash Can?" Boomer said, using the common Air Force slang term for the C-130 Hercules cargo plane. He laughed. "No way. She's just on the daily milk run, carrying some spare parts to one of our production facilities out in California." He waved the other man forward to the screens at his left side. He pointed down toward the sleek, jet-black, batwinged XCV-62 slowly taxiing out of Hangar Five. "No, *that's* the baby I knew you'd be interested in." He shrugged. "In this case, I figured it made more sense to clue you in up front, instead of writing endless reports explaining why this test hop was no big deal later."

"Your zealous cooperation with my surveillance team is always greatly appreciated, Dr. Noble," Sattler said.

"Just doing my bit as a loyal citizen," Boomer said virtuously. Sattler snorted, accustomed to hearing it but never really sure if Noble believed his own patter. "Okay, I guess that was a little over-the-top," Boomer allowed.

"Maybe a little," the FBI man said, smiling now. He nodded at the futuristic-looking aircraft as it swung toward the runway. "So what kind of plane *is* that? Some kind of new prototype stealth bomber?"

"The XCV-62 Ranger?" Boomer shook his head. "She's one of our old experimental aircraft, originally designed as a stealthy tactical airlifter. We lost that contract a few years back, and since then the Ranger's been in storage. So we're sending her up for a short checkout flight."

"And just why would you want to do that, Dr. Noble?" Sattler asked, sounding a little suspicious suddenly. "Why send an old aircraft like that up at this point?"

"It's no big mystery," Boomer assured him. "My bosses have heard rumors that the next defense appropriations bill may include money for a new stealth-cargo and airlift program. If the rumors pan out, they'd like to get a jump on the competition by being able to show we've already got a flyable contender. Hence my orders to make sure that's the case." Seeing the embarrassed look on Sattler's face, Boomer shrugged. "Okay, yeah, I know. You don't have to spell it out. Sky Masters is totally screwed right now as far as securing new government contracts is concerned. And I'm pretty sure the suits in corporate are fully aware of that, but they wanted it done anyway. My best guess is this is mostly a PR exercise to keep our shareholders happy."

The FBI agent nodded sympathetically. "The same kind of thing happens in the Bureau whenever Congress starts asking awkward questions about the size of our budget. We get frantic orders from on high to make some high-profile arrests, and pronto." He looked pained. "Lots of otherwise solid criminal cases go south when that happens."

Sattler pointed toward the batwinged stealth plane as it made its final turn onto the main runway. "So who drew the short straw and gets to fly that crate? Seems like that could be kind of dangerous if it's been sitting cold in a hangar for so long."

"You've heard the saying that there are old pilots and there are bold pilots?" Boomer said with grin.

"But there are no old, bold pilots," Sattler said, unable to conceal his pained expression. "Yeah, I've heard it before. Like about a thousand times since my team and I set up shop here. So?"

"Well, the old fart who's going to take the Ranger up this evening is a guy named Tom Rogers," Boomer said. "And he's sitting right over there."

Surprised, the FBI agent swung around. Rogers was seated at a console equipped with a joystick, throttles, and several large MFDs, multifunction displays. The gray-haired Sky Masters pilot wore a headset and was dressed in worn blue jeans, sandals, and a Tommy Bahama tropical shirt with World War II airplanes on it. Hearing his name, he looked up from his controls and sketched a mock left-handed salute.

"The XCV-62 can be configured for remote piloting," Boomer explained. "That's a Sky Masters specialty and it's one of our advantages when it comes to competing against some of the bigger defense contractors." His cell phone vibrated gently. He checked the message it displayed: *DCMP*. The text was from the crew of the C-130 that had taken off only minutes before, reporting that they'd completed their drop. He punched in a quick acknowledgment.

"Anything important?" Sattler asked.

Boomer donned an abashed grin. "Depends on how you look at it. I had to cancel a hot date tonight when this test flight came up. It seems the woman I'd asked out is kind of upset about that. As in 'see you later, jackass' upset. Probably because this is the third or fourth time lately I've had to stand her up for something work-related."

The FBI agent winced in commiseration. "It goes with the job, I guess."

"Seems to," Boomer agreed. Shrugging, he swung round toward Rogers. "How's she looking, Tom?"

The remote pilot glanced up from his displays. "Pretty good, Boomer," he said. "No problems so far."

"Then feel free to take her up anytime you're ready."

"Just running through my final checklist now," Rogers said. "Number two was a little slow coming up on taxi power, but it looks okay now." He was busy tapping his multifunction displays to set various controls and check different aircraft systems. When he was finished, he radioed, "McLanahan Tower, Masters Six-Two, number one, runway two-five, ready for takeoff."

"*Six-Two, McLanahan Tower, winds two-two-zero at twelve gusting to eighteen, cleared for takeoff runway two-five. Have a good one.*"

"Six-Two cleared for takeoff two-five." The XCV-62 began taxiing onto the runway.

With the FBI agent at his side, Boomer moved closer to the wall-size displays. Below them, the stealth aircraft finished lining up for takeoff. The aircraft stopped on the runway centerline. Slowly, with a steadily rising roar, the Ranger's four jet engines ran up to full military power.

"Compressors look good, temps look good, takeoff mode selected," Rogers muttered. "Heading, instruments, temps, safety check . . ." Below them, the XCV-62 roared down the runway, picking up speed fast. "Engines in the green, airspeed alive," Rogers intoned in a half voice, not on the radio. "Engines to idle, antiskid warning light out, engines to idle, stop straight ahead . . ."

"Who's he talking to?" Settler asked. "He doesn't have a copilot."

"He's talking to himself," Boomer replied. "He's running through a series of what-if scenarios in his head, already planning on what he will do in case this or that happens, and those readouts cue him in for the next what-if."

Just a thousand feet or so down the runway, Rogers muttered, "Vr . . . now. Rotating." The bat-winged aircraft nosed up slightly and a few short seconds later it leaped off the tarmac and into the night desert sky. "Gear down, go down. Land straight ahead."

Boomer heard the FBI man mutter "whoa" and grinned to himself. He glanced at the other man. "*That's* why we call the Ranger a short-takeoff-and-landing plane," he said, pointing at the black aircraft as it soared skyward after using barely one-seventh of the available runway. "She's designed to get in and out of small, improvised fields pretty much anywhere in the world."

Outside, the XCV-62 banked right, turning
west toward the nearby range of hills and mountains. "Gear up. Engines look good. Flight controls responding well," Rogers intoned behind
them. His hands danced across the controls,
making small adjustments with his joystick and
throttles. "All other systems nominal."

"So what's your plan for this flight, Dr. Noble?"
Sattler asked.

"Nothing complicated. Or long," Boomer assured him. His gaze was still fixed on the departing aircraft. By now, the Ranger was a small black
dot, barely visible against the rapidly darkening
sky and steep, brush-strewn ridgelines, highlighted by its computer-generated data block. "If
all stays well, we're going to take her up to fifteen
thousand feet or so, put her through a few basic
maneuvers, and then come back around for some
landings."

"But why fly this test when it's getting dark so
fast?" the FBI agent asked, more out of curiosity
than suspicion. "Won't that make your landing
more difficult—even with instruments and sensors?"

"It's our standard procedure when flying new-
type stealth aircraft," Boomer told him distractedly, still watching the XCV-62 as it cleared the
first ridge by a few hundred feet. "Makes it a bit
harder for outsiders, whether they're amateur aviation enthusiasts, corporate competitors, or Russian or Chinese spies, to get a really good look at
stuff we'd rather not show off just yet."

Thoughtfully, the FBI man nodded to himself.

"Trouble on the number one engine, Boomer," Rogers said abruptly. Both men swung toward him. "I've got a shutdown indicator," the gray-haired remote pilot reported. His voice was remarkably relaxed. His fingers flew across his displays and controls. "Boosting power on number two and cutting back on three and four. I'm going for an emergency engine restart."

"Christ," Boomer muttered. He turned around again, staring out the control-tower window. There, far off in the distance, the XCV-62, now wobbling visibly, disappeared behind another jagged ridge. The numbers on the electronic data block were unwinding at a rapid pace. He glanced back at Rogers. "You'd better abort, Tom," he said worriedly. "Get some altitude and then bring her straight back to the barn."

"Roger, Boomer," Rogers told him. His eyes were narrowed, quickly flicking back and forth between his displays, but his voice was calm and measured. "Number two's gone now," he said a few moments later, as matter-of-fact as if he was telling his wife that her toast had just popped out of the toaster. "Fuel pressure dropping. I've got failure readings on both the primary and second-ary port-wing fuel pumps. My airspeed and alti-tude are both dropping fast." There was a moment of strained silence. Boomer and Sattler watched in horror as more and more red indicators started to blink, and then they heard computerized terrain warnings . . . but only for a few seconds, and then Rogers breathed, "Oh, shit."

A bright flash erupted from behind a ridge off

to the west, lighting up the rapidly dimming sky for a brief moment. Low-light TV sensors automatically zoomed in to the area.

The remote pilot looked up from his console with a sour expression. "LOS, Boomer. Sorry."

"LOS?" Sattler asked. "What's that?"

"Loss of signal," Boomer said tiredly. "Tom, dump the telemetry to the secure server, then get up, take a break, and start making notes about your session. Not your fault, dude."

"What 'secure server,' Doc?" Sattler interjected. "You can't withhold anything from us, Boomer."

"Relax, Sattler," Boomer spat, obviously upset. "I'm not withholding shit from you. The standard procedure is to collect all of our telemetry data and store it. The storage is secure, but it doesn't mean it's restricted. I can grant access to anyone."

"I want access as soon as it's uploaded, Boomer," Sattler said. "I want immediate access."

"I need to make sure I have the data first, Sattler," Boomer said. "Then I'll pass it out. But I need to know I have it all first."

"That's not how it works, Boomer," Sattler said. "When you get it, I get it. That's the deal. You know it; I know it. Do it. What you have, I have, all of it, right *now*. Clear?"

He nodded toward the pillar of black smoke now curling up from behind the distant ridge on the monitors. "I just crashed a hundred-million-dollar prototype, Sattler," Boomer said, his voice breaking and his eyes distant. "I just lost a hundred mil. You want to share some of that loss? Be my friggin' guest."

XCV-62 RANGER CRASH SITE, WEST OF BATTLE MOUNTAIN
A short time later

FBI special agent Raymond Sattler swallowed hard as the twin-engine Bell 412 helicopter tilted sharply, circling low over the floodlit crash site. Always uneasy in the air, he found this hurried flight high into the craggy, pitch-black foothills west of Battle Mountain nerve-racking. Seeing Hunter Noble's grim features did nothing to calm his fears. Even knowing the Sky Masters aerospace-engineering chief was probably more worried about losing his job than he was about dying in a helicopter wreck wasn't much comfort.

A pattern of five small green beacons appeared ahead through the cockpit windscreen.

Sattler heard their pilot though the headphones he'd been given before takeoff. "I have the LZ in sight. Hang tight, guys. This may be a little bumpy."

Oh, swell, the FBI agent thought.

Slowing fast, the Bell helicopter flared in and landed on a rutted dirt track that ran along the ridge, close to where the Sky Masters stealth aircraft had crashed. It bounced once on its skids and then settled. Up front, in the cockpit, the pilot flicked a few switches. Immediately both engines began whining down.

Following Noble, Sattler climbed out of the helicopter and moved off into the darkness, climbing uphill toward an array of dazzling lights marking the downed aircraft. A chill wind out of the northwest seemed to cut right through the jacket he'd borrowed. Clouds were rolling in, gradually blotting out the stars.

The portable lights rigged up by Sky Masters emergency crews revealed a tangle of blackened, smoldering wreckage strewn across the slope. Men and women in silvery fire proximity suits moved through the debris field, using handheld extinguishers to put out small blazes or taking pictures and making notes.

To the FBI agent's untrained eye, it looked as though the batwinged stealth plane had slammed nose first into the ground and then exploded. He turned toward Hunter Noble. "Shouldn't your guys wait to start checking things out until one of the NTSB's investigative teams gets here?" The National Transportation Safety Board's "Go Teams" were groups of specialists charged with investigating major aviation accidents. Members on the duty rotation were expected to be reachable twenty-four hours a day, ready to head to any crash site as fast as possible.

Noble shook his head. "The NTSB won't be investigating this crash."

Sattler frowned. "Why not?"

"Because its investigators don't have the necessary security clearances, Agent Sattler," the other man said, with a sigh. He nodded toward the wreckage. "We built that XCV-62 with advanced stealth materials and dozens of other top-secret components. There's no possible way DoD could vet the NTSB guys in time."

The FBI agent nodded slowly, knowing he was right. Obtaining Top Secret security clearances could take between four and eight months. "Okay, then why not call in an accident team from the Defense Department? They must have specialists with the right clearances."

"I'm sure they do," Hunter Noble agreed. He shrugged his shoulders gloomily. "But the Ranger wasn't flying as part of an active military procurement program or competition."

"Which means what exactly?"

"It means the Pentagon won't waste a dime figuring out why the XCV-62 augered in," Noble said. "As far as they're concerned, we just lost an aircraft they never asked us for anyway. All they'll care about is that we secured the site and recovered every piece of our stealth materials and technology."

"What about your corporate insurer?" Sattler asked. "They'll demand an impartial investigation, won't they?"

The other man smiled wryly. "Nobody insures experimental prototypes, Agent Sattler. Not at prices anyone wants to pay. Even Lloyd's of London laughs in our face, and they insure dancers' knees and opera singers' vocal cords." Moodily, he scuffed at the ground with his boots. "Nope. Nobody else is going to want a piece of this action. Not even the Lander County Sheriff's Office."

"Why not?" Sattler asked, confused.

"Because the Ranger was unmanned, so nobody was hurt or killed in the wreck. On top of that, this is all Sky Masters–owned land," Noble explained. He winced. "No, this was a bet we made all on our own. So now we get to try figuring out what went wrong . . . using our own money. Which is going to make the board of directors really, really unhappy."

CHAPTER 15

Brad McLanahan couldn't help grinning like a maniac as the XCV-62 swooped and soared, climbing and diving as it streaked low over a broken, bewildering landscape of canyons, cliffs, buttes, and mesas at 450 knots. "This must be the world's longest roller-coaster ride," he said out of the corner of his mouth. "Sweet, isn't it?"

"You do know how to show a girl a good time," Nadia Rozek agreed dryly. She was sitting in the cockpit's right-hand seat, acting as his copilot and systems operator.

Brad laughed. Like the XF-111 Super Varks he'd flown into combat last year, the Ranger prototype was equipped with a digital terrain-following system. Between the detailed maps stored in its onboard computers and short, periodic bursts from its radar altimeter, they could speed across the ground at an altitude of just two hundred feet—even in this otherwise baffling maze of natural wonders.

He tweaked his stick slightly left, following the glowing visual cues displayed on his HUD. The Ranger banked slightly, racing past a sheer-walled mesa that rose high above them. It vanished astern in seconds.

An icon began flashing on Nadia's left-hand MFD. "We're receiving an encrypted transmission via satellite," she said crisply, tapping virtual "keys" on the display to decode the compressed signal. "Message reads: 'I owe you twenty.'" Puzzled, she looked across the cockpit at him. "What does that mean?"

"It means our deception plan worked," Brad said, with a sudden feeling of relief. "Boomer bet me ten bucks at two-to-one odds that it wouldn't."

In truth, even though it had been his plan, he was almost surprised that they'd actually pulled it off. *I must have shared more of Hunter Noble's skepticism than I realized*, he thought. In theory, setting up the fake crash had been comparatively simple and straightforward, but making it succeed in real life had required precise timing . . . and depended far more on luck than was usually wise.

First, they'd loaded up a C-130 with an assortment of aircraft components—bits and pieces from earlier XCV-62 mock-ups, four turbofan engines of the right make, and a couple of impact-resistant drop tanks full of fuel and rigged with command-detonated explosives. Then, while the real Ranger taxied out of Hangar Five, supposedly "remote-piloted" by Tom Rogers, the Hercules had flown low over a preselected point out of sight of McLanahan Airport and dumped the "wreckage" out of its cargo hold.

Once that was done and the real XCV-62 was in the air, the rest was comparatively easy. Brad had pretended to lose power to one of their engines and dropped behind the ridge. Triggering the explosive-rigged drop tanks after they'd flown past the crash site had created a nifty fireball, making it look as though the Ranger had slammed straight into the ground.

Nothing about their phony crash would have fooled an experienced accident investigation team. Not for very long, anyway. But Brad had insisted it would look convincing enough to fool the FBI agents keeping tabs on Sky Masters' activities, and it seemed he'd been right about that.

The navigation cues on his HUD slid sideways, indicating the start of their planned turn to the south-southeast. He toggled the stick, following the glowing cues until they were centered again.

"Next stop, a scenic stretch of sand across the border in Mexico," Brad announced.

Nadia checked her computer-generated map. They were heading for an improvised airstrip and refueling point set up by Scion operatives deep in the desolate Chihuahuan desert. From there, they would fly south across Mexico and then on to a tiny airfield on Colombia's Pacific coast, where they would fuel again and grab some much-needed crew rest.

She clenched her jaw. They were still half a world and more than twenty hours of total flight time away from her besieged homeland. Although she'd been frantically busy trying to learn the systems of this remarkable Sky Masters aircraft, she'd seen enough news to know that her country's situation was going from bad to worse with every passing day. Her parents assured her they were safe and well, but how much longer could that last as the Russians systematically crippled piece after piece of Poland's vital infrastructure?

OFFICE OF JASON RICHTER,
SKY MASTERS AEROSPACE, INC.,
BATTLE MOUNTAIN, NEVADA
That same time

Sky Masters CEO Jason Richter opened the door to his office and saw that all the lights were on and all of his window blinds were drawn tight. His mouth thinned. So he had company.

He went in, not entirely surprised to find Kevin Martindale already there waiting for him. As usual, the former president was accompanied by a hulking bodyguard.

"I see you've made yourself at home, Mr. President," Richter said pointedly. "Too bad I didn't know you'd be dropping by tonight or I would have arranged for some refreshments."

Martindale smiled. "You have my apologies, Dr. Richter," he said, with a perfunctory shrug.

"But I thought it best to keep a very low profile on this visit. Since I suspect you would prefer to avoid any unnecessary federal entanglements, that's as much for your company's sake as it is for my own."

The Scion chief glanced at his bodyguard. "You can wait outside, Carl. Mr. Richter may be irritated with me, but he is not homicidal."

The big man nodded silently and left, closing the door behind him.

"Where *do* you find those guys?" Richter asked. "Goons 'R' Us? Rent-a-Praetorian?" Martindale ignored his crack. He settled himself in one of the office chairs. Sighing to himself, Richter did the same. "Okay, Mr. President," he asked. "What can I do for you?"

"Now that the XCV-62 is safely on its way, I wanted to discuss our other big problem," Martindale replied.

"Patrick McLanahan," Richter realized. The other man nodded. Richter grimaced. "I've been analyzing the biometric data you've sent me over the past week or so."

"And?"

"I could have e-mailed you my findings," Richter said quietly.

"Certainly," Martindale agreed. His expression was somber. "But let's just say that I would prefer to hear bad news about a close friend and long-time colleague in person." He looked up. "And the news is bad, isn't it?"

Richter nodded slowly. "Yes, it is." He frowned. "There's no way to sugarcoat this, so here goes:

I'm certain the general is in grave danger. As is everyone around him."

"In what way, exactly?" the other man pressed.

"Piloting a Cybernetic Infantry Device may be keeping the general alive and physically healthy, but I believe it's also inflicting more and more psychological damage on him," Richter said flatly. "The mental strain and emotional impairment involved in living entirely inside a machine, without real, meaningful human contact, has to be enormous." He shook his head. "We designed CIDs for combat use, not as permanent habitats. Except for Patrick McLanahan, no human being has ever run one for more than twenty-four hours straight. So I have precisely zero data to use as a comparison."

"I'm well aware of that," Martindale said.

Richter nodded. "Just so you understand that I'm flying by the seat of my pants here, Mr. President. My background is in cutting-edge engineering, especially robotics—not in medicine or psychiatry."

"Consider your stipulations and caveats accepted," Martindale told him. "But medical doctor or not, you know more about CIDs and the stresses involved in piloting them than anyone else in the world." Slowly, reluctantly, Richter dipped his head, acknowledging the other man's point. "Is Patrick McLanahan insane?" Martindale asked bluntly.

"Not yet," Richter said. "At least not completely." He shook his head. "But I'd say he's headed that way. And fast."

He looked squarely at the other man. "I found

evidence in the data you supplied that the general is overriding the CID's health-monitoring software. He's deliberately preventing the robot from stabilizing his brain and body chemistry more and more often."

"Why on earth would he do that?" Martindale asked.

"My guess would be that General McLanahan believes he benefits from faster reaction times and reflexes."

"And does he?"

"In combat? Sure," Richter said. "But over the longer term, screwing around with your body chemistry and neurotransmitters like he's doing is pure, unadulterated poison."

Martindale sat silent for a moment, absorbing this news. "What can we do to stop this from happening?" he asked at last. "To keep him sane?"

"You have to pull him out of the robot," Richter said matter-of-factly. "And soon. Because if you wait too long, you're liable to have a hell of a mess on your hands." His expression was grim. "Imagine what could happen if General McLanahan lost the ability to control his emotions. Or to distinguish between friends and foes." He saw Martindale wince, obviously visualizing the political damage Scion and the whole Alliance of Free Nations would suffer if it became clear that one of their vaunted combat robots was in the hands of a madman.

"But if we pull him out of the CID, he'll die," the Scion chief pointed out grimly.

Richter nodded. "Yes." He frowned. "Or he may just slip into a permanent vegetative state."

"Which is as close to death as makes no real difference," Martindale said.

"True," Richter agreed.

Martindale scowled. "And we have no other option? There's nothing else we can try first?"

Richter hesitated, unsure of whether or not he should go any further down the road that had suddenly popped into his mind. Ethically speaking, experimenting with people's lives without their permission was strictly taboo. On the other hand, he thought, what did Patrick McLanahan really have to lose? He was pretty sure that the general would never knowingly want to risk losing his mind and putting others in danger.

"There *is* an alternative, isn't there?" Martindale said, watching his face.

"There may be," Richter admitted slowly. "But it's one hell of a long shot."

Martindale eyed him carefully. "I submit that our mutual friend's situation may be bleak enough to warrant taking chances. Even extreme chances," he said.

"Well, I've kind of been tinkering around with something new," Richter said slowly, frowning in thought. "Although really the device I'm working on is more for the civilian medical market. As far as I can tell, there aren't any military applications that make sense."

"Is this new device of yours something we could try on General McLanahan right away?" Martindale asked.

"Oh God, no," Richter said, abruptly appalled at his own train of thought. Proving a new technological advance was one thing. Using someone else as an expendable guinea pig, especially someone like Patrick McLanahan, was another. "All I have so far is a really raggedy-ass prototype. Between software glitches and hardware malfunctions, it still crashes about three-quarters of the time."

Martindale nodded. "I see." He frowned. "I assume a crash in this case would be bad?"

"Oh yeah," Richter nodded vigorously. "Bad as in fatal."

"And does this 'raggedy-ass' prototype of yours have a name, Dr. Richter?" the other man asked.

Richter hesitated again. "Well, yes, it does," he admitted at last, somewhat nervously. People were always telling him that the project and equipment names and acronyms he came up with sucked. "I've been calling it the LEAF."

Martindale showed no reaction to that, one way or the other. "Then let's discuss *exactly* what it's going to take to scrub the glitches out of this new machine of yours ASAP," he said firmly.

CHAPTER 16

Plump and balding, with a round, cherubic face, Yuri Akulov looked more like a baker than a spy. His amiable, harmless appearance had served him well during a long career with the KGB and later the FSB. Adversaries, whether foreign agents or rivals inside his own service, almost always underestimated his cunning, raw intelligence, and sheer ruthlessness. By the time they figured him out, it was usually too late. Foreign spies found themselves in prison, dead, or kicked out of Russia in disgrace. KGB and FSB colleagues who crossed him ended up in godforsaken backwater posts, guarding state secrets no one gave a shit about anymore.

Now Akulov used the same skills and deceptive appearance in his work as one of Igor Truznyev's top "security consultants." Asked by one of his girlfriends to describe the difference between being an FSB operative and working as a private consultant for the Zatmeniye Group, he'd cynically told her "about ten million more rubles a year. But if I kill anyone now, I have to be a bit more cautious."

Working in the private intelligence sector was also more challenging, he allowed. If pressed, you couldn't just whip out your state security ID and scare the hell out of potential sources or possible suspects like in the good old days. Instead, you had to rely on your wits, the ability to tell convincing lies, and, all too often, a willingness to mimic the patience of a saint.

Take this most recent assignment, for example. It was easy enough for Truznyev to order him to discreetly pierce the web of secrecy cast around Russia's cyberwar operation. Carrying out those orders, without getting caught, had proved a lot harder. None of his contacts inside the FSB turned out to know much about Gryzlov's plans or wanted to risk the president's wrath.

What had emerged from a series of careful, oblique conversations was that senior FSB officers were incredibly envious of Major General Arkady Koshkin's growing power and influence. That didn't surprise Akulov. Even in his day, Koshkin had been derided, behind his back, as Moscow's "Langleyite," because of his worship of technology over tradecraft. To FSB veterans, that was the same mistake made so often by the American CIA.

But now Gennadiy Gryzlov had allowed Koshkin to create his own fiefdom, this mysterious Q Directorate. That was bad enough for his detractors. What was worse was that Russia's president seemed to have given Koshkin and his computer geeks a blank check.

"He even bought a nuclear reactor, for God's sake!" one of Akulov's old comrades had groused. "I can't get funding to recruit more agents in Washington, D.C., and that *durak*, that jackass, spends billions of rubles to buy a fucking reactor from Atomflot!" Then, aware that he'd probably said too much, the FSB officer had suddenly clammed up.

But at least the man's momentary indiscretion had put Akulov on a new scent, one he'd followed from Moscow far into the frozen north—all the way to Murmansk, the headquarters of Atomflot, a state-owned company responsible for Russia's fleet of nuclear-powered icebreakers. More cautious inquiries inside the company, along with a number of bribes, had finally led him to Atomflot senior nuclear supervisor Ivan Budanov.

Budanov, his sources told him in whispers, had been away for months earlier in the year, seconded to the Kremlin for some big secret project. Since then, he'd been lording his status as a man of mystery over his coworkers.

For a time, Akulov had thought he'd need a complicated cover story to explain why he wanted to talk to the nuclear engineer. Fortunately, it turned out that Budanov was both an egomaniac and a binge drinker. Just the hint that Akulov represented other Russian military and intelligence outfits who were interested in his "widely appreciated expertise" sufficed to lull the Atomflot engineer's suspicions. Akulov's offer to pay for a night on the town had sealed the deal.

What he hadn't counted on was Budanov's ability to drink massive quantities of vodka for hours on end, all while telling incredibly dull and pointless anecdotes involving every shipborne reactor project he'd ever worked on. And Akulov, hiding his boredom behind a mask of cheerful comradeship, had reeled from bar to bar with the engineer. It had been an agonizing experience. He'd smiled and nodded and laughed and pretended to match the other man drink for drink, in the hope Budanov would finally let something useful slip about Q Directorate's secret nuclear power plant.

All to no avail.

Then, when the bars finally closed, Budanov had drunkenly insisted they go back to his dingy apartment to close out the night with a bottle of what he called "the good stuff." It was a miracle the man was still alive, let alone in a responsible position, Akulov thought disgustedly. Still faking good cheer, he perched on a sagging sofa watching as the buffoon downed yet another shot.

"*Nu, vzdrognuli!* Here we go again!" Budanov slurred. He raised his dirty glass to Akulov with a huge, lopsided grin. "And here's to all the sweet girls I've screwed together over the years!"

It took Akulov a few moments to understand that the Atomflot engineer was now referring to the reactors he'd helped build as "girls." Sighing inwardly, he raised his own glass to the other man with an equally shit-faced smile. *Maybe I can just push him out the window*, he thought bleakly. Budanov's apartment was only on the second floor, so the fall probably wouldn't kill him . . . but the drunken bastard would certainly freeze to death before anyone found him.

"To your sweet girls!" the ex-FSB agent agreed, deciding to try one last time before bailing out and returning to Moscow with his tail between his legs. "Especially the last one, eh? That must have been something to see."

"Definitely," Budanov said. He shook his head. "Now, there was a weird job, I can tell you. Assembling a reactor designed for a twenty-three-thousand-ton icebreaker way down deep inside a fucking mountain, imagine that!"

Akulov restrained the sudden impulse to hug the other man. *Finally*, he thought in relief. Carefully, he leaned over and poured more vodka into Budanov's glass. "What mountain was that, Ivan?"

With a sly smile, the nuclear engineer shook his head. "I can't tell you that," he said thickly.

"It's a secret, eh?" Akulov sat back, tapping his nose.

"You've got that right, Yuri," Budanov agreed. Then he laughed. "But what I mean is, I really *couldn't* tell you where that mountain is, even if I was allowed to."

The Atomflot man shrugged. "See, those state security guys put my team on a sealed train with the reactor components, along with a shitload of armed guards. Then, three days later, once we got to some blacked-out station in the sticks, they hustled us into trucks and dropped the flaps. When they finally let us out a couple of hours later, we were parked in some big-assed tunnel deep underground."

Akulov whistled softly. "Damn. *Eto piz'dets.* That's fucked up."

Budanov nodded. "Yeah, it was pretty crazy." He shook his head. "Worse than the patrols I hear those nuclear-missile submarine sailors bitching about. We never saw a thing outside the caves where we assembled the KLT-40. Imagine spending sixteen weeks without a breath of fresh air or a glimpse of the sun. And not a goddamned drop to drink the whole time!"

Akulov shook his head in mock sympathy. Inwardly, he exulted.

At last, he had some of the clues Igor Truznyev wanted so badly. It would take a lot more digging, but at least now he knew where he could find the next link in the chain leading to Q Directorate's hidden cyberwar complex.

WOLF SIX-TWO, OVER THE MOROCCAN-OCCUPIED WESTERN SAHARA
The next day

Thirty nautical miles and four minutes after crossing the Atlantic coast of Western Sahara, the Iron Wolf stealth transport aircraft zoomed over a flat, almost featureless expanse of sand and rock called the Río de Oro. The Ranger's batwinged shadow, elongated by the rays of the rising sun, rippled behind it across the desert floor.

"RDY-3 Pulse-Doppler radar detected at two o'clock. Estimated range is fifty miles and closing," the XCV-62's computer warned. *"Detection probability low."*

Major Nadia Rozek frowned. She punched up a menu on her threat-warning display and scanned through it fast. Several years ago, the Royal Moroccan Air Force had upgraded its aging Dassault Mirage F1 fighters with new Thales RDY-3 radars, cockpit electronics, antimissile flare and chaff defenses, and weapons capabilities. The French aerospace and defense multinational claimed its RDY-3 systems were more capable than the AN/APG-type radars that originally equipped America's F-16 Falcons and F-18 Hornets.

She glanced at Brad. "Should I activate SPEAR?" she asked.

Like many advanced Sky Masters aircraft, the Ranger carried the ALQ-293 Self-Protection Electronically Agile Reaction system. When active, SPEAR transmitted precisely tailored signals designed to dupe enemy radars. By altering the timing of the pulses sent back to a hostile radar, it could trick a hostile set into believing the XCV-62 was somewhere else in the sky—anywhere but where it actually was.

Brad shook his head. "Let's stay quiet for now. At least until we get some firmer indication that Mirage really has us on his scope."

He fought down a yawn. They'd been in the air for more than eight hours since taking off last night from a tiny strip in Colombia. Even with all the automation built into the Ranger's flight controls, that was a long stretch for any pilot. It was even longer when you added in the strain involved in making a difficult midocean aerial refueling rendezvous with a Sky Masters KC-10 Extender tanker.

"Okay-dohkay," Nadia said, deliberately mangling the Americanism. That earned her a tired grin. But she kept her display set on the SPEAR system's controls anyway, just in case.

"RDY-3 now at twelve-o'clock. Range is fifty-five miles and opening," the XCV-62's computer reported. *"Detection probability nil."*

Nadia breathed out. "The Mirage is turning away."

"That guy is probably just up flying a racetrack pattern patrol along the cease-fire line," Brad said. "He's not out hunting for us."

She nodded. After the Spanish left in 1975, Morocco had moved in to take control over this territory. That had set off a brutal, sixteen-year-long war waged between the Moroccan government and the independence-minded Polisario Front. A cease-fire finally negotiated nearly thirty years ago—well before she was born—was still holding, but neither side took anything for granted.

Something struck her. "I thought Mr. Martindale received permission for us to use Morocco's airspace?" she said. "Was I merely paranoid to worry about being spotted?"

"Nope," Brad said firmly. "Sure, Martindale got a thumbs-up from the king. They've been personal friends since he was president. But I doubt the word percolated very far down the Moroccan chain of command. With Stacy Anne Barbeau gunning for Scion and all its works, plausible deniability is the name of the game."

Nadia snorted. "Ah, the old '*ta rozmowa nie miala miejsca*,' 'this conversation never happened' routine."

Brad laughed. "Exactly. It wouldn't make sense for the king to risk antagonizing Washington by openly siding with us."

"So we *do* want to avoid detection?" Nadia said.

"Definitely." Brad yawned again. He peered out through the windscreen, studying the wasteland stretching ahead of them. "Which is why we need to set down soon. This bird is plenty stealthy against radar. But Boomer was right. In broad daylight, we're no more invisible than any other aircraft."

"Yes," Nadia agreed. She checked her navigation display. "I confirm that we are roughly two minutes out from Point Bravo."

That matched the indicators appearing on Brad's HUD. Point Bravo was their next stop. It was another makeshift airstrip and refueling station set up by a Scion advance team—this time out in the middle of the Western Sahara, some of the least habitable and least inhabited territory on earth.

"Let's make sure they're awake and ready for us," Brad ordered.

Nadia opened a com window and typed in a short query, which the Ranger's computer automatically encrypted, compressed, and then transmitted via satellite uplink. "Signal sent."

Seconds later, her MFD pinged. "Point Bravo

confirms they are operational," she reported.
"Winds are eight knots, from the north. No haze
or blowing sand reported."

When they were ten nautical miles out, Brad
saw a series of bright green beacons blinking on
the desert floor—marking the location of the improvised Scion airstrip. "Configuring for landing," he announced, tapping in a quick command
on one of his two displays. He started throttling
back.

Control surfaces on the trailing edge of the
Ranger's wing whirred open, providing more
lift as their airspeed decreased. More hydraulics whined below their feet. The airlifter's nose
gear and its twin wing-mounted bogies were all
coming down.

"Gear down and locked," Brad reported, seeing
the indicator on his HUD turn solid green.

"One nautical mile out," Nadia said, keeping
her eyes fixed on the navigation display.

The airstrip, which was really just a roughly
level patch of ground that had been quickly
cleared of brush and loose rocks, loomed ahead,
growing ever larger through the windscreen.
Off to one side, Brad could make out five or six
parked vehicles, including a fuel tanker, and several camouflage-draped tents.

"DTF disengaged," he said, turning off the
XCV-62's digital terrain-following system. He
chopped the throttles almost all the way back.
"Landing . . . now."

The Ranger dropped out of the sky and touched
down with a modest jolt. Trailing plumes of dust

and blown sand, it bounced and bucked as it rolled down the strip, slowing fast as Brad reversed thrust; brakes were useless on this surface. They came to a complete stop just over a thousand feet from their touchdown point.

Fighting off a sudden wave of fatigue, Brad and Nadia methodically ran through their various checklists, verifying that all of the Ranger's systems were shut down. Outside the cockpit windows, they could see a truck racing in their direction, carrying camouflage netting that would be draped over the XCV-62 to conceal them from aerial observation during the day. Satisfied at last, Brad unbuckled his safety harness and stretched. Beside him, Nadia did the same.

"Now we grab a bite to eat and get some shut-eye," he said. "And then, when it's dark, we'll head for Romania and the Scrapheap."

"And from there to home," Nadia said quietly. "To Poland."

CHAPTER 17

NIZHNY NOVGOROD RESEARCH INSTITUTE OF RADIO ENGINEERING

Several hours later

A highly detailed digital map showing the region around Moscow covered the auditorium's wall-size screen. Green symbols and circles showed the locations, estimated detection ranges, and missile kill zones for each of the multiple S-300 and S-400 surface-to-air missile battalions deployed around the Russian capital.

"Early warning radar reports a formation of high-speed aircraft bearing two-four-five," a young-sounding voice said over the auditorium's speakers. *"Direction of flight is zero-seven-zero. Range three hundred thirty kilometers. Speed nine hundred kilometers per hour. Altitude unknown."*

A set of blinking red icons flashed onto the map, not far from the town of Roslavl. They crawled across the map, heading straight for the heart of Moscow.

"*Sound air-raid alert,*" a second voice said. Deeper and more resonant, it was identified by a caption at the top of the screen as that of Moscow's air-defense commander. "*Interrogate that formation.*"

"*Negative IKS from inbound aircraft,*" the first voice replied.

The gaggle of high-ranking military officers and defense-industry officials crowded into the auditorium sat up straighter. IKS, *identifikatsion-nyy kod samolet,* was the transponder code used by aircraft to identify themselves as friendly to radar sites and fighter interceptors. It was the Russian equivalent of the IFF, identification friend or foe, system used by Western militaries. Negative IKS was an almost sure sign the aircraft heading for Moscow were hostile.

"*Estimated range to probable 96L6E acquisition?*" the air-defense commander asked. The 96L6Es were 3-D all-altitude acquisition radars deployed with Russia's most advanced S-300 and S-400 SAM units. As soon as these radars picked up the incoming aircraft and determined their altitude, they could pass their data to the 30N6E and 92N2E target-tracking and missile-guidance radars belonging to each firing battery. Once that was done, the SAM units could begin firing their long-range missiles.

"*Thirty kilometers.*"

Heads nodded inside the darkened room. At the speed those enemy aircraft were moving, they would be in range of the outermost target acquisition radar in less than two minutes.

As the seconds ticked down, the blinking red icons drew ever nearer to Moscow.

"All surface-to-air missile batteries report they are standing by. They are ready to fire on command," the first voice said again, sounding more excited now. *"Handoff to 96L6E complete! Hostile altitude is two hundred meters! Formation size is ten-plus hostiles. Types unknown. Enemy formation now increasing speed to one thousand kilometers per hour."*

The assembled officers and officials tensed. At any second now, salvos of long-range missiles would begin rippling skyward, reaching out to destroy enemy aircraft with relative ease.

"Second Battery, 210th Air Defense Regiment reports solid lock on hostiles. Ready to attack!"

Suddenly the red icons speeding toward Moscow vanished.

"What the hell?" someone exclaimed.

"Contact lost," the first voice reported, seconds behind the situation shown on the map. *"Radars are attempting to reacquire."*

Minutes later, the icons representing the incoming enemy air strike blinked back on. But they were in a different location now, well to the north of their previous plotted position and fifty kilometers closer to Moscow.

Again, the longer-range SAM acquisition radars cycled through the process of handing off data to their batteries' target-tracking and missile-guidance radars. And again, as soon as the defenders were ready to fire, their radars mysteriously lost all contact with the hostile aircraft.

Now, though, the green symbols representing several different SAM units flashed orange. Some went black.

"Our forces are under missile attack!" a panicked voice yelled over the speakers. *"They report multiple impacts which have destroyed many radars and SAM launchers!"*

The hostile icons reappeared suddenly on the map. But this time they displayed the enemy attack formation far south of its earlier reported position and scarcely a hundred kilometers from the center of Moscow.

"I think we've seen quite enough, Doctor," Colonel General Valentin Maksimov, the tall and powerfully built commander of Russia's Aerospace Forces, muttered to the much shorter man sitting next to him.

Dr. Nikolai Obolensky nodded. "Indeed, General," he said in a dry, precise voice.

Everything about Obolensky, from his close-cropped gray hair and tortoiseshell eyeglasses to his unfashionable black suit and drab brown tie, marked him as an old-fashioned academic. Some would have gone further, pegging him as a washed-up professor of mathematics from some minor university. That would have been both unkind and inaccurate.

In reality, he ran the Nizhny Novgorod Research Institute of Radio Engineering (NNIIRT)'s software lab—overseeing the development of the target acquisition and identification programs used by Russia's most advanced and lethal SAM systems. Though it had been years since he had done any serious software development himself, Obolensky had proved his managerial talents by successfully shepherding a number of vital projects to completion, and doing so on budget and on time.

"End simulation, Anya," the NNIIRT lab chief said into the wireless mic attached to his lapel. Behind him, in the projection room at the back of the auditorium, his assistant obeyed.

The digital map display froze, still showing the appalling hole torn in Moscow's outer air-defense network. It also showed that the enemy strike force was now well within air-launched missile range of Russia's capital. The lights came up, revealing a sea of unhappy faces.

Obolensky moved to the front of the auditorium. "This was a computer-generated simulation of what might happen if the Poles and their Iron Wolf mercenary allies conduct an all-out attack on Moscow. It represents our best estimate of the tactical advantages conferred by their use of netrusion technology and an array of stealth drones." He smiled thinly. "As you have seen, they are considerable."

Maksimov nodded bitterly. During last year's short war with Poland and its hired high-tech warriors, he'd watched in horror while several of his most advanced fighter squadrons and SAM battalions were savaged—often without being able to even fire a shot in reply, let alone score any kills. The sensor data they'd gathered on the enemy's netrusion systems and drones represented the only silver lining in that black cloud of slaugh-

ter and humiliation . . . and that was a very slender
thread to which to cling for solace.

"Now let me show you what will happen once
we deploy the software upgrades developed by my
lab here at NNIIRT," Obolensky told them. He
moved to the side, away from the screen and
looked up toward the projection booth. "Reboot the
simulation, Anya," he ordered. "Run FAVORIT/
TRIUMF variation 19 point 17c."

The lights dimmed again.

For a time, the sequence of events played out
just as it had earlier. Enemy aircraft were detected
and then vanished almost as soon as firing solu-
tions were first achieved. But that was the end
of any similarity. Now the icons showing the attacking force reappeared much faster, and they
were much closer to their earlier estimated positions. Halfway through the war game, Russia's
S-300 and S-400 SAM batteries were in action—
firing missiles at confirmed enemy targets. Most
missed, lured astray by the array of close-in defenses employed by the Poles and their hirelings.
But, ultimately, as almost always in war, quantity
proved to be a quality all its own. The equation
was simple: if you fired enough missiles at a given
number of targets, you were bound to score hits.

Colonel General Maksimov sat enthralled,
watching computer-generated Polish and Iron
Wolf bombers, fighters, and drones disappear.
Now, though, instead of vanishing behind their
technological cloak, they were blinking off
the display as they were shot down by Russian
surface-to-air missiles. His SAM units took ca-

sualties too, but the fight this time was far more even. In the end, the whole enemy air formation was wiped out. Best of all, they were blown out of the sky before they could launch any of their own offensive weapons toward Moscow.

When the lights came up, he stood to applaud Obolensky, a move slavishly imitated by his subordinates and by the other defense-industry officials who depended on the weapons contracts he approved.

"You have worked wonders, Doctor," Maksimov boomed. "For years, we have been at the mercy of this vaunted netrusion technology of the Americans. Their planes, and now those of the Poles, have flown unchallenged over our beloved Motherland. But now you have uncovered their secrets, and learned how to defeat our enemies."

Precise as always, Obolensky shook his head. "Short of capturing one of the aircraft employing this technology, I'm afraid its innermost secrets will remain outside our grasp."

Annoyed at being contradicted, Maksimov scowled down at the shorter man. He waved at the images shown on the screen. "Then what have you shown us? A lie? A wishful computer fabrication?"

"Not in the least, General," the lab chief assured him. He smiled. "The new upgrade we've just demonstrated represents a significant improvement over our existing defenses. In the past, once the enemy blinded or spoofed our radars, it could take as long as two or three minutes to regain an accurate picture of the air battlefield."

"Which is a lifetime in combat," Maksimov

growled. "In two minutes, a modern fighter-bomber might be as far as fifty kilometers away from where it was last detected."

Obolensky nodded. "To address this problem, my team identified two separate approaches. First, we've greatly speeded up the rate at which our target acquisition and identification software comes back online after suffering a so-called netrusion attack. And second, our upgrade significantly enhances the software's ability to sort out decoy drones from actual combat aircraft and air-launched weapons."

"How much faster? And in plain Russian, please," Maksimov asked. He shrugged his massive shoulders. "Remember that I am an old war-horse, not a computer scientist."

"The enemy can still blind our radars or launch waves of decoy drones to cloud the radar picture," Obolensky explained. "But now we can pierce this concealing cloak in as little as thirty to fifty seconds."

"To what effect?" Maksimov asked bluntly. "In the real world."

"We estimate this software upgrade will increase our Pk, the probability of kill, for S-300 and S-400 missile launches by up to thirty percent," Obolensky said with serene confidence. He turned and pointed at the situation now shown on the screen. "And that increase in combat efficiency, Colonel General, represents the margin between watching Moscow battered into burning, bomb-gutted ruins . . . and victory."

Maksimov lowered his head briefly, conceding the point. Much as he disliked appearing uninformed in front of others, he admired the little man's willingness to stand up to him, and the self-assurance he exhibited. "Then I gladly stand corrected, Doctor," he said with a forced smile. "But that leaves me with one last question."

Obolensky raised an eyebrow. "Yes, General?"

"How soon can this program upgrade of yours be deployed to my surface-to-air missile regiments?"

"We should be able to transmit a final, completely debugged version to your headquarters in Moscow within forty-eight hours," the NNIIRT lab chief assured him. He shrugged. "After that, its final distribution to the appropriate air-defense units will be up to your staff."

Maksimov nodded. He shot an inquiring glance at his senior military aide, Major General Viktor Polichev. "Well, Viktor?"

Polichev pursed his lips, pondering the logistics involved. "Once we get our hands on this NNIIRT software update, our headquarters IT specialists should be able to make the necessary copies in short order. And we can send them out to every S-300 and S-400 regiment by special courier."

"You suggest we use courier delivery?" Maksimov asked, unable to hide his surprise. "Wouldn't it be faster to distribute this update online, using our data links to each regimental headquarters?"

"Perhaps, sir," his aide said. Then he shrugged.

"But in light of recent events, I think it might be wiser to avoid relying too much on electronic communication."

Maksimov nodded slowly, thinking about the tidal wave of computer-caused havoc currently sweeping across Eastern and central Europe. Polichev was right. If nothing else, President Gryzlov's cyberwar campaign showed the dangers involved in trusting vital information to the vagaries of the Internet.

"An excellent point, Viktor," he said at length. "Organize your courier chain at once. Sooner or later, the Poles and their Iron Wolf pirates are bound to strike back at us. And when that day finally comes, I want to be sure our SAM regiments are ready, willing, and able to swat them out of the sky!"

As the assembled military officers and defense-industry officials filed out, Dr. Nikolai Obolensky stood near the auditorium's exit, gravely acknowledging their congratulations. His briefing had been a triumph, both of showmanship and of substance, and he knew it.

The NNIIRT lab chief was well aware that many of the computer engineers who worked under him had little understanding of, or respect for, his skills as an administrator. Sometimes they even furtively passed around copies of the subversive American comic strip *Dilbert*, slyly identifying him with the comic strip's imbecile, pointy-headed boss. In their insular world, a man who no longer wrote lines of code himself was nothing but an officious, interfering bureaucrat.

Today's success should shake that ignorant view, he thought smugly.

Not one of his technically adept computer geniuses could possibly have "sold" their work so easily to an old Soviet-era dinosaur like Maksimov. Any briefing they put together would have opened with deadly dull PowerPoint slides and ended with a mind-numbing, jargon-filled recitation of intricate technical detail. By that time, the NNIIRT auditorium would either have been packed with snoozing generals or completely abandoned after the audience fled. Using a battle simulation to show off the upgrade's features had been his idea. And it had worked perfectly. Nothing so delighted men of Maksimov's kind as seeing enemy planes—even computer-generated ones—blown to pieces.

The crowd of officers and officials thinned and then vanished. Later in the day, they would meet again at one of Nizhny Novgorod's most expensive restaurants. The Research Institute's top brass had organized an elaborate lunch for their distinguished guests and customers. And there, celebratory toasts would ratify yet another programming triumph for Nikolai Obolensky and his software-development team.

He smiled to himself, imagining the paeans of praise and new perks his superiors were sure to shower on him.

Suddenly aware that he was under observation, Obolensky looked up. A striking redhead in uniform had stayed behind the rest. Her shoulder boards bore the three stars of a colonel. She stood a few feet away, eyeing him with a wry smile of her own.

He blushed, feeling slightly awkward at having been caught so obviously daydreaming. Embarrassed, he cleared his throat. "May I help you with something, Colonel . . ." His voice trailed off as he realized he did not know her name.

"Nechaeva. Tatiana Nechaeva," the redhead said crisply. "And I think you will find that I am the one who can help *you*, Dr. Obolensky." Seeing his confusion, she handed him her identity card.

Obolensky stared down at the card. It declared that Colonel Tatiana Nechaeva was an officer in the FSB's counterintelligence service. His eyes widened a bit in surprise. He had always pictured secret-police agents as hulking, unsmiling brutes. Meeting one who was a shapely, extremely attractive woman came as something of a shock. Still puzzled, he handed her ID back. "I'm afraid I don't quite understand," he admitted. "How is it that you can help me?"

Nechaeva shook her head. "Not here, Doctor. Not in public." Her gaze was cooler now. "This is a matter of urgent state security."

He froze briefly. "A matter of state security? But—" Seeing her mouth tighten in annoyance, he stopped talking.

"I won't remind you again, Doctor," Nechaeva said sharply. "I strongly suggest we move this conversation to your office."

Obolensky bobbed his head in hurried agreement. "Of course, Colonel. At once." He gestured toward the hallway. "Please, follow me."

Somehow, his small office looked messier than he remembered. It also smelled strongly of both dust and pipe tobacco. With a murmured apology, he cleared away the stacks of file folders and manuals piled up on his only other chair.

Primly, Nechaeva sat down. She waited to speak until he closed the door and uneasily took his own seat. "First, you must understand that everything I am about to tell you stays in this room," she said sternly. "This information is classified at the highest level. Revealing it to anyone else is punishable by life imprisonment or execution. Is that clear?"

Obolensky swallowed hard and nodded. "Yes, Colonel. I understand."

"Good," she said, suddenly relaxing. "I apologize for all the theatrics, Doctor. But I'm afraid they are necessary."

"Why is that?" he asked nervously.

"Because it appears that foreign spies have targeted NNIIRT and especially your section," Nechaeva told him.

His eyes widened again. "Spies? Here? Trying to penetrate my lab?"

"Apparently, your good work is appreciated far beyond our Motherland's borders," Nechaeva said.

"My God," he murmured shakily. He looked at her. "But how do you know this, Colonel? Have these spies been trying to break into our facility? Or bribing some of my staff?"

"Nothing so old-fashioned," she replied.

"Then how—"

"We have observed several attempts to break through the security firewall guarding your lab's computer system," Nechaeva said flatly.

"Our firewall?" Obolensky shook his head. "Excuse me, Colonel, but that is not possible. The institute's information-technology specialists would have informed me at once of any such hacking efforts."

"You think it impossible?" Nechaeva said coolly. She nodded toward the computer on his desk. "Then I will show you what we have discovered, Doctor. You have system administrator privileges for the lab's computer network, do you not?"

He nodded slowly. "Yes, of course, but I . . . well, I almost never use them. Having such access is a formality, mostly. Because of my rank."

"Naturally," she agreed. Then she shrugged. "I suppose I should not expect the head of a computer software lab to pay close attention to the security of his own systems."

Obolensky flushed at her obvious sarcasm. Recovering, he fumbled around in one of his desk drawers until he found the laminated card with the necessary password and user-ID information. He showed it to her.

"Very good, Doctor. Now sign in as an administrator and bring up your denied-access log for the following times," Nechaeva commanded, rattling off a succession of specific days, hours, and minutes.

He obeyed, bringing up a dense wall of text

showing that several different attempts had been made to penetrate the lab's firewall at those moments. He glanced through the data and then shrugged his shoulders. "This is not evidence of any hacking, Colonel," he said confidently. "Even a cursory look reveals these are simply instances where the computer systems the institute uses for routine day-to-day business accidentally contacted our lab's secure network. This happens quite often, usually when someone hits 'reply all' to an e-mail which contains one of our secured addresses. Or occasionally when one of the administrative staff sends out a general memo to all departments, including ours, without first obtaining the necessary permissions."

Nechaeva smiled thinly. "I suggest you examine those supposedly 'internal' IP addresses more closely."

Nettled, Obolensky did as she suggested. What was she driving at? he wondered. His eyes moved from IP address to IP address, now paying careful attention to every detail. This time he saw the problem. The blood drained from his face. He looked away from the screen in horror. "Those are not genuine internal IP addresses," he sputtered. "Those queries are coming from the outside, camouflaged as one or another of our business-side computers."

"Clever, isn't it?" Nechaeva said quietly. "By mimicking known internal IP addresses so closely, these foreign agents were able to hide their hacking attempts from any routine firewall check."

"Clever? No. It's diabolical," he muttered. He

turned back to his computer, still staggered by what he now saw. "Who is doing this? Who do these spies work for?"

Nechaeva shrugged. "The American CIA? Our 'friends' in Beijing's Ministry of State Security? The Poles? It is impossible to say for sure."

"This is terrible. It's a disaster. A complete nightmare," Obolensky stammered. His mind was busy working through the consequences of a security breach. "My God, every piece of advance military-grade software that we've developed is at risk."

"True enough," Nechaeva said bluntly. Then she patted him on the shoulder. "If it's any consolation, we do not think these hackers have been able to penetrate your computer security. At least not yet."

"But they'll keep trying," he realized.

She nodded. "Oh yes. And they will succeed, probably sooner rather than later—unless additional precautions are taken."

Obolensky seized on that hope. "I'll contact our IT people immediately," he promised. "They can strengthen the firewall . . . and institute more rigorous monitoring of those access logs."

Nechaeva raised a finely sculpted eyebrow. "You would trust those who have already failed to detect these attempted intrusions? Or who, perhaps, deliberately decided not to report them to you?"

"What are you hinting at?" he demanded, turning even paler if that was possible. "Are you implying that some of the institute's own people may be in league with these spies?"

She smiled coldly. "I have said nothing of the kind, Doctor."

"But you think it is possible?"

Nechaeva shrugged again. "I merely suggest it might be wiser not to rely too heavily on your own resources. Not when faced with an espionage threat of this caliber and magnitude."

"Then what *can* be done?" Obolensky asked desperately, sounding like a drowning man thrashing about in the hope of rescue. "Earlier, you said you were here to help me. What did you mean by that?"

She reached into her uniform jacket and took out a USB flash drive. He could see the double-headed eagle emblem of the FSB embossed on the small device. "Our best cybersecurity specialists have devised a more advanced set of defenses for your network, Doctor. Their work will add a new and virtually undetectable layer to your existing firewall." Her mouth twisted in a cold, cruel smile. "Best of all, these defenses will instantly alert us to any new attempts to breach your security—enabling us to trace these hackers back to their lair."

"And then what?" Obolensky wondered.

"If, as I suspect, they are operating on our soil, we will capture them if possible. If not, we will eliminate them," Nechaeva told him brusquely.

He shuddered. Something in this beautiful woman's voice hinted that she would enjoy personally killing the foreign agents trying to break into his secure networks. He found such ferocity frightening. "Kills" in his professional world were antiseptic, largely a question of watching blips disappear from a glowing screen.

Still pale, Obolensky took the flash drive from her and plugged it into his computer. Immediately a dialogue box popped open. "*Prodvinutaya Programma Kiberbezpasnost.* Advanced Cybersecurity Program. Run Y/N?" He typed in yes and then entered the password necessary to approve the program for use throughout the lab network.

For less than a minute, the tiny device quietly clicked and whirred. When it fell silent, he ejected it and gave it back to Nechaeva.

She dropped it back into her pocket. "Thank you, Doctor," she said, without any apparent emotion. "The state appreciates your cooperation in this matter. Just as it also requires your utmost discretion."

Obolensky nodded quickly. "I understand fully, Colonel," he assured her. "No one else at NNIIRT will hear about this. Not from me."

"For your sake, I hope that is true," Nechaeva said. A thin, icy smile flitted across her face and then vanished. "It would be a great shame for Mother Russia to lose a man of your intelligence and ability."

NIZHNY NOVGOROD
A short time later

Several blocks from the Research Institute for Radio Engineering, Colonel Tatiana Nechaeva paused at a street corner to check her surroundings. To a casual observer, she was merely making sure she could cross safely.

Her eyes flicked in all directions. No one suspicious was in sight. She was clear.

Walking quickly in the cold, Nechaeva crossed to the other side of the narrow, tree-lined street. Halfway down the block, she turned into an alley running beside a run-down brick apartment building. After one more quick check to confirm that she wasn't being followed, she used a key to unlock the building's battered metal service door and went in.

Her nose wrinkled against the rank odor of uncollected trash. The dented, rusting garbage cans lined up along cement-block walls were overflowing, surrounded by plastic bags stuffed with rotting food scraps, dirty diapers, and broken bottles. Sanitation wasn't the strong suit of the apartment building's part-time superintendent. On the other hand, neither was poking his nose into the affairs of his tenants. All things considered, she thought, his laziness and lack of interest in anything but making sure his rents were paid on time was a net plus.

So were the other tenants, a mix of working families and single men employed in the city's factories and other businesses. During the daytime, the adults were either out at work or asleep after pulling exhausting night shifts. Their children were either in school or day care. All of which added up to a building where no one wondered about, or even noticed, the strange spectacle of a uniformed colonel in the FSB coming and going at odd hours.

Nechaeva took the dingy, garbage-strewn rear staircase to the small apartment she'd rented on the second floor. Most of the lightbulbs were burned out, so she used her smartphone as a flashlight to avoid stepping in the worst messes. At the door to her apartment, she rapped four times, then used her key and went straight in.

A young man wearing jeans and a sweater swiveled away from the computer he'd been using. "I'm inside their system, Sam!" he said in glee. "I've got total access to everything in the NNIIRT lab network. I went straight through their firewall without so much as a peep." He shook his head in disbelief. "But I still can't believe this loco scheme of yours actually worked!"

Samantha Kerr grinned back at him. "There's always a way in. Sometimes you pick the lock. Sometimes you figure out where they hid the key. And sometimes you just con them into opening the door for you."

She unbuttoned her heavy uniform coat and tossed her officer's cap onto a chair. "Have you snagged that target acquisition and identification upgrade yet?"

The younger man nodded. "No sweat. A copy's already on its way to our tech guys at Scion."

"Is there any way the Russians can detect what you've been doing?" Sam asked. "Or spot you when you go back in?"

"Not in a million years," he told her confidently.

"The passkey program that nice Dr. Obolensky installed for us includes a cleaner function."

"Good," she said seriously. "Because I have a hunch Mr. Martindale is going to have more work for us very soon."

CHAPTER 18

RUSSIAN RAILWAYS, STAFF OFFICES, MOSCOW
Later that night

Unlike his colleague Yuri Akulov, Taras Ivchenko looked like a man to be reckoned with. Tall, broad-shouldered, and square-jawed, the former intelligence officer had played ice hockey from the age of five up through his graduation from Moscow State University. On the ice, his ferocity and daring allowed him to score more goals than other players, while also spending more time in the penalty box and hospital emergency rooms. He'd stopped playing hockey after the KGB recruited him. Instead, he'd channeled his aggressive instincts into the more exciting game of espionage.

Over the course of his career with the KGB and later the FSB, Ivchenko had become a master of black-bag operations. His elite team of burglars had broken into more than a dozen Western embassies and consulates, stealing secrets, planting listening devices, and accumulating information on cryptographic methods that helped crack some of the codes and ciphers used by the Americans and their allies.

Now he was using those same skills on behalf of Igor Truznyev.

Breaking into the ultramodern building housing Russian Railways' central staff offices had been child's play in comparison to the exploits of his glory days. The security guards hired by the state-owned railroad firm spent most of their time and energy trying to stop employees from pilfering computers and other expensive equipment. The idea that a visitor might stay past normal working hours and then break into a senior executive's office would have struck them as ludicrous. Who would be dumb enough to risk going to prison doing something so pointless? After all, the Kalanchevskaya Street building wasn't a bank or even a repository of precious secrets.

But they were wrong.

So far in their joint investigation for Truznyev, Ivchenko and Akulov had been impressed by the thoroughness with which President Gryzlov and Major General Koshkin had camouflaged Russia's cyberwar operation. Between them, the two men had gone to great lengths to keep any knowledge of their Perun's Aerie complex within a tightly restricted circle. They'd even made sure that databases belonging to the FSB, the Kremlin, and Russia's armed forces contained no electronic records of its construction, location, defenses, or staffing.

Any foreign spy service poking and prying in

all the usual ways would never pick up any actionable intelligence about the massive cyberwar center. They might not be able to confirm that it even existed.

Taras Ivchenko grinned to himself, imagining the stunned looks on Gryzlov and Koshkin's faces if they ever learned how their carefully spun web of secrecy had been penetrated. Despite all their technological prowess, they'd overlooked the simplest of things—ordinary human weakness and the information routinely collected and stored by any modern railway company. First, the drunken babbling of Ivan Budanov, the Atomflot engineer, had revealed that a special mixed freight and passenger train was used to move nuclear-reactor components from Murmansk to the Perun's Aerie complex. From there it was simply a question of gaining access to Russian Railways' signal and traffic logs. Every train moving anywhere along the sixty-two thousand kilometers of Russia's railroads under centralized control automatically triggered a computer-generated report whenever it passed through a signal or a station.

Which was what brought Ivchenko to Konstantin Apraksin's office in the middle of the night. As a senior Russian Railways executive, Apraksin had unrestricted access to its entire corporate database. Best of all, like many computer illiterates, he kept a helpful cheat sheet with all of his passwords and user names taped to the side of his desktop monitor.

Patiently, Ivchenko clicked through page after page of Murmansk freight-yard records. He was looking for any train departures that matched the range of possible dates Akulov had picked out of Budanov's vodka-soaked memories.

A third of the way through, his eyes narrowed. Train Number 967 seemed a possible fit. That was a three-digit code used to identify mixed freight and passenger trains, although it was usually reserved for short-haul commuter runs. He clicked on the number, opening up more detailed records.

"*Kush!* Jackpot!" he murmured.

Number 967 included four heavy-duty electric locomotives. That was no commuter train. Just as revealing was the small tag that told the rail-control system to award it top priority along all sections of high-density track. Nor was there a slated destination. The only thing that didn't fit was its cargo—listed as imported factory machinery supposedly brought in through the city's warm-water port.

Ivchenko shook his head in disgust at such sloppiness. Imported machinery? That was a damned thin cover story. Then he reconsidered. It was probably good enough to fool any railway inspector who checked the train's freight cars. One jumble of steam pipes, pumps, conduits, turbines, and generators probably looked like another to the untrained eye.

Slowly, carefully, he began searching through the database—painstakingly tracking the progress of special Train Number 967 as it made its way from Murmansk south to St. Petersburg and from there to Moscow. At Moscow, it turned west onto the Trans-Siberian Railway and then north toward Volgoda. At the Konosha rail hub, Number 967 stopped briefly to replace its electric freight locomotives with diesel engines, and then continued northwest on the nonelectrified line to Pechora and Vorkuta.

Ah, he thought, *here we go*. Both cities were near the foothills of the northern Ural Mountains.

As it happened, Pechora was the end of the line for Train Number 967. The station logs showed that it arrived and was shunted off to a siding. And from that point on, it simply vanished.

Smiling to himself, Ivchenko closed the files he'd opened and turned off the computer. Between them, he and Akulov had narrowed down the location of the Perun's Aeria cyberwar complex. It was located somewhere in the Urals near Pechora. And that was close enough for nongovernment work, the former FSB officer thought.

He supposed Truznyev might want someone to actually visit the distant city to dig up more, but he would strongly recommend against that course. Gryzlov and Koshkin may have missed this particular hole in their security, but neither would be foolish enough to leave Pechora itself unwatched. As soon as anyone connected to Truznyev's private espionage network stepped off a plane or a train in Pechora, alarms would start ringing all the way from the Urals to the Kremlin.

Besides, Ivchenko thought, why bother? Once he reported in, his boss would have all the information he needed to make trouble for Gennadiy Gryzlov, should he decide that was either necessary or might be profitable.

IRON WOLF SQUADRON, POWIDZ, POLAND
Several hours later

Brad McLanahan finished taxiing the XCV-62 off the runway and into one of the squadron's largest camouflaged aircraft shelters. By the time he and Nadia finished their postflight checklists, the hangar doors were already closed.

Martindale and Whack Macomber were waiting for them at the foot of the Ranger's crew ladder.

"Well, how did it fly?" Martindale demanded, not wasting any time on pleasantries. "Is the Ranger really as capable as Jon Masters claimed it would be?"

"Why yes, thank you, Mr. Martindale. It is very nice to see you too," Nadia said bitingly. "So kind of you to ask."

Macomber chuckled—he enjoyed watching the smug, condescending, lordly former U.S. president receiving a shot from someone who wasn't afraid of his power or authority.

To his credit, the older man ducked his head in apology. "Forgive me, Major," he said, with a disarming smile. "I know that you and Brad are tired, but the situation's a bit tense here . . . and I've missed you both."

Brad decided to let that bit of politician's insincerity pass without further comment. Personally, he figured it was just as well that Nadia wasn't carrying her sidearm. She probably *wouldn't* have shot Martindale, but she might have scared the crap out of him. After logging more than twenty hours of total flight time and ten thousand nautical miles, they were both pretty frazzled.

Instead, he patted the underside of the wing just above his head. "She's a beaut, sir," he said. "The XCV-62 may not handle like a high-performance jet fighter, but she's a heck of a lot more agile than the B-2 bombers I've flown in Sky Masters simulators—despite having the same kind of tailless configuration. And based on the real-world fuel-consumption figures we saw, my guess is the Ranger has significantly more range than Uncle Jon claimed."

Macomber laughed quietly. "That bastard always did like to play it close to his vest."

"It's a good sales technique," Martindale allowed, with a slight smile of his own. "Always deliver more than you promised."

Folding her arms, Nadia tapped her foot impatiently on the floor of the hangar. They all turned to look at her. "You said the situation was bad, Mr. President," she reminded Martindale. "How bad?" Her eyes were worried. "Have there been new cyber attacks? Is our power grid still down?"

"I said *tense*," the older man corrected her gently. "Which isn't quite the same thing."

"But close enough, for fuck's sake . . . sir," Macomber muttered.

Martindale shrugged. "I won't argue semantics, Whack." He turned back to Nadia and Brad. "We've made some limited progress in restoring the electrical grid in Poland and the other AFN nations. Between my Scion experts and the various national CERT teams, we've flushed the Russian malware out of all the infected transmission-control computers. But it's going to take a lot longer to restore everything."

"If the viruses are gone, why not bring everything back online right now?" Brad asked.

"Because the initial power surges and blackouts fried a shitload of generators and slagged several hundred kilometers' worth of high-voltage transmission lines," Macomber said bluntly. "That kind of equipment doesn't exactly grow on trees."

"Sadly, no," agreed Martindale. "President Wilk and the other alliance leaders are buying replacement generators and supplies of transmission line wherever they can, but the fact remains that we're lucky if most of the major cities have electricity eight to ten hours a day at the moment."

"And the outlying areas?" Nadia asked. Her grandparents lived in a small village outside Kraków. "How long until they have power?"

"It could take weeks. Maybe months," Martindale told her.

"Jesus," Brad muttered.

Martindale nodded. "Which is why the leaders of the AFN are gathering in Warsaw tomorrow evening for an emergency summit. Under the pressure of this unrelenting wave of cyberwar attacks, confidence in the alliance is fraying. President Wilk wants to remind his fellow presidents and prime ministers that we have considerable military and technological capabilities of our own. That's why Piotr wants us there too—all of the top people in Scion and the Iron Wolf Squadron."

"Does that include my dad?" Brad asked quietly. "Because I notice he's not here to welcome us back to Poland."

"I've got the general out running maneuvers with Charlie Turlock and Captain Schofield's team," Macomber said quickly. "He was kind of going stir-crazy just sitting around the base. So I figured it would be better to keep him busy doing useful stuff."

Stir-crazy or just plain crazy? Brad wondered. At least his dad wouldn't be charging around with a load of live ammo during a training exercise.

"Your father is invited to the summit," Martindale said. He looked pensive. "But I've cautioned against bringing him openly into any discussions. Word that he was still alive would almost surely leak out—"

"Which could push Gryzlov right over the edge," Brad realized. Over the past several years, the Russian president had conducted a reckless personal vendetta against the McLanahans—a vendetta triggered long ago when an air strike commanded by Patrick McLanahan killed Gryzlov's own father. Scion psychologists who'd studied the Russian's behavioral patterns believed he would be willing to go to almost any lengths to make sure the older McLanahan was dead, no matter how much collateral damage he inflicted on innocents or even on his own people.

Martindale nodded. "Exactly. This underground war we're locked in is bad enough. There's no point in setting off an escalation beyond our ability to manage or withstand."

"And that works the same way in reverse, doesn't it?" Brad asked, eyeing the other man narrowly. "I mean, right now my dad would jump at the chance to take a shot at Gryzlov."

"That's true," Martindale agreed. "Hearing him pushing for an all-out counterattack on the Russians could easily backfire against us with the other alliance leaders. They might begin to wonder if we were only interested in dragging them into a war of revenge that might destroy us all."

Brad grimaced. "Yeah, and that's exactly the propaganda line Moscow's been pushing . . . that we're all fanatical warmongers."

"President Wilk sees the dangers," Martindale said. "So you and Major Macomber here will serve as the Iron Wolf Squadron's official representatives. We'll keep your father out of the room, but close by for consultation on any . . . tactical questions."

"You'd better make sure he isn't carrying any live ammunition," Brad said reluctantly.

Macomber snorted. "Hell, he's not going to be carrying any weapons. Period. Plus, I'll have Charlie suited up and along as a backup, just in case your dad decides to crash the meeting. Literally."

"Yeah, he does get a kick out of smashing through walls," Brad said, with a wry, sad grin.

After Martindale left, Whack Macomber walked Brad and Nadia over to the base living quarters.

Brad fought down a jaw-cracking yawn. He was

just about out on his feet. *Man, I'm going to need a few hours of shut-eye and some hot food before I start feeling halfway human again,* he thought. Then he felt Nadia's hand slip into his. Her fingers gently caressed his palm. Suddenly feeling more awake, he caught the playful sparkle in her beautiful blue-gray eyes.

Okay, he decided with a lazy grin, maybe sleep could wait.

"There is some good news in this mess," Macomber told them. "The AFN politicos may be getting antsy, but most of the ordinary civilians are hanging tight. If that son of a bitch Gryzlov was hoping to provoke more riots and looting, he must be pretty goddamned disappointed right now."

"Thanks to martial law?" Brad asked.

Macomber shook his head. "Not really. Sure, a few skinheads and other troublemakers got popped early on, but mostly the troops are busy distributing emergency supplies and making sure the civvies don't freeze to death."

Nadia raised an eyebrow in surprise. "That *is* surprising."

"Because so many Poles panicked when the banking system crashed?" Brad said.

She nodded. "I thought the chaos would be worse this time. Especially since the damage was so much more widespread."

"You can thank the Russians for that," Macomber said, with a quick, humorless grin. "At first, the banking crash looked like a royal fuckup by the big, bad capitalists that everybody loves to hate on. But when the power grid went down . . . well, then this crap started to look like enemy action. And most folks in this part of the world really do *not* enjoy being pushed around by Moscow."

"Gryzlov overplayed his hand," Brad realized.

Macomber nodded. "Yeah, that's the way it looks." He shrugged. "For now anyway. But the longer this cyberwar crap goes on without us being able to hit back, the more impatient they're going to get."

"So you think my dad's right?" Brad said. "That we need to punch back twice as hard?"

"Right in the sense that we should drop into Moscow and start shooting up the place? No," Macomber said, shaking his head. "But right in the sense that we're not going to win this thing staying curled up in a defensive crouch? Hell, yes."

CHAPTER 19

VORANAVA, BELARUS
The next morning

Snow fell out of a lead-gray sky, slowly covering the roads, woods, and fields around Voranava, a small town just thirteen kilometers south of the Lithuanian border. Spraying dirty brown slush behind them, a steady stream of trucks roared along the highway just outside the town. European Route 85 ran all the way from Lithuania to Greece.

A few blocks inside the town, two big semi-trailer trucks with Lithuanian license plates were parked outside a dreary apartment complex. A hand-lettered sign on the locked front door of the complex's ramshackle community hall read ZA-KRYTO DLYA UBORKI, Closed for Cleaning.

Inside, a small group of hard-eyed, tough-looking men in civilian clothes lounged around the dingy interior. Three were playing cards. A fourth sat smoking a cigarette while idly polishing a wickedly sharp combat knife. The fifth man, their commander, Major Pavel Berezin, sat off at a table by himself. His hand rested on a secure cell phone.

They were members of Vympel, or Pennant, a Spetsnaz unit controlled by Russia's FSB. Most Spetsnaz troops in Vympel were assigned to counterterrorist and nuclear-security missions. These five men were different. Highly trained and skilled in close-quarters combat, long-range marksmanship, explosives, and foreign languages, they formed a small elite team organized to conduct covert sabotage operations—both at home and abroad.

Berezin checked his watch for what seemed like the hundredth time in as many minutes. Were the higher-ups in Moscow getting cold feet? It wouldn't be the first time that one of his nation's political leaders, even a man as ruthless as President Gryzlov, aborted a high-risk operation right before it was due to kick off.

He scowled at the thought. A cancellation now would certainly improve his team's chances of surviving the next couple of days, but it would also be enormously frustrating. He and his men were proficient at dealing out death and destruction, and they relished any chance to do so. Desk soldiers and rear-area jack-offs didn't sign up with Vympel. His second in command, Captain Andrei Chirkash, sourly characterized these last-minute mission aborts as "whore farts." "You're all up and ready to go, right," Chirkash would grumble. "But then, just as you start to get into your groove, she cuts a real stinker. And that's the end of the match. No shot. No goal."

The cell phone chirped twice, interrupting his gloomy thoughts. Berezin snatched it up. "*Akrobat Odin.* Acrobat One."

"This is Inspektor Manezha, Ringmaster," the gruff voice of Major General Kirill Glazkov, commander of the FSB's V Directorate said. "Execute *Mor* Variant Six. Confirm."

"I confirm *Mor* Variant Six," Berezin said crisply.

"This mission is critical," Glazkov said. "So make no mistakes, Pavel. Understand?"

"*Da, ya ponimayu!* Yes, I understand," Berezin replied. "We are moving now. Acrobat out." He powered down the phone and slid it into his rucksack. He brought his fingers to his lips and whistled. The sharp sound brought the rest of his team to their feet.

"Listen up!" Berezin told them. "The mission's on. Everybody grab your gear and board the trucks."

While the others slung their packs and moved toward the door, the Spetsnaz major pulled Chirkash aside. "If we get separated in traffic, Andrei, make sure you stick to the schedule, okay? The timing on this one is damned tight. We don't have a lot of room for error."

"So I understand," his second in command replied. "But I hate relying on a bunch of long-haired *komp'yutershchiks*, geeks, this much," he groused. "One little screw-up by those clowns could land us in the shit, buried up to our necks."

Berezin grinned back at him. "It could, Andrei. And I don't like depending on them either. Still, if you've seen the news, those techno-twerps are really handing the Poles and their little friends a high-tech ass-kicking." His smile turned feral. "And pretty soon we'll get to do the same thing, only the old-fashioned, up-close-and-personal way, eh?"

THE KREMLIN, MOSCOW
That same time

The conference room adjoining President Gennadiy Gryzlov's office was crowded. His most senior national security advisers were there, including Sergei Tarzarov, his foreign minister; his occasional mistress Daria Titeneva; Viktor Kazyanov, the minister of state security; and Gregor Sokolov, his defense chief. They sat tensely in chairs arrayed around a large table while their most trusted aides lined the walls.

Gryzlov himself prowled back and forth, too full of energy to sit idly while waiting for the news from Belarus. A small part of him also enjoyed observing the worried faces of Titeneva, Sokolov, and the others as they swiveled back and forth, following his every move. Good God, he thought in cold contempt, they were like frightened sheep watching a lean and hungry wolf circling closer and closer.

A soft chime sounded from somewhere among

his uneasy cabinet ministers. Gryzlov stopped pacing.

Viktor Kazyanov gulped and grabbed at the desktop computer set on the table in front of him. For a moment, he stared down at the message it displayed. Then, clumsily, he typed in an acknowledgment.

"Well?" Gryzlov demanded.

"That was Glazkov," Kazyanov stammered. "He confirms that *Operatsiya Mor* Variant Six is under way. His Spetsnaz team is on the move."

Gryzlov nodded calmly. "Very good, Viktor." His gaze sharpened. "Are Koshkin's people ready?"

"Yes, Mr. President," the other man confirmed.

Satisfied, Gryzlov dropped into his own chair. He looked down the length of the conference table, studying the sea of nervous faces for a moment longer. Then he laughed. "For God's sake, cheer up. You all look as though I'd just signed your death warrants."

There was a moment of pained silence.

At last, Daria Titeneva spoke up. "We are worried, Mr. President, because this sudden escalation of *Operatsiya Mor* could easily jeopardize Russia's interests and international reputation."

"How so?" Gryzlov asked easily, still smiling.

She frowned. "Up to now, the cyberwar attacks Koshkin's experts are conducting have been indirect and deniable. While others may suspect our involvement in these attacks on banking systems and electricity-supply networks across Eastern and central Europe, no one can prove it. But this

Variant Six of yours is far more direct. If it goes wrong in any way—"

"Why assume that Berezin and his men will fail?" Gryzlov interrupted. "Why be so defeatist?" Titeneva flushed angrily.

"The foreign minister is merely pointing out the serious risks this gambit entails, Gennadiy," Sergei Tarzarov said quietly. He leaned forward. "She is right to do so. So far, Koshkin's viruses and malware infections have inflicted significant political and economic pain on our enemies. Best of all, they have done so without real cost to us. It is not defeatist to advocate continuing a successful strategy."

Gryzlov waved the older man's warning away. "Bah!" he scoffed, staring around the table. "You all make the same mistake. As usual, you confuse tactics and strategy."

Tarzarov's lips thinned, a sure sign of irritation.

Gryzlov smiled. *So there is still a man alive in there, after all*, he thought in amusement. *Sergei may present that withered mask and dry pedant's voice to the world at large . . . but prick him, and he bleeds.*

Seeing the confusion on their faces, he sighed. Sometimes it was maddening to realize how dense and unimaginative even those closest to him could be. "Koshkin's viruses are a tactic," Gryzlov explained, with mock patience. "They are only one means to an end. Nothing more. Already it is clear that the damage they do is only temporary. Besides, as the Poles and other nations increase their Internet and computer security—with the help of these Scion mercenary specialists—the effectiveness of our hacking attacks will rapidly diminish." He pointed at Tarzarov. "Tell me, Sergei . . . what are we trying to achieve with this cyberwar campaign?"

"The destruction of this Polish-led alliance," the older man replied tonelessly.

"Precisely!" Gryzlov snapped. Suddenly he slammed his fist down on the table, rattling water glasses. Sokolov and Kazyanov turned pale. Titeneva and Tarzarov were made of sterner stuff . . . they barely flinched. "This war is *not* about screwing around with Polish bank accounts or turning off the lights in Warsaw, Budapest, and Riga. Our strategic aim is to smash the so-called AFN to pieces. And then, with Piotr Wilk and his fascist cliques tossed on the ash heap of history, we will be free to reclaim our traditional dominance over Eastern and central Europe."

Tarzarov frowned. "We do not question your objectives, Gennadiy. Only the hazards you seem willing to run in pursuit of those ends."

"All war involves danger," Gryzlov retorted. "And in the end, those who are too afraid to act boldly still die—only without any lasting accomplishment or reward." He glared around the table. "This is the time to strike harder. For this brief instant, the Poles and their allies are teetering on the brink of panic and political collapse. Which means this is the moment to push them off the cliff."

Slowly, halfheartedly, Tarzarov and the others nodded.

Even their reluctant consent would suffice, Gryzlov decided. But for now it would probably be best to keep the rest of his plans to himself. The revelation that *Operatsiya Mor* was only the first step in an even more complicated, daring, and dangerous scheme would undoubtedly terrify them.

ŠALČININKŲ BORDER-CONTROL STATION, LITHUANIA
A short time later

Snug in his heated kiosk, state border guard Sergeant Edvardas Noreika looked up at the dark, overcast sky. Snow flurries swirled down and danced across the highway and surrounding woods, sent spinning by a bitterly cold east wind. The weather was turning ugly fast, he thought. Thank God, the powers that be in Vilnius had put restoring electricity to Lithuania's border checkpoints at the top of their priority list. But the local villagers, including his own family, were in for a long, brutal cold stretch.

A chime sounded, signaling the arrival of the next two vehicles in his queue. He looked up. Both were long semi-trailer trucks with Lithuanian plates. The camera set up outside his kiosk flashed twice, capturing a digital image of each truck's license plate. Using his computer, Noreika checked the numbers against his booking list. They matched.

To cut down on the traffic congestion that plagued Lithuania's border checkpoints, especially those with Belarus, the government had instituted a system that allowed truckers and other drivers to book a scheduled crossing time. The automated system even allowed certain vehicles, those registered to precleared Lithuanian businesses and corporations, to avoid the usual customs inspections and paperwork.

Sergeant Edvardas Noreika loved the system since it cut back on much of the dull, routine paperwork that used to bog down every shift. Preclearances also allowed the station's border guards, along with their customs-department colleagues, to focus more closely on foreign-owned cars and trucks and those that they suspected might belong to smugglers and other criminals.

A large green checkmark appeared next to each license-plate image on his computer display. Both trucks had passed the preclearance process. He tapped a key, sending the captured imagery to the Ministry of Finance and the Ministry of the Interior in Vilnius. Then he slid open the window of his kiosk, shivering in the sudden blast of cold air, and waved the semitrailers on through.

As the first truck rolled slowly past, Noreika greeted the driver with a grin. "*Sveiki namo, vaikinai.* Welcome home, guys. How was Greece?"

The trucker, a tough-looking man in a leather jacket, laughed. "Too sunny for my taste." He gestured at the snow now falling more heavily. "Who could resist our glorious winters?"

"Me, for one!" Noreika joked. Then, with a

final wave, he slid his window shut and turned back to check the next vehicles waiting up in his queue.

A couple of minutes later, his computer crashed—freezing in midscreen as it exchanged data with the central government network in Vilnius. "*Šūdas.* Crap," he muttered. He switched the signal light outside his kiosk to red and got on the phone.

"The whole system is down, Sergeant," his superior told him, sounding harried. "Vilnius says a huge denial-of-service attack just knocked out most of our servers. What's worse is there's also some kind of computer virus loose in the database. It's already erased all the information we collected today."

Noreika whistled. What a mess. "How long will it take to get the system back up?"

"God only knows," the other man said. "Not anytime today, that's for sure."

"Sweet Christ," Noreika muttered. "What do I do in the meantime? I've got one mother of a lot of trucks stacking up along the highway."

"You pull on your jacket and gloves, Sergeant," his supervisor growled. "And then you leave your nice cushy kiosk and do your job the way you were trained, with a logbook, a pencil, your brain, and your eyes."

In all the confusion over the next several hours, it never occurred to Edvardas Noreika to connect the two big semi-trailer trucks he'd cleared through his control point with the malware infection raising hell in Vilnius.

* * *

A couple of kilometers up the road, Spetsnaz lieutenant Mikhail Kuritsyn checked the text he'd just received. He glanced across the cab at the driver, Major Pavel Berezin. "Ringmaster confirms the Vilnius network is down, sir."

"*Khorosho*. Good," the major said, keeping his eyes on the road. "It's nice to know that Koshkin's geeks managed to pull off phase one without stepping on their dicks."

Kuritsyn nodded. He turned away, hiding a lopsided smile. Like Captain Chirkash, Berezin was a technophobe. The lieutenant suspected the major had never met a computer he didn't want to put a bullet in.

Idly, he swiped at the truck cab's passenger-side window. As the weather turned even colder, it was starting to fog up. His hand froze in midmotion.

They were driving through a narrow belt of forest. There, in among the trees, he could see tracked vehicles parked under camouflage netting. They were American-made M113 armored personnel carriers. Several dozen soldiers in winter camouflage parkas were gathered around tiny field stoves, heating food or boiling water to make tea or coffee.

"Don't look now, but we have company, Major," Kuritsyn murmured.

"Relax, Mikhail," Berezin said. "Our friends out there belong to the Grand Duchess Birutė Uhlan Battalion." He chuckled. "They're deployed to protect Lithuania against an invasion by those dastardly Russians."

"The ones who wear uniforms, you mean," Kuritsyn said, matching the major's sarcastic tone. "Not like us."

"Invade Lithuania? Us? Perish the thought, Lieutenant," Berezin said with a grin. "Remember, we're just passing through."

PODWOJPONIE BORDER-CONTROL POINT, POLAND
Several hours later

Although it was still early afternoon, it was already getting dark. Bright arc lights gleamed ahead. They were coming up to the Polish border checkpoint. Headlights flickered dimly in the distance, showing long lines of cars and trucks backed up waiting for permission to enter Poland.

Berezin spun the wheel slightly, turning into the lane reserved for Polish-registered vehicles. Traffic there was moving, inching ahead in fits and starts. He and Chirkash had switched their Lithuanian license plates and registration documents for those from Poland not long after leaving Vilnius.

When they reached the head of the line, he rolled down his window and offered his papers to the young Polish Customs Service officer who'd flagged him over to her station. Her breath steamed around her as she jotted down information in a thick logbook. "When did you leave Vilnius?" she asked.

"This morning," Berezin told her. "Right after breakfast." He shook his head. "Man, things are screwed up on the Lithuanian side of the border. Their computers are down and it took us an hour to clear customs."

She nodded. "The same thing's going on here." She shrugged. "It's a good thing you're Polish. We'll have you out of here in a jiffy."

"I appreciate it," the Spetsnaz major said. He jerked a thumb at Kuritsyn. "So does my nephew. He promised his girlfriend he'd be home in time for a late dinner."

The customs officer pointed toward the long trailer behind their cab. "So what's your load?"

"Furniture," Berezin replied. "A consignment of oak desks, bed frames, and dining room sets."

"Furniture? With this cold snap hitting and all the power outages, you might get a higher price selling it for kindling," the young woman said with a bitter smile.

Berezin matched her expression. "I'll bear that in mind."

"And what's your destination today?" she asked, still taking notes.

"Warsaw."

She nodded, handing back his papers. "Well, you should have an easy time of it from this point on. The snow's not too bad yet, so the roads are still clear."

With that, she waved them on through the

checkpoint. Berezin pulled back onto the highway and drove south. Behind them, the truck driven by Andrei Chirkash pulled up to the same customs officer.

Sitting next to the major, Kuritsyn pulled out his secure cell phone and sent another short text, this one informing Ringmaster, Major General Glazkov, that they were proceeding toward their designated operational area.

OVER RUSSIA
Several hours later

Cruising at forty thousand feet, Kalmar Airlines Flight 851 flew onward over Russia at 490 knots. The Boeing 777-300ER was on a long-haul red-eye flight from Shanghai in the People's Republic of China to Helsinki, Finland. A large majority of the hundred and fifty or so passengers aboard were Chinese business executives headed west to explore new investment opportunities or oversee existing ventures. More than six hours after takeoff, most of them and some of the flight attendants were dozing in their seats, lulled by the pervasive roar of the wide-body jet's powerful twin GE90-115B turbofan engines.

Far off to the north, a few lights signaling the presence of small towns or cities dotted an otherwise pitch-black landscape. Apart from that, there was nothing to catch the attention of anyone peering down at the passing countryside. This part of Russia just west of the Urals was almost uninhabited—a vast region dominated by primeval forests and swampland.

In the cockpit, Captain Kaarle Markkula ran through a routine check of the engine readouts shown on the large color flat-panel LCD display set squarely in the middle of the instrument panel. Everything was normal.

To his right, First Officer Tuomas Saarela muttered something incomprehensible in his sleep, twisted awkwardly against his shoulder straps, and then drifted off again without ever really waking up. His mouth fell open as he snored.

Markkula shook his head in envy. Saarela was one of those lucky people who seemed able to fall asleep almost anywhere in the blink of an eye if given half a chance. Night flights were the younger man's favorite, since their passengers only wanted to grab some shut-eye themselves. They never wanted or expected the usual running monologues from the flight deck that were the bane of most airline flight crews' existence.

For one brief second, he was sorely tempted to take to the 777's intercom. "On your right, you will see a vast expanse of nothing at all," he could say. "And for those of you on the left side of the aircraft, you are fortunate enough to observe even more emptiness."

Instead, the Kalmar Airlines captain once more busied himself with scanning through his instrument readouts and displays. He decided to let Saarela sleep until they were ready to begin their descent toward Helsinki. Since they were still almost nine hundred nautical miles out from the Finnish capital, that wouldn't be for at least another ninety minutes or so.

What neither Kaarle Markkula nor anyone else aboard the 777 noticed was the large, twin-engine jet aircraft steadily closing on them from above and astern. Its navigation and running lights were off, rendering it almost invisible against the night sky.

ABOARD THE TUPOLEV 214-R ELECTRONIC INTELLIGENCE AIRCRAFT, OVER RUSSIA
That same time

The Tu-214R was Russia's most advanced electronic intelligence aircraft. Bulges studded its fuselage, containing the sensors and antennas that allowed it to intercept, analyze, and record a wide range of enemy radars, radio transmissions, and other forms of communication.

For more than a week, its flight crew had practiced intercepting and flying undetected in ever-closer formation with a number of different foreign and domestic airliners traversing Russian airspace. But tonight's mission was not another drill. This was the real thing.

Inside the Tu-214R's darkened main cabin, two dozen Russian Air Force officers occupied the computer and electronic intelligence workstations lining the sides of the fuselage. Specially selected from among the top graduates of the Zhukov Air and Space Defense Academy in Tver, they were each expert in different fields of signals intelligence collection and analysis. None of them really understood why they were operating so far inside Russian airspace, where all they could detect were friendly radar emissions and radio and cell-phone traffic. Ordinarily, their aircraft flew intelligence-gathering missions along the periphery of potentially hostile nations—including flights that took them right up to the edge of American airspace.

Despite their curiosity, the Tu-214R's regular crew avoided paying too much attention to the two men seated at a console close to the cockpit. Orders from the top were clear: showing excessive interest in these men or their work would earn the culprit a one-way transfer to a remote outpost above the Arctic Circle.

One of the pair appeared much younger than the other air-force officers around him. A mop of unkempt hair hung low over his wrinkled, ill-fitting flight suit. He sat hunched over a computer keyboard, peering intently at a series of numbers and characters scrolling up across his display. His companion, older and more polished, wore the twin-headed eagle shoulder flash of the FSB.

The young man hissed in annoyance. "The signal is still too weak. This is crap. I can't work with static. I need a coherent data stream." He glanced away from his screen. "Tell the pilot he needs to get closer, much closer."

"I'm sure that Colonel Annenkov is doing his best, Stepan," the other man said mildly.

"Well, his best right now isn't damned well good enough," the young man said irritably.

"What's the point of my wasting all this time riding around in this glorified sardine can if this jet jockey and his guys can't do their jobs?" His voice rose higher. "If these air-force zeroes are too gutless to do what's necessary, we should just return to base."

"Calm down," the FSB officer said, unruffled. "I'll see what I can do." He clicked his mike. "Colonel, this is Major Filatov."

"Go ahead," the pilot's tense voice said in his headphones.

"Our specialist requests that you continue your approach. He needs a stronger signal from the target."

"Does your pet *komp'yutershchik* want me to rip a hole in their fucking fuselage so he can just run a data cable into their flight-management computer?" Annenkov asked acidly.

Filatov permitted himself a pained smile. Acting as the intermediary between Koshkin's hacker and the Tu-214R commander was never a pleasant task. In their own ways, both were highly skilled, but neither had much patience for anyone outside his respective closed fraternity. "I hope that will not prove necessary," he said calmly.

Slowly, carefully, Annenkov edged closer to the unsuspecting 777, careful to stay slightly above the bigger jetliner to avoid hitting any wake turbulence.

Major Filatov listened to the conversation between Annenkov and his copilot as they maneuvered.

"Two hundred meters, sir."

"Understood. Coming up a little on the throttles," Annenkov replied, the strain evident in his voice.

The Tu-214R bucked, catching a minor curl of turbulence coming off the wide-body passenger jet's wings.

"Airspeed now nine hundred twenty kilometers per hour. Range to target is one hundred fifty meters," the copilot reported.

"Easing back on the throttles," Annenkov said.

"Range now one hundred meters and holding."

Suddenly the young computer hacker stabbed a finger at his display. Lines of code had flashed onto the screen. "Ah! There we go!" His fingers rattled across his keyboard.

"Can you break in?" Filatov asked.

The younger man sneered, still intent on his work. "This is not a movie, Major. There is no way to 'break in' to a computer system on the fly, merely by typing. What I'm doing is uploading a special hacking tool I developed for this mission. It's a program designed to exploit weaknesses I've already identified in Kalmar's security protocols."

Filatov fought for patience. "Will this special tool of yours do the job?" he asked.

"It already has. I'm inside their system," the hacker said smugly. "Their protocols were childish. That 777's computer is predisposed to accept what it believes is navigational data from satellites."

Triumphantly, he tapped a key. More lines of code scrolled across his display, too fast to read, and then disappeared. He swiveled to face his

FSB handler with his arms folded across his chest. "Mission complete, Major."

Filatov breathed out. He keyed his mic again and relayed the good news to the Tu-214R's cockpit crew.

Gradually, the twin-engine Russian spy plane decreased its speed, falling farther and farther behind until it was a safe distance from the Kalmar Airlines passenger jet. Then it banked away, disappearing into the pitch-dark sky.

CHAPTER 20

THE BLUE HALL, PRESIDENTIAL PALACE, WARSAW
That same time

Polish troops in full combat gear were deployed around the elegantly classical Presidential Palace—guarding every entrance of the enormous, floodlit building. Squads of riot-control police backed them up. Two-man BOR sniper teams were posted on the surrounding rooftops. Tracked Leopard 2 main battle tanks and eight-wheeled Wolverine armored personnel carriers were stationed at every major intersection around the palace. As a final precaution, F-16 Vipers patrolled the skies over Warsaw, ready to react immediately to any Russian air strike.

With every major political leader in the Alliance of Free Nations in Warsaw for this emergency summit, Piotr Wilk and his government were taking no chances with security. This meeting had to go off without a hitch.

It was crucial that the AFN's leaders craft a united response to Russia's clandestine cyberwar onslaught. Otherwise, as the wave of malware attacks against vital infrastructure continued, Moscow's increasingly obvious attempts to pick off the alliance's weaker, less stable members might start bearing fruit. Rumors were already circulating about possible parliamentary impeachment proceedings against Romania's president Dumitru.

The presidents and prime ministers had assembled in the palace's Blue Hall. They were seated around a long conference table. Senior aides and translators filled the rest of the large chamber. Portraits of two of Poland's greatest patriots, Prince Józef Poniatowski and Tadeusz Kościuszko, looked down at them from the hall's ornately decorated walls.

Wearing his rifle-green Iron Wolf Squadron jacket, collared shirt, and black tie, Brad McLanahan sat stiffly in a chair placed directly behind Polish president Piotr Wilk and Martindale. Whack Macomber had the seat on his left. Nadia Rozek, stunning as always in her full dress uniform as a major in Poland's Special Forces, sat on his right.

Throughout the long, wearying discussions— most of them conducted in English, since that was the one language common to most of the AFN's leaders—Brad had been all too aware that the three of them were there mostly for symbolic purposes. Their task at this summit was to act as living, breathing reminders that Poland and its allies possessed formidable military and technological powers of their own. Or, as Whack had memorably put it during one of the brief recesses, "It's like we're sitting here with a big red sign that says 'In Case of a Shooting War, Break Glass and Send These Guys out to Bust Some Russian Heads.'"

"And do you mind that?" Brad had asked.

"I don't mind the part about busting heads," Macomber had growled. "But I hate being window dressing. And I hate wearing a fricking uniform. On top of all that, spending too much time around politicians gives me hives."

The memory brought a smile to Brad's face, which he quickly suppressed. Symbols of high-tech military might were not supposed to grin like idiots.

"This is Wolf Two. Check. Check," Charlie Turlock said quietly. Her voice sounded over the tiny, lightweight, and almost invisible radio earpiece he wore. Whack reached into his jacket pocket, found the slim tactical radio there, and squeezed the squelch button once, confirming that he'd heard her.

Superficially, Charlie's brief signal was a routine test to make sure their communications were working properly. In reality, she was letting him know that his father was under her observation and still appeared to be in control over his actions and emotions. The two CIDs were concealed in a large room down a corridor from the Blue Hall. Some of Major Stepniak's best BOR agents were posted on guard outside.

If President Wilk thought it necessary to

stiffen the spines of any of his alliance peers, he planned to show them the lethally agile combat machines—whose nature and capabilities remained the stuff of myth and rumor to almost everyone outside a tight-knit group in Poland. Even Brad's intervention to prevent a full nuclear meltdown at Cernavodă had yielded little hard data, since the press had been kept far enough back to render their pictures and videos little more than a succession of blurred, grainy images.

Privately, Brad hoped the Polish president would find a way to avoid summoning the CIDs. In his judgment, the risks were just too high. It would be one thing for the leaders of the alliance to see they were defended by remarkable war machines. It would be quite another for them to believe one of those deadly robots was in the hands of an uncontrolled madman.

As much as Brad hated to admit it, with every passing day, Patrick McLanahan acted less and less like a human being trapped inside a robot and more like a soulless automaton focused entirely on war and killing. He'd tried to talk to his father several times since returning from Nevada. Nothing had worked. His attempts had either been met by utter silence or by repeated demands that they push for violent, unrelenting action against the Russians.

He swallowed hard, fighting down a wave of sorrow. For the first time since learning two years ago that his father was miraculously alive, he felt the same pangs of loss he'd experienced when he'd believed the older man dead.

OVER THE GULF OF FINLAND
A short time later

Kalmar Airlines Flight 851 had just crossed the Karelian coast, heading west over the Gulf of Finland on its way to Helsinki-Vantaa International Airport. The wide-body 777 was now just 130 nautical miles from its destination.

"Kalmar Eight-Five-One, St. Petersburg Control," came the radio transmission from the Russian air-traffic controller, "thirty miles from OKLOR intersection, descend and maintain flight level one-zero-zero, contact Helsinki Approach, one-two-nine-point-eight-five, have a nice evening."

Captain Kaarle Markkula clicked his mike. "Thirty miles from OKLOR, descend and maintain flight level one-zero-zero and contact Helsinki Approach, Kalmar Eight-Five-One, good evening." The first officer changed frequencies, and Markkula keyed his mic and spoke: "Helsinki Approach, Kalmar—"

Triggered by the frequency change, the malicious code planted in the 777's computer systems went active. In the blink of an eye, it locked the flight controls and cut power to the radios. Every LCD display in the cockpit went black.

Markkula's eyes widened. *"What the devil . . . ?"*

"Did we just lose power?" his first officer, Saarela, blurted out.

Markkula glanced up at his overhead instrument panel. "The left and right IDG generators show as on. The APU generator is not running.

And the battery standby switch is set on auto." He frowned. "We should have plenty of power. But something's definitely haywire. I'll switch to the backup generators."

At that moment, the malicious code embedded in their computers took control over the 777's pressurization system. It closed the engine bleed valves that supplied pressurized air to the flight deck and cabin while simultaneously opening all of its outflow valves. In seconds, air pressure inside the wide-body jet plunged, plummeting toward lethally low levels. At the same time, the aircraft's interior temperature dropped fast, falling more than 140 degrees Fahrenheit.

Gasping, straining to breathe, Markkula and his first officer grabbed their oxygen masks and fumbled to put them on. Back in the main cabin, startled passengers and flight attendants scrambled to don their own emergency masks. Unfortunately for them, the malicious code in command of the 777's computers had already disabled the aircraft's emergency oxygen systems. A few flight attendants thought to pull out and activate emergency walk-around oxygen bottles, but they took too long and were soon overcome by hypoxia. Within fifty seconds, all 174 people aboard the huge jetliner lost consciousness. The outflow valves closed again, sealing off the deck and cabin from the outside air.

Meanwhile, the Russian malware continued working, feeding a new preplotted course into the airliner's automated pilot. Slowly, the huge

Kalmar Airlines 777 banked, turning southwest toward Estonia.

Inside the Finavia Air Traffic Control Center at Helsinki, one of the controllers saw the blip representing Kalmar Flight 851 veering off its filed flight plan. He keyed his mic: "Kalmar Eight-Five-One, Helsinki Approach, I show you three miles south of course. Fly heading two-eight-five, vectors to OKLOR intersection. Over."

There was only silence.

He repeated his order, more forcibly now. Again, there was no reply from the jetliner, which was now at least sixteen nautical miles off course. He heard nothing on the emergency radio frequency. Nor had its transponder codes been altered to indicate a possible hijacking, radio failure, or some other major problem.

The Finnish controller frowned. He punched the button to open the direct telephone line for his opposite number in Russia's St. Petersburg Control Center. "This is Helsinki Approach. Do you have radio contact with Kalmar Eight-Five-One?"

"Negative, Helsinki. We handed that flight off to you three minutes ago."

"I have no contact with Kalmar Eight-Five-One," the Finn said tersely. He checked his radar screen again. On its present course, the 777 was now roughly fifty nautical miles from the Estonian coast. "I am declaring an emergency. Better advise air defense. We might have a disabled or hijacked crew situation."

"Understood, Helsinki," the Russian said. "I will pass the word to my higher authority."

Two Su-27 fighters were on routine patrol over the Gulf of Finland, flying a lazy racetrack pattern at five thousand meters to conserve fuel and stay out of Finnish or Estonian airspace. Nominally, they were operating out this far in the highly unlikely event the Poles or their Baltic states allies launched a surprise, over-the-water air strike on St. Petersburg. In truth, this was just a show-the-flag exercise intended to flex Russian muscle over international waters near the Motherland's borders.

The only thing about this assignment either of the two fighter pilots appreciated was that it gave them a chance to get in a few flying hours. Otherwise, it seemed a tedious waste of time, fuel, and engine life-span.

Aboard the lead Su-27, Major Alexei Rykov tweaked his stick slightly to the right, beginning yet another gentle, curving turn. One more hour, he thought gloomily. One more hour spent endlessly looping around and around above the frigid waters of the gulf. Not that they could even see much of anything up here. The moon wouldn't rise for another two hours and a thick band of clouds stretched from horizon to horizon below them. Aside from a few tiny, blinking lights identifying commercial airliners crisscrossing the gulf and the Baltic region at high altitude, the two Russian fighters seemed to be all alone in a vast black sky.

"*Zamok Lead, this is Petrozavodsk Control,*" a voice crackled through his headphones.

"Control, this is Castle Lead. Go ahead," Rykov said. Petrozavodsk was their home airfield.

"*I have an emergency intercept mission for you, Castle,*" the controller said.

Rykov came fully awake, listening carefully. "Ready to copy," he responded.

"*Fly heading three-zero-zero, climb to eight thousand meters,*" the controller ordered. "*Your target is a Boeing triple-seven, Kalmar Airlines, not talking with controllers, range five-zero kilometers. Intercept, attempt contact with the flight crew, and turn it toward home base.*"

"Castle Lead copies. Castle?"

"*Two,*" his wingman replied immediately.

Rykov brought his Su-27 around in a tight, climbing turn—throttling up to increase speed as he soared toward eight thousand meters. The Kalmar wide-body appeared on his radar, about forty-five kilometers ahead. He locked on to it and peered ahead through his HUD. There, right where his steering cues pointed, he could see its red beacon flashing, tiny at this distance.

"Let's close as quickly as possible, Anatoly," he radioed his wingman. "That big mother out there is going to cross into Estonian airspace in a few minutes. And I don't want to be tagging along behind when it does."

"*Two,*" the other pilot replied. "*You don't think*

the Kurats *will give us a warm welcome?" Kurats* was the derogatory Russian slang for "Estonians."

Rykov grinned under his oxygen mask. "The only warm welcome we're likely to get from our Estonian friends would include a few heat-seeking missiles." He leveled out and accelerated smoothly, turning onto a heading that would bring him up behind the 777 jetliner.

"Well, they've got dick-all to do it with," his wingman scoffed. *"What can they send up? A few Czech-made training jets?"*

"Sure, but don't forget the Poles and the Lithuanians are backing them up with shiny, upgraded F-16s," Rykov pointed out. "So let's stay polite, okay, Anatoly?"

"Da, Lead," his wingman grumbled.

The two Su-27s streaked onward through the night sky. Rykov saw the flashing red beacon atop the Kalmar Airlines plane grow larger with astonishing rapidity. To avoid overshooting the big jet, he chopped back his throttles and started a flat scissors maneuver, banking back and forth across his line of flight, to shed excess airspeed.

Once that was done, he slid slowly up alongside the big airliner. His eyes narrowed, intently studying the 777 while flying just one hundred meters off its starboard wing. He moved ahead, now flying level with the airliner's cockpit. For a moment, he thought about trying to get close enough to look in through its windows and then dismissed the idea as far too risky. Instead, he flashed his navigation lights several times, trying to attract the attention of the pilots.

There was no response. The Kalmar Airlines jet kept flying southwest, straight and level at more than nine hundred kilometers per hour.

Frowning, Rykov keyed his mike. "Petrozavodsk, this is Castle Lead. We have intercepted the target. The 777's main passenger cabin interior lights are on. There are no signs of any obvious damage. Repeat. There are *no* signs of external damage. But I cannot see any movement aboard the aircraft and I have not been able to contact the flight crew."

"*Acknowledged, Castle,*" the controller said. There was a brief pause. "*Warning, Castle Lead. We show you only sixty seconds out from Estonian airspace at your present course and speed.*" Rykov bit down on a startled curse. Fixated on maneuvering so close to the enormous wide-body airliner without colliding, he'd completely lost track of his current position. "*Fly heading zero-six-zero, vectors for your refueling anchor.*"

"Acknowledged," Rykov said, rolling his Su-27 into a tight turn directly away from the lumbering 777. In less than a minute, the huge civilian aircraft was just a distant, flashing red speck—shrinking rapidly as the airliner flew steadily southwest toward Estonia.

"*What was that all about?*" his wingman radioed, sounding slightly shaken. "*How the hell does anyone lose control over a mother-humping mammoth that big?*"

Rykov shrugged. "I have absolutely no idea, Anatoly," he said, frowning. "Fortunately, it's no longer our problem."

AFN NORTHERN AIR OPERATIONS CENTER, KABATY WOODS, WARSAW
A short time later

The Kabaty Woods was a nature preserve on the southern outskirts of Warsaw, just a few kilometers southeast of the city's Chopin International Airport. Stands of century-old oak, maple, hornbeam, and linden trees intermingled with younger fruit trees. Wild boar, deer, and foxes roamed the woods.

The Northern Air Operations Center lay near the western edge of the park, surrounded by a wall topped with razor wire. A plaque honoring the Polish code breakers who had first cracked Nazi Germany's Enigma ciphers had been erected at the outer entrance. There were a few separate buildings on the surface, but most of the center was buried deep underground. Multiple levels housed command, intelligence analysis, and communications facilities dedicated to controlling air-defense operations in Poland and the Baltic states. A subordinate unit, the 21st Command and Guidance Center, was responsible for the defense of Warsaw itself.

Far below the surface lay the center's crowded combat operations room. Consoles fitted with radar displays, secure communications links, and computers were set on three stepped tiers facing a series of large screens. Officers and senior enlisted men from the Polish Air Force and its Baltic state allies manned these consoles around the clock.

Major General Czesław Madejski hurried into

combat operations, still knotting his tie. His gray hair was tousled. As deputy commander of the center, he had been pulling long duty shifts while his superiors were tied up at the AFN summit. "What's up, Reinis?"

Colonel Reinis Zariņš was a Latvian Air Force intelligence officer. He pointed to a map display showing the region from Finland to northern Poland. A long red line slanted southwest from a point just off Russia's Karelian coast. It ended in a blinking dot marked *KA851* about halfway across Estonia. More codes—*FL250*, *225*, and *490kts*—showed its tracked altitude, course, and speed. "Approximately twenty minutes ago, this Kalmar Airlines flight inexplicably departed its filed flight plan . . ."

Madejski listened closely to the Latvian's summary of recent events. When the colonel finished, he scowled. "And no one's been able to contact the flight crew or any of the passengers?"

"No, sir," Zariņš said. "Radio calls go unanswered. The airline says it's trying to call passengers using cell-phone numbers it has on record, but every call placed so far goes straight to voice mail."

The general rubbed at his unshaven jaw, studying the map. "Are we looking at a possible oxygen-system or pressurization failure?"

The Latvian nodded. "That would match the available evidence, sir. Although any problem must be internal—since the Russian pilots reported no signs of external damage or fuselage breach." He shrugged. "But even so, the pilots should have been able to use their own separate emergency oxygen bottles to stay conscious while diving toward a safe altitude."

"Which would mean one hell of a lot of things went wrong all at once," Madejski muttered.

"Yes, sir," Zarinš agreed bleakly. "Assuming a total failure of all pressurization and emergency air-supply systems, everyone aboard that 777 would be unconscious by now."

The general nodded. At twenty-five thousand feet, the time of useful consciousness without supplemental oxygen was somewhere around forty to sixty seconds. Death was not likely—climbers summited Mount Everest regularly above twenty-six thousand feet—but pilots certainly couldn't control their planes. Which implied the Kalmar Airlines jetliner was effectively a "zombie" flight—one doomed to fly along its present course until it ran out of fuel and fell out of the sky. He said as much to Zarinš.

"That seems likely, General," the Latvian concurred. He gestured at the display again. "That plane took off from Shanghai with a full load of fuel. Based on its track and speed, we estimate it will leave our airspace in minutes, cross the Baltic, traverse Germany, France, Spain, and Portugal . . . and then crash somewhere in the mid–South Atlantic in approximately eight hours."

"Those poor people," Madejski said heavily. He sighed. "We'd better pass the word to our opposite numbers in NATO. That 777 is going to hit German airspace in roughly fifty minutes."

"Sir!" one of the duty officers said suddenly.

"The aircraft is changing course! Look!" He pointed at the screen.

Madejski and Zarinš stood rooted in surprise as the Kalmar Airlines flight altered its heading from 225 degrees to 200 degrees, more south than southwest. The indicator showing its estimated altitude shifted from *FL250* to *FL245*. On its new heading, the jetliner would fly across Latvia, Lithuania, and cross the Polish frontier in just twenty-six minutes.

"Somebody must still be alive aboard that aircraft," the Polish Air Force general said grimly. "And in at least partial control."

"So it seems," Zarinš murmured. He turned to his superior. "We have two F-16s currently on combat air patrol over Warsaw, sir. Should I order them to make the intercept?"

Madejski frowned, running through his options. Then he shook his head. "No, Colonel. Not when there's a chance this is some sort of feint to draw away our fighter cover from the capital." He looked at the Latvian. "What do we have on alert status at Minsk Mazowiecki?"

"Two more F-16C Vipers," Zarinš said crisply. "The pilots are Colonel Kasperek and Captain Jaglieski."

Despite the gravity of the situation, Madejski smiled. Trust Pawel Kasperek to set a good example for his pilots by taking one of the most widely despised alert slots in the whole rotation. He swung toward the junior officer manning the closest console. "Connect me with Colonel Kasperek, Lieutenant."

"Yes, sir," the younger man said. He punched in a number on his secure phone. "This is the AOC Combat Operations, Colonel," he said tersely. "I have General Madejski on the line for you."

The general took the phone. "Pawel, this is Czesław. Listen. I need you and your wingman in the air. We have a crazy situation developing—"

Up on the big map display, the blinking dot identified as Kalmar Airlines Flight 851 crossed into Latvia.

CHAPTER 21

OVER POLAND
A short time later

Colonel Pawel Kasperek banked into a hard left turn, rolling onto a course that would bring him up behind Kalmar Flight 851. He strained against the g-forces he was pulling and shoved his throttles higher to avoid bleeding off too much airspeed in the turn.

The computer-generated navigation cue he was following slid fast toward the center of his HUD. He rolled back right, leveling out. There, about seven kilometers ahead, he could see the wide-body jet's flashing red top beacon and the red and green navigation lights on its port and starboard wings. Numbers glowing on his HUD showed that the airliner was at 7,000 meters. But it was descending at a rate of around 400 meters per minute. The 777's speed had also increased to more than five hundred knots.

"Air Operations Center, this is Tiger Lead," Kasperek said into his mic. "I have a visual on Flight Eight-Five-One."

"Center to Tiger Lead," he heard Major General Madejski say. *"You are cleared to approach with caution."*

"Acknowledged, Center," Kasperek said. He radioed his wingman. "Hang back and cover me, Tomasz."

Jaglieski sounded surprised. *"Two."* Then: *"You think that 777 is a bandit? An enemy?"*

"I don't know," Kasperek admitted. His mouth tightened to a thin line. "All I know is that something must be very wrong aboard that aircraft. If the passengers and crew are all dead or incapacitated, it should not be maneuvering. And if someone is still alive on board, why haven't they responded to anyone who's tried to contact them?"

"Copy," his wingman said. *"Very well, Lead, Two's in trail."*

Gently, Kasperek pushed his throttle forward, boosting power from the F-16's GE-F110 turbofan engine. His airspeed climbed from five hundred to six hundred knots. He wanted to overtake the big passenger jet, not zip past it without being able to see anything.

When he got closer, he began shedding velocity, gradually matching speed with the enormous civilian airliner. Two hundred meters off the 777's huge port wing and still moving a few knots faster, he began sliding in—drifting closer and closer to the other aircraft, but always ready to break away at the first sign of danger.

One hundred meters. Kasperek was coming level with the airliner's cockpit. He shed a little more speed, trying to match that of the 777. Sweating now under his oxygen mask and helmet, he tweaked the stick a tiny bit to the right. Eighty meters. Sixty meters. He leveled out again, now just fifty meters off the bigger jet's nose. The cockpit windows were dark. Darker, he thought, than they should be. Up this close, he should be able to see the glow from instrument panels and displays. But there was nothing.

He tried repeatedly flashing his navigation lights, hoping to draw some response. This close, his F-16 must be visible to anyone in the cockpit or anywhere on the huge aircraft's port side. He craned his head around, watching closely for any sign of movement in the windows.

Nothing.

The 777 flew straight on, deeper into Polish territory, and gradually losing altitude.

"Center, this is Tiger Lead," Kasperek said into his mic. "No joy on contact. I see no signs of life aboard Flight Eight-Five-One." He thought for a moment. What else could he try? "Recommend I make a close pass across the aircraft's nose to try to shake them awake—assuming anyone aboard is still alive."

For several more seconds, there was silence. Then Madejski said, *Very well, Tiger Lead. Your recommendation is approved.*

Kasperek broke away from the larger jet, separating to a safe distance. Then he pulled back on the stick, throttling up at the same time. His

F-16 climbed fast, soaring well above the 777. He craned his head around to the right, keeping his eyes on the big jetliner. With one gloved hand, he set his countermeasures system so that it would dispense flares only.

His eyes narrowed as he focused all of his mental energy on lightning-fast estimates of angles and relative velocities.

Now.

Pawel Kasperek yanked the F-16 to the right and dove—slashing down out of the night sky just ahead of the big passenger jet. White-hot magnesium flares spun away behind his fighter, briefly turning the night as bright as day. Tumbling through the air in his wake, they formed a rippling curtain of fire directly across the path of the oncoming airliner.

The 777 lumbered on as though nothing had happened.

Kalmar Airlines Flight 851 was now just 120 kilometers from Warsaw.

NORTHERN AIR OPERATIONS CENTER
That same time

Captain Jerzy Konarski manned one of the consoles in the crowded Combat Operations Center. The radio transmissions from the two F-16s crackled through his headset, but more as background noise than anything else. Colonel Kasperek and his wingman were engaged in a local intercept. His own responsibilities tonight were broader, more operational than tactical.

Konarski's job was monitoring the readiness status of the MiG-29 and F-16 fighter squadrons deployed to three of Poland's most important air bases—Malbork, Minsk Mazowiecki, and Łask. To aid him in this task, he had secure computer and phone links to each squadron and base.

His console LCD showed a map of Poland. Graphic tags attached to each base showed the number of aircraft on alert, a number that had doubled in the past several minutes due to the orders he'd relayed. Counting the fighters already on combat air patrol over Warsaw, nearly a quarter of Poland's most modern interceptors were now manned and ready to take off at five minutes' notice. He tapped a key, sending this information to the main map display.

Konarski sat back in his seat, free for a bit to pay more attention to the aerial drama taking place about one hundred kilometers north-northeast of the underground operations center.

"The 777 has altered course very slightly," he heard one of the F-16 pilots say. *"Its new heading is two-zero-four degrees. The aircraft is still descending at four hundred meters per minute. We'll be in the cloud layer very soon."*

That was odd, Konarski thought. Since departing from its filed flight plan, Flight 851 had only changed its heading once. Why would it do so again now? Curious, he leaned forward again. His fingers danced across his keyboard, opening a program that would project the jetliner's currently plotted track out into the future. A red line appeared on his map display. It slanted south-southwest straight through the heart of Warsaw.

Suddenly dry-mouthed, he entered the 777's observed rate of descent. The red line abruptly shortened. It ended in a blinking red cross tagged *Altitude 0*. Hastily, the young Polish Air Force officer toggled the controls of his display, zooming in on the projected impact site.

Konarski felt the blood drain from his face.

Flight 851 was currently on course to crash into Warsaw's Presidential Palace. If nothing changed, the huge wide-body jet was going to slam with enormous explosive force directly into the building where President Wilk and the other top leaders of the Alliance of Free Nations were gathered. His computer displayed one more horrifying result of its calculations: *Estimated Time to Impact—7 minutes, 25 seconds.*

With shaking hands, Konarski scooped up the red emergency alert phone. "I need to speak to Major General Madejski. Now!"

PRESIDENTIAL PALACE, WARSAW
That same time

President Piotr Wilk fought hard to maintain his composure. The trouble with most politicians, he thought, was that they instinctively loved the sound of their own voices. No matter how urgent the crisis, or how serious the situation, too many of his peers seemed to believe the same rhetorical skills that had carried them to political victory could be applied to questions of military strategy and tactics. It was as though they believed Winston Churchill's magnificent speeches played a bigger role in the defeat of Nazi Germany than did the RAF, the 8th Air Force, and George S. Patton's 3rd Army.

So far they'd spent hours wrangling over how to respond to Russia's escalating cyberwar offensive. While most members of the alliance agreed they needed to do *something*, there was no consensus on what that something might be. No one, not even Wilk, believed Gryzlov's armed forces could be defeated in any open conventional war. Even with support from Scion and the Iron Wolf Squadron, the best they could hope to achieve was a costly stalemate. Nor did pursuing a diplomatic path, whether through the United Nations or some other international forum, look any more promising. Without more evidence of direct Russian responsibility, no other major power wanted to risk getting pulled into a clash between Moscow and its smaller neighbors to the west.

In fact, Wilk thought bitterly, if Martindale's sources inside the U.S. intelligence community were right, President Barbeau had already decided to stand aside—no matter what happened in Europe. Her only interest now seemed to lie in strengthening America's own cyberwar capabilities. He was sure Barbeau would come to regret this shortsighted, isolationist policy, but by then it might be too late for Poland and her beleaguered allies.

Grimacing inwardly, he forced himself to set aside his impatience and pessimism. If nothing else, no one had yet proposed yielding to Moscow's thinly disguised ultimatums. Already the member states of Alliance of Free Nations had shown more resolve than Gennadiy Gryzlov could have anticipated when he launched his secret war. Refusing to surrender might not amount to much, but every passing day bought more time to strengthen their cyberwar defenses.

So far, they'd stopped one intended Russian attack. Polish and Scion CERT teams had found several pieces of suspicious malware in water treatment plants around the AFN—neutralizing them before they could dump dangerous levels of chemicals into the water supply. But while that was a victory, it was a victory they had to keep secret. No one wanted to encourage any more panic by revealing how close Moscow had come to contaminating the drinking-water supplies for millions.

Kevin Martindale, of course ever suspicious, had another theory. "I think we were *meant* to discover those cyberweapons," the American had said quietly. "It's another means of upping the pressure on us without causing so many civilian casualties that the U.S. or other NATO powers feel compelled to intervene. Gryzlov wants us to know that he could make things worse if we don't fold soon—much worse."

That was possible, Wilk thought, though it seemed excessively Machiavellian even by Gennadiy Gryzlov's standards. What was certain was that standing entirely on the defensive was a recipe for eventual defeat. No matter how many cyber attacks their improved defenses parried, the Russians were bound to find weaknesses they could exploit. In a one-sided war of this kind, the attacker held all the cards.

Some of the other AFN leaders knew this too.

"There must be a way we can hit back at the Russians," Sven Kalda, the prime minister of Estonia, said heatedly. "If not openly, then covertly—using cyberweapons of our own." He stared pointedly at Martindale. "I have heard your arguments urging caution in the past. And I understand them. But there comes a time when inaction is more dangerous than action. We have all contributed significant resources to hire Scion's military and technical experts. Well, I think it is high time Mr. Martindale and his people began earning their keep."

Martindale stirred in his seat. He frowned. "With respect, Mr. Prime Minister," he began. "I want to fight back just as much as anyone else in this room, but—"

Suddenly the huge doors at the far end of the Blue Hall burst open—smashed inward by a large, human-shaped robot. Striding on deceptively spindly-looking legs, the gray-and-black Cybernetic Infantry Device strode fast toward the conference table. A second Iron Wolf fighting machine followed the first.

For a moment, there was only stunned, absolute silence.

Wilk jumped to his feet. Down the corridor behind the two CIDs, he could see two of Major Stepniak's BOR agents staggering groggily back to their feet. They must have tried to stop the Iron Wolf robots from breaking in. His jaw tightened. This interruption was a direct violation of his orders.

"You must evacuate this building, Mr. President!" the eerie, synthesized voice of the first war robot said. "Now!"

"CID One is right, sir," the second machine, the one piloted by Charlie Turlock, said quickly. "We've been monitoring a fast-developing situation. It's urgent that we get you all out ASAP."

Around the Blue Hall, a clamor of voices rose, as prime ministers, defense chiefs, and other leaders protested this sudden, unauthorized, and seemingly senseless intrusion into their summit. They got to their feet, each talking louder and louder in a futile bid to be heard amid the turmoil.

Wilk's phone buzzed sharply, signaling an incoming Priority One call from Major General Madejski at the Air Operations Center. He answered it curtly. "Yes? What's the situation, Czesław?"

His face lengthened as Madejski rapidly summarized the emergency. "How long do we have?" Wilk demanded.

"The hijacked plane is now only four minutes out," the deputy air defense commander told him.

"Very well. Patch me through to Colonel Kasperek," Wilk ordered. He lowered the phone for a moment, filled his lungs, and then roared. "Quiet! Everyone shut up!" Into the sudden shocked silence, he said, "Our metal friends are right. We must evacuate. Immediately." Turning to Major Stepniak, he snapped, "Contact the troops outside. I want armored personnel carriers at all the palace exits at once. Cram as many people inside them as you can!"

Slowly at first and then faster, the worried-looking AFN leaders began filing out through the shattered doors, shepherded by the two enormous CIDs. Wilk moved with them, surrounded by Stepniak and his other BOR bodyguards. The younger McLanahan, Nadia Rozek, Martindale, and Whack Macomber were right behind him.

His phone buzzed again. *"Colonel Kasperek here,"* Wilk heard the young air-force officer say, through a buzz of static and the roar from his F-16's engine.

"Listen to me carefully, Pawel," Wilk said, making an effort to speak with precision and care while he hurried toward the nearest exit, moving in a sea of increasingly frightened politicians and senior aides. The word that they were in imminent peril was spreading fast through the crowd. "I order you to shoot that aircraft down. Immediately." For a second there was nothing but static-filled silence. "Do you understand your orders, Colonel?" Wilk asked sharply.

"Sir, if that 777 has been hijacked, there may be more than a hundred innocent people aboard, all of them citizens of other nations," Kasperek protested.

"And even if they are already dead, we're over War-saw's outer suburbs. Shooting it down now may cost dozens of lives on the ground."

"I'm well aware of the risks, Pawel," Wilk said grimly, cutting the F-16 pilot short. "I take full responsibility for this decision. Now carry out your orders. Destroy Flight 851 *now*! Before it is too late!"

OVER THE OUTSKIRTS OF WARSAW
That same time

Sick at heart, Colonel Pawel Kasperek rolled his F-16 Viper in behind the Kalmar Airlines 777, at least according to the radar steering cues fed to his HUD. They were descending through a thick layer of cloud, so right now the sky outside his cockpit was nothing but a dark, roiling blur.

He held the toggle switch on the right side of his stick, selecting his AIM-9X Sidewinder heat-seeking missiles. That wide-body jet two kilometers ahead in this swirling, blinding sea of water vapor was so big that one missile hit might not be enough to bring it down in time. In his headphones, he heard the warbling tone that indicated the first missile he'd selected was locked on target.

His F-16 broke out of the clouds and into clear air. The red beacon on top of the 777 was still rotating, flashing rhythmically in the darkness. Beyond the big passenger jet, Kasperek could see the glowing lights of Warsaw looming ahead.

He swallowed hard, knowing he might be about

to kill more than a hundred innocents. What if they were all wrong about what was happening aboard that airliner? What if the pilots or others aboard were just trying desperately to land safely somewhere? Reluctantly, his gloved finger hovered over the weapons release button. "*Zdrowas Mario, laskis pelna Pan z Toba . . .*" he murmured, repeating the words he'd learned by heart as a child. "Hail Mary, full of Grace, the Lord is with thee . . ."

But then, before Kasperek could fire, the huge jetliner suddenly dove—plunging toward the darkened ground now less than two thousand meters below. "*Co u diabła . . .* what in *hell . . .* ?" He mashed the mic button: "Control . . . Mr. President, that airliner appears to be in a steep dive!"

"*Good work, Pawel,*" Wilk radioed. "*It was for the best, believe me. We had no other choice.*"

"But, sir, I did not fire on it!" Kasperek shouted into his oxygen mask, his eyes bulging in horror. "I did not launch! The airliner suddenly started a dive!"

"*Is there any sign that it is trying to recover?*" Wilk radioed breathlessly after a short pause. "*Is it out of control? Is it damaged?*"

"I see no smoke or fire!" Kasperek responded. "I see no—"

Still moving at high speed, the 777 plowed nose first into a patch of farmland and smashed on through a thin belt of woodland—shedding engines, wings, and torn pieces of fuselage as it cartwheeled across the earth in a searing cloud of flame.

"Oh my God," Kasperek said softly, appalled by what he'd just witnessed. He banked into a hard, rolling turn, fighting against the high g-forces he was pulling in order to get a clearer view of the crash site.

The mangled wreckage of Kalmar Airlines Flight 851 had come to rest in what looked like a shallow, industrial pond not far from several large commercial buildings. Fires fed by burning jet fuel danced across the impact-torn ground and among the torn and splintered trees. More flames, smoke, and steam boiled away from the crumpled fuselage lying half buried in water and mud.

Colonel Pawel Kasperek was sure of one thing. No one could possibly have survived that crash.

CHAPTER 22

Brad McLanahan sat tight while Piotr Wilk's W-3 Sokół VIP helicopter orbited low over the crash site and then leveled out, coming in to land not far from the tangled, still-burning wreckage of the doomed airliner. Flashing red, blue, and white lights lit the darkness in all directions. Fire trucks, police cars, and other emergency vehicles were parked almost at random across the surrounding fields. More were arriving along every road. Crews in protective suits were spraying fire-retardant foam across the wreckage. Searing heat waves rippled across the scarred fields. Jet fuel burned at nearly eighteen hundred degrees Fahrenheit.

Where the fires were out, dozens of other first responders moved cautiously across fields strewn with gruesome debris—looking for any signs of life or clues that could shed light on this disaster. Bright camera lights showed that television news crews were busy broadcasting breathless reports to a horrified world.

For a split second, looking down from the air, Brad was reminded of the time he and a childhood friend had lobbed a firecracker onto a large anthill. When the wisp of smoke drifted away, they'd watched hundreds of ants silently milling about in apparent confusion. In an eerie way, this bustling, frenetic scene looked much the same.

Their helicopter touched down.

Led by Major Dariusz Stepniak, four BOR agents slid the side doors back and jumped down. Cradling Radon MSBS-5.56B short-barreled assault carbines, they fanned out to cover Piotr Wilk as he climbed out of the helicopter. Instantly, all the chaos and noise from outside rushed in—the sounds of roaring flames, static-laden radio transmissions, shouted orders and questions, and wailing sirens. And just as suddenly the whole scene came back into focus for Brad. This was all real.

Nothing in his days as a Civil Air Patrol cadet had prepared him for the scope of this disaster. As gruesome as it had been, finding the wreckage of a small private plane could not compare to seeing the slaughterhouse left by the crash of a huge commercial jet carrying nearly two hundred passengers.

Brad, Nadia, Macomber, and Martindale followed the Polish president as he and his bodyguards hurried across to a temporary command center set up near one of the fire trucks. Several men and women were gathered around a pair of folding tables and chairs, manning laptop computers or issuing orders via cell phone and walkie-talkie. One of them, a burly man in a heavy winter coat, greeted Wilk with a nod. "Mr. President, my name is Mariusz Brodski. I'm the senior investigator on scene for PKBWL."

PKBWL was the Polish acronym for its government aircraft-accident investigative agency—the equivalent of America's National Transportation Safety Board.

"I assume the news is bad," Wilk said grimly.

"Yes, it is," Brodski agreed. "We have not found any survivors from Flight Eight-Five-One." He indicated the burning wreckage scattered over several hundred meters. "Nor will we, I fear. The impact was too violent. It would require a miracle for any passenger or member of the crew to live through such an accident."

Wilk nodded. "From Colonel Kasperek's reports, I expected as much." He braced himself, obviously expecting more bad tidings. "How many casualties were there on the ground?"

"None, by great good fortune," Brodski reported, almost in disbelief. He pointed north, where twinkling lights marked a small town. "If that 777 had crashed even a few seconds earlier, it would have torn right through the center of Radzymin, killing and injuring hundreds of our people."

Brad whistled under his breath. "So there's the miracle for tonight." He saw Nadia and the others nodding in agreement.

"It appears so, Captain McLanahan," Wilk said. He turned back to Brodski. "Have your teams found the jet's black boxes yet?"

The larger man shook his head. "Not as yet. Once all the fires are out, my investigators will begin probing what remains of its fuselage. We will also drag the pond." He grimaced. "I have reviewed the radar data. It tells us very little. We will need whatever information remains intact on the flight recorders to have any serious hope of learning how this accident occurred."

Brad and the others nodded their understanding. The 777's black boxes, if they were still intact, could provide them with everything from cockpit voice recordings to instrument readings. Without that kind of data, it was highly unlikely they would ever definitively zero in on what went wrong aboard the Kalmar Airlines flight. Given how long it had flown without apparent difficulty, engine problems could be largely ruled out—as could avionics trouble. Unfortunately, that left a wide range of other possibilities, many of which would be virtually undetectable in the midst of so much impact and fire damage.

"I will make sure you have every resource you need," Wilk told Brodski. His expression was bitter. "One thing is clear to me. This terrible incident was no accident. It was very carefully arranged."

"By the Russians," Martindale said flatly.

"Yes," Wilk agreed. He shrugged. "Only a fool would assume random chance, considering how precisely this airliner was targeted on our summit."

Brad thought about that. The Polish leader's

suspicions made sense. No decent human being would turn a passenger jet into a weapon. Unfortunately, Gennadiy Gryzlov had never shown the slightest ounce of human decency. But then why had the hijacked airliner crashed short of its intended target? For that matter, where would Russia's leader find men or women willing to kill themselves on his behalf? More Chechens? Maybe a thorough probe of Flight 851's passenger and crew manifest would turn something up.

Major Stepniak moved closer to Wilk. The BOR commander looked worried. "I understand your need to see this crash site for yourself, sir," he said. "But we should go. And go *now*."

Wilk raised an eyebrow. "Why is that, Dariusz?" He gestured to the burning wreckage. "Whatever further evil Gryzlov intended is moot at this point." He patted the bulky body armor the major had insisted he don in the helicopter on the way out. "Besides, I'm wearing this contraption, aren't I?"

"The situation here is too uncontrolled," Stepniak said stubbornly. "Which makes it too dangerous. Anyone could be here in the middle of so much chaos. And with just four men, I cannot possibly establish an effective security perimeter."

To his surprise, Brad found himself silently agreeing with the major. There was something weird about this, he thought. If the Russians had somehow electronically hijacked the Kalmar Airlines flight, there was no good reason for it to have crashed so suddenly—still more than twelve miles from its intended target. What was it that his father had said once, during some long-ago hike or camping trip? *Oh yeah*. "Sure, the enemy may screw up from time to time, but that's never the safe way to bet," he muttered. "The thoughts of Chairman McLanahan."

Nadia was the only one who heard him. She nodded tightly, appearing as worried as Stepniak. Then she looked around, focusing her attention first on the crash site itself and then on the surrounding fields, woods, and buildings. From the cold, determined expression on her face, Brad guessed she was suddenly evaluating the scene as a potential battlefield.

"I think Major Stepniak's caution is justified," she told Wilk, still scanning their surroundings. "You should return to Warsaw, Mr. President."

The major nodded gratefully to her. He moved even closer to Wilk. "Please, sir, come back to the heli—"

Abruptly, Stepniak was thrown forward in a spray of blood and shattered bone—hurled against Piotr Wilk by the impact of a high-caliber bullet directly between his shoulder blades. Both men went down in a heap.

Crack!

In rapid succession, more shots rang out. Hit squarely by sniper rounds, two more BOR agents toppled, already dead or dying.

For a split second, Brad stood frozen, shocked into immobility. Then Nadia knocked him off his feet. She dropped flat beside him, hugging the frozen ground. "Shit," she snarled, in English. "This is an ambush, not an accident."

Macomber and Martindale were prone not far away. Caught completely by surprise, Brodski and the other accident investigators stood rooted in horror. The last surviving BOR agents scrambled toward Wilk and Stepniak. They knelt beside the downed men. One of them swung round. "The president is still alive!" he snapped. "We need to pull him out of here."

A blinding flash outlined one of the ground-floor windows in a solidly built brick-and-cement building about two hundred meters away.

"Down!" Nadia yelled. She buried her face in the earth. So did Brad.

A rocket-propelled grenade streaked out of the darkness and slammed into Wilk's Sokół heli-copter. It exploded, torn apart in a huge ball of orange-and-red flame. Twisted pieces of rotor and torn fuselage flew outward from the center of the blast. One large, razor-sharp chunk of shrapnel decapitated a kneeling BOR agent. Smaller frag-ments ripped right through the other bodyguard's chest and torso. He flopped backward, bleeding out in seconds from several horrific wounds.

"Jesus," Brad muttered, taking it all in. Stepniak and his men were dead. Most of the Polish acci-dent investigators were down too—either killed or wounded when the helicopter blew up. All across the crash site, policemen and emergency crews scattered, bolting for cover as high-caliber rifle rounds smashed windshields and thwacked into bodies. Terrified screams rose above the crackle of flames and wail of sirens.

"We can't stay here!" Nadia said through gritted teeth. "This is a kill zone! We have to find cover."

Macomber nodded. "I'm on it!" The big American leaped to his feet and raced toward the nearest vehicle, a midsize red Volvo fire engine. Despite his size, he moved like the wind, dodging from side to side to throw off the aim of any sniper trying to nail him. Without slowing down, he threw himself up and into the driver's seat.

Another bullet blew out the Volvo's rear cab windows, spraying pieces of safety glass in all directions. Macomber threw the fire engine into gear. The red truck lurched forward, rolling between them and the enemy-occupied buildings.

More bullets smashed into the moving vehicle. Some hit the water tank. Other rounds ricocheted off the engine block, tumbling away trailing sparks.

Satisfied that he'd blocked the line of fire, Whack dropped out of the Volvo's bullet-riddled cab and sped back toward Brad and the others. He threw himself flat as a second RPG round blew the front of the fire engine into a blazing wreck. Smoke billowed skyward, thickening as the flames fed on diesel fuel and lubricating oil.

"That is their first mistake," Nadia said. She bared her teeth in a cold, deadly smile. "May it not be their last."

Brad nodded. Between the flames and the smoke pouring off the wrecked vehicle, the shooters out there were going to find it difficult to spot them using either night-vision gear or thermal sights.

Staying low, he and Nadia quickly worked

their way over to Martindale and Macomber. The two older men were kneeling beside Piotr Wilk. Whack glanced at them. "He's unconscious, but breathing. There's no blood. His armor must have deflected the bullet after it punched through Stepniak."

Brad breathed out, hugely relieved. Everyone knew that the gutsy Polish president was the linchpin of the whole Alliance of Free Nations. If he were killed, the coalition would likely fragment under continued Russian pressure. And without its allies, there was no way Poland or the Iron Wolf Squadron could hold off an all-out ground or air offensive launched by Moscow. Bowing to Russia's demands would have been the only realistic option. Which was undoubtedly that bastard Gryzlov's plan, he realized. He felt sick. Somehow Gryzlov had orchestrated the cold-blooded murder of well over a hundred people aboard that doomed 777— all as part of a complex scheme to lure Wilk out into the open where assassins could nail him.

"Drag the president into better cover," Nadia ordered. She nodded toward the cluster of police cars and other emergency vehicles scattered across the farm fields behind them. Bodies littered the frozen soil around them, but the vehicles provided more places to go to ground while waiting for rescue. "Then contact Major General Domanski. Make sure he understands the situation and has his reaction force on the move."

Macomber nodded. Domanski was the Polish Land Forces commander responsible for security around the Presidential Palace. He'd organized a battalion-size task force of tanks, mechanized infantry in armored personnel carriers, and helicopters as a backup for the other troops deployed on guard duty. It would take time to get Domanski's troops out here, but the sooner they were alerted, the better. "Okay, that makes sense," he said. "But what are *you* planning to do in the meantime?"

She reached across one of the dead BOR agents and picked up his Polish-made assault carbine. "I am going hunting, Major Macomber."

Brad grabbed a second weapon. "Me too," he said firmly.

Whack frowned. "Well, hell," he muttered. "I can't let you have all the fun, Major Rozek." His eyes narrowed. "Brad, you'd best go with Mr. Martindale instead. Help him get Wilk to safety."

Nadia shook her head. "Saving the president is our top priority. His life is not expendable. Until Domanski's troops arrive, he needs the best protection available. And that means you," she told Macomber.

Whack scowled. "Are you saying that you two are expendable?"

"Not if I can help it, Major," Nadia said with a wry smile. "But while I am willing to risk my life to capture or kill these assassins, I am not willing to risk that of my nation's leader." She reached out and put a hand on Brad's shoulder. "We will do what must be done."

More shots rang out above the wail of sirens and the moans of the wounded. Using vehicles as cover, some of the police were firing back at the nearby buildings. Unfortunately, their service-issue pistols and shotguns were no match in range, accuracy, or firepower for the weapons being used by the enemy. Snipers were picking off the out-gunned police one by one.

"Much as I admire all this 'after you, Alphonse. No, after you, Gaston' one-upmanship, we'd better start moving," Martindale said shakily. For once, the former president looked his age and more. He wasn't used to finding himself on the sharp end of combat situations.

Reluctantly, Macomber nodded. He looked at Brad. "If you get yourself killed, just make sure it wasn't because you did something stupid, okay? Because God only knows how I'd explain that to your dad."

Brad lowered his head, trying to hide the sorrow he felt. In his heart, he suspected his father now saw him—and all the other humans around him—more as tools or weapons to be employed in a struggle against Gennadiy Gryzlov and his regime. Did the man trapped inside the machine even remember that he had a son?

NEAR THE PRESIDENTIAL PALACE, WARSAW
That same time

Riding inside the cockpit of Wolf Two, Charlie Turlock frowned, listening to the confused radio chatter streaming across local police and fire frequencies. While her CID's computer provided a running, simultaneous translation to English, it couldn't untangle fragmentary and often contradictory reports. Every circuit was jammed with voices yelling about exploding helicopters, frantic calls for medical help, and reports that shots were being fired.

She scanned her displays. Nothing bad was happening in her immediate area. Before he left for the Flight 851 crash site, Whack Macomber had ordered her to escort one of the convoys of armored personnel carriers evacuating AFN leaders from the palace. Right now those Polish troop carriers were unloading their high-ranking passengers outside the postmodern University of Warsaw Library building, about five hundred meters east of the palace. Heavily armed soldiers and police were on hand to guide the assorted prime ministers, cabinet officials, and aides inside.

With a twitch of a finger, Charlie ordered her CID to switch to the channel she used to communicate with Brad McLanahan. "Wolf Two to Wolf External, report your status."

There was no reply. Nothing but the hiss and crackle of static.

That wasn't really surprising, she told herself. The Kalmar Airlines plane had gone down almost twenty kilometers from her current location. Half of Warsaw lay between them, so Brad's small tactical radio probably couldn't pick up her signal through all the interference.

Nevertheless, she was getting really worried. Confusing as they were, the emergency transmissions she was hearing suggested something really bad was going down at that crash site. She opened another channel, this one a direct link to Major General Milosz Domanski. "Wolf Two to Watchman Six Actual."

Domanski replied at once. *"Watchman Six Actual. Go ahead, Wolf Two."*

"Submit I redeploy immediately to the Eight-Five-One crash site," Charlie suggested.

"Negative," Domanski said flatly. *"Without weapons, your intervention might be futile. Besides, my troops are already assembling. I will have transport helicopters en route to the scene in fifteen minutes."*

Charlie thought about protesting his order. Domanski was one of the best young commanders in Poland's ground forces—bold, highly intelligent, and a daring leader. But no one except those trained to fight them could really appreciate what a Cybernetic Infantry Device could do, even without normal weapons. She resisted the temptation. The Polish military officer had a lot on his plate right now. The last thing he needed was a protracted debate with a foreign subordinate.

"Very well, Watchman," she said. "CID One and I will continue our current escort assignments."

Patrick McLanahan's CID was guard-dogging another convoy—this one heading farther south to the solidly built Fryderyk Chopin University of Music. Since she was supposed to be keeping an eye on Brad's increasingly erratic father, Charlie hadn't been too happy about that. In the situation, though, the separation had made tactical sense. Their CIDs' sophisticated sensor arrays could give the Polish soldiers guarding each column of evacuees extra warning of any attack—just in case Gryzlov had anything else up his sleeve besides trying to slam a passenger jet into the Presidential Palace.

She frowned. It looked increasingly like they were right to worry about what more the ruthless Russian leader was up to. Unfortunately, it also seemed that they'd seriously misjudged his real plan.

Domanski's irritated voice broke into her thoughts. *"I concur, Two. But perhaps you should pass my order to your comrade! He has abandoned his post!"*

"Excuse me?" Charlie said in surprise.

"Police units guarding the Śląsko-Dąbrowski Bridge are reporting that a 'devil machine' just broke through their cordon. It is racing west across the bridge at high speed," the Polish general snapped. *"Where exactly is that robot of yours going, Wolf Two?"*

Swearing under her breath, Charlie zoomed in on her tactical display. The blip representing Patrick McLanahan's CID was right where it should be, guarding a major road junction near the music school—more than a kilometer south of the bridge Domanski was talking about. For a split second, she relaxed. But then her eyes narrowed. Why wasn't that blip moving? The general's robot should be prowling the whole area around the evacuation center, sweeping every possible avenue of attack with its sensors.

Even as Charlie watched, the blip faded and disappeared. "Oh, you clever boy," she murmured unwillingly. Somehow, Patrick must have managed to hack into her system, substituting a sensor "ghost" in place of the genuine position data his computer was supposed to be feeding to her through their secure link. And now the link was down, cut off on his end.

"CID One, this is Wolf Two," she radioed. "What the hell are you up to?"

Nothing.

Oh, shit, Charlie thought. The general must have been monitoring the same frantic radio signals from the crash site. And he'd decided to intervene—orders or no orders. She switched back to Domanski's frequency. "Watchman, this is Wolf Two. CID One is acting on his own initiative. His actions are totally unauthorized."

While speaking, she turned and started running toward the bridge—dodging oncoming trams, buses, and cars with unnatural grace. Soldiers, policemen, and civilian gawkers lining the street stared in openmouthed amazement as her Iron Wolf robot sprinted past them at high speed.

"Should I order my forces to stop this machine?" Domanski demanded.

"Negative, Watchman!" Charlie shot back. "That's my job. I am in pursuit. Wolf Two out!"

CHAPTER 23

NEAR RADZYMIN
A short time later

With the Radon assault carbine she'd picked up tucked securely against her right shoulder, Nadia Rozek ghosted ahead down a row of snow-dusted fir trees. Moving as quietly as he could, Brad McLanahan followed in her wake. Not far ahead, through a gap in the tree line, he could see what looked like a warehouse or maybe some kind of factory building. Several minutes and several hundred meters after breaking away from the crash site, they were coming up on the eastern flank of the small industrial complex occupied by Gryzlov's assassins.

As soon as Martindale and Whack dragged Piotr Wilk into cover among the bullet-riddled police and fire vehicles, Brad and Nadia had made their own move. There was only one other way out of the kill zone set up by the Russians—a frantic dash through the wreckage of the downed 777. For what seemed an eternity, they'd dodged and twisted through a smoke-filled hell strewn with jagged, burning metal, smashed passenger seats, torn suitcases and carry-on bags . . . and smoldering, horrifically mangled bodies.

Brad swallowed hard against the sour, acid taste of bile. *Keep it together,* he told himself. This was no time to dwell on the horrors they'd witnessed.

Nadia dropped to one knee, close to the trunk of one of the fir trees. She waved him up to join her.

"See anything?" he whispered.

She shook her head. "No. But unless they are complete fools, they must have someone guarding this approach."

"Maybe they've bugged out already?"

A flash lit the sky to the northwest, followed by the dull *WHUMMP* of an explosion. The would-be assassins had fired another RPG round.

"Or not," Brad allowed.

Cautiously, he peered out from under the overhanging branches. There, about fifty meters ahead, he could see the building they'd been moving toward. There were no windows on this side. Beyond it was another industrial-looking structure, with a paved opening between them.

Thinking fast, and trying to remember what he'd seen from Wilk's helicopter when they flew in earlier, Brad sketched out a rough map in the dirt. They were on the east side of a complex made up of several buildings. Two, including the one nearest to them, overlooked the crash site. Other buildings formed a rough square, crisscrossed by several roads. He thought he remembered seeing several big trucks and smaller cars parked behind the building most likely to be occupied by Gryzlov's killers. The road they could see from here ran straight to that lot.

Nadia leaned closer, studying his crude sketch. She nodded and then scratched an X near the parking lot he'd identified. "That is where I would post my sentry," she said. "Guarding my escape vehicles while also covering this exposed flank."

Brad raised an eyebrow. "Just one guy?"

She shrugged. "I do not think this is a large force. No more than four or five men total perhaps. Certainly no more than six."

"Based on what?" he asked, more curious than skeptical. Over the past year, he'd trained some for ground combat, but this was Nadia's special province far more than it was his.

"I counted the shots," she said with a slight smile. "I do not believe there were ever more than three or four men firing at us."

"And if you're wrong?" Brad countered. "If we're up against like ten guys?"

"Then we are going to die," Nadia said, very seriously. She shrugged. "The odds are bad enough as it is, even if I am right."

"Yeah," Brad murmured, looking down at his rough map. As it was, they were going up against a force of heavily armed, hardened Russian assassins—with a total of two 5.56mm assault carbines and sixty rounds of ammunition between them. "You sure we shouldn't wait for backup?" he asked.

"I wish we could," Nadia said. "But I fear the enemy will be long gone before help can arrive. These men are professionals, not half-trained terrorists."

He nodded. This Russian scheme was too elaborate for its creators to have overlooked the need for an escape plan. He was willing to bet the assassins had people in position to warn them as soon as a serious Polish reaction force started heading this way. Trying to find them, once they slipped away into the surrounding towns and suburbs or into Warsaw itself, would be like hunting barehanded for a needle in a haystack—as long as you assumed the needle was both mobile and poison-tipped. "Too bad we don't have more firepower," he grumbled.

"That is a problem," Nadia agreed. "But I may have a solution." Setting her carbine down, she scrabbled around in the dirt for a moment. "There we go!" she said, holding up her finds. She sounded pleased.

Brad looked down in dismay. He looked back up. "A couple of rocks? You're seriously proposing we go after the bad guys using *rocks*?"

"They are only rocks," she said, grinning, "from a certain point of view."

Spetsnaz sergeant Ivan Ananko lay prone close beside one of the two huge semi-trailer trucks the team had driven into Poland. Carefully stripped of anything that might lead investigators back to Russia, both rigs would be left behind when

Major Berezin and the rest of them bailed out of this place. In the meantime, their big tires provided Ananko with useful cover and concealment.

He scanned the road to his east, watching for any sign of movement between the two buildings at the far edge of this small office and light-manufacturing complex. The PCS-5M passive night sight attached to his Polish-made Beryl assault rifle intensified every photon of ambient light, turning the darkness of night into a green-tinted, slightly grainy version of daytime.

Every weapon and piece of equipment they carried on this mission was either manufactured in Poland, used by Poland's armed forces, or readily available in-country. Personally, Ananko thought that was overkill. No one in their right mind was going to believe the Polish president had been assassinated by his own soldiers. But orders were orders.

"Akrobat Pyat', *Acrobat Five, to One*," a voice crackled through his headset. That was Sergeant Dmitry Savichev, the fifth member of their team. The lucky bastard was currently comfortably ensconced in a plush hotel room overlooking Piłsudski Square. The site of Poland's Tomb of the Unknown Soldier, this vast open plaza was named in honor of the soldier and statesman Marshal Józef Piłsudski, one of the founders of modern Poland. Over the years, it had been used for outdoor papal masses and other important ceremonials. Tonight, it was crowded with Polish military helicopters and armored vehicles.

"*One to Five,*" Major Berezin replied. "*Go ahead.*"

"*The Poles are waking up, One,*" Savichev said. "*Their helicopters are spooling up. And I can see at least two infantry platoons forming up, ready to board soon. I estimate you'll have more company than you want in about fifteen minutes.*"

"*Understood, Five,*" Berezin said. "*Keep me posted.*"

Ananko knew what was coming next.

"*Acrobat One to Acrobat Two and Three,*" the major continued. "*Prepare to withdraw on my command. We'll kill Poles for another couple of minutes and then break contact.*"

The sergeant heard Captain Chirkash and Lieutenant Kuritsyn acknowledge. He thought Chirkash actually sounded disappointed. Now, there was a bloodthirsty son of a bitch, he thought approvingly. Stories floating around the barracks claimed the captain had a private collection of dried human ears he'd collected while fighting in Chechnya, Ukraine, and other hot spots. Wild as that sounded, Ananko knew the rumors were accurate. He'd seen Chirkash collecting some of his "trophies" after they'd slaughtered some Ukrainian troops in an ambush a few years back.

"*One to Four,*" Berezin continued, addressing him now. "*Any trouble out there?*"

"Negative, Acrobat One," Ananko said into his throat mic, still peering through his rifle's night sight. "No hostiles. No movement of any kind."

"*Very good. Prep the SUV now, Sergeant,*" Berezin ordered. "*When we move, we're going to want to move fast—not fart around waiting for the engine to warm up. Clear?*"

"Totally clear, Major," Ananko said. He lowered his assault rifle and scrambled to his feet. "I am moving now. Four out."

Still cradling the rifle, he stepped out of the shadow of the semi-trailer truck he'd been using as cover. The black Hyundai Tucson slated for their escape was a compact SUV. A couple of years ago, this model had been one of the best-selling new vehicles in Poland. Which meant it wouldn't stand out like a sore thumb when they drove off and tried to blend back into Warsaw's ordinary civilian traffic.

Ananko turned toward the SUV. It was parked close to a fire door leading into the machine shop and parts warehouse occupied by the rest of the Spetsnaz team. The keys were already in the ignition. The sergeant smiled. Soon they'd drive away, leaving nothing but dead and wounded Poles and confusion behind. Cover story or not, the lesson would be clear. *Nobody fucks with Mother Russia*, he thought coldly.

And then two small objects arced out of the darkness. One landed with a clatter near the semi-trailer. Another hit the asphalt only a few meters away and bounced toward him.

"*Granat!* Grenade!" someone shouted in Polish.

Oh, shit, Ananko thought, caught completely by surprise. He whirled away from the nearest grenade and threw himself prone.

It didn't go off.

Instead, he heard movement up the road behind him. Frantically, the Spetsnaz soldier wriggled around. He swung his assault rifle up . . . too late.

Flashes erupted in the night.

Hit multiple times by 5.56mm rounds fired at close range, Ivan Ananko fell forward on his face, dead before he knew what had happened.

Brad McLanahan dropped to one knee, facing the building. He sighted down the short barrel of his Radon carbine. Anyone poking his head out through that door was going to take a bullet.

Nadia moved ahead. She went prone near the body of the Russian sentry they'd killed. Quickly, she stripped the corpse of anything that looked useful, including extra ammunition, weapons, and other gear. Then she scampered back to Brad.

Her teeth flashed white in the darkness. "No more rocks," she said, handing him a small cylindrical object. Weighing less than a pound, it was a Polish-made RGZ-89 antipersonnel grenade.

"Sweet," Brad agreed, smiling back.

"But this is even better," Nadia told him, holding up the handheld tactical radio she'd found. She turned up the volume a bit—not much, just enough so they could both hear the bursts of speech crackling through it.

"*Akrobat Odin ko vsem Akrobatov. Byli sdelany. Davayte s'yekhat'!*" said a voice over the radio.

"They're coming out," Nadia hissed.

Brad hefted the grenade she'd handed him. "Then I say we give these guys a warm welcome."

Posted at one of the windows inside the machine shop, Major Pavel Berezin squeezed off one last shot. A Polish police officer who'd been bravely, if futilely, returning their fire with his service pistol fell backward with a huge hole blown open in his chest.

Satisfied, the Spetsnaz officer laid down the bolt-action, magazine-fed Tor sniper rifle he'd been using. The .50-caliber long-range rifle was too bulky and slow for use in close-quarters combat. In its place, he picked up his backup weapon, a 9mm PM-84 submachine gun.

Then he turned and walked away from the window, squeezing between a pair of large metal-cutting machines to come out into a small open space not far from the fire door. Plastic bins full of metal shavings and finished pieces were stacked along the nearest wall. More machines of various types stretched down the length of the building, interspersed with tool racks and shelving.

Chirkash and Kuritsyn were already there, waiting for him.

"All set?" Berezin asked.

Chirkash nodded. For once, the captain's normally sour face wore a contented smile. He was one of a very small minority among professional soldiers, a man who took real pleasure in killing.

Kuritsyn, on the other hand, looked pale and drawn. This was the young lieutenant's first operational mission and his nerves were showing. "Did we get him?" he asked. "Did we kill Wilk?"

"I nailed him with my first shot," Berezin said confidently. "Some clown got in the way, but they both went down hard." He pushed the talk switch on his radio. "Acrobat Four, this is One. Stand by. We're heading your way."

Nothing.

"Four, this is One," the major said again. "Do you copy?"

Berezin felt cold. Where the hell was Sergeant Ananko?

"Maybe the little prick's got the stereo cranked all the way up inside that fucking SUV," Chirkash growled. "And can't hear you over that shitty rap music he likes."

"You really think so?" Berezin snapped.

"Fuck no," Chirkash said. "I think we've got company. Somebody out there got smart, swung around behind us, and then got the drop on Ananko."

The major nodded, rapidly evaluating their tactical situation. He scowled. Put simply, it sucked. Right now they had no way to tell how many enemies were waiting beyond that fire door. Sure, there were other exits from this building, but they were all noisy, garage-style roll-up doors. Opening one of those would be like sending up a flare, saying "here we are, come and kill us."

Don't overthink it, Berezin told himself. The longer they let themselves be pinned down inside this building, the more likely they were to run into police roadblocks. Or worse yet, elements of that heavily armed and well-trained reaction force heading their way. Right now, though, any Poles waiting in ambush were probably only police officers—good enough perhaps against petty criminals and looters, but not really up for a fight against elite Spetsnaz troops.

"Okay," he told the others. "We go out hard and fast. Kuritsyn, you take point and move left. Chirkash, you go second and clear the right side. I'll take out anyone in the middle. Got it?"

Both men nodded.

"Then let's go," the major snapped.

The three Russian commandos swung into a tactical stack, lined up front to back to the right of the fire door.

Sweating now, Kuritsyn unclipped a grenade from his tactical vest.

Berezin shook his head. "No grenades, Lieutenant," he said dryly. "Not unless you're planning to walk out of here on foot."

Abashed, the younger Spetsnaz officer put it back. In trying to nerve himself up for battle, he must have forgotten that their vehicles were parked right outside the door—close enough so that any grenade blast was likely to damage or destroy them. Instead, Kuritsyn pressed up against the panic bar that would open the fire door, with his submachine up and ready.

"One. Two. Three," Berezin counted down. "Move!"

Everything around him began slowing down as adrenaline flooded his system, speeding up his reflexes.

Yelling, Kuritsyn slammed the door open and started to charge outside. Before he cleared the threshold, an assault rifle stuttered, firing short, earsplitting two-round bursts. Splinters flew off the doorframe. Shot in the chest and stomach, the lieutenant crumpled.

Chirkash whirled into position over Kuritsyn's body, firing back on full auto. The submachine gun hammered back against his shoulder as spent shell casings tumbled away. In that same instant, an olive-drab cylinder sailed through the door. It smacked into Chirkash's left arm and bounced off to the side.

Berezin saw the grenade drop into one of the plastic bins full of metal shavings. His eyes widened. He started to throw himself down.

WHUMMPP.

The blast hurled him sideways with enormous force. He lost his grip on his submachine gun and slammed hip first up against one of the big cutting machines. Pain sleeted through him, turning the world red. For a split second, he lay curled up, dazed and hanging on to consciousness by a bare thread.

Then, through ringing, almost deafened ears, Berezin heard the sound of high-pitched, shrill screams. Shaking his head to try to clear his confused mind, he forced himself to his knees and looked toward the door.

What he saw was horrifying.

Caught by the full force of the blast, Andrei Chirkash had been hit by hundreds of grenade fragments and sharp-edged metal shavings. His face was a blood-soaked mask, with streaks of white bone showing beneath the lacerated flesh. His ears had been torn off, along with most of his hair and scalp. For a second longer, the horribly wounded Spetsnaz captain screamed in agony—

and then, mercifully, he fell silent and slumped back, dead.

Berezin staggered upright with his back against the machine. He looked down at himself, suddenly aware that his own clothing was shredded and streaked with blood. Bright metal flakes protruded from small puncture wounds across his arms and chest. Like his submachine gun, his Walther P99 pistol was gone—either ripped away by the explosion or dragged out of his holster when he was thrown across the floor.

"Hell," he mumbled. Slowly, awkwardly, he fumbled for the concealed combat knife sheathed behind his back.

Fast footsteps rang on concrete.

The major looked up in time to see a tall, broad-shouldered man charging toward him.

Brad McLanahan crashed through the open doorway and saw the bloodied Russian dragging out a knife. His finger started to tighten on the trigger, but then he reconsidered. They needed a prisoner, someone who could be used to finger Gennadiy Gryzlov for all this butchery.

This bastard would do.

Without thinking further, he flicked the carbine's selector switch to safe and dropped the weapon. Then he lunged ahead, driving inside the other man's reach at top speed.

The Russian tried to slash at him, but he was slower than he should have been—probably still feeling the effects of the grenade blast. Brad slid to the outside, caught the other man's wrist in a left elbow hook, and then brought his right hand over on top, exerting even more pressure. Shoving down with all his strength while spinning through an arc, he yanked his opponent off balance. The man stumbled forward, right into a knee strike into his stomach and then another quick groin kick.

The knife clattered to the floor. Brad swept it away with his foot.

Still holding the armlock, he shoved the gasping, barely conscious man down onto the concrete—pressing his face flat against the unyielding surface. He looked back over his shoulder in time to see Nadia Rozek rush in with her own rifle at the ready.

She swung through a semicircle, checking to make sure all their enemies were dead or down. Then she turned back to Brad with a frown. "Charging in like that, on your own, was . . . most unwise."

"Well, yeah," he agreed, unable to keep a shit-eating grin off his face. "But you've got to admit it worked."

Almost against her will, Nadia offered him a slight, crooked smile in return. "They say fortune favors the brave. Perhaps it also favors the foolhardy once in a very long while." She nodded toward the wounded man he'd pinned. "You had better search that one for holdout weapons. I will cover him for you."

Nodding, Brad released the Russian's arm and

crouched down beside him. Briskly, he ran his hands over the prisoner's shirt and pants, checking for a concealed pistol or other knives. Some of the sharp metal flakes embedded in the other man's wounds snagged his fingers, drawing blood. "Cripes," he muttered. "This guy's a walking pincushion."

"Our medics can stitch him up," Nadia said flatly. Her wry smile vanished, wiped away by memories of the carnage and cold-blooded murder they had witnessed tonight. The expression in her eyes was icy. "Which is more than this swine deserves." Her finger tightened on the trigger. "In fact, maybe I should just put him out of his misery right now."

Uh-oh, Brad thought. Warily, he rose to his feet. "Much as I might agree in other circumstances, I kind of went to a lot of trouble to take this guy alive. Killing him now, before he can answer any questions . . . well, that seems like a waste."

Nadia exhaled sharply, almost as though she were waking up out of a nightmare. Her finger eased up on the trigger. She nodded tightly. "Yes. That is so. For now, we should call for backup and—"

"Move aside," an eerie, electronically synthesized voice interrupted. "Now."

Startled, Brad and Nadia swung around.

With a shriek of torn metal, a tall, man-shaped combat robot ripped the fire door off its hinges. The door went sailing away into the darkness, landing somewhere in the parking lot with a crash. Then, bending low, the CID squeezed its way inside the machine shop. Bits of broken brick and cement block pattered down around it.

Brad moved toward the machine with his hands out, palm first. "Hey, Dad," he said, trying not to sound nervous. "It's okay. We've got this."

"I said, move aside," the CID snarled. It stalked forward.

Brad gulped, staring up at the enormous machine as it loomed over him. "Dad, what the hell are you—"

Abruptly, the CID swatted him aside with one casual blow, much like a man shooing away some annoying insect. Sent flying, Brad crashed into the wall and dropped to the floor. Pain, white-hot and rimmed with fire, flared through every part of his body. It was impossible to breathe. The room around him flickered weirdly and then went black.

Coldly furious with the insolent fools who'd tried to obstruct him, Patrick McLanahan strode over to where the dazed prisoner lay bleeding on the concrete. He leaned over, grabbed the Russian with both hands, and then hoisted him high into the air. "Who are you?" he growled. "What's your name? Your rank? Your unit? Who ordered this massacre?"

Large, articulated metal fingers tightened their grip—drawing a gasp of pain from the man he held aloft.

Though white-faced with terror, the Russian shook his head. "You cannot interrogate me this way," he stammered. He hissed in agony as the

powerful hands holding him squeezed harder. "As
a prisoner, I have rights. I refuse to—"

Patrick's hands tightened convulsively, snapping the Russian's spine and neck as though they
were matchsticks. The man's eyes bulged out. His
mouth fell open. Then he shuddered once . . . and
died.

Enraged, Patrick tossed the corpse aside and
turned away in disgust. His vision display showed
a young woman cradling the body of the man he'd
hurled out of his path only moments before.

She looked up at him in sorrow. Tears ran
down her face. "What have you done, General?"
she asked in anguish.

He froze in horror, suddenly seeing clearly for
the first time in months. The woman was Nadia
Rozek. And the man he'd struck down without a
moment's hesitation was his own son.

An hour later, Patrick stood outside in the darkness, well away from the Polish soldiers, police, and
emergency medical teams who were busy clearing
away the dead and tending to the wounded. Another CID, this one piloted by Charlie Turlock,
waited not far away.

He winced. Charlie had followed him all the
way out from Warsaw. But she started too far
behind him and arrived too late.

The lights of the ambulance carrying Brad
away vanished in the distance.

"The kid's tough. He'll be okay," a voice said
quietly.

Patrick looked down at Whack Macomber. He swallowed hard. "I hope so. But this was my fault. I lost it. I got so focused on nailing that Russian son of a bitch that I lost my situational awareness."

"Situational awareness? That's bullshit and you know it, General!" Macomber exploded. He continued coldly. "You lost a hell of a lot more than your grasp of the tactical position. You damned well slid over the edge into full-on kill-crazy. And not for the first time, either."

Patrick stiffened. "You're way out of line, Major."

"No, I'm not," the other man snapped. "Remember how you butchered those Chechens who mortared us at the base? You didn't just take them out. You ripped them apart, limb from limb. Christ, General, their blood and guts were splattered all over that damned metal can you're riding."

"I had to act fast," Patrick said stubbornly. "Combat's not pretty, Whack. You know that."

"Yeah, I do," Macomber agreed. His expression hardened. "But I also know the difference between combat and wholesale slaughter. You crossed the line, General. And now you not only just killed a prisoner we urgently needed to interrogate . . . you beat the crap out of your own kid . . . without even recognizing him."

Patrick stayed silent, not sure how to respond to that.

"I've seen the medical readouts from your CID," Macomber continued. "You've been systematically screwing around with your brain chemistry, probably thinking you're boosting your fighting efficiency. And maybe that's so . . . but it's also driving you insane." His voice grew softer, but more urgent. "You've gotta face the facts, General. Riding that big metal machine full-time is keeping your physical body alive, but what's that worth if it kills your humanity?"

Patrick felt a sudden spike of anger. No one could know what he'd endured since he woke up inside one of Scion's combat robots, trapped and unable to survive for more than a few hours outside the machine. Yes, he'd been rescued from death, but at a terrible price. He clenched his jaw. How dare Macomber criticize him? Without conscious thought, the fingers one of his huge metal hands curled into a fist.

The other man looked straight up at him, apparently unfazed. "What's your plan, General? Are you gonna smack me around too? The way you just did to Brad?"

Patrick froze, suddenly aware of the murderous impulses flooding his mind. Memories of the things he'd done and been tempted to do in recent weeks rose in a dizzying, shameful cascade of gruesome images. Behaviors and ideas he had believed rational at the time stood revealed as nothing more than the expression of raw, uncontrolled rage and desire for revenge—no matter what the cost to himself or to those who relied on him. It was like awakening from a terrible nightmare, only to learn that he had not really been dreaming. He shivered, suddenly feeling cold despite the CID's precisely calibrated environmental systems.

Worst of all was the realization that this brief

moment of moral clarity was likely to be fleeting. He could no longer hide from the truth. Macomber was right. Life inside this machine, isolated from other people, was steadily robbing him of his essential humanity.

He'd put this day of reckoning off for three long years. But maybe the problem with living on borrowed time was that the hidden costs kept piling up—climbing higher and higher until they were beyond any one man's ability to pay. "It's time, isn't it, Major?" Patrick said slowly, unsteadily. "Time to pull the plug."

Macomber nodded sadly. "Yeah, General, it is," he agreed. "You can't ride that damned machine anymore. You're putting too many other lives at risk."

CHAPTER 24

PEOPLES' FRIENDSHIP PARK, MOSCOW
The next day

With his hands behind his back and his head bowed in thought, Igor Truznyev paced around the statue of Miguel de Cervantes given by Spain to the Soviet Union in exchange for a statue of the Russian literary genius Aleksandr Pushkin. Somehow, it seemed bitterly ironic to set a memorial to the author who'd created Don Quixote in the midst of a park extolling friendly relations among nations. After all, the so-called Knight of the Sorrowful Countenance was famed for acts of folly and mad illusions. Had some long-dead Soviet bureaucrat intended a discreet bit of subversive commentary by plopping this statue down here? Or, was the juxtaposition simply the product of official ignorance?

His lips thinned in irritation. If Sergei Tarzarov's choice of a setting for this clandestine meeting was meant as a humorous commentary on their present situation, it struck him as one in very poor taste—especially under the circumstances. He checked his watch. Where was the man, anyway? It wasn't like him to be late for a rendezvous, even one he hadn't sought himself.

The high-pitched noise of a yapping dog drew Truznyev's attention to an old pensioner hobbling along a nearby path. The elderly man, stooped over and twisted by arthritis and age, was being yanked along by a tiny, long-haired terrier that seemed to want to poke its small black nose into every snowbank or mound of dead leaves.

"*Podchinyat'sya*, Mischa," the old man snapped. "Obey!" He shortened the leash, tugging the little dog back to his side. Turning off the path, he shuffled closer to the Cervantes statue. "Well, Igor?" he demanded. "What is so urgent? It was not easy to slip away from the Kremlin today."

Truznyev shook his head in disbelief. He knew that Tarzarov enjoyed practicing the art of disguise as a means of throwing potential tails off his scent, but this was a first. "A dog?" he asked. "You brought a dog with you to a secret meeting?"

The older man shrugged his narrow shoulders. "Why not? Two men talking together in the midst of a field shouts 'conspiracy' to the whole world. But a man walking his dog and meeting a friend? What could be more commonplace . . . and boring?"

"Perhaps," Truznyev allowed, still frowning. "But make sure you keep the beast away from my shoes. They were handmade for me by Cleverley's in London."

"And thus astonishingly expensive, I suppose?" Tarzarov sniffed.

"Of course."

Gryzlov's chief of staff shook his head with a sly smile. "Some might find your spending habits excessively ostentatious, Igor."

"At least I pay my own bills and with my own money," Truznyev retorted. "While your lunatic protégé piles up debts that will be paid by all Russians—in blood, in prestige, and in treasure."

"Gennadiy is not mad," Tarzarov said. "He is undoubtedly aggressive, and perhaps more prone to rely on luck than I think wise. But that is a far cry from insanity."

"You think so?" the bigger man said heatedly. "Hitting the Poles and their allies with cyberweapons made some sense. It offered gains at comparatively little cost." He scowled. "But attempting to assassinate the Polish president? And murdering nearly two hundred people, many of them important Chinese businessmen, simply as a means of baiting the trap? That was pure madness! Especially since his ridiculous scheme failed so miserably."

Tarzarov said nothing. His face showed no emotion one way or the other.

"You know that I'm right, Sergei," Truznyev pressed. "This harebrained failure puts us all in peril—you, like the rest of those in Gryzlov's inner circle, most of all." He waved a hand at their surroundings. "How do you suppose the world will react when it learns Russia was responsible for this atrocity? Everything we have gained over the past few years is now at risk!"

"There is no proof we were involved," Tarzarov said mildly.

"How so?"

"The Spetsnaz team was sanitized before it infiltrated Polish territory," the older man explained. "Their records no longer exist."

"Their military records, you mean?" Truznyev asked.

Tarzarov shook his head. "*All* of their records, Igor." He shrugged again. "Effectively, Major Berezin and the three others who were killed at the crash site were never born. They never lived. They are nothing—not even the ghost of a memory."

"And their families?" Truznyev shot back. "What about them? You can fiddle with paperwork and databases all you like, but their parents, siblings, wives, and children can each tell a different tale if they talk to the wrong people."

The older man's eyes were hooded, impossible to read. "Their families have been . . . *cautioned*," he said. "Besides, they are under constant observation."

"Meaning what?" Truznyev snapped.

"Should any of them forget their duty to the state . . . well, accidents happen," Tarzarov replied smoothly. Seeing the slightly appalled look on the other man's face, he offered a crooked smile. "As you yourself pointed out, Igor, the stakes are high.

And extraordinary dangers require extraordinary responses, do they not?"

With an effort, Truznyev recovered his poise. There were moments when he forgot how cold-blooded and vicious the old Kremlin insider could be if he thought it necessary. It was a useful reminder that he was not the only ruthless player in this game. "It is easy enough, I suppose, to contemplate killing defenseless old men and women and children," he said cuttingly. "But there is still evidence outside your control. Evidence that will enrage Beijing and the rest of the world when it is analyzed and published."

"You refer to the black boxes from the jetliner?" Tarzarov asked.

Truznyev nodded.

"I have been assured they will show only a series of unexplained faults in various systems aboard the aircraft," the older man said, though he sounded a bit less certain now. "Nothing that can be linked conclusively to us."

"Nothing except for the *remarkable* coincidence that these random 'faults' caused the 777 to crash *precisely* where a team of trained assassins lay in wait," Truznyev said with heavy sarcasm.

Tarzarov eyed him narrowly. "Supposition is not proof, Igor. As you, of all people, should know."

For a moment, Truznyev felt cold. What did the other man mean by that? Was he growing suspicious about the true causes of last year's war with Poland? If so, he was in more danger than he had realized. Or was it just a stab in the dark by a man who knew full well that secrets, many of them deadly and disreputable, were Truznyev's stock-in-trade?

"For now, Beijing is turning most of its diplomatic wrath on Warsaw," Tarzarov went on. "After all, it is clear that Wilk's government was fully willing to shoot down the Kalmar Airlines flight with so many of its nationals aboard—even though it was unclear whether they were still alive or not."

"That won't last," Truznyev said tightly. "President Zhou and his government are not fools."

"Probably not," the older man agreed. "But I cannot say the prospect of Beijing's anger greatly dismays Gennadiy. After all, according to the evidence you provided, the Chinese were responsible for luring us into war with Poland in the first place. When set next to the losses we suffered in men and matériel, the deaths of a few score of their business executives are nothing."

Truznyev fell silent for a moment. This was dangerous ground. He was the one who had ordered faked evidence of the PRC's involvement planted to hide his own role in the terrorist campaign Gryzlov had originally blamed on Warsaw. Perhaps he should back off and pretend to accept the defenses Tarzarov offered for his protégé's reckless actions. Then he reconsidered. *You're riding on the tiger's back, Igor,* he thought. *Keep a firm grip, or you'll be eaten.*

Gryzlov had blundered badly by trying to kill Piotr Wilk so clumsily and with so much collateral damage. And for all of Tarzarov's bluster, he could tell the older man knew it too. Maybe this was the moment to demonstrate that their most precious secrets were not as safe as they dreamed. And, at the same time, to continue the process of sowing discord between Gryzlov and his long-suffering adviser. Three years ago, Tarzarov had allied himself with the younger man. This was another opportunity to make the old Kremlin power broker wonder if he'd tied himself to a loser after all.

"You dance past the true state of affairs with remarkable grace, Sergei," he said caustically. "I congratulate you."

Tarzarov flushed angrily.

"But we are old comrades, you and I," Truznyev went on. "So I feel compelled to ask what the president plans to do next. Now that his impatience and carelessness have made such a mess, will Gennadiy cut his losses like any sensible man and call off this covert war? Before it escalates out of control? Or will he push on obsessively, demanding still more wondrous cyberweapons from Koshkin's army of *komp'yutershchiks* locked away in the Urals? In that secret mountain complex he's dubbed 'Perun's Aerie'?"

Visibly shocked, Tarzarov stared back at him. "Where did you hear that name?"

Ah, so Akulov and Ivchenko were right, Truznyev thought. The look on the older man's face was confirmation enough. He smiled. "You forget who you are dealing with, Sergei, as does your new master. Remember, I ran our nation's intel-

ligence services for years. Did you really believe
the movement of so much sophisticated equipment, including a supercomputer and a nuclear
reactor, would not leave behind traces my people
and I could uncover?"

The little dog at Tarzarov's feet chose that moment to begin whimpering and whining, either
bored from doing nothing while the humans
talked and talked . . . or frightened by something
in the tone of their voices. Or perhaps spooked
by some movement neither of the two men noticed.

"*Tikho!* Quiet!" the older man snapped at the
dog. Then he looked up at Truznyev. "But I
could say the same to you, Igor," he said coldly.
"This private espionage of yours comes dangerously close to treason. I warned you earlier about
prying into state secrets that were no longer your
province. It appears you did not take me seriously
enough. I will not warn you again."

The old man is bluffing, Truznyev thought. He
must be. "I am no traitor," he retorted. "If I were,
I'd have sold what I know to the Americans. Or
to the Chinese, for that matter." He shook his
head in disgust. "Nor am I the madman whose
vendetta against the Poles now threatens our vital
national interests."

Angrily, Tarzarov glared back at him. "So now
I suppose you expect me to pay you—either for
your silence, or for the details of how you learned
so much that was top secret?"

Absorbed in their fierce argument, both men
again failed to spot the small birdlike shape cir-

cling overhead, picking up and retransmitting their conversation.

THE WHITE HOUSE, WASHINGTON, D.C.
Several hours later

National Security Adviser Edward Rauch sat slumped in his chair while the president skimmed through his preliminary report on the Kalmar Airlines crash and the apparent attempt to kill Piotr Wilk. He felt drained. The first news from Poland hit the Internet around the dinner hour, East Coast time. And those early, confused reports had triggered a frantic scramble by the interagency working group he'd taken over from Luke Cohen. Analysts from the CIA, NSA, the Pentagon, the State Department, and Cyber Command had worked through the night, assembling and evaluating every scrap of reliable information.

President Stacy Anne Barbeau closed the folder with a decisive gesture. She looked across her desk at Rauch. "How sure of this are you?"

For a second, he thought about running through the usual litany of caveats and cautions appropriate to any intelligence assessment, but then he saw the look in the president's eyes. She was definitely operating in "no bureaucratic BS" mode. He sat up straighter. "As close to certain as I can get, Madam President."

"Hell," Barbeau muttered. She tapped the

folder with one finger. "You really believe the Russians somehow hacked the airliner, killed everyone aboard, and then deliberately crashed it outside Warsaw—just so they could take a shot at Wilk?"

"Yes, ma'am," Rauch said. He shook his head. "I know it sounds crazy, but it's the only scenario that comes close to fitting the known facts."

"Yeah, well, crazy seems to be what Gennadiy Gryzlov does best." Barbeau pursed her lips. "Do the folks at Cyber Command have any idea of how the Russians could have pulled this off?"

"Not yet," he admitted. "They're subjecting the computer and flight-control systems Kalmar Airlines uses to intensive analysis, checking for vulnerabilities and possible back doors—but that's going to take more time."

"So we can't prove any of this?" Barbeau asked.

"Probably not to the standards of any criminal court of law," Rauch said carefully. "But the circumstantial evidence is so strong that we could certainly make a solid case for diplomatic purposes. If we took this to the UN or to the NATO Council, we'd pick up a lot of support."

For a moment, he thought the president would go for it. She leaned back in her chair with her eyes closed. She was obviously deep in thought—probably running through possible scenarios of how going to the UN or NATO might play out, both domestically and overseas. But then she shook her head. "And what would that get us, Ed? All we'd end up doing is pissing off the Russians for no real purpose. That game's not worth the candle."

"But, Madam President—"

"No buts, Ed," Barbeau said flatly. "There's no goddamned point in openly accusing Moscow of mass murder and attempted assassination. It would just make us look weak. You don't make those kinds of claims unless you're ready to go to the mat over them. And since we are most definitely *not* going to support the Poles or go to war for them, it would be really stupid to ratchet up tensions with Russia, wouldn't it?"

Rauch nodded, though unwillingly. Privately, he suspected she was more concerned about appearing foolish in front of American voters than she was about seeming weak abroad. From the moment she'd been sworn into office, Stacy Anne Barbeau had argued that the United States should focus more attention and resources on its own interests here at home. Her political rhetoric and most of her defense and foreign policy revolved around a determination to avoid being dragged into conflicts overseas. Standing up now to accuse Gennadiy Gryzlov of being responsible for crashing the Kalmar Airlines flight and trying to kill another national leader would require conceding that her long-held beliefs and policies were either inadequate or mistaken. Admitting error was not a course she could easily embrace.

"So we do nothing?" he asked, trying hard not to reveal his dismay. If the Russians committed an atrocity like this and got away scot-free, where would it end? Looking the other way might work in the short term, but it could lead to a catastrophe if Moscow kept pushing the envelope—taking bigger and bigger risks in the belief the United States would stay passive in the face of any provocation.

"That is not what I said," Barbeau told him. "I said we weren't going to commit ourselves *openly*, that's all."

Seeing the confusion on his face, she sighed. "Look, Ed, it's pretty clear that Gryzlov is nuts, right?"

He cleared his throat. "His behavior is certainly erratic, amazingly arrogant, and belligerent, Madam President. Whether it rises to the level of actual madness is beyond my ability to judge."

Barbeau raised an eyebrow.

"Okay, yes. He's nuts," Rauch agreed. "Or as close to it as makes no real difference."

"Exactly," the president said in satisfaction. "Which is why we're not going to do anything overt—at least not right now. Opposing a lunatic like Gryzlov without the means of finishing him off would be like poking a tiger in the eye with a padded stick. All you do is make the tiger mad. Understand?"

"Yes, ma'am," Rauch agreed quickly, still not entirely sure what she was driving at.

"So when we're done here, I'm going to put in a call to Sara Murchison over at the Hoover Building," Barbeau said, with a thin smile. "You with me so far?"

Rauch nodded. Murchison was a former federal prosecutor and the current director of the FBI.

"And I'm going to tell her to call off all the agents she's got riding herd on Sky Masters and the other companies affiliated with that asshole Martindale," Barbeau finished.

"You're lifting the restrictions on arms sales to Poland?" Rauch asked, not quite sure what she meant.

The president looked disgusted. "Oh, hell, no, Ed. The restrictions stay. At least on paper. That way the Russians can't bitch about us supporting Poland or any of the other AFN countries." She looked smug. "From our perspective, it'll be the best of both worlds."

Now he saw what she intended. While it would still be technically illegal for anyone to sell weapons or arms technology to the Poles and their allies, without active enforcement those restrictions were a dead letter. If Sky Masters or some other corporation wanted to deal with Wilk, they could . . . though at the risk of exposing themselves to serious legal jeopardy if the Barbeau administration reversed course again later. In effect, Piotr Wilk and his American mercenaries could buy the arms they needed, but only if they were willing to pay wildly inflated prices.

Rauch kept a tight rein on his own expression. He understood why this convoluted course of Machiavellian inaction appealed to Barbeau. It let her poke a finger in Gryzlov's eye, though in a totally deniable way. And, at the same time, it still inflicted significant financial pain on the Poles,

Martindale, and the others she despised and distrusted.

But from a real-world perspective, the president's proposal was too cute by half. Whatever Gennadiy Gryzlov planned to get out of this cyberwar of his, the Russian leader sure as hell wasn't playing for small stakes. He certainly wasn't going to be deterred by subtle hints and unserious threats left hanging unsaid. Every day the United States sat on the sidelines was another day this crisis would only intensify.

For the first time since being named as Stacy Anne Barbeau's national security adviser, Ed Rauch began seriously considering the need to update his résumé.

CHAPTER 25

**SECURE RECOVERY WARD, MILITARY
INSTITUTE OF MEDICINE, WARSAW**
The next day

Supported by Nadia Rozek's strong right arm, Brad McLanahan limped out of the large passenger elevator. The doors slid shut behind them. His nose wrinkled at the faint antiseptic smells wafting out of the ventilation system and from behind closed doors. Hospitals made him twitchy. He always associated them with bad news, especially news involving the deaths of friends and loved ones.

A squad of Polish Special Forces soldiers in body armor guarded the corridor leading to President Wilk's private room. A stern-faced captain stepped in front of them. "Your identification cards, please," he demanded.

Silently, Nadia and Brad handed their IDs to him. The captain scrutinized them carefully, painstakingly double-checking their faces against their official pictures. Then he handed the cards back and examined a typed list given to him by an equally grim-looking noncom. "Headquarters has approved your visit, Major Rozek and Captain McLanahan," he said, sounding somewhat disappointed.

"I am glad to hear it, Captain," Nadia said coldly. "Since I happen to know the president himself asked us here this morning. And the last time I looked, he outranked even Brigadier General Pawlik."

Brad winced. Baiting pissed-off guys armed to the teeth with American-made M4A1 assault rifles and German-manufactured MP5 submachine guns might not be the best option right now. The near success of Gryzlov's assassination attempt had humiliated the men and women of Poland's elite armed forces units and law enforcement agencies. And like most security professionals caught with egg dripping off their faces, they were reacting both with hyperaggressiveness and a strict attention to protocol.

Fortunately, the other man ignored her sarcasm. Instead he handed them each a large yellow badge marked VISITOR. "Wear these at all times while you are in this wing of the hospital," he warned. "My troops are under strict orders in this regard."

"They'll arrest anyone without a badge?" Brad guessed.

"Arrest? No," the Special Forces officer said. His eyes were cold. "Anyone found without the proper clearance will be shot without further warning."

Brad whistled silently. The Poles were taking the definition of *tight security* to a whole new level. He carefully clipped the visitor badge to his Iron Wolf uniform jacket.

When they pushed open the door into Wilk's room, they found the Polish president propped up comfortably in a hospital bed, reading through memos and e-mails on his laptop. Kevin Martindale stood nearby, doing the same on his smartphone.

Wilk looked up with a tired smile. "There you two are!" He waved a hand around the hospital room. "Welcome to my prison cell."

"It is for your own good, sir," Nadia said severely. "Your injuries may not be life-threatening. But that does not mean it is wise to bound around as though nothing had happened."

The Polish president started to shrug and then stopped with a stifled gasp. His smile turned crooked. "So it seems, Major Rozek," he admitted. "But it could have been much worse. If poor Dariusz hadn't stepped in front of the bullet meant for me, the doctors tell me I would probably be dead."

Brad and the others nodded. Penetrating Major Stepniak's armor and body had slowed the sniper round just enough for Wilk's own vest to absorb the impact—though at the cost of several broken ribs.

"Which is why we need to talk," Martindale said. He slid his phone away. "Gryzlov just upped the ante big-time. If it hadn't been for Whack

Macomber and Major Rozek and Brad over there, we'd *all* be dead, not just you, Piotr."

Wilk nodded. "Undoubtedly. Which is why I plan to award our three friends the Order of the Military Cross."

Brad was startled. The Military Cross was one of Poland's highest military decorations, usually conferred only for distinguished service, courage, and sacrifice in actions against terrorism. Earning that kind of medal had been the subject of a lot of his childhood daydreams. Having a father who had been one of the U.S. Air Force's most highly decorated officers could do that to you, he thought wryly. For a moment, he allowed himself to imagine what it would be like wearing that crown-surmounted cross with its blue-and-red ribbon. And how proud it would have made his dad. But then he shook his head, dismissing the fantasy.

"Whack and Nadia definitely deserve any medal you choose to award, Mr. President," he said quietly. "But I think you should leave me out of it."

Surprised, Nadia turned toward him. "What? How can you say that, Brad? Your courage is beyond question!"

"It's not that," Brad told her. "Well, not entirely, anyway." He shrugged his shoulders. And then, like Wilk earlier, he grimaced as the pain from his injuries flared up.

The other man noticed. "You too?" he asked.

Brad offered him a forced grin. "I'm only bruised as hell, sir. Nothing's broken. I'm popping painkillers every few hours, but otherwise

I'm fine." He knew the dark patches under his eyes and the sadness he couldn't entirely conceal said otherwise, but Wilk seemed willing to let it go at that.

Instead, the Polish president contented himself with nodding toward a chair. "Nevertheless, I suggest you take a seat, Captain McLanahan. Before you collapse, I mean," he said. "And then you can explain why I should not reward your gallant service to my country."

Nadia pulled the chair over closer and helped Brad sit down. He flushed slightly, embarrassed at showing so much weakness. "It's not that I don't care about the medal, Mr. President," he said. "I do. In fact, I'm deeply honored by the offer."

"But?" Wilk prompted gently.

"Publicly awarding the Military Cross to a McLanahan would cause a firestorm in Russia," he explained. "We already know Gryzlov's got a bug up his ass about my dad . . . well, about my whole family, really. I think things are bad enough right now without setting off his crazy revenge complex all over again."

Martindale sighed. "God knows, that's true enough."

Wilk shook his head. "Nevertheless, I am disinclined to offer a heckler's veto to the bloodthirsty butcher who has murdered so many innocents and caused my country so much grief." He held up a hand, forestalling further argument. "We can discuss that later. For now, we need to decide how we will respond to this most recent Russian atrocity."

"We must strike back, sir," Nadia said sharply. Her tone was fierce. "And the sooner the better."

Brad nodded his agreement. "Turtling up isn't working. Not when Gryzlov keeps escalating. If we sit around waiting for his next move, we're only going to wind up hurting worse than we are now." He tried to sit up straighter, working hard to ignore the stab of pain triggered by the sudden movement. "Stuff my dad proposed— like hitting the Kremlin with a CID-led strike force—is way too risky and extreme, but he was right that we've got to bloody Gryzlov's nose. It's the only way we're going to make that Russian bastard think twice about pushing this war to the next level."

"I concur," Martindale chimed in. "Which leaves the problem of picking the right target. Blowing the snot out of some random Russian military base with a CID raid might be satisfying, but it won't move the needle much."

"Or at all," Brad said quietly. "I bet Gryzlov sees even his own troops and weapons as just pieces on a chessboard. To his way of thinking, he can trade pawn for pawn all day long without breaking a sweat. Or better yet sacrifice a pawn or two for a shot at our king," he said, looking at Wilk. "Like he did a couple of days ago. Those Spetsnaz guys had an escape plan, but I doubt Gryzlov shed any real tears after we killed them."

Wilk nodded, looking troubled.

"Plus, a limited attack on an easy target might only give the Russians the excuse they want to escalate beyond cyber attacks and terrorism into all-out war," Martindale said grimly. "A war we are not ready for and cannot win."

"Pinprick raids won't do the job," Brad added. "If we go into Russia, we have to hit something that's key to Gryzlov's plans or power base. The only way we might be able to make him back off is to smash an installation or a military capability that's seriously important to him. And to the Kremlin insiders who keep him in power."

Wilk nodded again. "Very true." He rubbed at his jaw in thought. "I know you have all heard the recording of the most recent meeting between those two snakes in human form, Igor Truznyev and Sergei Tarzarov. Unwittingly, their argument provides us with the information we need to select a target." He looked around the room. "I propose we strike at this mysterious cyberwar installation the Russians call Perun's Aerie. As the place where Gryzlov has concealed his computer hackers and their equipment, *it* is our logical point of attack."

The Polish president went on, ticking off his points one by one. "Wrecking this Russian cyberwar facility will accomplish three objectives. First, it will diminish Gryzlov's ability to wage his war of machines and malicious code. Second, it will show him that we can find anything he hides. And third, it will prove there is *nothing* he defends that we cannot destroy."

"Well, yeah, that's all true," Brad said. He frowned. "But there's one big problem left: actually zeroing in on the damned place. With all due respect to Mr. Martindale's agents in Moscow, nothing they overheard was very specific. Learning that this Perun's Aerie complex is buried inside a mountain is just fine and dandy. Trouble is, there are one hell of a lot of mountains in Russia."

"So we go to Truznyev," Martindale interjected quietly. "It's obvious that he's got a pretty good line on the location of that base."

Caught off guard, Brad, Nadia, and Wilk stared at him in surprise.

Nadia broke the silence first. "Go to Truznyev? How exactly? Do you propose that we simply ask him politely?" she snapped. "Or try to bribe him?"

"Not quite, Major Rozek," Martindale said with an impish smile. "Actually, I have something a little more devious in mind."

"Devious how?" Brad wondered.

"Getting Truznyev to spill what he knows won't be especially easy. Or very safe," Martindale admitted. "But while there are risks, I think it's our best shot at obtaining the information we need to formulate a solid attack plan. Here's what I propose . . ."

When Scion's gray-haired chief finished sketching out his concept, the rest of them sat speechless for what seemed an eternity. Then, very slowly, Nadia smiled. *Uh-oh*, Brad thought. He knew that pleased and predatory look. In training, it usually meant someone else was about to get the crap beaten out of them—either physically or mentally. In combat, it meant a bad guy was going down hard and usually fatally.

"Your scheme is *całkowicie niepoczytalny*," she told Martindale. "It's totally insane."

"Which means you approve," Martindale guessed.

"Oh yes," Nadia confirmed. "I love it."

He grinned and turned to Brad and Wilk. "What about you two?"

"If Major Rozek is in favor, how can I be opposed?" Wilk replied with a wry smile. "After all, her tactical sense and daring just saved my life. If she sees promise in this crazy plan of yours, I'm willing to accept her judgment."

Brad nodded. "Count me in."

"Good," Martindale said in satisfaction. He turned back to Nadia. "Can your Special Forces units provide the more, ah, 'volatile' gear my people will need?"

"We should be able to," Nadia said, pondering the question. Then she shrugged. "But if not, I'm quite sure Major Macomber and Captain Schofield can pull a few pieces of Iron Wolf equipment out of their sleeves that should do the trick."

Once their meeting with Wilk and Martindale broke up, Brad and Nadia rode the elevator back downstairs. Neither felt much like speaking. The planning session had been a welcome distraction. But now it was time to face a much sadder duty.

Still wrapped in silence, they got off on the floor occupied by the hospital's intensive care unit. There were no guards on this dimly lit floor,

only somber doctors and nurses who moved quietly about their rounds—working diligently to
save those who might be healed and providing
palliative care to those who were dying.

They joined Whack Macomber in an almost
deserted hallway near the rear of the ICU. The
big man stood at a bank of windows, looking in on
a small private room.

Patrick McLanahan lay motionless in a hospital bed, hooked up to a bewildering number of
IV drips, monitors, and other machines. His eyes
were closed. A ventilator whirred rhythmically,
steadily pumping air into lungs that no longer
functioned on their own.

Brad swallowed hard. The lump in his throat felt
baseball size. He hadn't seen his father in the flesh
for more than two years. That was something he'd
yearned for, even dreamed about. But not like this.
Not seeing the man who had always been so *alive*,
always so physically and mentally intense, reduced
to this skeletal, silent, unmoving husk.

"It's a hell of thing," Macomber said. His voice
rasped. "Your dad was always such a tough, contrary
son of a bitch, I thought for sure he'd go out riding
some crippled bomber down in flames, fighting to
regain control right up to the last damned second."

"Me too," Brad agreed sadly. He felt tears well-
ing up and tried not to let them come. He felt Nadia's arm slide around his waist. "How long has
he got?"

Macomber shook his head. "The doctors won't
make any predictions. Not explicitly, anyway." He
leaned forward, pressing his big hands up against

the windows. "But your dad's in a coma now. They say his body is just slowly shutting down— one system at a time. Without support from the fricking robot, nothing works on its own."

"God," Brad whispered.

"Yeah," Macomber said grimly. "So who knows? Two days? Three? No more than four at the outside."

CHAPTER 26

Ivan Ulanov, Gryzlov's private secretary, politely ushered Major General Arkady Koshkin into the president's inner office. The head of Q Directorate fought hard to conceal his apprehension about the likely outcome of this cyberwar conference.

After the spectacular success of its opening salvos, *Operatsiya Mor* was beginning to bog down. The Poles and their allies must have found and neutralized the pieces of malicious code Russia's hackers had embedded in their railroad and air-traffic control networks. Instead of the expected spate of train crashes and air accidents caused by their viruses, Koshkin and his hackers saw nothing. Over the same period, several efforts to reinfect the Polish banking system had been intercepted by new cybersecurity protocols. The efforts the AFN and its mercenary technology specialists were making to tighten their security were paying off. And while Q Directorate's hackers had played their parts in the recent airliner hijacking and assassination attempt to perfection, there was no doubt that Variant Six as a whole had failed to achieve its intended objective.

A patient leader might accept these less-than-stellar results as the inevitable friction involved in the first use of any cutting-edge weapons technology. Unfortunately, no one could say that patience was one of Gennadiy Gryzlov's virtues.

To Koshkin's astonishment, Gryzlov jumped up from behind his desk and came around to greet him with a firm grip and a friendly smile. "Arkady! It's good to see you looking so well," the president said.

Still wary, the Q Directorate chief allowed himself to be led over to a group of comfortable chairs surrounding a small coffee table. Viktor Kazyanov and Gregor Sokolov were already seated. He could tell that the ministers of state security and defense were equally puzzled by the president's evident good mood. Failures of any kind usually sent the younger man into towering rages that were hard on his subordinates and office furniture.

When Gryzlov took his own chair, Kazyanov cleared his throat nervously. From the gloomy look on his broad face, the intelligence chief knew he was treading into deeper, shark-filled water, but he couldn't think of any safer alternative. "Mr. President, I deeply regret the inability of Major Berezin and his team to complete their mission, but—"

Gryzlov cut him off in midsentence with an offhand gesture. "Save the abject bowing and scraping for another time, Viktor," he said. He shrugged. "Variant Six was always a high-risk enterprise. True, I would have been delighted to see that fascist piece of shit Piotr Wilk dead, but I guess some of life's pleasures must be deferred to another day." His expression turned frostier. "At least Berezin and the rest of his direct-action team had the decency to get themselves killed, rather than be taken prisoner."

"Yes, sir," Kazyanov agreed. "Only the lookout man, Sergeant Savichev, escaped. He is exfiltrating now, through Germany."

"You think he will succeed?" Gryzlov asked.

Kazyanov nodded. "I do, Mr. President. Savichev is a highly experienced operative. I expect him back in Moscow within forty-eight hours."

"Very good," Gryzlov said. "You'll have your people thoroughly debrief him, I presume? To get some sense of how Berezin and the others muffed their assignment?"

"Yes, sir."

Gryzlov nodded casually, apparently satisfied. "Excellent. But once you've squeezed every last bit of information out of Sergeant Savichev, I want him *disappeared*. So thoroughly removed that it will be as though he never existed. There must be no slipups. No loose ends. Do you understand me, Viktor?"

Plainly rattled, Kazyanov hurriedly agreed. "Yes, Mr. President. Absolutely."

Despite himself, Koshkin shivered. It was one

thing to know intellectually that Gryzlov was callous and coldhearted. It was quite another to hear him so dispassionately order the death of a brave and loyal soldier, a veteran whose only real fault was to have survived when all his comrades were killed. He risked a furtive glance at the ministers of defense and state security. They showed the same sense of scarcely concealed foreboding. How safe were any of them around Gennadiy Gryzlov?

"Let's move on to pleasanter topics, shall we?" Russia's president said easily. He looked around the circle of anxious faces with a wry smile. "Oh, cheer up, gentlemen. I'm not going to order your heads chopped off." Koshkin and the others responded to his quip with dry, dutiful laughs. "At least not yet," Gryzlov said reflectively.

They stopped laughing.

His smile grew broader. "By now you must have realized that *Operatsiya Mor* is only the preliminary phase of a much larger plan." He raised an eyebrow at their evident confusion. "No?" He shrugged. "You surprise me. I thought it was obvious that so large an expenditure of our resources for so little potential gain made no real sense."

This cavalier declaration staggered Koshkin. Was the president really serious? How could he so easily dismiss destroying the Polish-led Alliance of Free Nations and destabilizing Warsaw's government as minor objectives?

Gryzlov read his bewildered expression and laughed. "Come now, Arkady! Apply that fine mind of yours more fully to the question. In the broader strategic sense, was it wise to have revealed the existence of your directorate's revolutionary new cyberweapons this way, by employing them against the Poles and their allies—instead of saving them as a surprise for more dangerous and powerful opponents? Especially when we could have achieved many of the same results through more conventional military and political means?"

Koshkin thought about that. What Gryzlov said was accurate, he realized. By now, every country with any advanced technological capability was racing to develop defenses against Russia's cyberweapons—along with computer viruses and pieces of malicious code of their own. And, if nothing else, *Operatsiya Mor* so far had shown that these weapons, while incredibly destructive when used intelligently, were not invincible. He had been so caught up in the excitement of seeing his brainchildren put to work that he had never stopped to question the president's first choice of targets. He frowned. But if Gryzlov knew all this going in, why had he pushed so hard for the cyberwar attacks on Poland and its allies in the first place?

Again, Gryzlov must have read his mind. "Now you begin to ask the right questions! Well, better late than never, eh?"

Koshkin felt his face redden in embarrassment. Over the course of a long career in Russia's intelligence services, he had grown used to believing himself to be the smartest man in any room. It was humiliating to realize the president had manipulated him so easily—simply by playing on his own eagerness to prove the foolishness of those who had scoffed at his cyberwar theories.

Gryzlov shook his head. "Don't let it distress you, Arkady. Your weapons have proved their worth beyond doubt. More important, their successes have set the stage perfectly for the rest of my broader plan."

At that, Gregor Sokolov sat forward. So far, the minister of defense had been conspicuous by his silence. It was no secret that he was one of those who had mocked the idea that computer viruses and other cyberweapons would ever play a significant role in war. "And what exactly *is* your plan, Mr. President?" he asked carefully.

"First, understand that what you hear today is to go no further than the walls of this office," Gryzlov said in reply. "*Nothing* will be committed to paper or to any electronic form of communication. No memos. No reports. No analyses. No e-mails. No texts. Nothing. Is that clear?" Koshkin and the others nodded. "Nor will you discuss any aspect of this plan with any of your subordinates or colleagues. Or even among yourselves outside my presence," Gryzlov went on. His voice was implacably cold and utterly precise. "The punishment for violating my orders on this subject is death. *Vy ponimayete?* Understand?"

Again, they nodded, though somewhat more slowly this time. What the president proposed was completely unprecedented, even when one took his deep-rooted paranoia about spies—especially those controlled by the American mercenary Martindale—into account. This level of classification was also dangerous. If there were hidden flaws in Gryzlov's scheme, restricting any knowledge of its very existence, let alone the details, to such a small circle made it far less likely they would be found before it was too late.

Satisfied that he had their acquiescence, if not their full comprehension, Gryzlov laid out more of the details of what he intended. He spoke persuasively and forcefully, and the scope of his ambition was, quite literally, breathtaking. It was also, Koshkin admitted to himself in silence, the logical—though almost insanely daring—response to the humiliating defeats periodically inflicted on Russia by enemies armed with superior technology. It also explained much about the Perun's Aerie complex that he had never completely understood.

When Gryzlov finished, they each sat quietly, inwardly considering the implications of his proposed high-stakes, winner-take-all gamble.

Koshkin broke the silence first. "When can we expect this next phase of your plan to go into effect?"

Gryzlov shrugged. "That depends entirely on the Poles and their Iron Wolf mercenaries. In the meantime, we will press ahead with *Operatsiya Mor* as previously agreed, inflicting as much damage as possible even in the face of their strengthened cyber defenses."

"We could leak the information you want them to have," Viktor Kazyanov suggested tentatively.

Gryzlov shook his head. "No. That would be the worst thing we could do. For all their many faults, Piotr Wilk and this American trouble-maker, Martindale, are not simpletons. Knowledge too easily obtained would only make them suspicious." He smiled. "But our enemies are resourceful. I am confident they will solve the riddle I've set before them—in one way or another."

UNDERGROUND PARKING GARAGE, DOMINION TOWER, MOSCOW
Later that night

Deep in thought, Igor Truznyev stepped out of his private elevator and into the first floor of the Dominion Tower's two-level underground parking garage. A blast of cold air greeted him.

Absentmindedly, he buttoned up his thick winter coat. His conversation yesterday with Sergei Tarzarov had not gone according to plan. For all his native cynicism and hard-won experience, the old man had proved unexpectedly loyal to that shallow, impetuous fool, Gennadiy Gryzlov. Instead of acknowledging the validity of Truznyev's criticisms, he had steadfastly focused on the security breach Truznyev and his paid spies had ripped open. A breach Tarzarov stubbornly characterized as potentially treasonous. In the end, they had parted on bad terms, each persuaded of the other's folly.

Truznyev scowled. Losing Tarzarov's trust permanently would be bad on many levels.

First, it would be bad for business. Unofficial commissions from the old man represented a significant fraction of Zatmeniye's net profits.

More significantly, it would make the task of oust-
ing Gennadiy Gryzlov and reclaiming power in
the Kremlin far more difficult. It was no secret
that the assorted and sordid group of politicians,
generals, and business oligarchs who backed the
younger man did so largely because they believed
Tarzarov could keep his wilder impulses under
control. Without his backing, Gryzlov would be
vulnerable. With it, he was probably safe. Worst
of all, if Tarzarov began seriously investigating the events of the past year or so, it was possible he could dig up damning evidence against
Truznyev—evidence Gryzlov would gladly use to
rid himself of a potential rival.

The former Russian president shook his head
in frustration. Much as it galled him, he was probably going to have to go hat in hand to the old man
and apologize. To sweeten the deal, it might even
be necessary to toss him a bone—the name and
methods used by one of the agents who'd cracked
Gryzlov's security, either Yuri Akulov or Taras
Ivchenko. Breaking faith with his own people like
that would be unfortunate, but it was better that
one of them should suffer than Truznyev himself
face unwelcome and possibly lethal scrutiny.

Well, he thought, tomorrow would be soon
enough to decide if he needed to go that far to win
back Tarzarov's favor. Perhaps he could dream up
a less humiliating and less costly plan overnight.

"Your car is waiting, *Gospodin Prezident*," his
senior bodyguard said deferentially. Like most of
the ex-FSB and KGB agents he employed, Leonid
Perov always addressed him as "Mr. President."

Drawn out of his dark thoughts, Truznyev looked up. Sure enough, his Mercedes S-class limousine sat idling a few meters away. The other two guards assigned to his inner security detail were already in position on the other side of the car, ready to intervene against any perceived threat. "Thank you, Leonid," he said.

The sudden sound of a car door opening echoed through the garage.

Startled, Truznyev swung his head toward the sudden noise. At this late hour, the parking garage was usually deserted. Perov and the other bodyguards went on alert. Their hands darted inside their coats, reaching for the miniature PP-2000 submachine guns each carried in a concealed shoulder holster.

A slender woman with short blond hair climbed out of the back of a black sedan parked near the garage exit ramp. She wore a long gray winter uniform coat. Her shoulder boards bore the single star of a major. Though her features were attractive, her expression was dour. Settling her peaked officer's cap firmly on her head, she strode briskly toward Truznyev.

Well, this was interesting, he thought, watching her approach. Whose emissary was this pretty but rather daunting Amazon? It had to be someone official. The license plates on that black sedan belonged to the number series reserved solely for government use. He made a small gesture, signaling his security guards to stand down. Relaxing slightly, they took their hands off their weapons and politely stepped aside.

"Can I help you, Major . . . ?" he asked.

"Chernova," she said brusquely, flashing an FSB identity card. "And yes, Mr. President, you can." She nodded toward the waiting sedan. "Minister of State Security Kazyanov asks that you accompany me to his office."

Truznyev raised an eyebrow at that. Of all the possibilities, he would have put Kazyanov near the bottom. Russia's intelligence chief was the prototypical yes-man, the last person he would have expected to risk contacting Gennadiy Gryzlov's deposed rival. "Viktor wants a meeting? At this hour?" He frowned. "Why not simply phone me?"

"The matter is of some urgency," Chernova told him. She lowered her voice. "And discretion."

Truznyev pondered that. Given the internecine rivalries Gryzlov habitually encouraged among his subordinates, it was likely that Kazyanov's phone calls were monitored—either by ambitious underlings or by others in the Kremlin. If the minister of state security truly wanted to avoid calling unwelcome attention to a clandestine meeting with someone out of official favor, arranging it this way made sense.

But be cautious, Igor, he told himself. *Don't jump to conclusions.* While he was confident that Tarzarov's anger with him could be managed, there was no denying that this sudden invitation to Kazyanov's lair—once his own—was unsettling. On the other hand, he thought, was it likely that Tarzarov would trust the intelligence chief to handle his dirty work? He shook his head. That was absurd. Of all the men in Gryzlov's inner circle,

Kazyanov was the one the old Kremlin power broker viewed with utter contempt.

"Is this an official matter?" Truznyev probed further.

Major Chernova shook her head. "No, Mr. President," she said matter-of-factly. "I am authorized to say that the minister requests this meeting as a personal favor 'between old friends of long service to each other.' He has also instructed me to tell you that it will be 'a strictly unofficial consultation on certain unfortunate current events.'"

Truznyev smiled inwardly, amused by the pompous phrasing so typical of the other man. In truth, the only thing he trusted about Viktor Kazyanov was his abject willingness to toady to those in power. On the other hand, he thought, maybe Gryzlov's hyperaggressiveness and manic behavior were finally beginning to rattle those closest to him. If nothing else, the failed attempt to assassinate Poland's president must have shown them that they were led by a madman. If so, some of the rats who'd helped oust him as president in favor of the younger man might be scouting around for a safe way off Gryzlov's foundering ship of state. Which meant putting up with Kazyanov's mewling might be worth his while.

He nodded to the major. "Very well, I accept the minister's invitation." But there was no point in being stupid about this, he decided. Some precautions were clearly in order. He turned to Perov. "You can take the car to my apartment, Leonid. Wait for me there," he said. "Tell Katya I'll call her later."

Expressionlessly, Perov nodded. "Tell Katya" was a code phrase meaning "follow me in case of trouble." "Yes, Mr. President," he murmured. "Your orders will be obeyed."

With that, Truznyev allowed Chernova to usher him to her waiting sedan. Politely, she held the rear passenger door open for him.

"Thank you, Major," he said with a smile.

"It is my pleasure, Mr. President," she said sincerely, suddenly appearing much less staid and somber and far more . . . approachable.

Still smiling, Truznyev slid into the backseat. There were worse prospects in life, he thought smugly, than a quiet drive with a beautiful young woman in uniform. If the truth be told, he was growing somewhat bored with his current mistresses. Perhaps it was time to branch out again. Besides, seducing one of Kazyanov's underlings might prove useful as well as pleasurable.

But instead of climbing in beside him, Chernova closed the car door firmly and walked around to get in the front, next to the driver. Taken aback, Truznyev frowned. What was this? Abruptly, he realized he was not alone in the passenger seat.

A big, beefy man in an immaculately tailored suit nodded politely to him. "*Dobriy vyecher.* Good evening."

Truznyev's mouth fell open in surprise. Who the devil was this clown? Alarmed, he reached for the door handle and then felt a sharp, stabbing pain in his thigh. Looking down, he saw that the big man had just jabbed him with a hypodermic. Suddenly he felt dizzy, as though he were falling into a bottomless pit. His vision blurred. His weirdly numbed fingers fumbled with the door handle. *Christ*, he thought in panic, *I have to get out of this car. I have to signal Perov for help.* But it was too late. The world grew darker with astonishing speed and then everything went completely black.

"And now *dobroy nochi*," the big man said coolly. "Good night." With one large hand, he held the unconscious Igor Truznyev upright in the seat.

The black sedan pulled away and drove up the ramp and out of the Dominion Tower garage.

CHAPTER 27

ON THE THIRD RING ROAD, MOSCOW
That same time

The black sedan turned right onto a wide, six-lane boulevard—heading toward the Third Ring Road, which circled around Moscow. Hotels, shopping malls, and apartment buildings blurred past in a succession of twinkling lights seen through a curtain of softly falling snow.

In the front passenger seat, Samantha Kerr took off her peaked officer's cap and ran her fingers quickly through her short-cropped dyed hair. She put her radio earpiece back in and clicked the transmit button. "Firebird to Gray Wolf. We're on the move."

The driver of their chase car, posted several blocks back, radioed back. "Understood, Firebird. We have eyes on you."

She glanced back across the seat at Marcus Cartwright. The big man had just finished fastening a seat belt to keep Truznyev from slumping over. Instead, the Russian lolled back against the headrest with his mouth sagging open. "Everything okay back there?"

Cartwright nodded. He had his fingers on the former Russian president's wrist, checking his pulse. "No problems so far. His pulse is strong. His respiration appears normal."

"That's a relief," Sam said. "This guy's a pig, but I know Mr. Martindale would rather we delivered him alive instead of as a corpse."

The drug they'd used on Truznyev was a Scion-crafted derivative of fentanyl—a fast-acting opioid analgesic. While there were a range of dangerous potential side effects, medical specialists who'd studied what was known of the Russian's health history had been fairly confident he could tolerate the drug's effects without suffering permanent damage. It wouldn't keep him unconscious for more than an hour or two, but by then they could arrange for longer-term sedation under more carefully controlled conditions.

Their sedan swung onto the access road that paralleled the main Ring Road and accelerated.

"Gray Wolf to Firebird," the chase car radioed. "You have company. A black Mercedes S-Class. The plate number is 'A 145 KH.'"

Sam Kerr frowned. That was Truznyev's personal car. She turned back to Cartwright. "His goons are following us."

"You're sure?" the big man asked mildly.

"Yep," she said flatly. "The turnoff to his apartment was three blocks back. They blew right past it." She frowned. "He must have slipped a code phrase in when he gave them their orders."

"Probably," Cartwright agreed. He pursed his lips. "So Comrade Truznyev here has finely honed survival instincts. That is too bad, though not entirely unexpected." He shrugged his shoulders. "Still, it's a shame when an operation gets messy."

He leaned forward, speaking to the driver. "We'll move to Plan B, Davey."

"Got it, Mr. Cartwright," David Jones said, carefully noting street signs as they flashed past in the darkness and falling snow. At the right moment, he exited the Ring Road, turning onto a broad, tree-lined street flanked by well-maintained four- and five-story-high apartment buildings. The black Mercedes limousine swung in behind them, now just about ten car lengths back.

Sam Kerr pulled out her smartphone and tapped in a short text message: *KRAK ENG*. Then, carefully holding her finger hovering over the send button on the screen, she kept her eyes fixed on the side-view mirror. "We're prepped and good to go," she told Cartwright and Jones.

Several blocks down the avenue, they turned again, this time into a narrow, dingier street running behind some of the apartment buildings. Trash dumpsters, mounds of blackened snow and frozen slush, and parked cars lined both sides of the road. A small orange reflector taped to the outside of one of the dumpsters gleamed brightly in their headlights.

They drove on past.

Behind them, the Mercedes accelerated, obviously moving to close the gap now that they were caught in a confined space without room for any fancy escape maneuvers. Sam's eyes narrowed as she began counting down, watching the headlights of the car behind as it drew closer. "Three. Two. One," she murmured, and then pushed the send button.

Fifty meters behind them, a small, soda-can-size plastic tube packed with C-4 dangled from the side of the marked dumpster. The Krakatoa-shaped demolition charge detonated with a blinding flash. A massive shock wave slammed straight into a thin, inverted copper plate set at the mouth of the plastic tube—instantly transforming it into a mass of molten metal flaring outward at hypersonic speed. Hit broadside, Truznyev's black Mercedes was blown apart, ripped into a blazing heap of pulverized metal and plastic.

"Problem solved," Samantha Kerr said evenly. She slipped her phone back into her uniform coat and turned back to Cartwright. "But the heat's going to come down hard on this one, Marcus. I think it's high time I disappeared. Along with the rest of my team."

The big man nodded. "Quite true, Ms. Kerr. Once we part company at the rendezvous point, activate your exfiltration plan." He offered her a crooked grin. "After all, there's no point in spoiling the beauty of the thing by lingering too long where you're likely to be wanted . . . at least by the Russian security services. Davey and I will take our sleeping friend here the rest of the way."

Minutes later, their sedan turned onto the M2 Motorway, heading south out of Moscow. Police and fire sirens wailed in the distance, converging on a plume of oily black smoke rising into the night sky.

OSTAFYEVO INTERNATIONAL BUSINESS AIRPORT, SOUTH OF MOSCOW

An hour later

Ostafyevo lay roughly twenty-seven kilometers south of Moscow's Third Ring Road. Originally owned by the Russian Ministry of Defense, the airport was now operated by Gazpromavia, a subsidiary of Gazprom, the giant, state-controlled natural-gas corporation. Much smaller than any of the other Moscow-area airports, it was used mostly by chartered flights and by corporate jets owned by favored international and domestic companies. Its two-thousand-meter-long concrete runway could accommodate aircraft ranging from Learjets to Boeing 737-700s and Sukhoi Superjet-100s.

Marcus Cartwright's black sedan, again carrying its regulation license plates, pulled up alongside a small but elegant, mirrored-glass terminal. Even this late, all the lights were on. Ostafyevo ran on international time, welcoming flights from Europe, Asia, and the Americas at all hours. The big, beefy man, back in his Klaus Wernicke persona, climbed out from behind the steering wheel.

With a smile, he handed the keys and a fat tip to one of the hovering valets. "Put my automobile in long-term parking, please, Dmitry," he said. "I may not be back for a few weeks."

With a pleased grin, the young Russian made the banknotes disappear. "At once, Herr Wernicke," he replied.

A utility van pulled in behind the sedan and David Jones got out. He moved around to the back of the van and yanked open its rear doors, revealing two large crates. Each crate already bore inspection seals from Russia's Federal Customs Service. Imperiously, the slender man waved a handful of waiting airport cargo handlers over. "These go to Herr Wernicke's private jet," he said. "But be careful with them, mind you. They're fragile."

They hurried over and began muscling the crates out of the van and onto the snow-dampened pavement.

Leaving the matter in the short Welshman's capable hands, Cartwright entered the terminal to handle the rest of the formalities for their departure. He moved straight to the main desk. An airport official in a jacket and tie looked up at his approach. "Welcome to Ostafyevo, Herr Wernicke." He checked his watch. "Right on schedule, as always."

Cartwright laughed. "We Germans are nothing if not precise," he said in Teutonic-accented Russian.

"I hope your visit to our country was pleasant?" the Russian asked obsequiously. It was widely known that the Kremlin smiled on Tekhwerk, GmbH, thanks largely to its role in supplying otherwise-difficult-to-obtain Western high-technology equipment useful for both civil and military applications.

"Extremely pleasant," Cartwright told him. "And very profitable." He slid a folder across the desk. "I trust that you will find my shipping and customs paperwork in good order?"

With a pleased smile, the Russian smoothly pocketed the sealed envelope discreetly tucked away inside the folder. "Everything is in perfect form, Herr Wernicke," the official assured him. "As always." He checked a monitor on the desk. "In fact, your baggage is being loaded aboard the aircraft now. There should be no trouble with an on-time departure."

"Even with this snow?" Cartwright asked. "I thought there might be a weather delay."

The airport official's smile widened. "All the runways have been thoroughly plowed and swept, Herr Wernicke. Remember, while you Germans may be the most punctual of all peoples, we Russians certainly know how to handle a few centimeters of snow."

Not long afterward, Marcus Cartwright and David Jones lounged comfortably aboard a nine-passenger Dassault Falcon 50 corporate jet—flying west out of Russia. Behind them, in the aircraft's baggage hold, a heavily sedated Igor Truznyev slept on, securely strapped inside a shipping crate.

CHAPTER 28

A PRISON CELL
The next day

Slowly and painfully, Igor Truznyev clawed and fought his way back up out of oblivion. He opened his eyes and then closed them again for a moment, feeling light-headed and utterly disoriented. He tried to move and found it impossible. Where was he? What had happened? Had he been in some kind of accident? Was this a hospital?

But then his memories flooded back. The memories of Kazyanov's strange invitation. Of climbing into that sedan. And then the sharp sensation of that needle plunging into his thigh. He swallowed in sudden panic. He'd been drugged!

His eyes opened. He took a deep, shuddering breath and regretted it straightaway. It was cold. So cold that the very air seemed full of ice crystals that stabbed and hacked and slashed all the way down his throat and into his straining lungs.

Truznyev stared down at himself. Clad in a

threadbare, sweat-soaked shirt and rough, ill-fitting trousers, he was strapped upright on a tiled metal table. Everything else around him was almost completely dark, with only glimmers of light seeping under a heavy steel door set in a dank concrete wall. Beyond the ragged sound of his own labored breathing and the thudding of his heart, there was only silence—an oppressive, all-encompassing silence like that of the grave. Fear crawled down his spine.

This was no hospital.

He had seen places like this before—places where soulless, cold-eyed men tortured other men and women, systematically reducing them to broken, barely human husks emptied of all knowledge and hope. He had been one of those cold-eyed men himself, in his younger days.

Straining futilely against the straps that bound him in place, Truznyev fought to regain control. *This is a mistake*, he told himself. *A terrible mistake.* Or maybe, he thought wildly, it was only some horrible nightmare.

And then, with a harsh, rippling crackle of electricity, a spotlight flared on—spearing him in its stark white glare, as though he were a cockroach caught crawling along a kitchen countertop. Squinting painfully against the pitiless, blinding light, he could only blink away tears.

"You are a traitor, Igor Ivanovich Truznyev," a flat, emotionless voice said, from the shadows behind the light.

All Truznyev could make out of the other man were a pair of highly polished boots. He swallowed and then tried to speak. "That is a lie," he stammered. "I am no such thing. I—"

"You will be silent," the voice said brutally. "Your crimes are no longer hidden. They stand revealed for all to see. Last year, at your orders, Ukrainian terrorists murdered numerous loyal Russian officers. Under your direction, these same terrorists committed acts of sabotage designed to drag this country into a war with Poland under false pretenses. Hundreds of our countrymen were killed in this war and thousands more were wounded. Tens of billions of rubles of valuable military hardware—missiles, aircraft, armored vehicles, and artillery—were lost. And then, simply to camouflage your role in luring the Motherland into this disastrous conflict, your agents murdered a Chinese intelligence officer and planted evidence suggesting Beijing's involvement. You were willing to destroy decades of delicate diplomatic rapprochement—to set us again in enmity against a nuclear-armed neighbor— and for what? Just to try to save your own skin."

Sweating now, despite the cold, Truznyev shook his head repeatedly, trying desperately to signal his denial of each accusation as it was made. Inwardly he felt mounting despair as the litany of his crimes unfolded, including details, dates, and names known only to a few of those he had covertly manipulated and corrupted—many of whom he had believed were dead, murdered at his own orders. Someone had betrayed him, but who?

"So, yes, you are a traitor, Igor Ivanovich," the voice said, now sounding disgusted. "A vile, stinking, and evil traitor. A traitor willing to betray his own people for sordid profit and the deluded hope of personal political gain."

Increasingly terrified, Truznyev retched, tasting the sour, acid taste of bile. "Where is my advocate?" he demanded feebly. "You cannot hold me incommunicado like this. Under the constitution, I have rights! I am entitled to a defense lawyer."

"You have no such rights, Igor Ivanovich," the voice said implacably. "Nor are you entitled to counsel. Your trial is concluded. You have been found guilty, and the sentence is death."

"No! That is not possible!" Truznyev protested shrilly, more afraid than ever. His voice cracked. "This is a farce! I am a former president of the Russian Federation! I am no traitor! I am a loyal servant of the state. I demand to speak to Sergei Tarzarov! Or to President Gryzlov himself!"

With a squealing, grinding sound, a view port slid open on the cell door. There, framed in the narrow opening, Truznyev saw Gennadiy Gryzlov staring in at him with a stern, unblinking expression. His breath caught in his throat. "Mr. President," he pleaded, reduced to babbling brokenly, almost incoherently, as his terror mounted. "Gennadiy. You are the son of my old friend and comrade Anatoly. Please, I beg you—"

Without speaking, the younger man turned away. The view port slid shut.

"Your appeal has been heard. And denied," the voice behind the blinding lights said tersely. "By order of the president, your sentence will be carried out without further delay."

The lights went out.

In the darkness, Truznyev felt a powerful hand grip his arm, followed by the sharp prick of a needle. He began screaming hoarsely, frantically writhing against the straps that bound him to the metal table. He was still screaming when the world fell out from under him and he lost consciousness.

THE WOODS
Sometime later

Again, Igor Truznyev swam groggily up out of blackness. His hands and feet were no longer bound. He staggered upright, forcing himself off his knees. Woozily, he spun slowly through a half circle, trying to make sense of his surroundings. What was this place? Branches laden with pine needles brushed past his face. All color seemed to have been leached from the world, leaving only shades of black and white and gray.

He was in a forest, he realized. It was night and he was somewhere deep in a forest choked by snow. An icy wind whipped right through his threadbare prison clothes, stabbing deeply. His feet were numb. His teeth chattered, rattling so hard that he could not keep his mouth closed.

"You have gone far enough, dead man," a harsh voice said from behind him.

Dazed and barely conscious, Truznyev turned slowly.

The blue-tinted halogen headlights of an automobile flicked on. Silhouetted against their glare, he could make out three men in heavy military overcoats. They cradled assault rifles.

Oh God, no, he thought.

"Make ready!" the voice snapped.

Their assault rifles came up, aiming straight at his chest.

"No! Please! No!" Truznyev screamed, overwhelmed by panic. He dropped to his knees in the snow with his arms spread wide. "Don't kill me! Not like this!" he begged.

But then, suddenly, an enormous black-and-gray shape lunged out of the forest. It raced into the midst of his would-be executioners in a blur of lethal precision and speed—trailing a whirlwind of snow and splintered branches. In what seemed a single blurred instant of murderously efficient motion, the machine slaughtered them. Bodies went flying in all directions. Bright red blood sprayed across the snow.

Truznyev stayed frozen, his eyes wide in horror.

Towering above the broken corpses of the men it had just butchered, the robot stood motionless for a moment. Then its six-sided head swiveled through an arc, as though it were a wolf sniffing the air for the scent of new prey.

With a soft, hydraulic whine, the huge machine turned in his direction, reaching out with large, articulated metal fingers. "You are Igor Truznyev," it said in an eerie, inhuman voice. "And I have come for you."

Terrified out of his wits, Igor Truznyev passed out.

OUTSIDE THE CID TRAINING SIMULATOR, IRON WOLF SQUADRON SECURE HANGAR, POWIDZ, POLAND
That same time

A large opaque dome occupied the center of the cavernous hangar. It looked oddly like one of the inflatable, portable planetariums used to bring astronomy shows to schoolchildren around the world. Power and fiber-optic cables snaked across the cold concrete floor, connecting the dome to an array of monitors and computers. Environmental systems hummed softly. Technicians moved quietly from machine to machine, checking various systems and adjusting controls as needed.

The dome contained a haptic interface module and a series of three-dimensional projectors, all tied into a sophisticated virtual-reality setup. Ordinarily the simulator was used to give prospective CID pilots a taste of what piloting one of the fighting machines was like—without risking damage to one of the hugely expensive robots at the hands of a rookie. Pilot candidates could run through a whole series of mock battle and training scenarios that would look, sound, and even *feel* real, thanks to the haptic interface.

But now the simulator had been reconfigured for a very different purpose.

Brad McLanahan stood next to Kevin Martindale, watching the Scion techs work in hushed silence. "You really think this scheme of yours is going to work?" he asked skeptically, eyeing the jury-rigged mass of cabling.

Martindale shrugged. "I certainly hope so," he said. Pointedly, he nodded toward the large digital clock mounted on one wall of the hangar. "Given the time constraints we face, the other means of . . . persuasion . . . available to us seemed even less likely to achieve results."

"Not to mention being even more ethically suspect," Brad said wryly.

"Indeed," Martindale agreed, without batting an eyelash. "So let's pray this succeeds, shall we? Because I am prepared to do *whatever* is necessary to get the information we need."

Brad nodded slowly. Not for the first time, he decided that Martindale was a very dangerous man. For now, the head of Scion was on the side of the angels, but the ease with which he contemplated cutting moral and ethical corners in pursuit of his goals was daunting. What was that line from Nietzsche he'd read in some philosophy class? Something about staring into the abyss too long and one day finding the abyss staring back at you? Well, Kevin Martindale had been dancing on the edge of the abyss for a long, long time.

"Excuse me, Mr. Martindale," one of the technicians said, coming up to report. "The subject has just lost conscious, as expected. We've started sedating him again."

"Very well," Martindale said. He looked up at the clock again. "Initiate the final phase of Program Lubyanka." Seeing the wry look on Brad's face, he murmured. "It seemed an appropriate title."

"Yeah, no kidding," Brad replied tightly. "I'll go make sure Captain Schofield's guys are set. And then I'll suit up."

He turned and walked away, wondering if a day was going to come when he and Martindale crossed swords. For both their sakes, he hoped not.

OVER POLAND
Sometime later

Igor Truznyev woke up again, this time feeling more rested and far more in control of his faculties. He felt warm, almost comfortable. That seemed . . . wrong, somehow.

He opened his eyes. Wrapped in blankets, he was strapped loosely to a stretcher. An IV tube was attached to his arm. A uniformed medic with a Red Cross armband finished checking his pulse, gave him a quick thumbs-up sign, and then sat back.

Truznyev lifted his head slightly, studying his surroundings. From the noise and vibration, he judged that he was in the troop compartment of some kind of military aircraft. Grim-faced men and women in snow camouflage uniforms sat in fold-down seats that ran down the length of the cabin. Both their uniforms and their weapons were unfamiliar.

His eyes widened when he saw the large, spindly-limbed combat machine squatting near the aircraft's sealed rear ramp door. Memories of the slaughter he'd witnessed suddenly crowded his mind. He started to shiver. He was in the hands of the Poles and their Iron Wolf mercenaries.

With a jolt, the aircraft touched down, bounced slightly, and then settled firmly. The roar of its engines diminished fast, spooling down into silence. At the same time, the ramp door whined open, revealing a barren stretch of tarmac and snow-dusted trees in the distance.

With that same startling grace he'd witnessed earlier, the tall robot unfolded itself and strode away with amazing speed. The snow-camouflaged troops followed it out, assembling in squads on the tarmac and then marching away at the double.

Once the ramp was clear, a medical team darted inside, lifted up his stretcher, and carried him outside. As they left, Truznyev got a better look at the aircraft, a large tilt-rotor emblazoned with a metal gray, red-eyed robotic wolf's head.

The medics set his stretcher down on the tarmac.

A well-dressed man with long gray hair and a neatly trimmed beard sauntered over and looked down at him. "Welcome to Poland, President Truznyev," the man said smoothly.

Truznyev recognized Kevin Martindale at once. Intelligence reports, rumors, and pure speculation about the former American president and his private military corporation occupied substantial space in official Russian intelligence databases and in those belonging to his own private consulting group.

He swallowed hard. "You—" he said hesitantly, not sure quite how to proceed.

"Extracted you from a rather nasty situation of your own making?" Martindale finished for him.

Wordlessly, Truznyev nodded, feeling humiliated. First, Gryzlov and now this American. How many others had uncovered the secrets he thought so carefully buried?

"Yes, we did," Martindale said flatly. "And at considerable risk and expense to ourselves." Coldly, he stared down at the Russian. "You know who I am, Igor," he said. "So you know that I am not a particularly charitable or forgiving man."

Again, Truznyev nodded.

"Good. Because you put yourself into this mess. And now you're going to have to buy your way out of it," Martindale told him. His expression hardened. "And if you can't, my people will dump you back across the border so that Gryzlov's killers can finish the work we so rudely interrupted. Is that clear?" Truznyev winced. He felt the color drain from his face. "Good," Martindale said, sounding satisfied, not waiting for a verbal response. He signaled the waiting medic. They lifted Truznyev's stretcher again and moved toward a waiting ambulance.

Martindale kept pace. "You're going to a pleasant, comfortable, and extremely well-guarded military hospital, Igor," he said with a slight smile. "And on the way, you and I are going to have a really thorough and *very* detailed chat about the cyberwar complex you folks call Perun's Aerie."

CHAPTER 29

THE KREMLIN
That same time

Sergei Tarzarov maintained a small office just down the hall from Gennadiy Gryzlov's more extensive suite. Unlike the president's elaborately furnished chambers, the chief of staff's working space was plain, almost Spartan in its simplicity. He made do with a metal desk, a single chair, an old-fashioned desktop computer, and a secure phone with direct links to the president and other major key players in the government. There were no decorations, no knickknacks, mementos, or personal photographs—nothing that might suggest he had any hobbies or interests beyond work or any weaknesses that potential rivals could exploit.

Now he sat alone at his desk, with the door firmly closed, moodily contemplating the mystery of Igor Truznyev's sudden disappearance. When the first police report of the bomb attack on the former president's limousine came in, he'd assumed Truznyev was dead, killed with his body-guards. That had prompted him to order an immediate high-priority investigation by the FSB's counterterrorism section. He'd also embargoed all news accounts of the incident. Until it was clearer why someone had murdered Truznyev, there was no point in feeding a speculative frenzy by domestic and foreign journalists.

But now it was clear that Igor Truznyev had not been inside his S-Class Mercedes when it was blown to hell. Surveillance camera footage retrieved from his office-tower garage showed him being accosted by a woman in uniform. After a brief conversation, he'd left the building in her car, followed moments later by his own body-guards in the Mercedes.

Unfortunately, the security cameras weren't equipped to record audio—apparently the result of a deliberate specification by Truznyev himself, as part of his own anti-eavesdropping precautions. Nor had the FSB's lip-reading experts been able to piece together anything useful from the footage. The angles were wrong, they said. The intelligence service's photo-interpretation experts were more certain they could extract information from the one grainy screen capture they'd made of an ID card shown to Truznyev by the mysterious woman. They were methodically working on the project, digitally enhancing the image over and over until it was clean enough to make out details.

Privately, Tarzarov doubted that would help much, if at all.

Preliminary searches through every Russian military- and intelligence-service database had failed to turn up a match. Whoever she really was, she was not on the books for any government agency. And the license plates on her sedan were faked. While the sequence of numbers and letters on them matched those reserved for official cars, that particular number had never been issued. Effectively, barring some lucky break, the FSB's investigative team had reached a dead end.

In the meantime, Truznyev himself had vanished completely. Checks at every airport, train station, and border crossing point were still in progress, but so far no sign of him had turned up. It was as though he'd been snatched off the surface of the earth by aliens.

Damn the man, Tarzarov thought. Was this disappearing act part of one of Truznyev's private spy games? The murder of his bodyguards made that seem unlikely.

Was it possible that he'd finally pushed one of his shadier rivals or even a onetime business partner too far? His Zatmeniye consulting firm certainly had its fingers in any number of different enterprises—many of which were not even remotely legal. And Russia's organized-crime syndicates were even more violent and unforgiving than their Sicilian or North American counterparts. If so, it was unlikely anyone would ever see Truznyev again, alive or dead. Permanently disposing of an inconvenient corpse was no great challenge for the Russian *Mafiya*, with its ready access to factory blast furnaces, cement mixers and construction sites, and vast stretches of empty wilderness.

Sergei Tarzarov's high forehead furrowed in sudden worry as he contemplated a far less appealing prospect. Truznyev dead was no great loss. Yes, the former president's services, political and diplomatic advice, and occasional tidbits of intelligence had been useful, but they were not vital. But what if he were still alive? And not only alive, but somewhere outside Russia—either as a prisoner or, more probably, a defector?

He grimaced. Truznyev dead might not be a problem. But Truznyev alive and spilling his guts was a potential time bomb. At their last rendezvous, the former president had made it abundantly clear that he knew far more than he should about Russia's top-secret cyberwar operations and infrastructure. And it was no secret that he hated and despised Gryzlov, the man who'd replaced him as president. What if he had decided to disappear, leave Russia, and then sell his information to the highest bidder?

Tarzarov's frown deepened. If that was the other man's plan, he would find no shortage of buyers with very deep pockets—ranging from the Poles to the Americans to the Chinese. Could Truznyev have arranged the murder of his own bodyguards to make it look as though he'd been kidnapped? It was perfectly possible, the older man decided. No man in Russia rose to such heights without being willing to sacrifice even his most loyal subordinates if necessary.

Almost of its own volition, his hand drifted to

the secure phone on his desk, hovering over the button that would connect him directly to Gennadiy Gryzlov. If there were any possibility that Truznyev was selling their cyberwar secrets to a foreign power, it was his duty to give the president the bad news.

But then his hand drew back.

Think carefully before you leap into the unknown, Sergei, he thought. Decades spent up to his neck in Kremlin intrigue had imparted a very basic lesson: bearers of bad tidings were rarely rewarded. There were other considerations too. Briefing Gryzlov would necessarily entail revealing more than might be wise about his dealings with Truznyev. Russia's president, while supremely self-confident, was also deeply paranoid. How would he react to learning that his trusted chief of staff and closest confidant had been holding clandestine meetings with the man he'd deposed? Would he see the value derived from maintaining such contacts? Or would he see them as evidence that Tarzarov might be plotting against him?

Without hard evidence of Truznyev's real fate, it made no sense to take such a risk now, he decided. If allegations made by the former Russian president started showing up in the Western press, they could easily be dismissed as the disgruntled ravings of a failed leader. In time, any effects on international opinion they produced would fade—buried by the news of some pop star's drug overdose or another petty scandal.

The chance that Truznyev's information might be used for military purposes was a more serious threat. If the former president really had defected, he certainly knew enough to allow his new masters to pinpoint Russia's buried cyberwar complex. But even with that information, could anyone really hope to launch a successful attack so deep into the Motherland's territory? It seemed unlikely to Tarzarov. Not unless they were willing to send so large a strike force that it would represent an open declaration of all-out war against Russia. And not even the Poles were that crazy.

Besides, he reminded himself, Gennadiy was supremely confident that the defenses around the Perun's Aerie complex were impregnable. Under the circumstances, Tarzarov concluded, wisdom dictated a course of waiting to see precisely how events unfolded.

NATIONAL GEOSPATIAL-INTELLIGENCE AGENCY, FORT BELVOIR NORTH AREA, NEAR SPRINGFIELD, VIRGINIA
That same time

Intelligence analyst Kristin Voorhees came back from lunch and entered her cubicle. The first thing she noticed after sitting down at her computer was that someone had futzed with her ThinkGeek *Firefly* magnetic word set. Clipped to one of her cube's partitions, the board came with an assortment of words and suffixes used in dialogue from the cult-classic science-fiction series, and she was fond of arranging and rearranging them while noodling with complex database problems.

In and of itself, the futzing wasn't a problem. She'd made it clear that her colleagues were welcome to reset the board whenever the spirit moved them. Many of them did, especially during those all-night shifts during a major international flap—when it seemed like every U.S. intelligence agency and administration senior executive was screaming for more satellite imagery and analysis.

No, it wasn't the fact that the words had been rearranged while she was gone that caught her attention. It was what they now spelled out: *Gorram wobble-headed doll caper.*

Her breath caught in her throat. She'd been activated.

Years ago, while Voorhees was still just a computer-science postdoc interviewing to join the NGA, she'd been recruited by Scion as an unpaid sleeper agent. She'd never regretted her decision. Where so much of the U.S. intelligence community seemed bogged down in bureaucratic sloth and political infighting, former president Martindale's private military and intelligence outfit had been out fighting the good fight—relentlessly opposing the enemies of the United States and the whole free world.

Then again, she thought wryly, feeling her heart pounding in her chest, as a sleeper agent, she'd never been asked to take any risks. Not until now. Her Scion handlers had only expected her to do the best job possible for the NGA, earning promotions and steadily working her way up into positions of higher and higher responsibility.

And now here she was, one of the agency's data stewards charged with maintaining its huge archives of highly classified satellite imagery, maps, and other intelligence information. Her post gave her high-level, read/write access to those databases, and now it was time for her to use that power on behalf of Scion.

For a moment, Kristen Voorhees was tempted to shuffle the words on her Firefly board back into random patterns and pretend the activation signal had never been delivered. That would be the safest course. If she were caught and convicted, the lightest prison term she could probably expect was something on the order of the two-year sentence handed to another government intelligence analyst caught passing classified satellite photos to *Jane's Defence Weekly* back in the mid-1980s. But given President Barbeau's long-standing feud with Scion and Kevin Martindale, her fate was likely to be a lot worse.

Deep in thought, she pulled off her glasses and absently polished them with the untucked tail of her blouse. Doing time in federal prison was not an appealing prospect. She was pretty sure that convicts weren't allowed access to computers for anything but e-mail.

But she knew she couldn't really just walk away. Not in good conscience. Anyone who followed the news knew that Russia was on the march again in Eastern and central Europe—using cyberwar weapons and terrorism to brutalize the small democracies America had turned its back on. Whatever Scion was interested in had to be related to that ongoing battle.

She sat up straighter and put her glasses back on.

Resolutely, she turned back to her keyboard, logged in with her access codes, and then entered a single, short command—a command that triggered a small piece of code buried long ago in the primary database operating software. In turn, this subroutine opened a tiny back door, a secret way into every NGA archive that could be used remotely by Scion intelligence operatives. For the next six hours, Martindale's agents would have free, virtually undetectable, entry into every agency database. After that, the subroutine would erase itself until its next activation, sealing the back door and deleting any record of what she'd done.

At least that was how it should work in theory, she thought. But no one knew better than she did that systems as large and complex as those used by the agency had peculiar, little quirks all of their own. It was entirely possible that this Scion foray would leave traces the agency's counterintelligence people would spot on their next security sweep. And if that happened, Kristen Voorhees was going to be neck-deep in trouble with a capital *E*, as in "violation of the Espionage Act."

With a sigh, she turned back to her list of regular assignments and started work again. If they did come to slap the cuffs on her, she could at least try to make life a little easier for her successor.

HEADQUARTERS, RUSSIAN AEROSPACE FORCES, MOSCOW
That same time

"*Da*, Mr. President!" Colonel General Valentin Maksimov said into the phone. "I understand. My forces will be ready for any eventuality."

He hung up and looked at his senior military aide, Major General Viktor Polichev. "The president has ordered us to prepare for the likelihood of limited air and missile hostilities along our western and northwestern borders."

The other man raised an eyebrow. "Based on what? Our intelligence reports show no signs of increased combat readiness by the Poles or their allies. Or by any of the NATO powers, for that matter."

"The president did not see fit to share his reasoning with me," Maksimov said with a wry smile. "But I suspect he thinks the recent assassination attempt on President Wilk may have consequences."

"Yes, that seems likely," Polichev agreed. "It is a pity that our FSB and Spetsnaz colleagues were so clumsy." He frowned. "What exactly does the president expect us to do? Put our air-defense forces on full alert?"

"Fortunately not," Maksimov said.

Polichev looked relieved. And for good reason. Raising the alert status of their fighter squadrons, radar units, and SAM regiments would set off alarms in defense ministries across Europe and even in the United States. Of itself, that was no real problem. However, in the aftermath of the crude attack on Poland's president, going on high alert could trigger an unwanted sequence of actions and reactions from both sides. Like many Russian Aerospace Force officers itching to avenge their combat losses last year, Polichev had no problem with fighting the Poles. But that didn't mean he wanted to blunder into a shooting war by accident because some trigger-happy pilot or missile officer got careless. "Then what are your orders?" he asked his chief.

"Have your couriers finished distributing the new target-acquisition-software upgrade for our S-300 and S-400 forces?" Maksimov wondered.

"Deliveries to our units in the Eastern and Central Military Districts are continuing," Polichev said. "But all our SAM regiments in the Western and Southern Military Districts have already been upgraded."

Maksimov nodded in satisfaction. Those were the regions most vulnerable to attack by enemies equipped with "netrusion" technology and stealth drones. The Chinese did not possess such weapons, at least not yet. "I want you to schedule a rotating series of battle drills at the regimental level starting tomorrow, Viktor," he said firmly. "That should help our missile troops shake off the cobwebs and learn the ins and outs of these new programs."

"Yes, sir," Polichev said. "Should I inform the various foreign military attachés?"

Maksimov thought about that. To avoid unnecessarily raising international tensions, it was standard practice to brief other governments on major military exercises. "Go ahead. But, Viktor?"

"Yes, sir?"

"Make sure no one says anything about the software improvements we've made. And keep them well away from any of our command centers," Maksimov cautioned. "As far as our foreign friends are concerned, we will say these are simply routine drills to check equipment readiness. Let them draw their own conclusions about our real intentions."

Polichev nodded. It was all part of the complicated game of diplomatic and military signaling so common in relationships among the great powers. By announcing its series of SAM drills in advance, Russia was acting as though nothing out of the ordinary was happening. But at the same time, the short notice with which those same exercises were called also sent a message that Russia's armed forces were alert and able to defend their country if attacked.

If all went well, they would make the Poles and their American mercenaries think twice about seeking revenge. And if not . . . well, Russia's air-defense forces in the sectors most likely to be attacked would be ready and waiting.

CHAPTER 30

**IRON WOLF SQUADRON HEADQUARTERS,
33RD AIR BASE, NEAR POWIDZ, POLAND**
The next day

Brad McLanahan looked around the oval conference table. Counting Piotr Wilk, who was joining them by secure video link from his hospital room, the key members of the joint Polish–Iron Wolf command team were here. All but one.

For a moment, his vision clouded. The medical team monitoring his father's deteriorating condition sent him reports every few hours or so. All of them said pretty much the same thing: "The general's life is moving peacefully to its close."

Earlier, one of the doctors had tactfully suggested removing Patrick McLanahan from life support—a suggestion Brad had heatedly declined. "I may not be able to save my dad's life," he'd snapped. "But I am damned well *not* going to kill him. As long as he isn't in unbearable pain, you're going to give him every chance to fight this last battle in his own way and go in his own time. Is that clear?"

Nadia had intervened at that point, dragging the ICU physician off for an intense, private conversation in fast-paced Polish. From the apprehensive look on the man's face when they'd parted company, he guessed she'd put the fear of God, or at least Major Nadia Rozek, into him.

Martindale's voice drew him back to the present.

"We have a confirmed target," the gray-haired chief of Scion said quietly. "Thanks to the clues provided by our 'guest,' the regrettably still-breathing Igor Truznyev."

"And what did you promise him in return for this information?" Wilk asked. His eyes were steely, unforgiving.

"His life, nothing else," Martindale said bluntly. He offered them a thin, humorless smile. "Truznyev was in no condition to ask for anything more." He shrugged. "Of course, now that he's betrayed Gryzlov's secrets, he has no leverage at all. And over time, I'm sure we'll think of a great many more interesting questions to ask him—questions he will be in no position to dodge."

Brad nodded to himself. Truznyev was doubly screwed. Even if the Russian ever figured out that he'd been tricked, it was too late now. The first time he balked, all the Poles had to do was threaten to hand him back to Gryzlov's people, along with a brief précis of the classified information he'd already spilled.

"Good," Wilk replied. He sounded pleased. "I'm

sure we can find suitably uncomfortable quarters to keep him on ice for as long as we see fit."

Impatiently, Whack Macomber broke into the conversation. "Glad as I am to hear that piece of shit Truznyev is slated for more bad tidings of discomfort and woe, I'd kind of like to know more about this target Mr. Martindale mentioned." His expression was grim. "Because I have this bad feeling that it's not going to be real easy to hit."

Martindale nodded. "Ten out of ten, Major." He looked around the table. "I've had teams of Scion and Polish intelligence analysts working around the clock to confirm Truznyev's claims about the location of this 'Perun's Aerie' cyberwar complex. While he could not give us its precise coordinates, his information let our people zero in on the most probable site."

"Which is where . . . exactly?" Macomber pressed.

In answer, the Scion chief brought up a topographical map on one of the wall displays. It showed a rugged landscape of jagged, sawtooth ridges and mountains and glaciers, cut by narrow, winding river valleys. A red circle surrounded one of the peaks. "Here. Buried inside Mount Manaraga in the Nether-Polar Urals, about sixty-five nautical miles due east of the city of Pechora."

"Meaning?" prompted Brad.

Martindale zoomed the map out, showing the cyberwar complex's location in a broader geographic context. Mount Manaraga lay deep inside northern Russia, more than 1,400 nautical miles east of Poland, and only 250 nautical miles south of the frozen Barents Sea.

"Oh, fuck," Macomber muttered, with an unhappy look on his hard-edged face.

Silently, Brad echoed the sentiment. That mountain was one hell of a long way inside enemy territory.

"How sure are your analysts of this?" Wilk asked, studying the same image repeated on a display in his hospital room.

"Just about one hundred percent," Martindale said. "Like I said, once Truznyev pointed us in the right direction, our people were able to do some discreet and focused poking around inside various National Security Agency and National Geospatial-Intelligence Agency databases. They hit pay dirt fairly quickly." He tapped another control, bringing up a succession of satellite images and short transcripts of intercepted Russian radio and phone conversations.

Several months-old satellite photos showed freight cars loaded with the spoil from underground excavations sitting on sidings around Pechora. Other images taken around the same time showed what might be traces of new roads built through the pine forests surrounding Mount Manaraga. Later photos showed no signs of those same roads. Either they had been destroyed, or more likely, better camouflaged.

Among the intercepts was a signal from Atomflot headquarters to the Ministry of State Security protesting an explained directive that Atomflot sell a naval nuclear reactor intended for one of its new *Arktika*-class icebreakers to "an entity under your ministry's control" at cost. A terse reply informed the state-controlled company that its protest had been rejected "at the highest authority" and that any further discussion of the issue was "forever foreclosed by Presidential National Security Decree 117."

Heads nodded slowly around the table, seeing the picture this was all painting.

"And then when our people went digging inside the corporate records of a Russian computer manufacturer named T-Platforms, we turned up a purchase order for an extremely powerful supercomputer," Martindale continued.

"A purchase order from who?" Brad asked.

"A company we've long suspected of being a front for the FSB," Martindale said.

"And where was this supercomputer delivered?" Nadia wondered.

Martindale smiled. "That's the curious fact of the dog that didn't bark in the night, Major Rozek. As far as T-Platforms' records are concerned, the computer was *never* delivered. But neither is it still in their inventory."

Nadia wrinkled her nose. "That was sloppy."

"It was," Martindale agreed. Then he shrugged. "On the other hand, without the added clues Truznyev gave us, we'd just be looking at another tantalizing dead end."

"How could American intelligence miss this secret project?" Wilk wanted to know. "With all these images showing new excavations and construction work around this mountain, I mean."

"Because it's like looking at one particular grain of sand on a whole beach," Martindale explained. "The major industry in this part of the Urals is mining. New tunnels and roads are a dime a dozen. The only reason my folks are pretty sure this isn't just some new commercial mine is the effort the Russians made to hide their tracks—along with the fact that there are no records of any mining claims registered for Mount Manaraga."

"And that was even sloppier," Nadia said.

"Maybe," Martindale replied. "But remember, our spy satellites take enormous numbers of images every day—more images than we have the ability to thoroughly analyze in anything approaching real time. More and more of the work is automated, but—"

"Computers only see what they've been programmed to look for," Nadia finished, sounding disgusted.

"Exactly," Martindale said. "In the old days, satellite intelligence analysts had to make bricks without straw, stretching tiny fragments of information to the breaking point to make a case. Now they're flooded with more and more imagery captured from wider and wider swathes of the earth. More images than they can possibly examine closely in any normal human lifetime."

"Which means analysts only focus on issues they've been tasked to address," Brad realized. "And nobody in the States had any idea Gryzlov was building this cyberwar complex in the first place."

Martindale nodded.

"All this is just peachy-keen," Whack Macomber said gruffly. "But assuming this fucking mountain really is what we've been looking for, do we have the slightest damn idea of what kind of defenses the Russians have deployed to protect it?"

"That's a good question, Major," Martindale said coolly. He tapped another control, bringing up two side-by-side images of the mountain. One was dated from more than two years ago, presumably before any serious construction began. The other was only several weeks old.

To Brad's untrained eye, they looked absolutely identical.

When he said as much, Martindale looked pleased. "Yes, they do, Captain McLanahan. That's why I had our best analysts dive in deep, scouring these images right down to the individual pixel. They wrote special programs to speed up the work. And this is what they turned up . . ."

With a muted flourish, Scion's chief clicked to another version of the second satellite photo. This one showed dozens of red circles scattered across the mountain's rugged slopes and the narrow valleys around it. "By very, very carefully comparing every square meter of terrain captured in these two separate images, our people were able to spot places where some kind of change—man-made change—had taken place. In some cases, the indications are as small as a boulder shifted a meter or so out of place, or a section of rock or soil raised slightly above where it was in the original images."

"Those are camouflaged weapons bunkers," Macomber said grimly.

"Most are. The others are probably sensor posts and concealed surface-to-air missile positions," Martindale agreed. He looked around the table again. "Which raises the very real question of whether we stand *any* chance of successfully attacking Perun's Aerie at all."

Brad frowned. "There's no way we can hit it successfully from the air," he said. "No combat aircraft or drone in our inventory has the range and penetration ability, let alone the ordnance load needed to do the job."

"Hell, even a big-ass tactical nuke would probably just scratch the surface," Macomber muttered.

Brad nodded. "Well, yeah, Whack, and as it happens, we're fresh out of nuclear weapons anyway." He saw Piotr Wilk and Nadia exchange glances. "Aren't we?"

Wilk shrugged. "Sadly, that is true, Captain. After winning our freedom from the communists, we relied entirely on the nuclear umbrella provided by the United States." He smiled lopsidedly. "It's only now beginning to occur to some of us that we may need to fill that rather large gap in our defenses. But acquiring such weapons is a much longer-term project."

"In which case, we really only have one option," Brad said quietly. "And that's a bolt-out-of-the-blue attack by Iron Wolf CIDs flown in on the XCV-62 Ranger."

"Oh, man," Macomber growled. "I knew I should have upped my fucking life insurance when I had the chance."

IRON WOLF FLIGHT LINE
Several hours later

Brad escorted Martindale into the large bomb-resistant hangar used to prep Iron Wolf aircraft and CIDs for combat missions. The massive concrete-and-reinforced-steel building was a sea of purposeful activity and noise.

In one section of the hangar, an Iron Wolf ground crew swarmed over the black, batwinged XCV-62 Ranger, checking the stealth STOL transport's engines, avionics, and other systems. Off to the side, Whack Macomber and Captain Ian Schofield were putting together an assortment of small arms and other weapons. Schofield and four of his most experienced recon troopers were going along to act as a close-in protection force for the Ranger while it was on the ground inside Russia. And over in the far corner, Charlie Turlock was supervising a team of technicians who were hard at work readying two of the squadron's remaining CID combat robots.

Brad spotted Nadia Rozek standing at the foot of the ladder Charlie was using. The dark-haired Polish Special Forces officer had her hands planted firmly on her hips. She also had an obstinate, thoroughly exasperated expression on her face.

"Uh-oh," he murmured.

Martindale saw where he was looking and winced. "Let me guess," he said. "You didn't tell her?"

"I was going to," Brad said, trying very hard *not* to sound like a kid explaining that his dog really had wolfed down his homework. "But other high-priority stuff kept coming up."

Nadia swung toward him as he came up. "Charlie says that *she* is piloting one of the CIDs, instead of me." Her eyes flashed angrily. "This mission is important to my homeland and to the entire alliance. It is my duty as a Polish officer to participate in this attack! Besides, you know very well that I have significant battle experience in these machines!"

Gracefully, Charlie slid down the ladder and dropped lightly onto the hangar floor. "Hi, Brad. Mr. Martindale," she said coolly. "I've tried telling Major Rozek the assignments are set, but she insists on bucking the question up to higher authority—which I guess in this case would be you, right? Since this is your plan and all?"

Brad nodded. *Don't turn and run*, he told himself. That would be cowardly. Besides, the way his ribs still ached, Nadia would just catch him in the first few meters. "Ms. Turlock is right, Nadia. I need you as my copilot and systems operator for the Ranger. No one else can do the job. No one else in the world has the flight time or experience with the bird that you do."

"I can do both," Nadia insisted stubbornly. "The CIDs will only go into action once we've landed. And I can have the machine up and running in minutes."

"And what happens if you get killed or wounded in the fight?" Charlie said, not sugarcoating it.

"CIDs aren't invincible, after all. Then Brad's stuck on his own trying to fly that aircraft out through an alerted Russian air-defense network. Hey, believe me, I get why you want to be in at the sharp end. Kicking Gryzlov's computer goons in the gonads should be sweet. But this is about sound tactics and focus. Putting our copilot into ground combat only adds another risk factor to the chances of mission failure."

Smart woman, Brad thought. Focusing on what was best for the mission was the surest bet to disarm Nadia's fierce combativeness and otherwise almost unyielding sense of patriotism and national honor.

Sure enough, though she still appeared irritated, Nadia also looked a bit more thoughtful.

It was time for him to chime in, Brad decided. "This is going to be a tough flight," he said. "Basically, our only chance to penetrate Russian airspace undetected is to go in really low and stay low most of the way—and do the same on our way out. That's nearly seventeen hundred nautical miles round trip. And low-altitude flying eats fuel fast, so we're gonna be operating right at the outside edge of our endurance. Which means I need to put everything I've got into keeping the Ranger flying right down the zone." He shook his head. "If we get jumped, I need you there beside me, running our defenses. Otherwise, we're toast."

Nadia grimaced, knowing he was right. As a stealth transport aircraft, the XCV-62 carried no offensive weapons—no air-to-air missiles, bombs, or even guns. Its defenses consisted entirely of the SPEAR system, chaff and flare dispensers, and two ADM-160B miniature air-launched decoys fitted in a small internal bay.

"Besides, Whack and I have fought as a team before, in Iran and Iraq and a bunch of other godforsaken places," Charlie went on. "So we know each other's moves inside out and that boosts our combat efficiency."

This time, Nadia bobbed her head slightly, though it was a grudging, very reluctant nod. "Perhaps, you are right," she said stiffly, through gritted teeth. "Though I wish—"

"Ms. Turlock, what on earth are you doing to these Cybernetic Infantry Devices?" Martindale interrupted, sounding appalled. He was staring up at the two twelve-foot-tall CIDs, which looked even more spindly and skeletal than usual. The Iron Wolf techs were busy removing whole sections of hexagonal-shaped thermal tiles and the wafer-thin electrochromatic plates layered over them.

Charlie shrugged. "We're stripping their thermal-adaptive camouflage and chameleon camouflage systems."

"And why in God's good name would you do that?" Martindale demanded. "Right before an attack on a heavily defended Russian base?"

"For three reasons," Charlie said patiently. She held up one finger. "Number one, because of snow. Have you seen the most recent satellite photos of that area, Mr. Martindale?" He nodded. "Then you know, sir, that the whole area is practically hip-deep in snow right now," she said. "And the one thing those really nifty chameleon systems *cannot* do is hide footprints."

"Oh," the gray-haired man said, sounding flummoxed.

Charlie nodded. "Yeah. *Oh*. See, I don't care how dumb your average Russian sentry is, I kind of figure the sight of a bunch of big footprints appearing in the snow will clue him into the fact that something bad is going down. Which brings me to reason number two." She held up a second finger. "It's cold there. Really, really cold."

"As in too cold for the CID's thermal-adaptive tiles to function efficiently," Martindale guessed, frowning now.

"Yep," she said. "There's no way we can cool the tiles down to match those external temps. Not without draining the CID's power supply in minutes."

"And your third reason?" Martindale asked.

"Weight," Charlie said simply. She shrugged her slender shoulders. "See there's no way we can expect a field resupply mission on this gig. Even if the terrain and tactical situation allowed it, there's no room for one of those handy little Wolf ATV cargo carriers in the Ranger. So Whack and I are going to have to hump in every bit of ammo, spare batteries, and all the other gear we'll need right from the get-go. Dumping the camouflage systems nets us the extra load-carrying capacity we require."

"Captain McLanahan?" a voice called across the hangar.

Brad turned and saw an Iron Wolf communications specialist trotting toward him. "What's up, Yeats?" he asked.

"This signal came in by radio," the specialist answered, handing him a message flimsy. "We just finished decrypting it."

Puzzled, Brad took the sheet. They were at a base with multiple secure telephone and data links. Why would anyone fall back on radio to send a message here? His eyes widened slightly as he read the signal.

He looked back up at the communications tech. "You've authenticated this?"

Yeats nodded. "Yes, sir. It checks out."

Nadia moved closer to him. "What's going on, Brad?"

"This is an urgent signal from President Wilk," he said, raising his voice slightly so the others could hear. "There's a new Russian cyberattack in progress. Cell-phone, Internet, and landline communications networks all across Poland and the rest of the AFN are crashing."

"Ah, crap," he heard Charlie Turlock mutter.

"You've got that right. Apparently, we're back to satellite phones and radio, until CERT teams can find and neutralize the viruses that are locking things up," Brad told them grimly.

Gryzlov had just landed another solid punch. Without reliable communications, everything from regular day-to-day business to public safety was in jeopardy. Robbed of the ability to call for help, innocent people were going to die—from heart attacks and strokes left untreated until it was too late, from house fires that spread unchecked, or from any one of a dozen other kinds of accidents where minutes could make the difference between life and death.

"What are the president's orders?" Nadia asked.

"We're authorized to strike the Russian cyberwar complex at the earliest possible moment," Brad replied. Fighting the weight of the responsibility he'd just been handed, he straightened up to his full height. "Which means we go tonight."

CHAPTER 31

NEAR OSTROWO, NORTH OF POWIDZ, POLAND
That evening

GRU major Leonid Usenko carefully lit another cigarette before turning back to the English-language crossword puzzle he was wrestling with this evening. It was from an American newspaper, the *Wall Street Journal*. He preferred the American style to those published in the British papers. The English crosswords, he thought, were maddeningly indirect, full of mysterious allusions that meant nothing to those who hadn't been educated at one of that nation's elite public schools, like Eton or Harrow. American puzzles, while often cleverly constructed, were far more decipherable—requiring only a solid knowledge of the language, American idiom, and popular culture.

For a moment, he considered sharing this insight with Captain Artem Mikheyev. The other intelligence officer sat at a table just on the other side of the tiny living room of the small lakeside vacation cabin they'd bought through a series of cutouts. But then he reconsidered. Mikheyev was hunched over his laptop computer, grumbling and swearing about something under his breath. One of the problems with any prolonged covert surveillance mission, especially when it involved living in relatively tight quarters, was that tempers naturally frayed over time. The younger man, especially, was feeling the strain. As a cybernetics and computer expert, he was supposed to have been on his way back to Moscow and his regular duties weeks ago. Instead, he had been ordered to stay on with Usenko and Rusanov while they maintained a distant watch on the Iron Wolf base and its activities.

Usenko bent back over his crossword. What was a seven-letter word for "a Roman legionary officer"? he wondered. Was it a—

Suddenly the front door burst open. Both Usenko and Mikheyev looked up in alarm. Usenko shot to his feet. "What the *hell* . . . ?"

Captain Konstantin Rusanov hurried inside and slammed the door shut behind him, breathless with excitement. The short, dark-haired man had been on duty observing activities at the airfield from a concealed vantage point. "Something's up," he panted. "The base is under complete lockdown, with troops patrolling along every meter of the perimeter fence. And the Iron Wolf mercenaries just launched an aircraft, of a type I've never seen before—some sort of new stealth craft from the look of it. It took off and then flew due north."

Usenko shoved his half-finished crossword puzzle aside. "Did you get a picture?"

Rusanov nodded. He dropped into the chair opposite the major and slid his smartphone across. On the surface, the phone looked very much like any of the major brands. Only close examination would reveal that its built-in camera was far more powerful than anything on the civilian market and that it included encryption technology that was beyond cutting-edge.

Usenko expanded the image with his fingers. His subordinate was right. At first glance, the batwing-shaped aircraft bore similarities to the American B-2 Spirit stealth bombers. But there were subtle differences. He looked up. "How big would you say this plane is?"

"Offhand?" Rusanov shrugged. "Smaller than a big strategic bomber, I would guess. But significantly larger than a fighter."

The major pursed his lips. That was an odd size, he thought—neither fish nor fowl. Well, perhaps the experts in Moscow could make something of it. "We'd better report this at once," he said.

Mikheyev got up from his chair. "That will be a problem," he said gloomily. "Our Internet service is down. And so are all cell-phone and landline networks. I can't find any connections anywhere."

"You're kidding," Rusanov blurted out.

"Unfortunately, I'm not," Mikheyev said. His mouth twisted in a crooked, sardonic smile. "I think our glorious Q Directorate comrades are up to new cyberwar tricks."

"Shit." Usenko took a long drag at his cigarette and then stubbed it out with an angry gesture. "Now would be a damned good time to have a satellite phone."

The others nodded. Unfortunately, the geniuses at the Ministry of State Security had prohibited the use of satellite phones by deep-cover operational teams, especially those tasked with spying on the Iron Wolf mercenaries and their CID combat robots. Two GRU agents taken prisoner last year in Poland and exchanged at the end of the brief shooting war had blamed their capture on the use of a satellite phone near one of those terrifying machines.

"If the Poles can't clear their communications networks sooner, we'll have to report this during our next scheduled radio-contact window," Usenko decided. He checked his watch. He scowled. "Which won't open for almost another four hours."

Their GRU team had a high-powered radio transmitter equipped to send compressed encrypted transmissions. Since even a short signal might still be picked up by Polish counterintelligence, it was a risky procedure. It was also a poor way of trying to send actionable intelligence. For security reasons, Moscow only listened for transmissions during certain set times. Signals sent outside those narrow communications windows would be ignored. They might even be treated as evidence that the Poles had captured Usenko and his subordinates and were trying to feed false information to Russia.

KEMIJÄRVI AIRFIELD, NORTHERN FINLAND
Sometime later

Two hours and nine hundred nautical miles after departing Powidz, Brad McLanahan brought the XCV-62 down for a smooth landing on Kemijärvi's fourteen-hundred-meter-long runway. He taxied off onto the apron, where a Scion maintenance, security, and refueling team waited.

This airport, just inside the Arctic Circle and deep amid Lapland's forests and lakes, was a good choice for an interim refueling stop. Used mainly by private jets, Kemijärvi was also an Arctic test site for UAVs, unmanned aerial vehicles, operated by Sky Masters and other manufacturers. Which meant that oddly configured aircraft were a relatively common sight here, far less likely to attract unwanted attention. As it was, their flight into the field had been logged as a cargo flight carrying equipment for the region's timber industry.

Quickly, he and Nadia Rozek ran through their postlanding checklists. Then he clicked the intercom, opening a channel to the troop compartment behind the cockpit. "How are things back there?"

"No problems," Whack Macomber told him from inside one of the two CIDs squeezed into the compartment alongside Schofield, his four commandos, and their weapons and gear. "Other than Charlie pestering me to ask if there's time for a quick drink at the airport bar."

Brad smiled. "Maybe on the way back." He glanced down at the fueling status indicator shown on one of his MFDs. "We should be gassed up and back in the air in about fifteen minutes or so."

Beside him, Nadia finished typing a short message on her left-hand display. She hit the send button. "I have informed Powidz of our arrival here and estimated time of departure," she reported. Seconds later, her MFD pinged, signaling the receipt of a new transmission via satellite downlink. Her fingers flew over the virtual keyboard, ordering their computer to decode the incoming signal. "It's an intelligence update from Martindale," she said. "So far, the Russians are sticking precisely to their announced schedule of air-defense exercises."

"That's mighty generous of them," Brad said with a quick, slashing grin. While he bet Gryzlov hadn't intended this sudden round of SAM and radar drills as anything but a bit of saber rattling, it had certainly made their mission planning a little easier. When they crossed into enemy airspace about ten minutes after takeoff from Kemijärvi, Russia's Aerospace Forces would be focused on testing their defenses around St. Petersburg—more than 350 nautical miles south. "Anything else?" he asked.

"There are no signs yet of any higher alert level anywhere along our planned flight path or in the region around their Perun's Aerie complex,"

Nadia read. "Also, Colonel Kasperek's covering force is completing its movement to the forward air base. His fighters will be fueled, armed, and on ready alert in sixty minutes."

Brad nodded. With luck, they would never need to call on Pawel Kasperek's F-16s for help. First, because that would mean things had gone really wrong. The whole point of this mission was to hit the Russian cyberwar complex by surprise, blow it to hell, and then get out while Moscow was still trying to pick up its drawers. And second, because there probably wasn't a lot the Polish fighter pilots could do except die gallantly if they were thrown into battle against Russia's S-300 and S-400 SAMs, Su-27s, and other advanced combat aircraft.

If it were up to him, he would have vetoed the idea of putting Kasperek's squadron on standby. But both President Wilk and Kevin Martindale had insisted—labeling it a last-ditch contingency option.

"Wolf Six-Two, you're fully fueled and good to go," the Finnish ramp manager said, less than twenty minutes after engine shutdown. "As the Scion maintenance team requested, the tower has cleared you for departure without further communication. No other flights are inbound or outbound. Good luck and Godspeed."

"Roger that, Kemijärvi Ground," Brad acknowledged. "Thank you for your assistance." Scion's close working and financial relationship with the Finns meant they could take off again without risking the routine aircraft-to-control-tower transmissions that could be intercepted by Russian SIGINT posts just across the nearby border. He glanced at Nadia. "All set?" She nodded tightly. "Okay, let's run through the take-off checklists and get this beast airborne, pronto." He opened the intercom channel to the troop compartment again. "Right, guys. This is it. Strap in tight. The ride's likely to get a little bumpy."

ÄMARI AIR BASE, JUST SOUTH OF THE GULF OF FINLAND, NORTHERN ESTONIA
That same time

Colonel Pawel Kasperek watched the last of his squadron's F-16C Vipers taxi into one of the camouflaged aircraft shelters built along the airfield's northern side. He felt himself relax. Not much. Just a bit. Whatever happened, at least his fighters were in position.

Ämari was an old Soviet-era air base, once home to a Russian naval aviation regiment flying Su-24s. Upgraded to NATO standards several years ago, the base was just a little over three hundred kilometers west of St. Petersburg—thirty minutes' flight time at the F-16's cruise speed. That put them practically on Russia's doorstep, at least by combat standards. Best of all, as far as he could tell, they'd managed this emergency operational movement without the Russians picking up so much as a whiff that something odd was happening.

His squadron's F-16s had been taking off in pairs from Minsk Mazowiecke at varied intervals over the past several hours. In and of itself, that was nothing out of the ordinary: fighter patrols over Warsaw had become a regular sight ever since the Kalmar Airlines crash. What was different was that each pair of Vipers, instead of climbing to orbit the Polish capital, had flown north at extremely low altitude—flying out into the Baltic and then turning northeast to Estonia along several different, precleared air corridors. That had kept them off Russian radar and held radio transmissions to an absolute minimum.

Bomb-handling trailers loaded with thousand-pound AGM-154A Joint Standoff Weapons, or JSOWs, and AIM-9X Sidewinder and AIM-120 AMRAAM air-to-air missiles, were already in motion—heading for the aircraft shelters. The ground crews flown in earlier on Poland's American-made C-130s were inside waiting to arm their planes with a mix of air-to-ground and air-to-air ordnance.

Kasperek turned to his Estonian counterpart, Lieutenant Colonel Inar Tamm. "So now we wait, Colonel."

"*Jah*. Yes," the other man said simply. Then he smiled thinly. "And perhaps we should pray too, eh?"

Kasperek nodded fervently. Ordinarily he wasn't much for prayer, but there were moments when you wanted to make sure you covered every possible angle. This was definitely one of them.

OVER NORTHERN KARELIA, RUSSIA
A short time later

One hundred and twenty nautical miles and sixteen minutes after crossing the Russian frontier,
the Iron Wolf stealth aircraft streaked low over
a landscape of dense snow-cloaked forests and
ice-covered lakes. Thousands of stars shimmered
high overhead, only partially obscured by thin
wisps of cloud.

Brad McLanahan pulled his stick a bit to the
right, banking onto a course that took the XCV-62
between two low tree-covered hills and then back
out over a dully gleaming expanse of ice. Cameras
set to cover the rear arc of their aircraft showed
roiling vortices of loose snow swirling in their
wake—ripped off the earth by the sheer speed of
their low-altitude passage. He frowned. By rights,
he ought to gain more altitude. If some eagle-
eyed Russian fighter pilot were on the prowl in
the skies above them, he might spot the glitter-
ing snow-crystal trail they were tearing across
an otherwise darkened countryside. If that happened, they were screwed.

Unfortunately, there were other, even more
compelling reasons for him to keep this bird right
down on the deck.

*"S-band search radar at eleven o'clock. Estimated
range is one hundred fifty miles,"* the Ranger's computer reported. *"Detection probability at this altitude
nil."*

"It's a 96L6E 'Cheese Board' system," Nadia

said, checking the signal characteristics shown on her threat warning display. "Probably operating with the S-300 regiment deployed to cover the submarine construction and repair yards at Severodvinsk."

"Yeah, that sounds about right," Brad agreed absently. He was almost entirely focused on following the HUD cues provided by their navigation and digital terrain-following systems. He pulled back on the stick a tiny bit as they left the ice lake behind—climbing slightly to clear the tops of the trees by just a couple of hundred feet. To avoid losing airspeed in the climb, he inched the throttles forward, feeding just a scooch more power to the Ranger's four turbofan engines.

"New S-band search radar at two o'clock. Range is one hundred sixty-five miles," the computer said suddenly.

"It's the same radar type," Nadia told him.

Brad nodded, keeping his eyes fixed on his HUD. "That'll be the radar around Petrozavodsk, guarding the interceptor air base there." He forced a tight grin. "This is what we call threading the needle."

Russia was an enormous country with around thirty-six thousand miles of land borders and coastline to guard. Even with a vast network of powerful air-surveillance radars, there was no practical way for Moscow to continuously monitor so large a perimeter. Instead, the Russians deployed their radars, SAM regiments, and fighter patrols to protect key sites like major cities, important military installations, and vital industries.

In theory, that made it possible for a small, highly stealthy aircraft to duck and dodge and bob and weave its way through the porous web of radars.

Plotting that kind of course was relatively easy against fixed radar sites. Unfortunately, the Russians also had a substantial force of highly mobile detection units, many of which could be up and running within minutes if ordered to activate. Sure, Scion and Polish intelligence analysts had done their best to plot a relatively safe route to Russia's Perun's Aerie cyberwar complex, but penetrating deep into Russian airspace without being detected was still a crapshoot.

CHAPTER 32

THE KREMLIN, MOSCOW
Ninety minutes later

Russian president Gennadiy Gryzlov read through the most recent reports from Koshkin's Q Directorate with a deep sense of pleasure. After several recent failures, his computer hackers were back on track. At last count, more than two-thirds of all the private telecommunications networks in Eastern and central Europe were down—causing havoc and hardship for tens of millions. He smiled to himself. For some reason, kicking enemies around always aroused him. Maybe he should summon Daria Titeneva for a celebratory romp around his office. His lush, full-bodied foreign minister might have deep misgivings about this cyberwar campaign, but he knew she also enjoyed being dominated. Yes, he thought lazily, bending Daria over his desk and having his way with her would end this day on a delightfully obscene note.

His phone buzzed. Irritated at being interrupted, he snatched it up. "What is it, Ulanov?"

"It's Minister of State Security Kazyanov, Mr. President," his secretary said. "He says it's urgent."

Gryzlov rolled his eyes. Dull, boring, timid Viktor Kazyanov was just about the last person he wanted to talk to right now. Then again, the intelligence chief was usually so nervous about pissing him off that whatever news he wanted to pass on might actually be important. "Very well," he snapped. "Put him through."

"Mr. President! Something is happening in Poland! We've just received a radio signal from—" Kazyanov started out, speaking so rapidly and so excitedly that he was almost tripping over his own words as they came spilling across the phone line.

"For God's sake, slow down, Viktor," Gryzlov said. "You sound like a demented clown!"

The other man stammered to a stop, took a deep breath, and then went on in a somewhat calmer tone. "Approximately four hours ago, our deep-cover GRU agents stationed near Powidz spotted intense activity at the Iron Wolf base. They report seeing an unidentified aircraft flying north at high speed. It has not yet returned."

"And this happened four hours ago?" Gryzlov said through gritted teeth. "So what the hell were your precious agents doing in the meantime? Washing their damned hair?"

"They were unable to report sooner," Kazyanov said simply. "Because our cyberwar operations have knocked out all the phone lines and Internet connections in their area."

"Oh," Gryzlov said blankly. That was a complication he had not foreseen. He gripped the phone tighter. "This aircraft? What can you tell me about it?"

Kazyanov gulped. "Not as much as I would like, sir," he admitted. "The signal from our team describes it as all black, with a batwing configuration."

"So, some kind of stealth aircraft," Gryzlov guessed.

"Yes, Mr. President," the other man agreed. "But from the rough estimate of its size, my analysts say it does not match anything in the known Polish or American inventory. It could be anything from a small strike bomber to a long-range covert reconnaissance drone."

"Very well, Viktor," Gryzlov said. "Inform me at once if you learn anything more." He hung up.

For a moment, he sat with his fingers pressed hard against his temples, deep in thought. What were the Poles and their American mercenaries up to? If they were executing some kind of attack or prestrike reconnaissance with this mysterious new aircraft, why fly north, instead of heading east toward Russia? Then he shook his head in disgust at his own foolishness, remembering what he'd told Koshkin and the others just a couple of days ago. "Wilk and Martindale are not simpletons," he muttered. Why should he expect them to do the obvious?

Gryzlov swung toward his computer and pulled

up a map of Poland, western Russia, and the neighboring countries. Assuming this new stealth aircraft had a cruising speed of somewhere between 700 and 950 kilometers per hour, where could it be now, four hours or so after taking off? Quickly, he began laying out possible flight paths on the digital map. After all, he thought, he'd originally trained as a bomber pilot. If he were tasked with planning a deep-penetration mission into Russia, what were the best options to evade radar detection? Then he reconsidered . . . Why cast his net so widely? While there were thousands of potential targets for an Iron Wolf retaliatory strike, only one was truly important in the present circumstances.

Confidently, he erased all but one of the hypothetical flight plans he'd drawn and then ran through his calculations again—estimating where the enemy aircraft could be . . . right *now*.

"*Sukin syn!* Son of a bitch," Gryzlov snarled, staring at the map. He grabbed his phone again. "Ulanov! Connect me with Colonel Balakin at Perun's Aerie!"

When the cyberwar complex's security chief came on the line, Gryzlov didn't waste time with small talk. "Listen carefully, Balakin. You may have visitors inbound."

"Is this a bombing raid, sir? Or . . ." The colonel hesitated. "An attack by those machines? By those combat robots?"

Gryzlov smiled unpleasantly. "I haven't the faintest idea, Colonel." He glanced back at the map on his computer screen. "But if I'm right, I have a hunch you'll find out soon enough."

"I understand, Mr. President," Balakin said, still obviously rattled. Then he rallied. "I will order the garrison to go on full alert and bring my outer warning station online."

NEAR KIPIYEVO, 250 KILOMETERS WEST-NORTHWEST OF PERUN'S AERIE, NORTHERN RUSSIA
That same time

Bundled up in his heavy winter parka, Captain Fyodor Golovkin sat drowsing by the heater in his operations van. Snores from the back told him that most of his troops were doing the same thing. No surprise there, he thought dully. This far north in winter, the nights lasted twenty hours. Between the near-perpetual darkness, the bitter cold, and the boredom of manning a radar unit continuously on standby, it was no wonder that he and his men spent most of their time practically hibernating.

An alarm buzzer jolted him more fully awake. "Sir! It's Colonel Balakin," said his senior sergeant, hurriedly scanning the message scrolling across his computer screen. They were linked to the Perun's Aerie complex by a direct fiber-optic cable. "We're ordered to activate the radar and begin scanning!"

For a moment, Golovkin couldn't take it in. "What? Now?"

"Yes, sir," his sergeant said, with far more patience than he would have shown to anyone of lower rank. "The colonel has set Warning Condition Red."

Golovkin's mouth fell open in surprise. If this was a drill, it must have been ordered by the highest command authority. And if it wasn't a drill . . .

Wide-awake now, he scrambled out of his chair. "Get up! Up, you lazy bastards!" he roared, his voice echoing through the crowded van. "We're on alert! Get the fucking camouflage netting off the antenna truck! Go!"

His crew hurried to obey, bolting outside into the frigid night air. Before turning to follow them, the captain swung back to his sergeant. "Power up the system, Proshkin! As soon as we've got the antenna erected, I want this radar fully operational. Understand?"

The sergeant nodded. He turned back to his station and began rapidly flipping a succession of switches. With a low hum, automated signals processing units, satellite navigation systems, and digital map displays started warming up.

Golovkin paused only to pull on his fur-lined gloves and then went outside into the darkness. He gasped as the raw, subzero cold hit him with sledgehammer force. But his men were hard at work, tugging and straining to pull snow-covered layers of antiradar and antithermal camouflage away from their radar antenna truck. With a creaking groan, the huge crane-mounted antenna itself rose slowly but steadily, scattering shattered chips and pieces of ice in all directions.

The captain stood watching it climb into the

air. With luck, they would be online and radiating in less than six minutes.

OVER NORTHEN RUSSIA
A few minutes later

Brad McLanahan peered through his HUD. The Ranger's advanced forward-looking night-vision camera systems turned the night into a green-tinged version of daylight. They were closing on the foothills of the Urals, a series of barren, boulder-strewn heights cut by twisting, tree-lined ravines.

"We are thirteen minutes out from the LZ," Nadia reported. Her eyes were fixed on the computer-generated map shown on one of her displays.

Brad nodded. They were a little over one hundred nautical miles from their planned landing zone—a two-thousand-foot-long clearing in the forest about ten miles from Mount Manaraga and Russia's buried Perun's Aerie cyberwar complex. For a second, his vision blurred. *Crap*, he thought. *Not now.* He blinked rapidly a few times. His vision cleared up. He frowned, glad his expression was hidden beneath his oxygen mask. Even with the aid of the XCV-62's digital terrain-following system, this prolonged nap-of-the-earth flight was testing his endurance.

"*New VHF search radar detected at ten o'clock,*" the Ranger's computer announced suddenly. "*Strong agile active frequency signal. Range estimated at thirty-three miles. Detection probability moderate.*"

Damn it, Brad thought. Where the hell did that come from? Nothing in their mission planning intelligence had identified a radar site anywhere near here.

"The radar is evaluated as a KB/Agat Vostok E-type," Nadia said. Her voice was tight. "Shall I activate SPEAR?"

"Negative," Brad said quickly. "If we use SPEAR, the Russians will know for sure we're coming. So let's see if I can shake this radar loose before it firms us up." Since it used longer wavelengths, VHF radar was extremely effective against stealth aircraft. The Vostok E system was a mobile, modern replacement for the old Soviet-era P-18 Spoon Rest units. But it was usually paired with faster L- and S/X-band fire-control radars as part of a SAM battery. What was this one doing out on its own?

"DTF disengaged," he said, turning off the Ranger's terrain-following system. He pushed the stick forward a bit, dropping the aircraft's nose. They descended from two hundred feet down to just a little over a hundred—almost brushing the treetops that flashed past and below them in a rippling blur. His teeth locked together. While flying this low at 450 knots, even a momentary loss of concentration would be fatal.

Heading east, they zoomed down one of the narrow valleys. Rocky heights rose sharply on both sides. An ice-covered stream twisted and turned down the floor of the valley.

"*VHF signal strength decreasing*," the computer reported. "*Detection probability now low.*"

"You did it!" Nadia said, exhaling.

Feeling a little safer now that they had higher ground between them and that Vostok radar, Brad switched the XCV-62's terrain-following system back on. It pulled them back up to two hundred feet. He unclenched his teeth. "Maybe. Maybe not," he told her. "Depends on how jumpy that radar crew is. And why they suddenly powered up." He shrugged his shoulders against his harness. "I'm pretty sure they got some piece of us, at least for a few seconds. Now, if we're lucky and that Russian crew was only running a routine test, they may think the blip they saw was just a systems glitch."

"And if we are not lucky?" Nadia asked softly.

"That's what has me worried," Brad acknowledged. He clicked the intercom, opening a channel to the troop compartment. In a few terse phrases, he briefed Macomber, Charlie Turlock, and the others on the situation.

"So," Macomber drawled, "it may be 'goodbye, surprise' and 'hello, hornet's nest?'"

"Could be."

"Care to give me any odds on which one it is?" Macomber asked.

Brad shrugged again. "Maybe fifty-fifty." He banked right, following the trace of the valley as it curved southeast. "Do you want to abort?"

"Hell, no," the other man growled. "If those Russian sons of bitches really are awake and waiting for us, skedaddling now won't improve the situation much. If we're gonna have to run a missile gauntlet on the way home, let's blow the shit out of Gryzlov's cybergeeks first."

"Charlie?" Brad asked.

"Suits me," Charlie Turlock said simply. "You know, not that I would *ever* say I told you so, Whack . . . but I feel compelled to point out that I *did* strongly suggest we stop for a drink at that Finnish airport bar first."

Despite his anxiety, Brad felt himself grinning. "Captain Schofield?"

"My lads and I are ready," the Canadian told him. "We're unstrapping now and getting our gear ready."

"That's kind of dangerous," Brad told him. "This could be a pretty rough landing."

"We'll take that chance," Schofield replied. "No offense, Captain McLanahan, but if we are heading into a hot LZ, my troops and I would rather like to get clear of this aircraft and into cover as quickly as possible."

"Understood," Brad said. The glowing numbers on his HUD altered slightly as the Ranger's computer recalculated their flight plan, based on their current airspeed and heading. "We're eight minutes out. Stand by."

NEAR KIPIYEVO
That same time

"Replay that sequence, Proshkin, but slow it down this time," Captain Fyodor Golovkin ordered. His sergeant obeyed. Together the two men watched the small blip suddenly appear on their radar display, waver, and then just as suddenly vanish. From start to finish, the blip was visible only for fifteen seconds. The captain pulled at his jaw. "What do you think?"

The sergeant shrugged. "We were still powering up, Captain. It could easily have been a false reading." His fingers drummed lightly on the side of his console. "But since we haven't been able to run our normal alignment, calibration, and other tests, who knows how out of whack this equipment is. Ordinarily, I'd say that we picked up something real. As it is, in these temperatures and with all that ice coating the ring element radiator—"

Golovkin nodded. He shared the other man's frustration and uncertainty. As part of the effort to hide the existence of Perun's Aerie, Colonel Balakin had ordered them to keep their radar completely off the air once it was deployed. Golovkin had argued that his equipment needed periodic checks to confirm its full operational readiness—especially in these harsh winter conditions. Unfortunately, the colonel had ignored his protests. Like many senior officers without a technical background, Balakin expected that fully activating complex systems like their Vostok E radar was as simple and foolproof as flipping a power switch.

He sighed. If only it were that easy. "How does the equipment look now?" he asked, still trying to decide what he should do about this possible contact.

"The antenna array seems okay," the sergeant admitted. His tone, however, strongly suggested that he wouldn't be surprised if bits and pieces started falling off in the next few minutes.

"Assuming that contact *was* genuine, what can you tell me about it?" Golovkin pressed.

The sergeant brought up the recorded sequence again and ran through it one more time. "We picked it up at about sixty kilometers," he said carefully. "I would estimate the contact's course as zero-eight-five degrees and its speed at more than eight hundred kilometers per hour."

"Right, so let's put that track on a map and then extend it along the observed direction of flight," the captain said.

Dutifully, the sergeant obeyed. During the fifteen seconds the blip appeared on their radar display, it had covered a little more than three kilometers before disappearing. Golovkin's eyes followed the projected track as it "stretched" almost due east—slanting toward the Urals on a course that took it within a few kilometers of Mount Manaraga and Perun's Aerie.

"Damn," he muttered. Still looking at the map, he picked up the direct line to Balakin's command post. It was answered on the first ring. "This is Captain Golovkin at the Kipiyevo radar outpost. I need to speak to the colonel. Right now!"

CHAPTER 33

IRON WOLF STRIKE-FORCE LANDING ZONE, NORTHWEST OF MOUNT MANARAGA
That same time

"We are two minutes out from the LZ," Nadia Rozek reported. On the surface, she sounded cool, totally unruffled. But Brad could pick up the tension hidden beneath her outwardly calm, thoroughly professional manner.

"I confirm that," he said. "I have the LZ in sight." Through his HUD, the clearing they'd picked out from satellite photos as a landing zone was a brighter green against the darker green of the surrounding forest. They were arrowing toward it at three hundred knots, flying low down a narrow gap cut through the tall, razor-backed ridge that formed an outer barrier to the Nether-Polar Urals mountain chain.

The irregular, roughly oval-shaped clearing was a little under two thousand feet long and only about five hundred feet across at its widest point.

Close study of the photos taken before snow covered the area had shown no signs of tree stumps or boulders that could tear off the Ranger's landing gear or rip open its fuselage. But Brad knew satellite photos were one thing. Reality might be quite another.

"Ninety seconds out," Nadia said. She tapped one of her MFDs, zooming in on the view through one of their forward-looking passive sensors. "No unidentified thermal contacts around the LZ."

Brad nodded tightly. *So far, so good*, he thought. While it was still possible that antithermal camouflage might mask Russian troops deployed around the clearing, it wasn't likely—not unless they'd been stationed there before this mission was even planned. And if that was the case, they were screwed any way you looked at it. "Give me a quick air-to-ground radar sweep of the immediate area, please," he told Nadia.

Using radar of any kind, even for a single pulse, this close to the Russian cyberwar complex was risky, but he needed to confirm they had a clear field ahead of them. The radar sweep should reveal any obstructions hidden beneath the snow . . . and any enemy troops, weapons, or vehicles hidden under camouflage.

"Sweeping now," Nadia acknowledged. She tapped a menu on her right-hand display once.

One quick tone sounded in Brad's headset as the XCV-62's radar pulsed once in air-to-ground mode. In milliseconds, the aircraft's computer analyzed the information received from the sweep and showed the resulting image as an overlay across his HUD. "Looks clear," he said. "We are go for landing."

"Go for landing," Nadia agreed. She tapped a key on one of her MFDs, alerting Macomber and the others in the troop compartment that they were on final approach.

Using a control on his stick, Brad scrolled a blinking cursor across the HUD and selected his preferred touchdown point. The navigation system updated his steering cues.

"Forty-five seconds," Nadia announced.

"I am configuring for landing," Brad said quietly. He entered a command on one of his MFDs and throttled back. The muted roar from the Ranger's four turbofan engines decreased fast.

Their airspeed dropped. Hydraulics whined out along the trailing edge of the XCV-62's wing. Control surfaces were opening to give them more lift as they slowed. There were more bumps and thumps below the cockpit as the Ranger's landing gear came down.

When he got the green light confirming that their nose gear and bogies were locked in position, Brad disengaged the terrain-following system and throttled back even farther. "Hang tight!" he warned over the intercom.

The Iron Wolf aircraft slid down out of the sky and touched down. Thick curtains of snow fountained to either side, hurled high into the air as the Ranger raced down the clearing. It bucked and bounced across the uneven ground hidden beneath the snowpack. Carefully, Brad reversed thrust—trying to shed speed as rapidly as possible without risking a skid on this slick surface.

They slid to a shuddering stop with only a couple of hundred feet to spare. "Everyone all right back there?" Brad asked over the intercom.

"Jostled around and bruised a bit, but otherwise fine," Ian Schofield said cheerfully. "Standing by to deploy once you drop the bloody ramp."

Smiling with relief, Brad fed just a little power to the engines and steered the Ranger through a tight 180-degree turn so that they were facing back the way they'd come, ready for an immediate takeoff. Then he throttled all the way down and hit the ramp release.

Schofield and his four commandos were out in seconds, fanning across the snow-covered expanse to take up covering positions around the stationary XCV-62. One of them lugged three Israeli-made Spike-SR man-portable antitank missiles. The others were equipped with a mix of sniper rifles and automatic weapons.

The two Iron Wolf CIDs exited right behind them—slowly unfolding out of the cramped troop compartment. They glided down the ramp and out into the snow with long, menacing strides. Packs stuffed full of extra ammunition, explosives, and other gear were slung across their backs. The lead robot swiveled its six-sided head toward the cockpit. "Wolf One to Wolf Six-Two," Macomber said. "Thanks for the ride. We're moving out now."

"Copy that, One," Brad replied. His chest felt

tight. "But be careful, Whack. If the defenses look too tough, don't try to bull on through."

"Don't sweat it, Six-Two," the other man said gruffly. "Charlie and I know what we're doing. We'll go in, shoot the crap out of a bunch of Russians, and boogie on back here before the survivors figure out what the hell just happened to them. Wolf One out."

With that, the two Iron Wolf robots turned and loped southeast at high speed.

THE KREMLIN
A short time later

Gryzlov listened intently while Colonel Balakin made his report. "Our radar station at Kipiyevo picked up one brief contact about thirty minutes ago," the colonel said. "But they say it vanished almost immediately. Within just a few seconds."

"Was their system knocked out or spoofed by the enemy's netrusion technology?" Gryzlov demanded.

"I don't think so, Mr. President," Balakin said. "The Vostok E crew reports no apparent interruption of their radar's normal operation." He hesitated. "However, Captain Golovkin has often warned of potential equipment problems caused by prolonged exposure to the winter elements. This fleeting contact may only be a false reading caused by a minor hardware malfunction or some software bug. Since we've seen no further signs of any enemy activity, that seems increasingly likely. In which case, I may have alerted my garrison unnecessarily."

Gryzlov's hand tightened around the phone. "Don't be an idiot, Balakin," he snapped. "You and your troops will stay on full alert until I decide otherwise. Is that perfectly clear?"

"*Da*, Mr. President," the other man agreed hurriedly.

"Keep your eyes and ears open wide, Balakin, if you want to live through the night," Gryzlov told him brutally. He disconnected and then punched the button for Ivan Ulanov. "Get me Colonel General Maksimov!"

Maksimov, his former instructor at the Yuri Gagarin Military Air Academy, sounded drowsy, almost half asleep, when he answered the phone. Impatiently, Gryzlov checked the time. His lip curled in disgust. It wasn't even that close to midnight yet. Maybe the old man really was past his prime and ready for the boneyard, along with the rest of the old Soviet-era relics.

"It looks as though Poland's Iron Wolf mercenaries have slipped right through your vaunted air-defense network, Valentin," Gryzlov said, not bothering to hide his scorn. "I want two of the alert Su-50 stealth fighters stationed at Syktyvkar heading for the Pechora area at once! Tell the pilots to go in hard and fast, with their radars active. They are to shoot down any unidentified aircraft they detect. Failure will not be tolerated. Is that understood?"

"I understand, Mr. President," the older man said. His voice was stiff. "But I must point out that sortieing our Su-50s with their radars powered up negates every advantage otherwise conferred by their stealth configuration and materials."

"I don't give a crap about stealth right now, Colonel General," Gryzlov said icily. "You've boasted that the Su-50 is the best combat aircraft in the world—faster, longer-ranged, and more maneuverable than the American F-35. You also told me its phased-array radar and other sensors could detect and track any enemy aircraft, no matter how stealthy. Were those lies?"

"No, sir," Maksimov growled, plainly stung.

"Then prove it," Gryzlov told him. "Get those precious fighters of yours off the ground and tell the pilots to go kill whatever they find."

CHAPTER 34

Major Wayne "Whack" Macomber's Cybernetic Infantry Device crouched low among snow-covered trees and boulders. Mount Manaraga's slopes climbed above him, rising to a jagged peak more than a mile high. A pulsing green dot on his tactical display marked the position of the Iron Wolf robot piloted by Charlie Turlock. She was about four hundred meters north of him, also concealed well in among the trees.

The pine forest they were using to cover their approach came to an end about five hundred meters dead ahead, right at the edge of a mile-wide bowl formed by two steep spurs extending out from Manaraga's main summit. There were no trees on those white slopes, just occasional patches of bare black rock and loose scree.

Looking uphill, Macomber could see a massive tunnel set into the flank of the northernmost spur. According to their intelligence, that was the principal way into the Russian cyberwar complex. Scion and Polish analysts suspected there were probably a number of smaller, secondary entrances and exits, but he and Charlie didn't have the time to scout for them. An overhanging ledge shielded this particular entrance from satellite or aerial observation. The tunnel was about two thousand meters from his current hiding place. Even scrambling upslope through deep snow, he could cover that distance in his CID in well under four minutes. He grinned sourly to himself. Or at least he could if it weren't for all the enemy weapons so carefully sited to lay down a deadly hail of fire on anyone moving up that bowl.

Data from his sensors poured into his mind. The robot's computers provided instant analysis of everything he "saw" and "heard"—whether in the form of thermal imagery, narrow-beam radar pulses, intercepted radio and cell-phone transmissions, and even sounds picked up by its incredibly sensitive microphones. A sea of targeting indicators flashed onto his display, each marking the position of a concealed Russian bunker or remote sensor.

The woods ahead of them were laced with IR-capable cameras, motion detectors, and tripwire-triggered flares. He shook his head. A mouse might make it through there without triggering an alarm, but nothing bigger would. At least not while those sensors were operational. And beyond the woods, those seemingly empty slopes were studded with camouflaged bunkers and buried minefields. They were also covered by emplaced ground-surveillance radars to pick up the slightest movement.

Macomber whistled softly, studying the results. He radioed Charlie Turlock. "Are you seeing what I'm seeing?"

"As in 'antitank guns, missile launchers, machine guns, and minefields under the snow, oh my!'?" Charlie said. "Yep, I sure am. Geez, you'd almost think these guys don't want any uninvited visitors."

"You would, wouldn't you?" Macomber said. He paused, listening to the simultaneous translation of a conversation between the Russian soldiers manning one of the nearby fighting positions. They were wondering if this sudden alert was just another drill or something more serious. "And it just gets better. Because it sure as shit looks as though these bastards are wide-awake and waiting for us."

There was a moment of silence while Charlie digested the information from her own sensors and obviously came to the same, sobering conclusion. "Well, that makes it more of a fair fight, right?" she said at last. The biometric data piggybacked onto her transmission showed that her heart rate had climbed slightly, but there was no real trace of fear in her voice.

Macomber forced a laugh. "Hell, I *hate* fair fights." He sighed. "But I guess this is where we earn the big bucks they're paying us."

"Hold on a minute," Charlie said, sounding surprised. "You're getting paid big bucks? Why wasn't I informed? Maybe I need to renegotiate my contract."

"Maybe so," Macomber agreed absently. His mind was busy refining the preliminary attack plan he and Charlie had developed before taking off from Poland—adapting it to the reality revealed by their sensor scans. All Martindale's satellite intelligence analysts could give them was an estimate of probable Russian defensive positions. But now they had it all—the precise location of every gun and missile bunker, all the minefields, and every remote camera and motion detector.

While Whack really hated squeezing himself into one of these CID steel cans for any length of time, he had to admit that the neural interface between the machine and his brain made tactical planning a snap. In just seconds, he could do work that would have taken a human staff officer an hour to finish. Focusing mentally, he ordered the robot's attack software to create a new set of target priorities. Then he divvied them up between their two Iron Wolf fighting machines. He flicked a finger, sending the revised battle plan to Charlie.

"Got it," she confirmed. Seconds later, she said, "Looks good to me, Whack."

"Okay, stand by," he ordered. "On my mark, we'll light 'em up and take 'em down."

"Copy that, Red Leader," Charlie replied, with a mischievous chuckle.

Smiling despite his tension, Macomber ran through one last systems and weapons check. Everything still looked good. *So stop stalling*, he told himself coolly. The longer he and Charlie dicked around out here, the more likely they were to be spotted by some sharp-eyed Russian sentry. The fact that the Perun's Aerie garrison was on alert suggested they'd somehow lost operational surprise, but they could still rock the enemy back on his heels by attacking now, before they were detected. "Commence blackout in five seconds," he ordered. "On my mark . . . Now."

He flexed his CID's right hand, activating its netrusion capabilities. Included among the sensors equipping their robots were active radars. And those radars could be configured to pump malicious code into enemy digital systems, computers, radios, telephone networks, and radars—commanding them to shut down or flooding them with false images. A wolfish grin flashed across his face. After all, there was a certain poetic justice in using the Scion variant of cyberwar against the Russians guarding this Perun's Aerie complex.

"Three . . . two . . . one . . ." he counted down. "Let's go!" He leaped to his feet and ran forward into the Russian detection grid. His radars powered up, pouring commands into the preset sequence of enemy sensors and computers. Off on his left flank, Charlie Turlock's CID was in motion, doing the same thing.

Across the forest and on the high mountain slopes above them, ground-surveillance radars went dead, knocked off-line. Radio communications dissolved into a blur of incomprehensible static. Cameras and motion detectors froze.

Macomber hurtled over a trip wire and unslung his electromagnetic rail gun. It whined shrilly, powering up. Still moving at nearly sixty kilometers an hour, he dodged around trees. The targeting reticle on his display centered on the slit of a Russian bunker. He fired.

CCRRACK! In a blinding flash of plasma, a small superdense metal projectile streaked toward the distant bunker, moving at more than Mach 5. Tall pine trees caught in its wake bent and shook. Blankets of snow and ice layered on their branches exploded into steam. The rail-gun projectile slammed into the camouflaged antitank missile position with enormous force. Torn apart, the concrete bunker vaporized— blown into a swirling cloud of shattered concrete and molten steel.

Charlie's 25mm autocannon stuttered, firing on full automatic. Dozens of HE rounds pounded the slopes ahead of them. Orange-and-red bursts rippled across the snow as the mines triggered by her burst detonated. A roiling curtain of smoke and dirt drifted across the bowl.

Laser targeting, Macomber's CID warning system indicated suddenly, coupling it with a shrill *BEEP-BEEP-BEEP*. *Threat axis ten o'clock.*

He accelerated and swerved to the left, hoping to shake off the laser painting him. He swiveled on the move, bringing his rail gun on target.

Launch detection, his computer announced calmly.

Trailing a plume of fire and smoke, a Russian Kornet laser-guided antitank missile speared past

Macomber's CID. It missed by less than a meter. Still dodging and weaving, he fired back.

The Russian bunker exploded.

Caught up completely in the fierce exultation of combat, Macomber charged onward. He was fully synched with the Iron Wolf robot's computer now. New targets appeared on his display. Each was coded by its perceived threat level and the weapon his CID evaluated as most likely to be effective. He fired again and again, using both his rail gun and 25mm autocannon as the circumstances and his battle software dictated. Charlie Turlock moved at his side, firing with equal poise and lethality.

One by one, the defensive positions guarding Perun's Aerie were knocked out, either left burning or in smoldering piles of heaped rubble. Together, the two CIDs raced up the mountainside, dashing safely through wide gaps Charlie had blown clear through the Russian minefield.

Five minutes after the battle began, it was over.

Macomber reached the enormous tunnel entrance and spun to cover Charlie as she lunged uphill, covering the last stretch. Everywhere he looked, he saw only death and destruction. Plumes of greasy black smoke curled away from wrecked bunkers. Fires crackled, fed by burning ammunition and missile propellant.

"Reloading," Charlie radioed. Her CID's metal hands blurred into motion, ejecting empty autocannon ammunition clips and rail-gun magazines and replacing them from the extra packs slung across her robot's back. "I'm back up," she announced.

Macomber did the same thing while she covered him. "What's your status?" he asked.

"I've used around sixty-five percent of my ammo stores," Charlie told him. "But my fuel cells and batteries are in good shape."

He nodded. That matched his own situation pretty closely. They were lower on ammunition than he would have preferred, but they should still be okay—depending on how much opposition they ran into inside the complex itself. "Any damage?"

Her robot actually shrugged its shoulders. "One of my thermal sensors is kaput. And I have some minor surface damage across my left leg. Nothing too bad."

"How did that happen?" Macomber asked.

"I ducked a missile and ran into a heavy-machine-gun burst instead," Charlie said, sounding irritated. She changed the subject, waving at the massive blast door that sealed the tunnel entrance. "So, what's the plan now?"

In answer, Macomber charged his rail gun. His CID's battle computer set a succession of aim points in a circular pattern across the blast door. Pausing only briefly between shots to let the powerful weapon cool and reset, he punched a series of holes right through the solid steel barrier. Pale fluorescent light streamed out through the new openings. Their edges glowed cherry red for a few moments, cooling fast in the below-freezing temperature.

"Oh, I like your plan," Charlie said gleefully. "I always thought the Big Bad Wolf had all the best lines." She pulled one of her equipment packs off her CID's armored shoulder and moved forward to the blast door. One by one, she quickly attached shaped demolitions charges to the inside edges of the holes his rail gun had blown.

When she was finished, they turned and darted away along the base of the ridge, plunging through deep snow until they were a few hundred meters away. Both CIDs crouched low. "Detonation in three, two, one," Charlie murmured. One of her fingers flicked, keying a precoded transmission.

With an earsplitting, ground-shaking *BANG*, her demolition charges went off simultaneously. In the middle of a bright orange flash that lit up the entire slope, they saw a large section of reinforced steel cartwheeling away through the air.

Before the echoes stopped bouncing around the surrounding peaks, the two Iron Wolf fighting machines jumped up and sped toward the tunnel. Bending low, they squeezed in through the ragged hole blown through the blast door.

They found themselves in a massive passage, more than large enough for their robots to stand fully upright. The first dozen meters were scorched and blackened by their demolition charges, but beyond that the corridor's walls and overhead lighting looked completely untouched, almost pristine. More tunnels and chambers branched off this central passageway.

No sounds reached their CIDs' audio pickups except for the low whir of a ventilation system circulating fresh air through the complex. "Knock, knock. Anyone home?" Charlie murmured.

"This sudden absence of any opposition does *not* make my heart grow fonder," Macomber growled.

"Maybe our big ka-boom scared the crap out of them," she suggested.

"Yeah, maybe," he said doubtfully. "Let's see if we can stir up any trouble. You take the left and I'll go right."

Weapons at the ready, the two CIDs moved down the tunnel—separating at the first intersection to prowl through the labyrinth of lighted corridors in search of Gryzlov's cyberwar "information troops" and their equipment. As they moved deeper into the Perun's Aerie complex, Macomber and Charlie dropped small radio repeaters at every turn to relay their signals so they could stay in touch.

Whack pushed deeper, moving faster through a maze of offices, briefing rooms, and living quarters as it became clear that Perun's Aerie was completely deserted. In fact, he thought worriedly, there was no evidence that this place had ever been occupied for any real length of time. There were no stores of foodstuffs. There were no pieces of clothing or personal belongings in any of the quarters. And there were no documents or operations manuals in any of the offices or briefing rooms. Charlie reported the same thing from her side of the complex.

They met outside another large steel door. This one had a biometric lock set into the rock wall beside it. Thick power conduits fed into the chamber behind the door. Their CIDs registered measurable amounts of electromagnetic-field radiation leaking out into the passage.

Looking down at the faintly glowing palm lock, Charlie wriggled the large metal fingers of her robot's right hand. "Methinks I'm not going to get a match here." She glanced at Macomber. "Want to apply a little rail-gun tough love to the situation?"

"Hell, no," he said. "The Russians have a nuclear reactor buried somewhere in this place. I'd really hate to find out the hard way that it was sitting right behind this door."

"Good point," Charlie agreed gravely, obviously imagining the havoc a superdense slug moving at Mach 5 could wreak on a reactor core and its cooling systems. Instead, she rummaged around in one of her packs and came up with a rectangular block of plastic explosive. "So I guess we do this the old-fashioned way. A little C-4 should do the trick."

Working swiftly, she layered chunks of the malleable plastic explosive over places where the hinges should be. Nonelectric blasting caps and short lengths of detonator cord tied into a section of flexible shock tube connected to an igniter finished the job. Satisfied, they moved away down the corridor and into cover at the nearest intersection.

"Fire in the hole!" Charlie said. Smoothly, she yanked the igniter ring. A puff of smoke eddied away. Seconds later, her charges exploded, blowing the door off its hinges.

Using the enormous strength of his CID, Macomber levered the twisted remains of the heavy door to one side. He entered the large chamber on the other side and stopped a few meters in.

Dozens of racks of computer components filled most of the center of the room. They were connected by fiber-optic cables and power conduits. Tens of thousands of lights blinked in regular patterns across thousands of nodes. A steady hum pervaded the chamber, seeming to indicate that the giant machine was running. His CID scanned the array and flashed a message: *Confirm TL-Platforms Supercomputer match. The computer is live, but configured for remote operation.*

Charlie Turlock moved up beside him just as Macomber came to a grim and very unwelcome realization. "Know what you're looking at?" he said bitterly.

For once, she didn't have a snappy answer.

"The world's biggest fucking piece of cheese," Macomber continued. He was mad at himself and it showed in his voice. "This whole place is a mousetrap. And *we* are the goddamned mice."

Charlie sighed. "Well, that sucks. I thought this seemed a little too easy." She glanced at the other Iron Wolf robot. "So do we just back away nice and slow?"

"No way," Macomber grunted. "A hundred to one, those Russian cocksuckers already know right where we are. So we might as well screw with their fricking bait." With that, he unlimbered his 25mm autocannon and opened fire.

Rack after rack of expensive electronic hardware shattered under a stream of armor-piercing rounds. Showers of sparks erupted on all sides, streaming from floor to ceiling. Small fires sputtered in the gutted remains of computer cores and processors.

Slightly mollified, Macomber put the autocannon away and rearmed with his rail gun. He spun toward the doorway. "C'mon, Charlie! Now let's get the hell out of here!"

SECURITY COMMAND POST, TWO KILOMETERS EAST OF PERUN'S AERIE
That same time

Deep inside a separate tunnel complex dug into one of Mount Manaraga's other spurs, Colonel Balakin and his staff stood staring in horror at their displays. Frantic work by some of Koshkin's experts had finally managed to flush the netrusion-implanted viruses out of their sensor network. Most of their remote cameras were still down, either damaged or destroyed in the Iron Wolf mercenary attack. But the few that were working revealed a scene of utter destruction. Every defensive position they had so laboriously constructed to protect the main entrance to Perun's Aerie had been obliterated in a matter of minutes. Hundreds of Russian soldiers were dead or dying. In this weather, the wounded would freeze to death long before any medical teams could possibly reach them.

And then a young Russian captain swung away from his own console in excitement. "Colonel!" he said excitedly. "The TL computer just went off-line!"

Balakin shook himself out of his funk. They still had time to retrieve something from this disaster—thanks, he was forced to admit, to President Gryzlov's foresight and cunning. Although his conventional defenses had been designed to stop any Iron Wolf attack outside the base, the president had insisted they have a contingency plan in the event the Poles and their American mercenaries reached the costly supercomputer itself. "Activate Plan *Zapadnya*. My authorization code is AZ-4985," he said crisply. "And signal Lieutenant Colonel Zykov to have his force stand ready."

The younger officer typed in the authorization code he'd been given. The lights above a small key inserted into his console flashed green. He turned the key. "Plan Deadfall activated, sir!"

CHAPTER 35

PERUN'S AERIE
That same time

Piloting her CID, Charlie Turlock followed Macomber out of the burning supercomputer room. They turned into the main tunnel, heading for the exit. Toxic smoke from burning plastics and rare metals drifted out behind them.

And then the whole Perun's Aerie complex suddenly shuddered, rocked by shock waves rippling inward at several miles per second. Bits of loose rock and concrete pattered down around the two Iron Wolf combat robots.

"Down!" Macomber roared. His CID crouched, covering its six-sided head and sensor arrays. Reacting just as fast, Charlie did the same.

WHUMMP. WHUMMP. WHUMMP.

The drumbeat roar of a series of powerful explosions followed, echoing and reechoing through the labyrinth of corridors and passages. Dust and debris hurled away from the blasts boiled through tunnels with astounding force.

Charlie felt her CID sway, rocked by the blast wave and hammered by small fragments of shattered rock. Minor damage and failure warnings flooded through her mind. *Hydraulic system function down six percent. Secondary thermal sensor acuity degraded. Left-hand actuator function slightly impaired.*

The fast-moving debris cloud shattered light fixtures in tunnels and corridors. Whole sections of the underground cyberwar facility were abruptly plunged into near-absolute darkness.

Slowly, Charlie's CID climbed back to its feet. Her thermal sensors showed the bright green image of Macomber's robot as it stood up at the same time. Everything else in the swirling, dust-choked air was a blur. Her low-light sensors were down, so she was forced to activate a spotlight. The dazzling beam speared through the darkness.

As the dust settled, things became clearer. The main entrance they'd been moving toward was completely sealed, choked off by hundreds of tons of rock blown down from the mountain above them. She frowned. Even using their CIDs' incredible strength, there was no way they could dig through that debris field. Not before they exhausted the power stored in every lithium-ion battery and hydrogen fuel cell.

"The Russians had demolitions charges rigged to collapse their tunnel entrances," Macomber growled. "Crap, I hate it when the enemy gets smart."

"Do you think they've sealed off every way in or out?" Charlie asked. She wasn't claustrophobic. No one who was truly afraid of confined spaces could pilot a CID. But that didn't mean she relished the prospect of spending an eternity trapped inside this mountain, like some weird, high-tech mummy.

Macomber's CID shrugged. "There's only one way to find out."

They turned away from the collapsed tunnel and trotted deeper into the complex. It quickly became clear that the Russians had blown in all of the entrances to Perun's Aerie—all but one.

"'Come out, come out, and let's play,' said the cat to the mouse," Charlie muttered as they edged cautiously toward the tunnel mouth. Grimly, Macomber nodded.

Set into the north-facing slope of the mountain, this secondary exit looked out onto a shallow, barren, windswept slope devoid of any potential cover. The camouflaged blast door that had once concealed the tunnel from satellite observation stood wide open.

Both CID computers began issuing immediate threat warnings. Their sensors were picking up a large enemy force on the move. At least twenty Russian T-90 main battle tanks were visible roughly a thousand meters away, maneuvering into firing positions on a low, boulder-strewn rise. Intermingled with the tanks were several 9K22 Tunguska armored antiaircraft vehicles—each bristling with 30mm cannons and surface-to-air missiles.

"Geez, Whack, these guys aren't exactly being subtle, are they?" Charlie said with forced good humor. Inside the CID cockpit, her eyes were troubled. "I think they're really pissed off at us for blowing up their nice new supercomputer."

"Could be," Macomber agreed. "Damn it, Charlie. I'm really sorry I got you into this."

"Nobody *got* me into this, Whack," she said with a low laugh. "Obviously I forgot Army Rule Number One—"

"Never volunteer for anything," he finished for her. He sounded pained, almost embarrassed. "Yeah, me too."

Brad McLanahan's worried voice broke in on their circuit. "Wolf Six-Two to Wolf One and Wolf Two. We lost your signal for several minutes. What's your situation?" Macomber filled him in quickly, not bothering to sugarcoat anything. Brad fell silent for several moments. Then he came back on the radio. "Hang tight where you are. I can try to bring the Ranger in for an emergency recovery. That slope beyond your position isn't a great landing site, but it might be doable."

"No way, Wolf Six-Two," Macomber said. "They'd knock you out of the sky in seconds."

Given the number of antiaircraft units already visible on that low rise, Charlie thought that "seconds" was being wildly optimistic. Her CID was also picking up radar emissions from behind the hill, signaling the presence of additional Russian mobile antiaircraft artillery and SAM vehicles. They'd blow the hell out of the XCV-62 before it got anywhere close to this side of the mountain.

"Could you pull back into the complex?" Brad asked. "And make them come to you?"

"Negative," Macomber said. "These guys show no signs of being that stupid. If Charlie and I try to fort up here, all they have to do is wait us out. Eventually, we'll run out of battery power—and then we're just sitting ducks. Besides, there's no way you can stay parked on the ground. If there aren't already Russian fighters on the way here now, there will be *muy pronto*."

"Understood," Brad replied.

"So we're going to have to break out to you," Macomber continued. "And listen, Brad, if we don't make it, get out fast. Don't screw around trying to play hero. This was a sucker play, so let's not give that bastard Gryzlov any more prizes than we have to, okay?"

Twelve miles to their northwest, Brad sat staring blindly out through the Ranger's cockpit windows. Slowly and very reluctantly, he nodded. "Got it, Whack. We'll let you come to us." He swallowed hard against a huge lump in his throat. "Good luck. Wolf Six-Two out."

Macomber's CID turned toward Charlie. "Listen close. When we go, shoot straight and fast. And keep moving. Don't stop for anything. Understand? If I go down, you keep running. Our only chance here is to smash a hole in their deployment and get clear before they're set."

She nodded. Then she stuck out her CID's hand. "Whatever happens, Whack, it's been a hell of an honor to serve with you."

He took it. "Amen to that, Charlie." Then he

let go and deployed his rail gun on one shoulder and his 25mm autocannon on the other.

She followed suit, frowning at the ammo read-outs her computer fed her. Well, what did it really matter? she thought with icy determination. This was a come-as-you-are war, after all. It wasn't like she was going to have time to stop to reload.

"You ready?" Macomber asked softly.

"I'm set," Charlie replied.

"Then go!" he ordered.

Together, the two CIDs burst out of the tunnel mouth, already veering apart to make it harder for the Russians to concentrate their fire. Accelerating fast, they charged downhill toward the still-deploying enemy tank companies.

Charlie's battle computer silhouetted one of the T-90s in red, identifying it as a priority target. The low-slung tank's main gun was swinging toward her. Almost quicker than conscious thought, she aimed her rail gun and squeezed off a shot.

CCRRACK!

Her round slammed into the T-90's turret, tore through, and punched out the other side—moving so fast that it vaporized the tank's reactive armor in a blinding white flash. Flames erupted from its mangled turret and hull as the air inside caught fire.

Off to the side, another Russian armored vehicle blew apart, hit by one of Whack's projectiles.

Charlie ran like the wind, shooting on the move. Her shoulder-mounted weapons were slewing back and forth like crazy—she followed maneuver cues so that the weapons could stay on target as she ran. Two more Russian T-90s slewed sideways, wreathed in fire and smoke. Another exploded downrange. Its mangled turret flew skyward, tumbling lazily end over end.

Recovering from the shock caused by their all-out attack, the surviving Russian tanks and other vehicles opened fire. Salvos of 125mm armor-piercing shells and 30mm cannon rounds streaked across the snow toward the speeding Iron Wolf combat robots. Their first shots missed, slashing past overhead or narrowly to either side before slamming into the mountain behind them. Pulverized rock splashed across the slope. Explosions, the tearing, ripping sound of small-caliber automatic weapons, and the sharp crack of smoothbore cannons echoed off the surrounding peaks.

Numbers flashed across Charlie's display. *500 meters to enemy battle position. 450 meters.* Microwaves suddenly lashed at her CID. The robot's neural link translated the sensation into something like hot needles stabbing her left side. *I'm being painted by a phased-array S-band radar,* she realized. There was no time to try spoofing it with her netrusion systems. Reacting instantly, she rolled away from the radar beam. Her 25mm stuttered, shredding one of a pair of tracked Tunguska antiaircraft vehicles just cresting a low rise off to the left. It shuddered and squealed to a halt with thick black smoke curling out from open hatches.

Its surviving companion fired back. Radar-guided 30mm rounds whipcracked through the air. Charlie's CID stumbled, hit several times across her torso and legs. Her composite armor held, but warnings flashed through her consciousness. *Hydraulic-systems damage. Fuel Cells Four through Seven down. Active radar off-line.* She swiveled fast, hearing servos and actuators grinding and whining in protest. Another burst from her autocannon destroyed the second Tunguska before it could hit her again.

Teeth set in a determined grin, she turned and ran on. But her CID was moving slower, laboring as the computer tried to compensate for her damaged hydraulics and reduced power supplies.

WHAAMM!

A 125mm tungsten alloy sabot round slammed into Charlie's CID with bone-shaking force—ripping off the arm carrying her autocannon. The impact sent her flying. She landed in a crumpled heap.

For a moment, she lay still inside the cockpit, groggily trying to comprehend what had just happened. Her display was a sea of red-and-orange failure and damage indicators. "Ah, crap," she muttered. "This is not good."

With an effort, Charlie wobbled back to her feet, trailing bits of wiring and shattered armor. Spatters of red hydraulic fluid stained the snow. Through the cascading failure warnings scrolling across her screens, she saw the Russian T-90 that had hit her rumbling closer. Its turret swiveled, bringing that big main gun to bear again.

She fired her rail gun. The T-90 exploded, torn open from end to end.

Rail-gun ammunition expended, her computer warned. *Hydraulics crippled. All sensors off-line. Power at fifteen percent.*

"I'm not going to make it, Whack," Charlie radioed. "This tin can is dying on its feet."

"Then set the self-destruct and bail out," Macomber urged.

"Already on it," she said crisply. *Initiate self-destruct sequence*, she ordered the CID's computer through her neural link. *Authorization Turlock One-Alpha.*

Self-destruct authorization confirmed, the machine replied. *Thirty. Twenty-nine. Twenty-eight . . .*

Time to get while the getting was good, Charlie thought. She squirmed out of the haptic interface, feeling fully human again as her awareness of the CID dropped away. *Eighteen. Seventeen. Sixteen.* Wriggling around, she punched the emergency hatch release. Nothing happened. She punched it again.

"Damn it," she murmured. She keyed her radio. "The hatch is jammed, Whack."

Four hundred meters away, Macomber turned toward her, taking out another Tunguska antiaircraft vehicle with a quick burst of 25mm armor-piercing ammunition. He was near the top of the low rise. Burning Russian armored vehicles dotted the hill. "Abort the self-destruct, Charlie," he said. "I'll come get you."

"It's too late, Whack, but thanks," she said, still determinedly working on the hatch mechanism.

There was no way she could reengage with the haptic interface in time. *Four. Three . . .* "See you on the other side—"

Her CID exploded in a huge ball of fire that lit the night sky for miles around.

With his face set like flint, Macomber swung away and accelerated to his CID's best remaining speed—determined to break clear of this murderous ambush or die trying. He darted past another smashed Russian T-90, veering sharply to put its flaming hulk between him and the enemy's surviving tanks. Moving at more than seventy kilometers an hour, he skidded down the rear slope in a spray of snow and fractured ice.

Just ahead he saw a meandering, ice-choked stream and then open ground. A stand of pine trees rose several hundred meters away, offering the promise of cover and limited concealment.

Macomber leaped across the stream, landed heavily on the ground beyond, and took off running. The woods were only three hundred meters away now. Flashes rippled like lightning across the distant horizon. *Artillery alert*, his CID reported. *Multiple 122mm howitzer rounds inbound. Impact zone is—*

The world around him erupted in fire and smoke. Huge fountains of dirt and rock soared high into the air, hurled skyward by exploding shells. Knocked off its feet by a near miss, his CID tumbled across the quaking ground. His rail gun, riddled by shrapnel, went flying, along with shards of broken composite armor. Swearing under his breath, he scrambled upright.

And went down again under the hammer-blow of another massive impact as a 122mm HE round detonated only meters away. More shrapnel punched into the robot's torso, arms, legs, and head. Damage readouts flickered across his static-laced displays in a blur of red.

Once more, Macomber pushed his damaged machine up and into an awkward, shambling gait. Most of his sensors were dead, along with all of his weapons. He staggered onward. That patch of pine forest was close . . . so damned close.

Movement at the edge of his failing vision display caught his attention. He turned . . . and saw another T-90 main battle tank grinding out of defilade to intercept him. Its turret whined round, slewing its 125mm smoothbore gun on target. Two wheeled BTR-82 troop carriers fanned out to either side of the Russian tank.

"Well, just fuck me," Macomber said tiredly. He focused on his link with the computer. *Initiate self-destruction sequence. Authorization—*

The T-90 fired its main gun.

Macomber felt himself slammed backward with colossal force. Everything around him flared bright red and orange and then faded to black.

When he came to moments later, he found himself curled inside the CID's shattered cockpit, staring up at the night sky. Hit by an armor-piercing round at point-blank range, his Iron Wolf robot had been blown in half. He fumbled with the straps holding him in place. There was no way he was just going to lie here and die. *Not in this fucking machine anyway*, he thought angrily.

Gritting his teeth against a sudden wave of pain, Macomber twisted out of the wrecked CID's torso and dropped into the snow, landing on his knees. Still dazed, he painfully lifted his head to look around. The two BTRs had halted not far away. Rifle-armed Russian troops were pouring out of their open hatches. Urged on by a shouting officer, they trotted in his direction. Wearily, Macomber staggered to his feet and assumed a fighting stance. Win or lose, these sons of bitches would know they'd been in a fight.

Some of the soldiers raised their weapons, but they did not fire. They moved in quickly, obviously more fascinated by the abandoned machine and not worried one bit about their quarry. Whack had enough strength to crush one trachea and break one arm. He heard a rifle drop to the ground and he scrambled to find it. But now, enraged, the rest of the soldiers swarmed over him like a pack of dogs bringing down a wild boar.

Macomber went down hard, hammered into oblivion by rifle butts and fists.

CHAPTER 36

IRON WOLF STRIKE-FORCE LANDING ZONE
That same time

Brad McLanahan had watched Charlie Turlock's CID beacon disappear from his tactical display in stunned disbelief. God only knew, he was no stranger to the violent deaths of people close to him. In the past couple of years alone, he'd lost plenty of friends and teammates. But it was still a shock to see someone like Charlie—so full of life and energy and joy—wiped out in the blink of an eye. He'd felt her death like the sharp, piercing blow of an ice pick driven straight into his heart. What made it even worse was realizing that it could easily have been Nadia piloting that robot, and feeling grateful that she was safe.

And now Whack Macomber's CID was down too, destroyed by the same brutally effective Russian ambush. The lump in his throat grew larger, threatening to choke him. Not for the first time lately, he wished he weren't too old to cry.

He stared out the cockpit windows. Outside, across the clearing, Ian Schofield and his commandos humped their gear and weapons back toward the XCV-62. Once they were aboard in a couple of minutes, he could take off—beginning the long, risky flight out of Russia with the news of their failure.

"Brad," Nadia said suddenly, sitting bolt upright. She'd been scanning through radio frequencies, using the Ranger's sophisticated computers, in an effort to figure out more of what the Russians were up to. "Listen!"

She switched the channel she'd been monitoring to his headset. Someone gabbling frantically in Russian sounded in his ears. He frowned. It sounded like a very excited junior officer making a report, but otherwise it was gibberish to him. He shrugged helplessly. "Sorry, I can't make it out."

"Major Macomber is alive!" Nadia said. Her eyes were almost completely closed while she translated on the fly. "This lieutenant is telling his colonel that they've taken a prisoner from the second mercenary robot they destroyed."

For a split second, Brad experienced a surge of hope. But then it faded, replaced by a horrible feeling of dread and helplessness. Alive as a prisoner of the Russians, Whack was probably worse off than if he'd been killed outright. Gryzlov had tagged the Iron Wolf Squadron as terrorists, even though they fought in uniform and for a recognized nation-state. The cold-blooded Russian leader would have no qualms about ordering Whack tortured for information about CID and other advanced Scion weapons technology and tactics. And after they'd squeezed him dry, they'd put a bullet in the back of his skull and dump his body in an unmarked grave.

SOUTHWEST OF PERUN'S AERIE

That same time

Flying at three thousand meters above the forests of northern Russia, two Russian Air Force Su-50 stealth fighters in dark and light blue camouflage raced northeast. Seen from a distance in daylight, their deceptive "Shark" paint scheme made them appear much smaller than they actually were. At night, they were almost invisible to the naked eye.

Colonel Ruslan Baryshev spoke into his mic. "Perun Security Command, this is Prividenye Lead. I am five minutes out from your position. Request situation update."

"Specter Lead, this is Security Command," an agitated voice acknowledged. *"We have defeated the enemy ground assault, destroying two of their combat machines. But our casualties are extremely heavy—as is the damage to our special complex."*

Baryshev grimaced. The quick briefing he'd received from Colonel General Maksimov before his fighters took off had indicated the extraordinarily high value President Gryzlov placed on this top-secret facility. Heads were likely to roll in the aftermath of this Iron Wolf attack—he only hoped his would not be one of them. He keyed his mic again. "What about the enemy transport aircraft? Have your radars or scouts pinpointed its location?"

"*Negative, Specter,*" the other man reported. "*Our radars were destroyed in the initial assault, along with our fixed air defenses. And unfortunately, we have no ground- or helicopter-based reconnaissance units currently available to search the surrounding area.*"

Better and better, Baryshev thought acidly. The situation on the ground sounded like a total clusterfuck—which meant it was up to him to find the surviving American mercenaries before they escaped.

So far, his Su-50's radar showed no unidentified contacts in the skies ahead. That wasn't surprising. To have penetrated this far inside Russia without being detected, any enemy aircraft would have to be fairly stealthy and able to fly safely at extremely low altitude. If so, he couldn't expect to pick up anything until they were much closer.

The other possibility, of course, was that the Iron Wolf aircraft was still parked somewhere on the ground, somewhere relatively close to the Perun's Aerie complex. He radioed his wingman. "We're going hunting, Oleg. Let's maximize our coverage. Deploy in line abreast. Five-kilometer spacing. I'm switching my radar to air-to-ground mode. You keep an eye on the sky, understand?"

"*Two,*" the other pilot, Captain Oleg Imrekov, replied. Even over the radio, he sounded dubious. "*It's going to be a bitch spotting anything in all that clutter up ahead.*"

Baryshev understood his wingman's skepticism. They were approaching the Urals at high speed. The brand-new N036 AESA radars equipping their Su-50s were marvels of Russian technology, but no fighter-size airborne radar in the world could hope to see through mountains. "Don't worry, Captain," he said. "Wherever these mercenaries are hiding, they'll have to come up into the open air sooner or later. And if they don't, we'll fly search patterns until we nail them on the ground."

THE URALS
That same time

"*Caution, two unidentified airborne X-band search radars detected,*" the Ranger's SPEAR threat-warning system announced abruptly, shockingly loud in the gloom-filled silence of the cockpit.

Jolted out of his funk, Brad muttered, "Hell." The Russians finally had aircraft up looking for them. Which meant they had to get out, and get out fast. Stealth characteristics or not, they were bound to be detected eventually—and on the ground, the XCV-62 was a sitting duck. He leaned forward, rapidly punching through takeoff checklist menus on his two MFDs. "I'm going for a fast engine start."

"Identify those radars," Nadia ordered.

"*Negative identification,*" the computer told her. "*Probable agile frequency signal. Stand by.*"

Her fingers flew across the virtual keyboard on one of her displays as she searched for possible matches. If those enemy radars were hopping frequencies too fast for the SPEAR system to identify, they were probably active electronically scanned array types. And those rapid frequency changes made it almost impossible to get a bearing and range to the emitter, let alone positively identify it from its signals alone.

On the other hand, she thought, there were only so many known X-band airborne radars in the Russian inventory. And there were even fewer AESA-types. Her finger stabbed at one of the screens on her MFDs—the N036 radars manufactured by Russia's Tikhomirov Scientific Institute of Instrument Design, or NIIP. That had to be it. Her eyes widened slightly as she realized those radars were only fitted to one type of combat aircraft. Alarmed, she turned back to Brad. "We are being hunted by Russian Su-50 stealth fighters."

"Swell," he said under his breath. "Nice of them to bring out the first team." He opened a channel to the Ranger's troop compartment. "Captain Schofield?"

"*We're aboard*," the Canadian-born commando officer said, sounding a bit breathless. Running through deep snow was hard work, no matter how physically fit you were.

"Good," Brad said. He tapped a control on his display. "Then I'm sealing the ramp." A high-pitched hydraulic whine penetrated the cockpit. "Strap in tight. We have company coming and this is going to get hairy real fast."

He entered more commands. Outside the windows, their four turbofan engines started spooling up. "All compressors are in the green. Engine temps look good," he said, studying the readouts.

Beside him, Nadia was running through her own checklists. "Preparing defensive systems. SPEAR is ready. Flares are set for K-74M2 heat-seekers. Chaff is configured for K-77M radar-guided missiles. Spinning up inertial navigation systems on both MALDs. GPS receivers are initialized."

Hearing her, Brad nodded to himself. That was smart. She'd identified the air-to-air weapons most likely to be carried in those approaching Su-50s' internal weapons bays. Their defensives would be preset for maximum efficiency against the most likely threats. Unfortunately, their options were very limited.

According to their intelligence, Su-50s configured for stealth flight usually carried two heat-seekers each. Russia's K-74M2 missiles were an advanced version of its R-73 infrared homing weapons, code-named the AA-11 Archer by NATO. In size, range, speed, and agility, K-74M2s were the equivalent of the American AIM-9X Sidewinders. That was bad enough.

The four K-77M radar-guided missiles carried by the Russian fighters were even more dangerous—better than anything in current U.S., NATO, or AFN service. Compared to American AIM-120 AMRAAMs, K-77Ms had one huge advantage: older missiles of this type carried a small, mechanically steered radar antenna in their noses to provide final guidance against a target during the seconds before impact. But sharp evasive maneuvering by an aircraft in those last few seconds could slip out of that narrow seeker beam faster than it could adjust, causing a miss. Unfortunately, the K-77M carried a phased-array terminal guidance radar in its nose. Since this radar was digitally steered, its beam could be adjusted thousands of times per second. Put simply, there was no way any final evasive maneuver could shake its lock. Stealth, jamming, and chaff were the only real defensive options . . . and even then the missile's phased-array guidance radar greatly reduced their effectiveness.

Struck by a sudden thought, Brad pulled up a digital map on one of his displays. Flying straight west with those Russian fighters up and looking for them would be suicide. They couldn't outrun those Su-50s or dodge every weapon they fired—not over northern Russia's vast, virtually flat expanses of forest. But heading east into the radar maze created by the jagged peaks and ridgelines of the Ural Mountains might help them evade detection. If missiles started flying, the cover offered by mountains might also give them a slim chance at survival. That wasn't much of a straw to grasp at, but it was better than nothing.

"Unidentified X-band signal strength increasing," the Ranger's computer reported.

Brad finished his takeoff checklist. "We're good to go," he said quietly. He throttled up to full military power. The XCV-62 started rolling forward, picking up speed. Carefully, he steered straight down the ruts his landing had ripped through the snowpack. Huge masses of compacted snow rippled off the ground behind the Ranger and blew apart into individual flakes, sent whirling through the air by the exhaust from its engines.

He held tight on course and felt the batwinged aircraft shuddering and bouncing as it raced faster and faster across the clearing. The woods on the far side grew larger with astonishing quickness. The airspeed indicator on his HUD climbed higher. *C'mon, baby*, he thought, *give me just a little more speed*. Now individual trees were starkly visible through the windscreen, looming closer and closer. "Vr . . . rotating!" he said, pulling back on the stick.

The Ranger's nose rose and it soared off the ground in a billowing cloud of vaporized snow. Still accelerating, the batwinged aircraft cleared the tops of the surrounding trees by a few yards and climbed higher. Its landing gear whirred smoothly up and locked inside with a few muffled thumps.

At a thousand feet, Brad banked sharply, rolling back toward the east at 450 knots. With the ice-and-snow-covered peaks rising ahead, starkly outlined against the night sky, he leveled off.

SPECTER TWO
That same time

Captain Oleg Imrekov frowned. At this speed, nearly eleven hundred kilometers an hour, he and

Colonel Baryshev were only two minutes out from the Perun's Aerie base. But their radars still weren't picking anything up—not in the air and not on the ground. How stealthy were these damned mercenaries? Were they already gone, well on their way out of Russia?

Suddenly a sharp tone sounded in his headset, alerting him to a possible detection. A green diamond appeared on his HUD. His infrared search-and-track system was picking up a heat signature almost due north. But the signature was very small, more like that of a missile than a full-size aircraft. It was moving east across his field of view at more than eight hundred kilometers an hour. *Well, hell*, he thought, that was far too slow for a missile. For a split second, his radar saw something in the same spot but then lost the contact.

"Lead, this is Two!" Imrekov snapped. "Stealth target bearing eleven o'clock moving to twelve at low altitude. Target is heading east toward the mountains at high speed. Range more than thirty kilometers. IRST contact only."

He pushed a switch on his stick. Two missile symbols appeared in the corner of his HUD. The two K-74M2 heat-seeking missiles in his Su-50's wing-root bays were armed and set for a single salvo launch.

"Acknowledged, Two," Colonel Baryshev said excitedly. *"Switching back to air-to-air mode. Do you have a shot?"*

Imrekov's eyes narrowed as he rapidly considered the question. Scoring a kill on a crossing target at this range, especially one with such a small heat signature, would be tough. Then again, if you didn't shoot, you couldn't score. "Affirmative!" he radioed back.

"Then you are cleared to fire, Two! See if you can rattle this mercenary's cage."

Without hesitating, Imrekov squeezed the trigger on his stick. One after another, two K-74 missiles dropped out of his fighter's internal bays and lit off. Trailing fire and smoke, they slashed across the night sky—arrowing toward the distant Iron Wolf target at two and half times the speed of sound.

"Warning, warning, IR missile launch detection at three o'clock," the Ranger's computer announced. *"Two missiles inbound."*

"Countermeasures ready," Nadia said. She had her head bent low, peering intently at her displays. "Time to impact estimated at thirty seconds." She transferred her data to Brad's HUD, providing a visual running countdown.

Brad nodded tightly. Some Russian son of a bitch was eager for a quick kill, because that was a hell of a long-range shot for heat-seekers. Their solid-rocket motors would have burned out by the time they reached him, meaning they would be flying solely on inertia. Plus, the geometry sucked. But he wasn't close enough to the mountains to use them as cover . . . and those K-74s were dangerous weapons.

One of the best ways to defend against a long-range attack like this involved climbing right away to force enemy missiles to bleed off more energy in their approach, making it easier to evade them at close range. Doing that now, though, would only increase the odds the Russians could lock up the XCV-62 on radar—which would expose them to a long-range attack by the far more lethal K-77 radar-guided missiles those Su-50s were carrying.

Well, he wasn't going to play that game, Brad decided. Instead, he kept straight on toward the mountains. "Stand by on countermeasures."

"Countermeasures ready," Nadia confirmed.

"Lead missile burnout," the computer reported. *"Time to impact is fifteen seconds."* A moment later. *"Trailing missile burnout."*

Now those K-74s were coasting toward him on inertia alone, Brad thought. Then the side of his mouth quirked upward in a wry grin. Well, at least, if you could call missiles tearing through the sky at more than sixteen hundred knots "coasting."

The missile-impact estimate on his HUD kept counting down. When it flickered to *4 seconds*, he snapped, "Countermeasures!" Nadia's finger stabbed at her display. Brad yanked the XCV-62 upward into a hard, tight, climbing turn—briefly handling the Iron Wolf aircraft more like it was a fighter jet than a transport. G-forces slammed him back against his seat. The color started to leach out of his vision, turning the world gray. The Ranger soared skyward, trading airspeed for altitude as it climbed.

Dozens of flares streamed out behind them, each a miniature sunburst against the black sky.

Decoyed away, the first Russian missile veered

off toward one of the tumbling points of fire and detonated. Slowing visibly, the second K-74 swung through the flare cloud and chased after the Iron Wolf transport as it climbed and turned. Every turn it made in a vain effort to home in on the evading aircraft ate more energy, until at last, out of airspeed and at the extent of its range, the Russian missile fell away—plummeting toward the darkened earth several thousand feet below.

Instantly, Brad rolled out of the climb and dove back toward the ground, again heading east toward the Urals. He throttled back to reduce their heat signature, allowing gravity to accelerate them as they plunged back down.

"Warning, warning, X-band radar locked on," the computer said.

Shit, Brad thought. He kept his eyes on the altitude reading sliding down the edge of his HUD. Five thousand feet. Four thousand feet.

"Engaging X-band radar," Nadia said from beside him. She tapped a display, directing their SPEAR system to try to jam or spoof the Russian airborne radar that had them zeroed in. "I show two Su-50s on our thermal sensors," she continued coolly. "They are fourteen miles behind us and closing at high speed."

"Understood," Brad said tightly. Suddenly his "brilliant" plan to backtrack deeper into the Urals didn't look quite as smart. There was no way he could outrun those enemy fighters. And how the hell was he going to outmaneuver them in this crate? The XCV-62 handled beautifully for a transport aircraft, but she wasn't built for dogfighting. That 4-g turn he'd just pulled was right at the edge of her performance envelope. In contrast, the Su-50s now in hot pursuit were some of the most maneuverable combat aircraft in the world.

The Ranger streaked east, still losing altitude fast. Three thousand feet. Twenty-five hundred feet. They roared low over a steep-sided ridge and dropped behind it. A wide valley opened up before them, running northeast deeper into the Urals. Brad rolled left to follow it.

"*X-band radar lock broken,*" the computer reported.

With that ridge crest between them and the Russians, they had a few moments' grace. It wouldn't last long, he realized. Those enemy fighters had two options, both equally dangerous: If their pilots were aggressive, they could go for a balls-out chase through this maze of ice and snow, relying on superior speed and maneuverability to close in for a better IR missile shot . . . or even drive into knife-fight range for a gun kill, using their 30mm cannons. If they were cagey, the Russian pilots could go high, using their powerful radars and IRST systems to cover every possible escape route out of the mountains. That way they could either vector in other fighters to finish the job—or make the kill themselves with long-range, radar-guided missiles as soon as fuel constraints forced Brad to break back west . . . out of cover.

"One Su-50 just popped over that ridge and is now dead astern," Nadia said. She had one of her displays cued to their rear-facing thermal sensors.

"Range is now eight miles. The trailing Russian aircraft is one mile behind the leader."

That meant they'd decided to chase him down themselves, Brad figured. That was no great surprise. That first long-range shot they'd taken at him signaled that these guys were aggressive as hell. A sharp tone from their SPEAR threat-warning system sounded in his headset. At this range, those X-band radars probably had him painted again. And the IRST systems carried by those enemy fighters certainly did.

He rolled back right, turning tightly down another gorge running east between two serrated spurs. The threat-warning tone cut off. More high ground rose steeply about three miles ahead, where this valley bent sharply back to the southeast.

"We can't run. We can't fight. And we can't hide forever," he muttered. "Which leaves—"

"Deception," Nadia finished for him.

"Exactly," Brad said. He slammed the Ranger into another tight, 3-g turn, following the trace of the gorge as it veered right. There, about five miles ahead, a rugged mountain summit soared steeply, sharp-edged in white snow and gray rock against the black, star-spangled night sky.

"I am laying in an evasion course for MALD One," Nadia said, straining forward against the g-forces to input commands on her display. "General heading?"

"East and then north," Brad told her. He flew on straight toward that huge peak. The mountain grew larger and larger with frightening speed—

spreading across the XCV-62's windscreen until it filled it completely.

"Course programmed," Nadia told him. Another warning tone sounded from SPEAR. "The lead Su-50 is now six miles astern and turning after us," she said. "He could fire at any moment."

Brad shook his head. "That guy already fired his only two heat-seekers at us. It's the trailer we have to worry about." His eyes narrowed, completely focused on the steep slope looming ahead. He could make out huge boulders now, half buried in ice and snow. This was going to be close . . . very, very close.

At almost the last possible moment, he pulled back sharply on the Ranger's stick—yanking the aircraft into a near-vertical climb. His left hand shoved the throttles forward, running the engines up to full military power. They soared skyward at high speed, roaring above the slope with just a few feet to spare. Another glistening rooster tail of swirling snow fanned out in their wake.

Still flying at more than four hundred knots, they cleared the top of the peak. Instantly, Brad rolled right almost inverted, causing the Ranger's nose to tuck sharply down the other side into a wide valley. Negative g's tugged him forward against his shoulder straps.

The warbling tone from their SPEAR system went silent. He'd put the massive bulk of that mountain and its millions of tons of rock between them and those pursuing Su-50s. They had maybe thirty seconds before the Russians could pick them up again.

Brad rolled back wings level and cried, "Launch the MALD!"

Nadia stabbed her display. "Launching!"

Bay doors whined open, and a small ADM-160B decoy dropped away from the Ranger. Its small wings unfolded as it launched. Then, powered by an ultralight turbojet engine, the MALD veered away, jinking wildly as it flew northeast above the mountain slopes. It went active, mimicking the radar signature and flight profile of their XCV-62.

Immediately Brad rolled away and dove, following the trace of the valley opening before them as it curved back west around the mountain. He throttled back to minimum power to cut their heat signature as much as possible. The roar from their engines faded away, replaced by the eerie, keening sound of wind as they glided down and down—slanting toward the ground at high speed. The needle-sharp tops of pine trees reached out toward them.

Far behind and above them, two blinding flashes lit the sky.

"Missile launch!" Nadia shouted. The leading Su-50 had fired K-77 radar-guided missiles at the fleeing MALD. Both missiles slashed through the darkness, curving northeast as they guided on their target.

Seconds later, another explosion seared the darkness. Bits and pieces of flaming debris tumbled toward the earth—scattering widely across the boulder-strewn slopes of another mountain spur miles away.

"The Su-50s are turning away from us!" Nadia

said exultantly. "They're flying north, toward the MALD crash site!"

Grinning like a lunatic, Brad jammed the Ranger's throttles forward to regain some control. He leveled out only a hundred feet above the treetops. The Iron Wolf aircraft zoomed westward down the valley—widening the distance between itself and the Russian stealth fighters now speeding away toward the wreckage of the decoy they had mistaken for their prey.

CHAPTER 37

Russian president Gennadiy Gryzlov listened to Colonel Balakin's recitation of his woes with growing impatience. Intellectually, he could understand the shock the other man felt in seeing more than three-quarters of his troops killed in a battle against just two combat robots. But it was a waste of time. War ate men and machines. That was its nature. What mattered was victory.

Finally, he snapped. "Look, I don't give a crap about your casualties, Balakin. We'll send their loved ones a medal and the usual bullshit letter of condolence, okay? Now, did you stop those Iron Wolf mercenaries who attacked Perun's Aerie or not?"

"Yes, Mr. President, we destroyed both machines," Balakin replied stiffly. "And we have a prisoner—one of the robot pilots."

A huge smile spread across Gryzlov's face.

"*Molodets!* Well done, Colonel! You should have reported that first." He spun round in his chair, crooking a finger at Sergei Tarzarov. The older man had just come into his office.

Tarzarov came forward and stood impassively in front of his desk, apparently waiting for instructions.

"Can the mercenary pilot you've captured be moved?" Gryzlov asked Balakin over their secure connection.

"Yes, sir," the other man answered. "It seems this man, an American named Macomber, was only lightly wounded when Zykov's tanks knocked out his machine. He suffered more injuries when my soldiers took him captive, but nothing too serious." From the sound of his voice, Balakin regretted that.

"See that your prisoner stays intact, Colonel!" Gryzlov snapped. "I don't want any slipups. I don't care how pissed off your troops are, you keep them under control! If the American dies, I'll have your entire command liquidated . . . including *you*. Is that clear?"

"*Ya ponimayu.* I understand," Balakin said, frightened now.

Gryzlov relaxed slightly, satisfied that he'd put the other man on notice. He knew how soldiers thought. It would have been all too easy for some junior officer or noncom, enraged by the death of so many comrades, to put a bullet in this Iron Wolf pilot and claim he'd been "shot while trying to escape." He swiveled back to his computer. "Good,

Colonel. You've done well so far. Don't foul up now, eh?"

"No, Mr. President," Balakin said.

"Then listen carefully," Gryzlov continued. "I want your prisoner at the aiport in Pechora within three hours. I'm sending an aircraft to bring him back to Moscow. Keep him safe until then. Out."

When he hung up, he looked across the desk at Tarzarov. "I'm putting this matter in your hands, Sergei. Head for Vnukovo immediately. Take a detachment of troops from the Kremlin Regiment with you. Use my personal Sukhoi Superjet 100." He grinned cruelly. "We might as well make sure our 'guest' is comfortable on his last flight, eh? But you can skip the in-flight caviar and vodka service."

Expressionlessly, Tarzarov nodded. "Very well." He looked back at Gryzlov. "But before I go, I should tell you that Colonel General Maksimov phoned me while you were talking to Balakin."

Gryzlov laughed. "So the old man's too upset to call me directly now?" His gaze sharpened. "Why? Did his precious stealth fighters muff the job of nailing that Iron Wolf transport aircraft?"

Tarzarov shook his head. "On the contrary, Colonel Baryshev and his wingman report downing an unidentified stealth aircraft in the mountains northeast of Perun's Aerie."

"Unidentified?" Gryzlov pounced on the qualifier.

Tarzarov shrugged. "Apparently the debris came down in very difficult terrain. Maksimov says it will take some hours before he can get a search-and-rescue helicopter to the scene to fully confirm the kill."

"How confident are they that this was the Iron Wolf aircraft?" Gryzlov pressed.

"Maksimov told me his pilots have completed several low-level sweeps of the surrounding mountains and river valleys," Tarzarov replied as confidently as he could, "without making any further contacts."

Gryzlov nodded slowly. In the circumstances, the obvious answer was probably right. There was no realistic way a subsonic stealth transport should have been able to survive for long when actively hunted by two of Russia's most advanced combat fighters. Still, there was no point in taking chances. "Contact Maksimov on your way to Vnukovo," he said. "Tell him I want fighter and Beriev-100 air-surveillance patrols up along our borders with Ukraine, Belarus, the Baltic states, and Finland—covering every gap in our ground radar coverage. If, by some miracle, that Iron Wolf aircraft slipped past his Su-50s, I want it detected and destroyed before it escapes our airspace."

PECHORA, RUSSIA
A short time later

Engines throttled way back, the Iron Wolf XCV-62 Ranger came in low and slow, almost skimming the earth as it flew south. The lights of Pechora and a couple of small adjoining towns twinkled to the southeast and to the west. Brighter lights were visible almost dead ahead, marking the location of Pechora Airport's nearly six-thousand-foot-long runway.

Brad McLanahan kept his eyes fixed on his HUD. He was pretty sure that the patch of waste ground he'd picked out earlier as a landing site was clear of major obstacles, but there was no way they could risk a radar sweep—even a short, single pulse—to check. One good thing was that there was a lot less snow hiding the ground this far out from the mountains.

"Gear coming down," he said, tapping in the commands that would set the Ranger's systems for a very short, rough-field landing. Wing-control surfaces opened wider, providing even more lift to counteract the extra drag from their landing gear. They dropped lower.

A thin belt of forest hid the lights of the airport. Brad was counting on those trees and darkness to screen their approach from any prying eyes. With all the Ranger's stealth features, the civilian approach radar at Pechora couldn't pick them up. There wasn't much he could do about noise, though the XCV-62 was pretty quiet.

Still, all of Gryzlov's closely guarded, top-secret activities around this area should have taught Pechora's civilians the value of ignoring the sounds of mysterious aircraft flying overhead. There was an old bomber and AWACS aircraft base, Pechora Kamenka, about sixteen miles west, but it had been decommissioned and its runways and facilities were in serious disrepair. So any cargo flights bringing personnel or equipment to the Perun's Aerie base had to be flown into the civilian airport. As an added precaution, though, Nadia was monitoring emergency channels, ready to warn him if she picked up any signs that the local authorities were sounding the alarm.

The bright green line marking his desired touchdown point appeared to slide toward them even faster as they descended. Brad's left hand hovered over the throttles. One hundred yards. Fifty yards. *Now*, he thought decisively. He pulled the throttles almost all the way back in one, smooth motion.

Robbed of the last bit of airspeed keeping her aloft, the Ranger dropped out of the sky and onto the empty field. The aircraft shook and rattled, jarred roughly from side to side, as they bounded across a rough surface of frozen earth, dead grass, and isolated patches of snow and ice. Every bump hurled Brad and Nadia against their straps and then slammed them back hard into their seats. Finally, they slewed to a stop with just a few yards to spare before they would have slammed head-on into the woods lining the southern rim of the clearing.

Sweating now, Brad swung the XCV-62 back through a half circle so that they could take off fast when the time came. And then, working together with practiced efficiency, he and Nadia quickly shut down the Ranger's engines and avionics. The frozen stillness of a winter night settled once more across the clearing.

Slowly, he breathed out. His hands were shaking slightly as they dropped back into his lap. "Jesus," he murmured. He glanced across at Nadia. Though her face still carried its usual determined look, she was paler now. "Sorry about that," he said softly. "That landing was a little hairier than I thought it would be."

She forced a crooked smile. "Yes, but I am sure you will get better with practice."

Shakily, he echoed her wry expression. "Sure hope so."

The intercom from the troop compartment buzzed. "Are you going to drop the ramp, Brad?" Ian Schofield asked. "Because my lads and I can't do much from in here."

"Hang on a second, Ian," Brad answered. He unstrapped himself. Nadia did the same. "We're coming back to you for a quick command conference."

Bulky in their winter camouflage and body armor, Schofield and his four commandos formed a half circle around Brad and Nadia. Their weapons and gear were securely stowed along the fuselage. The five Iron Wolf troopers were poker-faced.

"By now, you've probably figured that we're not back in Poland," Brad said quietly.

"Yeah, I thought that last little hop seemed fucking short," Sergeant Andrew Davis growled. The big man was Schofield's senior NCO and his second in command on this mission.

"Is there a reason you've disregarded Major

Macomber's last orders?" Schofield asked carefully. "Because I rather thought he was clear that we were to abort the mission and get out of Russia fast."

"Yes, he was." Brad nodded. He bared his teeth in a tight grin. "But as the mission pilot and air commander, I have two very good reasons for *altering* Whack's orders."

Schofield's stony expression softened a bit. "All right, I'm listening."

"Right now the Russian air defenses are bound to be on high alert," Brad explained. "Even if they still believe that decoy they blew to hell was us, they won't take any chances on being wrong. Which means they'll have fighters aloft and patrolling every egress route. Every search radar will be energized. And every SAM unit will be ready to shoot. So bolting for the border straightaway would only end up being a fast trip to nowhere."

The Canadian nodded slowly. "I see your point." He frowned. "But once the Russians get a better look at the remains of that MALD, they'll know we're still on the loose."

"Yep," Brad said. He shrugged. "Which could also work in our favor. Even if Gryzlov figures out his pilots were duped, the more time that passes, the more likely he'll believe we already made it out."

"And the more likely the Russians will be to lower their alert level," Nadia finished for him.

"But we can't stay on the ground here forever," Schofield pointed out. "Once the sun comes up, we're likely to become something of a curiosity. I imagine even the local yokels might wonder a bit at seeing a stealth aircraft parked in one of their fields."

"Which is why it's a darned good thing this is the winter," Brad agreed. He checked his watch. "Right now it's a little after zero-one-hundred hours, local time. Dawn isn't until zero-nine-hundred hours. Depending on our flight path, we need roughly three hours of darkness left when we take off—to minimize the chances of visual detection. So, barring something unexpected, like a Russian fighter sweep that comes too close or some fitness nut who decides to go hiking after midnight, we should be able to hang out here safely for a while."

Schofield nodded again. His eyes narrowed. "You said you had two reasons for changing the major's orders. I've heard one. What's the second?"

"Whack's not dead. The Russians took him prisoner after he bailed out of his CID," Brad said flatly, dropping his bombshell. The Canadian and his men had been outside, guarding the Ranger, when Nadia intercepted the enemy transmissions reporting the news.

Davis and the other commandos swore quietly, but vehemently. Like Brad, they knew what that meant for Macomber. A clean death in combat would have been a far better fate than prolonged torture and eventual execution.

Schofield, however, kept his eyes on Brad and Nadia. "Are you seriously proposing that we try to rescue him?" he asked, in disbelief. "With five soldiers and one unarmed transport aircraft?"

"I'm suggesting that we keep our options open," Brad countered. "Look, it's pretty clear we walked into an ambush custom-designed to capture or destroy the CIDs and their pilots, right?"

"Yes," the Canadian agreed bleakly.

"So that means Whack is Gryzlov's big prize," Brad argued. "Which is why I think it's probable that they'll fly him straight out of here for interrogation." He shrugged. "Once he's in Moscow, there's nothing we can do. But if we see an opening here—"

"The Russians will be cocky, savoring their triumph," Nadia added persuasively. Her eyes were angry, full of barely contained shame. "They believe we are either dead or running for our lives like whipped dogs. A sudden attempt to retrieve Major Macomber is the very last thing they will expect."

"Surprise or not, what you're proposing is one hell of a reach, Major Rozek," Sergeant Davis said. He jerked his chin at the Iron Wolf commandos around him. "My guys and I are good. Real good. But we're not fricking supermen."

Looking pained, Schofield coughed quietly.

Davis grinned. "Well, except for the captain over there. But you'll notice he left his cape at home."

"No one here is invincible," Brad acknowledged. "Major Rozek and I do have a rough plan we think might work, but this enterprise is not something I'd make an order." He smiled wryly, looking around the half circle of tough, veteran combat soldiers. "Even if I thought I could make that kind of order stick."

"So you're asking for volunteers?" Schofield said softly.

"I am." Brad nodded.

Davis shook his head. "Man, Captain, you really should have a sword like Colonel Travis. That way you could scrape a line across the deck here and dare us to step across it."

Brad laughed. "That'd be pretty dramatic, Sergeant. But this isn't the Alamo, where some could stay and some could go. So either everybody's in on this . . . or no one's in. There's no margin for error."

"Are you planning to consult with President Wilk or Mr. Martindale about this plan of yours?" Schofield asked. "Using a secure link?"

"We could," Brad said. He shrugged. "But I'm not going to. They'd only order us out."

"Which might be the wisest course," Schofield said.

"Probably," Brad agreed. He looked stubborn. "But they're not here. And we are. The way I figure it, that makes this our call."

"Yes, I suppose it does," Schofield said. He sighed. "Very well, Captain McLanahan, let's hear your plan. And then my lads and I will make our decision."

Several minutes later, the rear ramp of the Ranger whined down. Carrying their weapons and other gear, the five members of the Iron Wolf commando team moved out into the open and then disappeared into the woods—scouting southward to find concealed positions overlooking the runway at Pechora.

CHAPTER 38

PECHORA AIRPORT
Three hours later

Captain Ian Schofield and Sergeant Andrew Davis crouched in the cover provided by a thin clump of pine forest just west of the runway. From their concealed vantage point, they could see most of the airport buildings and infrastructure. The other members of his commando team, Mike Knapp, Karol Sikora, and Chris Walker, were deployed along the same belt of trees. The ground was too frozen to dig in, but fallen timber, rocks, and tree trunks offered modest protection. Like Davis, Walker and Knapp were Americans, veterans of the U.S. Special Forces before they joined Scion and Iron Wolf. Sikora was one of the Polish soldiers attached to the squadron.

The runway lights and beacons were lit, as were a number of hangars and other buildings. Airport workers bundled up in parkas were moving around the buildings and parked aviation fuel tankers.

"Wolf Six-Two, this is Wolf Three. It looks as though your guess was right. We see major activity here," Schofield radioed. "There's no scheduled flight this early in the morning, is there?"

"Negative on that, Three," Major Nadia Rozek's crisp, clear voice said in his earpiece. "Stand by."

From beside him, Sergeant Davis said, "I've got movement at my twelve o'clock. Six hundred meters out and closing. Multiple armored vehicles arriving."

Schofield swung his binoculars toward the indicated area. Three eight-wheeled BTR-82 armored personnel carriers came into view. Moving in column, they drove out onto the apron and then parked.

The side hatches on the middle troop carrier popped open. A squad of Russian soldiers dropped out onto the concrete. Two of them reached back in and roughly dragged Wayne Macomber outside, dumping him onto the ground like a sack of potatoes. Then they hauled him upright. The Iron Wolf major looked woozy. Dried blood streaked his bruised face and uniform. His hands were flexicuffed behind him.

The two other BTRs took up flanking positions about a hundred meters away on either flank. Turrets mounting their 30mm autocannons whined, rotating to cover the airport and its surroundings.

"Well, this is going to be a bit tricky," Schofield murmured, still watching through his binoculars.

Davis snorted. "No shit, sir." He peered

through the scope of his M24E1 sniper rifle. "We can probably nail two or three of those guys before they figure out we're shooting. But after that, all hell's going to break loose."

"Pechora Approach, this is Rossiya One-Zero-Zero, forty-eight kilometers out, level four thousand meters," a Russian voice said in Nadia Rozek's headset.

"Rossiya One-Zero-Zero, Pechora Approach," another voice replied. *"Turn right, heading one-two-five. Descend and maintain one thousand."*

She checked the flight indicator on her computer display and swung toward Brad. "There's a Russian passenger jet, a Sukhoi Superjet, coming in. They're going to land to the south. Which will take them right over our current position."

He nodded. "That's our guy." He started the XCV-62's engines and throttled up to full military power. "Let's get this crate off the ground, pronto."

The Ranger rolled out fast, bumping and rocking back across the clearing as it gained speed. Brad pulled off the ground at the first possible moment. Holding at less than two hundred feet, he throttled back again and banked into a long, slow turn, curving west over the Pechora River. In the sky off to the north, he could see the Russian airliner's bright white anticollision strobes as it came around toward the airport.

"Pechora Tower, Rossiya One-Zero-Zero, eight kilometers out, requesting visual approach to runway one-six," he heard the Russian pilot radio.

"Rossiya One-Zero-Zero, Pechora Tower, you are cleared to land," the controller replied.

Nadia keyed her mic, speaking to Schofield. "Wolf Three, this is Wolf Six-Two. Action imminent. Stand by." She leaned forward, bringing up a menu on one of her big multifunction displays. "Checking MALD Two. Programmed navigation course is set. All systems are green."

"Copy that," Brad said. He blinked away a droplet of sweat and throttled up just a tad, maintaining their airspeed as he tightened the turn. They were coming all the way back around to the east. The big Russian passenger jet appeared again, this time ahead of them, crossing from left to right as it descended toward the runway—flying low and slow with its landing gear down and locked.

Throttling back again, Brad swung onto a course that would intercept the Sukhoi Superjet. Their airspeed dropped to just a little over two hundred knots. "Range to target is three miles." He steadied up, keeping the much bigger airliner centered in their cockpit windscreen. This was going to take some really careful timing . . . and a hell of a lot of luck. His eyes narrowed, judging Sukhoi's rate of descent, and adjusting his own flight path to match. Down a little . . . up a little. He tweaked the Ranger's stick a bit to the right and then back again. There. "Launch MALD!"

"Launching!" Nadia said. Her finger tapped a display.

Their last ADM-160B decoy dropped out of the Ranger's internal bay. Its turbojet ignited. The MALD streaked straight toward the Russian passenger jet, arrowing ahead as its speed climbed toward six hundred knots.

Aboard the Sukhoi Superjet 100, Sergei Tarzarov tightened his seat belt, getting ready for what he knew from experience would be an unpleasantly rough landing. To avoid tipping anyone off about the secret work at Perun's Aerie, Gryzlov had decided against reactivating the much bigger military airfield at Pechora Kamenka. That meant all air traffic had to funnel into this small civilian airport. Its runway was long enough to accommodate this jetliner, but only by the narrowest of margins. Which meant the pilot had to bring them down right at the threshold and then brake hard and fast.

He frowned, again pondering Gennadiy's possible motives for sending him on the long flight to this dark and frozen wasteland. Retrieving a prisoner, even one so important, was a task better suited to a lower-ranking officer in the military or the security services. Was this some strange sign of the younger man's trust in his chief of staff's abilities? Or, perhaps more likely, was this a kind of rebuke for having doubted that the president's convoluted plan to ambush an Iron Wolf attack force could ever work? As a means of putting Tarzarov on notice that Gryzlov now viewed him as only one more underling to dominate—rather than as someone whose advice he would occasionally heed?

Excited voices broke into Tarzarov's increas-

ingly gloomy thoughts. Several of the soldiers
sent along to guard their Iron Wolf prisoner on
the return trip to Moscow were eagerly peering
out the windows, straining to see something in
the surrounding darkness. His scowl deepened.
Sending troops from the Kremlin Regiment was
another misstep on the president's part. They
were parade-ground soldiers, not trained jailers.
A handful of experienced FSB agents could have
handled the task more efficiently . . . and certainly
more discreetly.

Oh my God, he realized suddenly, Gryzlov must
be planning a spectacle for public consumption.
He would have television cameras waiting at Vnukovo when they returned—ready to broadcast
images of crack uniformed Russian troops marching a bedraggled Iron Wolf "terrorist" off his own
personal jetliner.

"Hey, what's that?" he heard one of the young
soldiers call out. "Some other plane?"

"If it is, it's coming right at us!" another said
nervously.

Startled, Tarzarov swung toward the nearest
window . . . just as the decoy drone slammed into
the side of the Sukhoi Superjet and ripped through
the fuselage in an expanding ball of fire. Carbon-
fiber composites shattered under the enormous
impact—sending lethal fragments sleeting
through the passenger cabin. Soldiers were torn
out of their seats and sent flailing through the air.
Sergei Tarzarov opened his mouth to scream, and
then died . . . engulfed by a tidal wave of flame
and shrapnel.

Streaming fire and smoke from the huge gash torn through its midsection, the Sukhoi Superjet rolled over and fell out of the sky. It smashed into the ground just short of the runway and blew up.

The Russian soldiers guarding Macomber had all turned to watch the big, twin-engine jetliner coming in for a landing. When it hit the ground and exploded, they stood frozen—staggered by the catastrophe. For a split second, the flash cast gigantic shadows of men and machines slanting down the runway. Ian Schofield felt the ground shake and rumble.

"Wolf team, this is Wolf Three. Execute. Repeat, execute," he said quietly into his mic.

Sergeant Davis's sniper rifle coughed quietly, echoed moments later by shots from Sikora and Knapp. Two of the Russians dropped like puppets with their strings cut. In a spray of blood, a third spun through a half circle and then folded over.

From farther down the tree line, Chris Walker fired one of his Spike-SR antitank missiles. The tiny missile streaked low across the runway and hit one of the BTR-82s right below its 30mm gun turret. The enemy troop carrier rocked back as the tandem-charge HEAT warhead ripped through its thin Kevlar-laminated armor and exploded inside. Flames ballooned out of every opening.

"Nailed him!" Walker whooped jubilantly over the circuit. He dumped the expended missile case and reached for another of the nine-kilogram, man-portable weapons.

Unfortunately, a gunner on one of the surviving BTRs was more alert than his comrades and had lightning-fast reflexes. The Russian spotted the small puff of smoke rising from Walker's position, spun his turret around, and fired a quick burst that cut the Iron Wolf commando in half.

"Damn it," Schofield muttered. Without those Israeli-made antitank missiles, they had nothing that could even scratch those two remaining Russian armored vehicles. Their gunners could stand off at leisure and pound this patch of woods into kindling.

"I'm on it," he heard Karol Sikora yell. With more guts than sense, the Polish Special Forces soldier broke cover, sprinting toward Walker's mangled body. One of the BTR turrets whined around, traversing fast toward him.

Suddenly the XCV-62 Ranger streaked low overhead, roaring down the length of the runway. Flares rippled into the air in its wake, streaming in all directions. Still burning, they bounced off the concrete and pattered down around the Russian vehicles.

Apparently believing that they were being strafed, the BTR gunners spun their turrets away—frantically tracking what they perceived as the more immediate threat. Tracer rounds streamered toward the black, batwinged aircraft as it rolled back to make another pass.

Beside Schofield, Sergeant Davis fired again, killing a fourth enemy foot soldier who had been pounding on the outside of one of the BTRs, trying to attract the attention of its crew. And then the armored car exploded. Hit broadside by another Spike missile, the gutted wreck sat motionless, wrapped in oily black smoke and sputtering flames.

Panicked, the driver of the last surviving Russian troop carrier popped his six 81mm smoke-grenade launchers. Gray clouds blossomed in the air, hiding the BTR from view as it reversed away at high speed—hightailing it for cover behind one of the distant airport buildings.

"That's our cue, Sergeant," Schofield snapped, leaping to his feet. He headed straight into the smoke with his Polish-made Radon assault rifle up and ready to fire. Davis scooped up his own carbine and plunged after him.

Moving fast across the runway, the two Iron Wolf commandos raced toward the spot where they'd last seen Macomber and his captors. They entered an eerie, half-lit world. The fires consuming the two destroyed Russian BTRs flickered red amid a thickening haze of black-and-gray smoke.

Schofield saw movement out of the corner of his eye. He spun to the side and threw himself prone. An assault rifle stuttered; 5.45mm rounds whipcracked over his head. He shot back at the flashes and heard a Russian screaming in agony. Davis fired a second three-round burst and the screaming stopped.

Breathing hard, the Canadian captain scrambled back to his feet. They moved on, deeper into the drifting smoke. Contorted corpses littered the concrete, sprawled in pools of blood.

"I found the major!" Davis shouted, dropping to one knee beside a man lying curled up on the ground. It was Macomber. The Iron Wolf sergeant laid his carbine down and pulled out a combat knife to cut the flexicuffs binding the big American's wrists.

Just then, more flashes sparkled in the smoke, accompanied by the crackling sound of rifle fire. Hit twice, once in the shoulder and once in the chest, Davis groaned loudly and collapsed next to Macomber.

Furious, Schofield returned fire, killing the Russian soldier who'd played dead long enough to bushwhack his sergeant. Then he turned and hurried over to Davis and Macomber. Both men were alive, though it was clear that Davis was badly wounded.

He took the sergeant's knife and slashed through Macomber's bindings. Then he rolled the big man over. "Can you move, Whack?" he asked urgently. "Because I need your help with the sergeant here."

"Hell, yeah," the American muttered groggily. "I can't see for shit. But I can move okay." He forced open a blood-caked eyelid and offered Schofield a painful grin. "Guess I can't court-martial you guys for coming back for me, can I?"

"It might be considered bad form," the Canadian agreed. Taking hold of Macomber's hand, he hauled the bigger man upright.

Then, dragging Davis between them, they staggered back through the smoke and out onto the runway—in time to see the Ranger touch down. The Iron Wolf transport rolled toward them, braking hard. Mike Knapp and Karol Sikora burst out of the forest on the other side, already loping toward the batwinged aircraft as its rear ramp whined down.

CHAPTER 39

THE KREMLIN, MOSCOW
A short time later

Slowly, Gryzlov put the secure phone down. He sat in uncharacteristic silence for several moments, digesting the incredible news Colonel Balakin had just relayed. Around the conference room table, the most senior members of his national security team sat frozen, plainly afraid of how he would react to this catastrophe. He had summoned them to this late-night meeting to share his triumph, the culmination of months of careful planning and intense effort. Now, instead, they were here at the very moment when the taste of victory turned to ashes in his mouth.

In the bad old days, those who served a Russian strongman like Ivan the Terrible or Stalin knew they could be exiled, imprisoned, or executed on a whim—savaged by a tyrant lashing out in the face of humiliation and failure. Not much was different under the rule of Gennadiy Gryzlov. Pun-

ishments meted out to those who fell out of favor
might carry a veneer of legality, but they were no
less arbitrary.

For now, Gryzlov ignored their fear. There
would be time enough later to savor his power over
Sokolov, Kazyanov, Titeneva, and the others—
power that had, if anything, just become even more
absolute. While he regretted Sergei Tarzarov's
death, there was no denying that the older man's
connections and carefully cultivated ties to Russia's business, military, and intelligence elites had
checked Gryzlov's authority and ambitions. Tarzarov's gray, shadowy presence inside the Kremlin had acted as a constant reminder of older days
and other leaders. Wittingly or unwittingly, he had
sometimes served as a rallying point for those who
feared their president's aggressive behavior.

But now the old man was gone. And most conveniently for Gryzlov, he'd been killed by Russia's
foreign enemies, rather than simply losing an internal Kremlin power struggle. For good or ill,
Gennadiy Gryzlov alone held the stage.

Which left the question of what to do about
this most recent foul-up by Russia's military, he
thought coldly. Losing the Iron Wolf prisoner
taken at so high a cost in men, matériel, and machines was bad. Watching the survivors of this
mercenary assault force escape to safety would be
infinitely worse.

Moodily, Gryzlov tapped the surface of his
tablet computer, transferring its detailed map of
Russia and its surroundings to the conference
room's huge flat-screen monitor. Green symbols

dotted the digital map, indicating the reported positions of friendly radar units, SAM regiments, fighter patrols, and AWACS aircraft. A slowly expanding red circle centered on Pechora showed the area within which the fleeing Iron Wolf stealth aircraft might be found. It was an extrapolation only, based on very limited observations of its maximum speed made by the two Su-50 pilots before they'd muffed their intercept.

He swung to face Colonel General Valentin Maksimov. The old man's square-jawed face was almost as pale as his short-cropped shock of white hair. The commander of Russia's Aerospace Forces looked every year of his nearly seven decades . . . and more. With Tarzarov gone, Maksimov probably sensed that his neck was on the chopping block. Angrily, Gryzlov stabbed a finger at the monitor. "Is that an accurate depiction of our current air-defense deployments and posture, General?"

Maksimov nodded heavily. "Yes, Mr. President." He lifted his massive shoulders and then let them fall in resignation. "By your orders, my headquarters situation plots are being fed to your personal computer in real time."

"That is unfortunate," Gryzlov said with undisguised contempt. "I had hoped you and your staff had simply screwed up on a minor technical question—rather than making so many obvious tactical and operational blunders."

Maksimov looked stunned. "I . . . I don't understand what you mean, Mr. President. Our forces are correctly positioned to—"

Gryzlov cut him off with a single, angry gesture. "Spare me your pathetic excuses, Maksimov!" he snapped. "You persist in making the same mistakes over and over again. Perhaps that is why your forces have had their asses handed to them so many times by the Americans! And now by these Iron Wolf mercenaries!" He waved a dismissive hand at the situation plot. "Look at it!" he demanded, glaring coldly around the table. "Do any of you see the error Maksimov and his clowns are making?"

Carefully blank faces met his gaze. No one spoke. When their president was in this kind of mood, there were no right answers.

Gryzlov smiled inwardly. Now more than ever, he suspected that his cabinet ministers regretted Sergei Tarzarov's death. Secure in his own position, the Kremlin chief of staff had never hesitated to intercede for his colleagues in the face of the president's rage. Now these sheep had no protector to shield from the darker impulses of their demanding master.

"No one?" he asked, with deceptive mildness. His eyes glittered. "Perhaps I should not be surprised. You are all disposed to inaction and idleness—even when the situation demands boldness and daring."

Unable to sit still any longer, Gryzlov rocketed up out of his chair and stormed closer to the large display. Dismissively, he swiped his hand across the radar, fighter, and SAM regiment icons shown clustered along Russia's borders. "Passive, wasteful, and, ultimately, futile barrier defenses!" he said scathingly. He sneered in Maksimov's direction. "You deploy your forces with all the skill of a child, General . . . and with a child's dependence on luck and wishful thinking. 'Perhaps our enemies will stumble into the kill radius of a SAM battery?' you imagine. Or, 'maybe one of my fighter patrols will somehow spot them before they sneak past?' you hope."

For a moment, watching Maksimov's face stiffen, he thought the old man would either fall dead of a stroke or finally fight back. But instead, the Aerospace Forces commander regained control over himself and simply asked, "Then what are *your* orders, Mr. President?"

So his old academy instructor was only another coward like all the rest, Gryzlov thought with some disappointment. There seemed to be no limit to how far he could push these gutless place-seekers. Mentally, he shrugged. If so, putting the next phase of his long-dreamed-of plans into action would be that much easier.

Confidently, he began rattling off new movement and engagement orders for Russia's air and missile forces. This time, there would be no easy escape for that fleeing Iron Wolf stealth aircraft.

WOLF SIX-TWO, OVER RUSSIA
Sometime later

Practically hugging the treetops, the XCV-62 banked right, turning to head northwest over a barren, almost completely uninhabited countryside of forests and frozen swamps—one virtually untouched by recorded human history. Occasional lights in the distance signaled the presence of small villages or logging camps, but otherwise everything was dark. Pechora and its burning, wreck-strewn airport lay far to the east.

"How are things in back?" Brad McLanahan asked Nadia, forcing the words out through clenched teeth. Every muscle ached. His flight suit was drenched in sweat. His vision seemed to have collapsed inward until all he could focus on was the green, softly glowing landscape visible through his HUD. The strain of flying this low and this fast for so long was draining his mental and physical reserves.

"Major Macomber is definitely concussed and has several minor wounds, but he is not in any immediate danger," Nadia answered quietly. "However, Captain Schofield says that it is urgent that Sergeant Davis receive advanced medical care and trauma surgery as soon as possible. He and the others have done all they can for now—but it will not be enough."

Brad nodded tightly. While the kit aboard the Ranger included medical equipment to stabilize most casualties, treating the serious wounds sustained by the Iron Wolf sergeant was beyond their ability. The best they could hope for was to keep him alive long enough to reach a skilled surgical team. "With some luck, we'll be on the ground in Kemijärvi in roughly sixty minutes."

"Warning, warning, multiple airborne X-band

search radars detected from ten o'clock to two o'clock," their SPEAR system reported abruptly. *"Evaluated as Su-27s and Su-30s. Range one hundred miles and closing. Probability of detection very low but rising."*

A row of red boxes flashed onto Brad's HUD, matching the computer's estimated bearings to those Russian fighters. They stretched across the horizon ahead of the Ranger—coming southeast at nearly four hundred knots like a moving wall.

"I count at least six Su-27s and another six Su-30s flying in line abreast," Nadia said. She peered down at her defensive displays. "I see no way to evade them on our present course."

Brad nodded grimly. Stealth or no stealth, those Russian fighter radars would pick them up if they got close enough. Turning north to try to go around them was a nonstarter. They'd run head-on into the network of radars and SAM defenses guarding Russia's Arctic naval and submarine bases. The big enemy air base at Petrozavodsk was almost due west. Heading southwest would take them into the middle of the layered defenses surrounding St. Petersburg. That left only one real option. And it sucked.

He banked into a left turn, coming back around to the south. "Plot a course that takes us far enough east of Moscow to stay out of its air-defense zone. And then another leg southwest, staying north of those Russian air bases at Lipetsk and Voronezh," he told Nadia. "We'll cross into Belarus and go direct to Warsaw."

She pulled up their navigation system and began

keying in commands. A new steering cue appeared on Brad's HUD, a little more to the southeast. He turned to follow it.

"We have enough fuel remaining to reach Warsaw on this new course, though only by a very narrow margin," Nadia said. Her voice was troubled. "But it adds two hours to our flight time, and—"

"Davis may not last those extra two hours," Brad finished for her. His jaw was set. "Look, it's my call, Nadia. My job is to get this crate home in one piece. And right now I don't see any other way to do that."

"I know," she said softly. "Making decisions that may cost lives is the price of command."

Brad said nothing. He only nodded. Now that it was too late, he was beginning to understand some of the stresses that had made his father seem so distant at times. If only they'd had more time to talk about important things, instead of school or sports or girls or even flying. Breathing hard, he fought back the tide of sorrow threatening to wash over him. *Hold it together,* he told himself. *Keep flying and don't look back. Not yet.*

They flew on in silence for several more minutes. More lights appeared on the horizon ahead of them. This part of Russia was still thinly populated, but they were heading toward its more settled regions.

"*Caution, unidentified L-band search radar detected. Radar is phased array, probable Beriev-100 AWACS aircraft,*" the computer told them abruptly.

"Son of a bitch," Brad said under his breath. He changed course slightly, veering a little more to the west to try to get some kind of rough bearing on the enemy radar aircraft.

Nadia's fingers danced across her displays. Her eyes narrowed in total concentration. "I estimate the Beriev is approximately one hundred miles due south of us," she said after several seconds. "At the moment, its apparent course is easterly."

"Yeah, that makes sense," Brad said. He frowned. "The Russians probably have that AWACS plane flying a racetrack oval. It's perfectly positioned to detect anyone trying to break south past Moscow. And I bet there are more fighters—probably a mix of MiG-29s and Su-27s—hanging with it with their radars off . . . ready to charge in for the kill."

He risked a quick glance at Nadia. "Somebody out there is reading my mind."

She nodded, looking worried.

"*Lima-band search radar, Beriev-100, eleven o'clock, ninety-five miles. Signal strength increasing,*" the SPEAR system told them.

"Shit," Brad muttered. He altered course again, turning southwest.

Just then their computer issued a new alert. "*Warning, warning, new airborne X-band search radars detected. Multiple sources from eight o'clock to four o'clock. Range one hundred and twenty miles.*"

"I identify those as Su-30 and Su-35 fighters," Nadia said. "They are coming west at more than four hundred knots."

The Russians had another line of combat aircraft booming in on them from the east, Brad realized. His mouth tightened as the fuzzy tactical picture suddenly clarified. "Crap," he said. "We can't go north or south . . . and we can't reduce our speed, not with those fighters coming up behind us. These guys are driving us, just like beaters in a big-game hunt. We're being herded straight into the St. Petersburg SAM belt."

"I concur," Nadia said tightly.

Several minutes later, multiple radars began lighting up across the horizon about two hundred nautical miles ahead of them, confirming his instincts. Their signature characteristics indicated they were the search and target acquisition radars for at least two regiments of S-300 SAMs and one of S-400 SAM launchers.

"Time until we hit the outer edge of their effective missile-engagement envelope?" Brad asked.

"Approximately ten minutes," Nadia told him.

Grim-faced, he nodded. "That's it, then, I guess. We'd better call home and report before it's too late." He glanced at Nadia and saw her biting her lip. He forced a grin for her sake. "Look, I'm not giving up just yet. I'll cut south or north before we hit that SAM barrier and try to blitz through whatever fighters the Russians have in our way. But we need to let Martindale and President Wilk know the score . . . just in case we don't get lucky."

"I understand, Brad," she said softly. She bent her head over her display again, opening a com window to enter a short situation report. Once she was finished, their computer took over. Quickly it encrypted and compressed her message to a single millisecond-long burst via satellite uplink. The system beeped. "Message sent," she said, sitting back with a resolute expression on her face.

OFFICE OF THE PRESIDENT, BELWEDER PALACE, WARSAW
That same time

Polish president Piotr Wilk finished reading the signal shown on his monitor. His eyes were dark with shame and anger when he looked up at Kevin Martindale. "I sent them into a trap."

Martindale shook his head. "*We* sent them into a trap," he corrected. "I was right there with you every step of the way. Gryzlov set us up perfectly. And we all fell for it. He rigged this game from the get-go. Either we did nothing and let his cyberweapons continue hammering us. Or he figured we'd react and send a strike force to hit what appeared to be his base of operations—which turned out to be one damned big kill zone. Destroying that Russian supercomputer and the programs they were creating on it will slow his hackers down some, maybe even a lot. But Gryzlov can buy another computer and programs can be re-created."

Frustrated, Wilk started to climb to his feet and then sat back down sharply, gritting his teeth against a wave of pain. His injuries were not fully healed yet. Only his own direct order as commander in chief had freed him from the hospital. "At least we have a fighting chance to get the survivors out," he said. "Signal Captain McLanahan and Major Rozek to use the Passkey cyberweapon your Scion experts have devised. I'll order Colonel Kasperek to send his F-16s in at the same time."

"I didn't brief the assault team on Passkey," Martindale said flatly. His face was completely expressionless. "The codes are in their computer as a subroutine in the SPEAR system, but set to self-destruct in the event the XCV-62 is shot down or captured. They don't know it exists."

"In God's name, why not?" Wilk asked, scarcely able to believe what he'd just been told.

"The risk that the team might be captured was too high," the American said stubbornly. He spread his hands. "And as things stand now, Passkey is our ace in the hole against the Russians if this war escalates further." His face darkened. "Hell, after this failed raid, it's practically the only card we have left."

"Meaning what, exactly?" Wilk demanded.

"Meaning, Passkey is essentially a onetime-use weapon," Martindale said. "It doesn't make sense to waste it saving one aircraft and its crew—no matter who they are and how much they mean to us personally."

"*I* will be the judge of that, Mr. Martindale," Wilk told him sharply. "Not you." Icily, he stared at the other man. "Unless, of course, you have decided that Scion will unilaterally break its contract with my country."

There was silence for several agonizing moments.

"No, Mr. President," Martindale said at last. "We honor our contracts. All the way."

"Good," Wilk told him. "Then listen to me very closely. Poland has a debt of honor to the Iron Wolf soldiers and airmen aboard that aircraft. It is a debt I intend to pay. Is that clear?"

Reluctantly, Martindale nodded. "It is."

"Very well, then," Wilk said. "Then you will signal Major Rozek and Captain McLanahan to activate Passkey at the appropriate time." He turned away from the American and picked up a secure phone. "Connect with me Colonel Kasperek at Ämari Air Base."

When the Polish F-16 squadron commander came on the line, Wilk said, "Pawel, get your Vipers in the air at once! *Wykonać Taran.* Execute Battering Ram."

OVER RUSSIA
A short time later

"Time to effective engagement envelope for those S-300 and S-400 SAMs is now only sixty seconds," Nadia reported, sounding frantic. Her fingers were a blur across her MFDs as she managed their defenses. "SPEAR is active, trying to engage and spoof the Russian radars. But there are too many of them! They are locking on too fast! And the systems I knock off-line are coming back on target very quickly—much more rapidly than they did last year when we bombed near Kaliningrad."

"Understood," Brad replied. Should he break left or right? he wondered. There sure as hell was no way he was going to fly straight down the throat of all those surface-to-air missile units.

"*Warning, warning, enemy fighters at three o'clock through nine o'clock increasing speed and closing,*" the Ranger said. "*Multiple target-tracking radars detected.*"

"Ah, hell." Brad resisted the urge to just close his eyes and let the Ranger auger in. The Russians weren't taking any chances. None at all. Between the Su-27s, Su-30s, and other fighters closing in from the flanks and rear and those SAMs out ahead, they were royally fucked.

Nadia's left-hand MFD pinged, alerting them to the receipt of a satellite transmission. "Message reads: 'Hold your course. Activate SPEAR Passkey subroutine,'" she said.

Puzzled, Brad asked, "Passkey? What the hell is that?"

"I do not know," Nadia admitted. She leaned forward against her straps, rapidly paging through menus on the MFD she'd set to handle their primary defensive systems. She paused uncertainly, with her finger hovering over the screen. "Here it is. But there is no indication of what this subroutine does! Only an initiate button."

"*Warning, warning, multiple X-band Tombstone and Gravestone target tracking radars locked on,*" the Ranger's computer reported. "*S-300 and S-400 missile launches imminent.*"

"Just bring it up," Brad said tightly. "Those Russian bastards are about to shoot. So whatever this Passkey thing does, it can't make things any worse."

Nadia tapped the button.

"New commands accepted. Transponders are set," the computer said coolly. *"Squawking Five-Zero-Five-Zero."*

"Jesus Christ!" Brad snarled, stunned. The Ranger's transponders were part of its IFF, or identification, friend or foe, system. When interrogated by a radar, its transponder automatically sent back a code identifying the aircraft and reporting its current altitude. That was fine in friendly-controlled air space or when operating openly under civilian air-traffic control. But turning them on in enemy territory, in a combat situation, was just about as loco as painting the XCV-62 bright yellow and flying around in lazy, slow circles. What the hell was Martindale playing at? "Okay, scratch what I just said," he growled. "Things just got worse."

Major General Anatoliy Kaverin, commander of the 2nd Aerospace Defense Brigade, stood at ease in his command post. His eyes were fixed on the displays showing the developing engagement—images he knew were being simultaneously transmitted directly to President Gryzlov and his national security team. He felt confident. The radio chatter passing between his firing units and their associated radars was thoroughly calm and perfectly professional.

He smiled. This was a far cry from the clusterfuck that idiot Konrad Saratov had presided
over last year in the Kaliningrad area. Whenever
the fast-approaching Iron Wolf aircraft managed
to blind or spoof one of his radars, the newly upgraded target identification and acquisition software provided by Dr. Obolensky's lab at NNIIRT
brought it back on line and on target within a few
seconds. Besides that, the sheer number of systems he had radiating made it impossible for the
mercenaries to deceive them all.

"Sir!" one of his staff officers said suddenly.
"The enemy aircraft has turned on its transponders."

Kaverin swung around toward him. "Is it using
our IKS system?" he demanded. That was one
possible trick he hadn't considered. It wouldn't
matter in the end, since he could order their own
fighters to back off and have his SAM units override the lockouts that would otherwise prevent
them from firing on nominally friendly planes.

"Negative, General," the younger man said,
sounding puzzled. "It's broadcasting an unas-
signed civilian code."

"Maybe somebody aboard panicked," Kaverin
said with a shrug. He smiled coldly. "So now it's
that much easier to spot them, eh?"

Another staff officer interrupted. "Sir! Batteries Four through Eight report solid locks. The
enemy is in range. They are ready to attack!"

"Commence firing," Kaverin said calmly. This
would be short and sweet.

What neither he nor anyone else in the 2nd

Aerospace Defense Brigade knew was the "5050" code the Iron Wolf XCV-62 was squawking was the detonation trigger for a Scion-designed logic bomb buried inside their upgraded target identification and acquisition software. The difficult and dangerous covert work done by Samantha Kerr and her team in Nizhny Novgorod was about to pay off. Unseen by any of the humans who thought they were in control, lines of malicious code spooled through their battle-management systems . . . executing one simple identification change as each surface-to-air missile launched.

"Missile launch!" Nadia called out in a tight, strained tone. She tapped frantically at her displays, desperately trying to jam or spoof the missiles being fired at them. "I show multiple missile launches."

Through the cockpit windows, Brad could see Russian surface-to-air missiles streaking aloft ahead of them, soaring skyward on pillars of fire and smoke. The incoming missiles curved toward them, closing fast as they accelerated toward Mach 6.

"Jesus," he murmured. His hand froze on the stick. No combination of desperate maneuvers or chaff could dodge or decoy that many SAMs. He was basically out of altitude, airspeed, and ideas. There was time for only one thing. He turned toward Nadia. She stared back at him, with her beautiful blue-gray eyes full of unshed tears. *"Kocham cię,"* he said softly. "I love you."

And then the first Russian missiles slashed right past them, still accelerating. The XCV-62 rocked wildly, buffeted by the wake of their passage.

"What the hell—" Brad blurted out. Miles behind them, explosions speckled the night sky. Those Russian SAMs were attacking their own fighters—knocking Su-27s, Su-30s, and Su-35s out of the air with contemptuous ease.

More smoke trails appeared along the western horizon, but these curved down toward the ground. Huge flashes rippled across the landscape, briefly turning night into day. Fires burned, glowing white-hot as they fed on missile propellant. In twos and threes, Russian radars and SAM launchers were destroyed—obliterated by the hundreds of bomblets packed inside each precision-guided AGM-154A Joint Standoff Weapon fired by Polish F-16s as they popped up off the deck.

Brad stared in amazement as icons filled his HUD, each indicating a Polish Viper squawking the same 5050 transponder code, a code that falsely identified them as friendly to the Scion-hacked Russian missile software. "Wolf Six-Two, this is Taran Lead," he heard Colonel Pawel Kasperek say through his headset. "The gate is down. I repeat, the gate is down. Welcome home!"

CHAPTER 40

THE KREMLIN, MOSCOW
A short time later

The silence in the crowded conference room was absolute, as though no one dared even breathe.

Gennadiy Gryzlov sat staring at the large display in wordless rage, watching helplessly as the icons representing his most advanced SAM regiments and jet fighters winked out. His hands shook, eager to choke the life out of someone—anyone. How could this be happening? Whose vile, unforgivable treason had turned Russia's own missiles against itself?

A phone buzzed sharply, breaking the appalled silence.

Ashen-faced with fear, Ivan Ulanov, his private secretary, picked it up. "Yes?" The younger man listened intently for a moment. If anything, his face turned even whiter. He gulped and turned toward Gryzlov. "Sir?" he said hesitantly. "It's the

American White House. Their president wishes to speak to you on a secure video link."

"Put her through," Gryzlov heard himself say, almost without thinking. Was that slut, Stacy Anne Barbeau, calling to gloat? Were the Americans somehow responsible for this disaster? His teeth ground together. If so, she would bitterly regret her insolence—and soon.

He saw Foreign Minister Daria Titeneva stir as if to protest and silenced her with a quick, ferocious glare.

The large monitor blanked and then came back up. But instead of President Barbeau, it showed a man with gray hair and a neatly trimmed gray beard perched nonchalantly on the corner of a desk. He was smiling, but the smile did not extend to his eyes, which were as cold and distant and bleak as the icy plains of Pluto.

Gryzlov sat bolt upright. The guy looked damned familiar. "Who the hell are you?" he demanded.

If anything, the mocking smile on the other man's face grew colder. "My name is Martindale," he said flatly. "Kevin Martindale."

"Martindale. Kevin Martindale." Gryzlov's eyes exploded in shock as he recognized the former American president.

Martindale gestured toward the unseen camera broadcasting his image. "I could apologize for this small deception, but I won't. Because it's extremely important that you realize that *two* can play this computer hacking game." His gaze hardened. "And that we play it better."

"What the fuck do you mean by that?" Gryzlov snarled.

"Come now, don't be coy, Gennadiy," the American said coolly. "We've all seen the handiwork of Major General Koshkin's hackers. And *now* you've just had one small taste of what my own specialists can accomplish. I really hope you enjoyed watching so many of your jet fighters go down in flames."

There were muted gasps around the room.

For a long moment, Gryzlov saw only red. Fury possessed him, raging through his otherwise rational mind in an uncontrollable flood. He bolted upright. "You fucking *bastard*," he growled. "If you want all-out war—a war red in tooth and claw— you can have it! My troops and tanks will—"

Martindale cut him off with a single, imperious gesture. "Oh, I wouldn't advise that, Gennadiy," he said disdainfully. He bared his teeth in a wolfish smile. "You've already lost control over your surface-to-air regiments and watched them shoot down more than a dozen of your best combat aircraft. How much more damage would you like to take today? And tomorrow? And the day after that?"

For another instant, Gryzlov teetered on the very edge of pure madness. But then, slowly, very slowly, the deeper implications of what the American had been saying sank in. He turned away from the screen and the watchful eyes of his advisers, suddenly thoughtful. It was clear that the Poles and their technologically advanced mercenaries had somehow suborned his air-defense systems.

How many other elements of his armed forces had they hacked? Were they inside his command links to the navy and the aerospace and ground forces?

And then another, even more terrifying thought occurred to him. Was what remained of his nation's strategic nuclear arsenal still under his control? He shivered suddenly, imagining nuclear-tipped missiles blasting out of their silos and off their mobile launchers . . . but aimed at Russia's own cities instead of its enemies.

Trying to hide his fear, Gryzlov turned back to Martindale. "What are you proposing?"

"Nothing too complicated," the other man told him bluntly. "You call off Koshkin's hackers—and disarm every cyberweapon still planted in the infrastructure of the Alliance of Free Nations. And in return, we agree not to blow the Kremlin, and the rest of Moscow, down around your god-damned ears."

Reluctantly, Gryzlov nodded. Perhaps it would be wiser to pull back now, and give his cyberwar experts time to strengthen their own defenses. Besides, he thought, more confidently, this was only a preliminary skirmish. He could sit back and count his gains, which were more substantial than this American knew. His eyes narrowed as he studied the other man. "Very well, I agree." He showed his own teeth. "But you should know that this isn't over, Martindale."

"Oh, I never thought it was, Gennadiy," the other man agreed. He shrugged. "After all, you're still breathing."

The monitor went black.

INTENSIVE CARE UNIT, MILITARY INSTITUTE OF MEDICINE, WARSAW
Several hours later

With Nadia Rozek at his side, Brad McLanahan stepped out of the elevator and onto the dimly lit hospital floor. Together they hurried down the corridors, heading for the small darkened room where his father lay dying. Escorted by Colonel Kasperek's fighters, they'd flown the XCV-62 direct to Warsaw's Minsk Mazowiecki military airfield—and then boarded a helicopter with the gravely wounded Sergeant Davis for the short hop to this trauma center.

Davis was in the operating room now, being worked on by some of Poland's best surgeons. While they cautioned that the road to full recovery would be long and difficult, they were confident that the Iron Wolf sergeant would survive his injuries.

So now, with his last duty to those in his command discharged, Brad felt able at last to focus on his own private sorrows. They turned a corner and entered the quiet, deserted hallway at the very back of the ICU.

But when they arrived at the bank of windows looking into what had been Patrick McLanahan's room, they saw only an empty bed. The tangle of complicated medical machinery was gone. The room had been stripped bare, right down to its plain linoleum floor.

They were too late.

Brad stared blindly at the vacant bed, trying . . . and failing . . . to come to grips with a future empty of his father's powerful presence. Slowly, unwillingly, he turned away. His eyes filled with tears. Nadia fell into his arms, quietly weeping herself.

"Hello, son," he heard a familiar voice say. "I'm sorry about giving you a shock like that. I planned to meet you before you got this far, but I move a little slower these days."

Startled, Brad looked up. He saw a human-size figure walking somewhat awkwardly down the hall toward them. It was a man. His torso, arms, and legs were supported by an exoskeleton coupled to a large backpack. A helmet enclosed his head, but through a clear visor, he saw his father's face—older and more lined—smiling back at him.

Scarcely able to speak, Brad stammered. "Dad! I thought . . . well . . . I thought you were dying."

"Me too, son," Patrick McLanahan said with a wry, lopsided smile. "Luckily, Jason Richter had one more little high-tech wonder up his sleeve, with some forceful encouragement from Kevin Martindale." He tapped the exoskeleton with one finger. "This thing. It's called a LEAF, a Life Enhancing Assistive Facility." He saw the pained expression on Brad and Nadia's faces and laughed. "Yeah, that's another of Jason's less artistic acronyms."

"Is this a new variant of the Cybernetic Infantry Device?" Nadia asked carefully. From the tone of her voice, Brad knew exactly what she was thinking. Was this machine some new monstrosity that would drive his father insane over time?

Patrick shook his head. "Not really. Oh, the

exoskeleton provides me with a little armor and I can access a few sensor capabilities, but that's about it. Most of this hardware is dedicated solely to keeping me alive and functioning." He offered her a rueful nod. "So my days as a combat pilot— either in the air or inside a robot—are over."

Then he flashed a warm, appealing grin, the kind of smile that Brad had missed seeing for a long, long time. "But I can get around pretty well now in the LEAF." His grin widened. "Hey, who knows? Maybe I'll even be able to dance at your wedding."

EPILOGUE

Trailed by his security detachment, Gennadiy Gryzlov strode onto a huge factory floor. An assembly line surrounded by computer-driven industrial robots ran down the middle of the enormous space. Dwarfed by their surroundings, a tiny group of scientists and engineers waited nervously near a pair of large doors at the end of the production line.

He joined them. "Well, what have you got?" he demanded.

One of the engineers keyed in a code, unlocking the doors. They slid smoothly aside. One by one, arc lights flared on—revealing a series of tall, motionless, human-shaped figures.

Gryzlov stood transfixed, hungrily staring up at the massive machines. They were more than ten feet high, with spindly arms and legs and elongated torsos. Smooth ovoids bristling with antennas and other sensor arrays took the place of heads.

Smiling now, he turned toward the senior scientist. "You have done very well, Dr. Aronov," he said. "I congratulate you."

The portly professor of cybernetics dipped his head in acknowledgment. "Thank you, Mr. President. My team and I have worked hard." He hesitated briefly. "But I confess that we would not have been able to achieve so much without being able to reverse-engineer so many systems." He shook his head in amazement. "I would never have believed the Americans were so far ahead of us in so many fields. It would have required many years of painstaking research and development to achieve similar advances in actuator, sensor, and battery technology."

Gryzlov nodded in satisfaction. While he would have preferred a live prisoner to interrogate, components salvaged from the Iron Wolf combat robots wrecked outside Perun's Aerie had proved their worth a thousand times over. "And the neural interface technologies required to make these war machines fully operational?" he asked. "Have you been able to re-create them?"

Aronov looked apologetic. "I am afraid the haptic control interfaces suffered too much battle damage for us to replicate them," he admitted. "My people have been working very hard on various alternatives, Mr. President . . . but without success so far."

Gryzlov waved a hand dismissively. "Don't be

too concerned, Aronov." He smiled coldly. "After all, we now know where to go to acquire the necessary information. When the time comes, you'll have what you need to bring these machines to life."

He nodded toward his guards, who ushered the scientists and engineers away—leaving him alone to revel in the knowledge that Russia would soon have its own lethal war robots. He smiled nastily, remembering Martindale's arrogant boasts. The man had sneered when Gennadiy Gryzlov had promised that this war was not over. Well, the days were fast approaching when he would redeem that pledge—and this time it would be a war fought entirely on American soil.